DEPRAVED HEART

ALSO BY PATRICIA CORNWELL

SCARPETTA SERIES

Flesh and Blood
Dust
The Bone Bed
Red Mist
Port Mortuary
The Scarpetta Factor
Scarpetta
Book of the Dead
Predator
Trace
Blow Fly
The Last Precinct
Black Notice
Point of Origin
Unnatural Exposure
Cause of Death
From Potter's Field
The Body Farm
Cruel and Unusual
All That Remains
Body of Evidence
Postmortem

NONFICTION

Portrait of a Killer: Jack the Ripper—Case Closed

ANDY BRAZIL SERIES

Isle of Dogs
Southern Cross
Hornet's Nest

WIN GARANO SERIES

The Front
At Risk

BIOGRAPHY

Ruth, A Portrait: The Story of Ruth Bell Graham

OTHER WORKS

Food to Die For: Secrets from Kay Scarpetta's Kitchen
Life's Little Fable
Scarpetta's Winter Table

Patricia Cornwell

DEPRAVED HEART

HarperCollins*Publishers*

HarperCollins*Publishers*
1 London Bridge Street
London SE1 9GF

www.harpercollins.co.uk

First published in Great Britain byHarperCollins*Publishers* 2015

First published in the United States by William Morrow,
an imprint of HarperCollins*Publishers* 2015

A catalogue record for this book is
available from the British Library

ISBN: 9780007552467

Printed and bound in Great Britain by
Clays Ltd St Ives plc

Designed by Jessica Shatan Heslin

To Staci

LEGAL DEFINITIONS of "DEPRAVED HEART"

Void of social duty and fatally bent on mischief.

MAYES V. PEOPLE, ILLINOIS SUPREME COURT (1883)

Depraved indifference to human life.

PEOPLE V. FEINGOLD, COURT OF APPEALS OF NEW YORK (2006)

The dictate of a wicked, depraved and malignant heart; *un disposition a faire un male chose;* may be either express, or implied in law.

WILLIAM BLACKSTONE, *COMMENTARIES ON THE LAWS OF ENGLAND* (1769)

Herr God, Herr Lucifer
Beware
Beware.

Out of the ash
I rise with my red hair
And I eat men like air.

SYLVIA PLATH, "LADY LAZARUS," 1965

CHAPTER 1

I GAVE THE VINTAGE TEDDY BEAR TO LUCY WHEN she was ten and she named him Mister Pickle. He sits on the pillow of a bed made military tight with institutional linens tucked into hospital corners.

The chronically underwhelmed little bear stares blankly at me, his black thread mouth turned down into an inverted V, and I must have imagined he'd be happy, yes grateful if I rescued him. It's an irrational thing to think when we're talking about a stuffed animal, especially when the person having these thoughts is a lawyer, a scientist, a physician presumed to be coolly clinical and logical.

I feel a confusion of surprised emotions at the unexpected sight of Mister Pickle in the video that just landed on my phone. A fixed camera must have been pointed down at an angle, possibly from a pinhole in the ceiling. I can make out the smooth fabric bottoms of his paws, the soft swirls of his olive green mohair, the black pupils in his amber glass eyes, the yellow Steiff tag in his ear. I remember he was twelve inches tall and therefore an easy companion for a speeding comet like Lucy, my only niece, my de facto only child.

When I found the toy bear decades ago he was toppled over on a scarred wooden bookcase filled with musty-smelling obscure coffee table tomes on gardening and southern homes in a boutique-y area of Richmond, Virginia, called Carytown. He was dressed in a dingy knitted white smock, and I stripped him. I repaired several tears with sutures worthy of a plastic surgeon and placed him in a sink of tepid water, shampooing him with antibacterial color-safe soap, then drying him with a blow dryer set on cool. I decided he was male and looked better without smocks or other silly costumes, and I teased Lucy that she was the proud owner of a *bare bear.* She said that figured.

If you sit too still too long my Aunt Kay will rip your clothes off and hose you down and gut you with a knife. Then she'll sew you up and leave you naked, she added gleefully.

Inappropriate. Awful. Not funny really. But after all Lucy was ten at the time, and her childish rapid-fire voice is suddenly in my head as I step away from decomposing blood that is brownish red with watery yellow edges on the white marble floor. The stench seems to darken and dirty the air, and flies are like a legion of tiny whiny demons sent by Beelzebub. Death is greedy and ugly. It assaults our senses. It sets off every alarm in our cells, threatening us with our very lives. Be careful. Stay away. Run for the hills. Your turn could be next.

We're programmed to find dead bodies off-putting and repulsive, to avoid them literally like the plague. But embedded in this hardwired survival instinct is a rare exemption that is necessary to keep the tribe healthy and safe. A select few of us come into this world not bothered by gruesomeness. In fact we're drawn to it, fascinated, intrigued and it's a good thing. Someone has to warn and protect those left behind. Someone has to take care of painful unpleasantness, to figure out the why, how and who and properly dispose of rotting remains before they further offend and spread infection.

I believe that such special caretakers are created unequally. For better or worse we're not all the same. I've always known this. Give me a few strong Scotches and I'll admit I'm really not quote *normal* and never have been. I'm not afraid of death. I rarely notice its artifacts beyond what they have to say to me. Odors, fluids, maggots, flies, vultures, rodents. They contribute to the truths I seek, and it's important I recognize and respect the life that preceded the failed biology I examine and collect.

All this is to say that I'm unbothered by what most people find upsetting and disgusting. But not by anything that has to do with Lucy. I love her too much. I always have. Already I feel responsible and to blame, and maybe that's the point as I recognize the plain vanilla dorm room in the recording that's just ambushed me. I'm the master designer, the authority figure, the doting aunt who put her niece in that room. I put Mister Pickle there.

He looks pretty much the same as when I spirited him away from that dusty Richmond shop and cleaned him up at the beginning of my career. I realize I don't remember the last time I saw him or where. I have no idea if Lucy lost him, gave him away or has him packed in a closet. My attention flickers as loud spasms of coughing sound several rooms away inside this beautiful house where a wealthy young woman is dead.

"Jesus! What is this? Typhoid Fucking Mary?" It's Cambridge Police Investigator Pete Marino carping, talking, joking with his colleagues the way cops do.

The Massachusetts state trooper whose name I don't know

is getting over a "summer cold" supposedly. I'm beginning to wonder if what he really has is whooping cough.

"Listen meat puppet. You fucking give me what you got? You get me sick? How about standing over there." More of Marino's bedside manner.

"I'm not contagious." Another salvo of coughing.

"Jesus! Cover your fucking mouth!"

"How am I supposed to do that with gloves on?"

"Then take them off dammit."

"No way. It won't be me leaving DNA in here."

"Oh really? Coughing doesn't spray DNA from one end of the house to the other every time you hack up your toes?"

I tune out Marino and the trooper, keeping my eyes on the display of my phone. Seconds tick by on the video and the dorm room stays empty. Nobody is there but Mister Pickle on Lucy's military-looking uncomfortable, ungenerous bed. It's as if the white sheets and tan blanket have been spray-painted on the narrow thin mattress with its single flat pillow, and I hate beds made as tight as a drum. I avoid them every chance I get.

My bed at home with its plush Posturepedic mattress, its high-thread-count linens and down-filled duvets is one of my most cherished luxuries. It's where I rest finally, where I have sex finally, where I dream or better yet don't. I refuse to feel shrink-wrapped. I won't sleep trussed up and restrained like a mummy with the circulation cut off in my feet. It's not that I'm unaccustomed to military quarters, government housing, lousy motels or barracks of one sort or another. I've spent countless hours in unwelcoming places but it's not by choice. Lucy is a different story. While she doesn't exactly live a simple spartan life anymore she also doesn't care about certain creature comforts the same way I do.

Put her in a sleeping bag in the middle of the woods or a desert and she's fine as long as she has weapons, technology and can bunker herself against the enemy, whatever that might be at any given moment. She's relentless about controlling her environment and that's another argument against her having a clue she was under surveillance inside her own dorm room.

She didn't know. Absolutely not.

I decide the video was filmed sixteen, at the most nineteen years ago with high-resolution spy equipment that was ahead of its time. Megapixel multicamera input. A flexible open platform. Computer controlled. Facile software. Concealable. Remotely accessible. Definitely New Millennium research and development but not an anachronism, not faked. It's exactly what I would expect.

My niece's technical environment is always ahead of its time, and in the mid- to late 1990s she would have known about new developments in surveillance equipment long before other people did. But that doesn't mean Lucy is the one who installed covert recording devices inside her own dorm room while she was an intern for the FBI, still in college and as excruciatingly private and secretive as she is today.

Words like *surveillance* and *spy* dominate my internal dialogue because I'm convinced what I'm looking at wasn't recorded with her knowledge. Much less her consent and that's important. I also don't believe it was Lucy who texted this video to me, even if it appears to have been sent from her In Case of Emergency (ICE) cell phone number. That's very important. It's also problematic. Almost no one has her ICE number. I can count on one hand the people who do, and I carefully study the details in the recording. It started playing ten seconds ago. Eleven now. Fourteen. Sixteen. I scrutinize images filmed from multiple angles.

Were it not for Mister Pickle I might not have recognized

Lucy's former dorm room with its white horizontal blinds shut backward like a nappy fabric or fur rubbed the wrong way, a habit of hers that's always driven me a little crazy. She routinely shuts blinds with the slats verso, and I gave up saying it's like wearing your underwear inside out. She argues that when the closed slats curve up instead of down it's impossible to see in. Anybody who thinks that way is vigilant about being watched, stalked, spied on. Lucy wouldn't let someone get away with it.

Unless she didn't know. Unless she trusted whoever it was.

SECONDS TICK BY and the dorm room is the same. Empty. Silent.

The cinder block walls and tile floor are primer-white, the furniture inexpensive with a maple veneer, everything plain and practical and prodding a remote part of my brain, a pain-saturated part of my memory that I keep sealed off like human remains under poured concrete. What I'm seeing on my phone's display could be a private psychiatric hospital room. Or a visiting officer's quarters on a military base. Or a generically bland pied-à-terre. But I know what I'm looking at. I'd recognize that moody teddy bear anywhere.

Mister Pickle always went where Lucy did, and as I look at his poignant face I'm reminded of what was going on with me during the long lost days of the 1990s. I was the chief medical examiner of Virginia, the first woman to hold that position. I'd become Lucy's caretaker after my selfish sister Dorothy decided to unload her on me. What was presented as a short impromptu visit turned into forever and the timing for when it all began couldn't have been worse.

My first summer in Richmond and it was under siege as a serial killer strangled women in their own homes, in their own beds.

The murders were escalating and becoming increasingly sadistic. We couldn't catch him. We didn't have a clue. I was new. The press and politicians thundered down on me like an avalanche. I was a misfit. I was chilly and aloof. I was peculiar. What kind of woman would dissect dead bodies in a morgue? I was ungracious and lacked southern charm. I wasn't descended from Jamestown or the *Mayflower*. A backslidden Catholic, a socially liberal multicultural Miami native and I'd managed to anchor my career in the former capital of the Confederacy where the murder rate per capita was the highest in the United States.

I never got a satisfactory explanation for the reason Richmond won the prize when it came to homicide and what sense it made for the cops to brag about it. For that matter I didn't understand the point of Civil War reenactments. Why would you celebrate the biggest thing you ever lost? I quickly learned not to give voice to such skepticisms, and when asked if I was a Yankee I said I didn't follow baseball closely. That usually shut the person up.

The exhilaration of being one of the first female chiefs in the United States quickly lost its thrill and the brass ring I'd grabbed tarnished fast. Thomas Jefferson's Virginia felt more like a stubborn old war zone than a bastion of civility and enlightenment, and it didn't take long for the truth to become abundantly clear. The former chief medical examiner was a misogynistic bigoted alcoholic who died suddenly and left a disastrous legacy. No seasoned board-certified forensic pathologist with a decent reputation wanted to take his place. So a bright idea occurred to the men in charge. What about a woman?

Women are good at cleaning up messes. Why not find a female forensic expert? It doesn't matter if she's young and missing the requisite experience to head a statewide system. As long as she's a qualified expert in court and minds her manners she can grow into the position. How about an overeducated detail-addicted work-obsessed perfectionistic Italian woman who grew up dirt poor, has everything to prove, is turbo-driven and divorced with no kids?

Well no kids *sort of* until the unexpected happened. My only sister's only offspring Lucy Farinelli was the baby on my doorstep. Except this baby was ten years old, knew more about computers and all things mechanical than I did or ever would, and she was a tabula rasa when it came to appropriate behavior. To say Lucy was difficult is like saying that lightning is hazardous. It's a statement of fact that will always be a given.

My niece was and is a challenge. Immutably and incurably. But as a child she was impossible and uncivilized. She was a genius aborigine, angry, beautiful, fiery, fearless, remorseless and untouchable, overly sensitive and insatiable. Nothing I might have done for her could have been enough. But I tried. I tried relentlessly against all odds. I've always feared I'd be a lousy mother. I have no reason to be good one.

I thought a stuffed bear might make a neglected little girl feel better and possibly loved, and as I watch Mister Pickle on the bed of Lucy's former dorm room in a surveillance video I didn't know existed until one minute ago, a low voltage shock settles into a generalized calm. I go flatline. I focus. I think clearly, objectively, scientifically. I must. The video playing on my phone is authentic. It's crucial I accept that. The footage wasn't Photoshopped or manufactured. I know damn well what I'm seeing.

The FBI Academy. Washington Dormitory. Room 411.

I try to pinpoint precisely when Lucy was there as an intern first and later a new agent. Before she got run off the job. Basically fired by the FBI. Then ATF. Then became a mercenary special operator disappearing on missions I don't want to know about before starting her own forensic computer company in New York City. Until she got run out of there too.

Then has become now, a Friday morning in the middle of August. Lucy is a thirty-five-year-old extremely rich technical entrepreneur who generously shares her talents with me, with my headquarters the Cambridge Forensic Center (CFC), and as I watch the surveillance video I'm in two places. Back in time and here in the present. They're connected. A continuum.

Everything I've done and been has pushed forward slowly and unstoppably like a landmass, propelling me into this marble foyer spattered with putrid blood. What's gone before has brought me exactly where I am, limping and in pain with a badly injured leg and a decomposing dead body near me on the floor. My past. But most importantly Lucy's past, and I envision a galaxy of bright swirling shapes and secrets in a vast inky void. Darkness, scandals, deceptions, betrayals, fortunes won and lost and won again, bad shootings, good ones and near-misses.

Our lives together started with hopes and dreams and promise, and incrementally got worse and better and finally not so bad and then pretty good until it all went to hell again this past June when I almost died. I thought the horror story was over forever and no longer foremost on anybody's mind. I couldn't have been more mistaken. It's as if I outran a speeding train only to be hit by it coming the other way around a bend in the tracks.

CHAPTER 2

HAS ANYBODY ASKED THE DOC?" THE VOICE BELONGS to Cambridge Police Officer Hyde. "I mean marijuana could do that, right? You smoke a lot of weed and get high and have some bullshit brainstorm like *how about I change a lightbulb while I'm naked?* That sounds smart. Right? Ha! Real damn smart, right? And you fall off the ladder in the middle of the night when no one's around and crack your head open."

Officer Hyde's first name is Park, a terrible thing to do to a child and he gets called every insulting nickname imaginable and returns the favor. To make matters worse Officer Park Hyde is pudgy and short with freckles and kinky carrot-red hair like a bad parody of Raggedy Andy. He's not in my line of sight at the moment. But I have excellent hearing, almost bionic like my sense of smell (or that's the joke).

I imagine odors and sounds as colors in a spectrum or instruments in an orchestra. I'm good at singling them out. Cologne for example. Some cops wear a lot of it and Hyde's masculine musky fragrance is as loud as his voice. I can hear him in the next room talking about me, asking what I'm doing and if I'm aware that the dead woman was into drugs, was probably *a psych case, a whacko, a frequent flying loony tune*. The cops are wandering around bantering as if I'm not here, and Hyde leads the charge with his boisterous clunky snipes and asides. He doesn't hold back, especially when it comes to me.

What's Doc Mort found? How is Chief Zombie's leg after you know . . . ? (whisper, whisper) What time is Count Kay returning to her coffin? Shit. I guess that's not a good thing to say considering what went down two months ago in Florida. I mean do we know for a fact what really happened at the bottom of the sea? We sure it wasn't a shark that got her. Or maybe she speared herself accidentally? She's okay now, right? I mean that really had to fuck her up. She can't hear me, right?

His words and not-so-quiet whispers are around me like shards of glass that glint and cut. Fragments of thoughts. Ignorant banal ones. Hyde is the master of dumb nicknames and comes up with dreadful puns, and I remember what he said as recently as last month when a group of us met at the Cambridge watering hole Paddy's to toast Pete Marino's birthday. Hyde insisted on buying me a round, on treating me to a *stiff drink,* maybe a *Bloody Mary* or a *Sudden Death* or a *Spontaneous Combustion.*

To this day I'm not sure what the latter is but he claims it includes corn whiskey and is served flaming. It might not be *lethal* but will make you wish it were he must have said five times. He dabbles in comedy, occasionally does stand-up in local clubs. He thinks he's quite entertaining. He's not.

"Is Doctor Death still here?"

"I'm in the foyer." I drop my purple nitrile exam gloves into a red biohazard bag, my Tyvek-covered boots making slippery sounds as I move around the bloody marble floor, staring at the display on my phone.

"Sorry, Doctor Scarpetta. Didn't know you could hear me."

"I can."

"Oh. I guess you heard everything I was just saying."

"I did."

"Sorry. How's your leg?"

"Still attached."

"Can I get you anything?"

"No thanks."

"We're making a Dunkin' Donuts run." Hyde's voice sounds from the dining room, and I'm vaguely aware of him and other cops walking, opening cabinets and drawers.

Marino's not with them now. I no longer hear him and don't know where he is inside the house and that's typical. He does his own thing and he's competitive. If there's anything to find he'll be the one who does, and I should be looking around too. But not now. My priority this moment is the image of *four-eleven,* what we used to call Lucy's FBI dorm room in Quantico, Virginia.

So far the recording is devoid of people, narration or even captions as it plays on second by second, offering nothing but the static image of Lucy's empty stark former quarters. I pay attention to the subtle background sounds, turning up the volume, listening though my wireless earpiece.

A helicopter. A car. Gunshots on distant firing ranges.

FOOTSTEPS AND I LISTEN CAREFULLY. My attention beams back into the real world, the here and now inside this historic house on the border of the Harvard campus.

I detect the hard rubbery tread of the uniformed cops walking toward the foyer. They don't have plasticized covers over their shoes and boots. They aren't investigators or crime scene techs, not Officer Hyde, not any of them. More nonessential personnel, and there have been plenty of them in and out since I got here about an hour ago, not long after thirty-seven-year-old Chanel Gilbert was found dead in the mahogany entranceway near the big solid antique front door inside her historic home.

How awful that discovery must have been, and I imagine the housekeeper letting herself in through the kitchen door just like she did every morning, she told the police. Instantly she would have noticed the extreme heat. She would have noticed the stench and followed it to the foyer where the woman she worked for is decomposing on the floor, her face discolored and distorted as if she's enraged by us.

What Hyde said is almost true. Allegedly Chanel Gilbert fell off a ladder while changing lightbulbs in the entryway chandelier. It sounds like a bad joke but it's anything but funny to see her once slender body in the early stages of putrefaction, bloated with areas of her skin slipping. She survived her head injuries long enough to have bruising and swelling, her eyes slitted and bulging like a bullfrog's, her brown hair a sticky bloody mass that reminds me of a rusting Brillo pad. I estimate that after she sustained her injuries, she was lying on the floor unconscious and bleeding as her brain swelled, compressing her upper spinal cord and eventually shutting down her heart and lungs.

The cops aren't suspicious of her death, not sincerely no matter what they discuss or claim. What they really are is voyeuristic. In their own unseemly way they're enjoying the drama and it's one of their favorites. *Blame the victim*. It must be her fault. She did something to cause her own untimely death, a death that was *stupid*. I've heard that word several times too and I'm not at all happy when people close their minds to other possibilities. I'm not convinced this is an accident. There are too many oddities and inconsistencies. If she died at some point late last night or early this morning as the cops suspect then why is decomposition this advanced? As I attempt to figure out time of death what keeps coming to mind is a Marino turn of phrase.

Cluster fuck. That's what this is and my intuition is picking up on something else. I sense a presence inside this house. A presence beyond the cops. Beyond the dead woman. Beyond the housekeeper who showed up at quarter of eight this morning and made a shocking discovery that ruined her day to put it tritely. I sense something that unsettles me and I have no empirical explanation for it and don't intend to say a word.

I usually don't share my so-called gut feelings, my intuitive flashes, not with cops, not even with Marino. I'm not expected to have any impression that isn't provable. In fact it's worse than that if you're me. I'm not supposed to have feelings and at the same time I'm accused of not having them. In other words a catch-22. In other words I can't win. But that's nothing new. I'm used to it.

"Ma'am?" An unfamiliar man's voice but I don't look up as I stand in the foyer, covered in white Tyvek from head to toe, my phone in my bare hands, the body of the dead woman several feet away near the upright ladder.

Profession unknown. Kept to herself. Attractive in a sharp off-putting way, brown hair, blue eyes based on the driver's license photo I've been shown. The daughter of a juggernaut Hollywood producer named Amanda Gilbert, the owner of this expensive property and on her way to Boston from Los Angeles. That much I know and it explains plenty. Two Cambridge cops and one Massachusetts state police trooper are now passing through the dining room talking loudly about movies Amanda Gilbert has or hasn't made.

"I didn't see it. But I saw the other one with Ethan Hawke."

"The movie that took twelve years to make? Where you watch the kid grow up . . . ?"

"That was kinda cool."

"I can't wait to see *American Sniper*."

"What happened to Chris Kyle? Unbelievable right? You come home from the war a hero with a hundred and eighty kills and some loser takes you out on the firing range. Sort of like Spider-Man dying from a spider bite." It's Hyde who's saying this as he and the other two cops hover near the staircase at the edge of the foyer, not coming any closer to me or the stench that holds them back like a wall of foul hot air. "Doctor Scarpetta? Like I was saying? We're making a coffee run. Anything for you?" Hyde has widely spaced yellowish eyes that remind me of a cat.

"I'm fine." But I'm not.

I'm not even close to fine despite my demeanor as I hear more gunshots and see the firing ranges in my mind. I hear the dull clank of lead slamming into steel pop-up targets. The bright chink of ejected metal cartridge cases bouncing off concrete shooting pads and benches. I feel the southern sun heavy on my head and the sweat drying beneath my field clothes during an era when everything was the best and worst it's ever been in my life.

"What about a bottle of water, ma'am? Or maybe a soda?" It's the trooper talking to me between coughs, and I don't know him but we won't get along if he insists on calling me ma'am.

I went to Cornell, to Georgetown Law and Johns Hopkins medical school. I'm a special reservist colonel in the Air Force. I've testified before Senate subcommittees and have been a guest at the White House. I'm the chief medical examiner of Massachusetts and director of the crime labs among other things. I didn't get this far in life to be called ma'am.

"Nothing for me thank you," I reply politely.

"We should just get a couple gallons of coffee in those cartons. Then there will be plenty and it will stay hot."

"A hell of a day for hot coffee. How 'bout iced?"

"Good idea since it's still *hot yoga* in here. I can't imagine what it was like earlier."

"An oven. That's what." More dreadful coughing.

"Well I think I've sweated a couple quarts."

"We should be wrapping it up pretty soon. An open-and-shut accident, right Doc? The tox will be interesting. You wait and see. She was stoned and when people are high they think they know what they're doing but they don't."

"High" and "stoned" are two different psychoactive states, and I don't believe weed is an explanation for what happened here. But I won't give voice to what's passing through my thoughts as the trooper and Hyde continue their ping-ponging quips and cranks. Back and forth. Back and forth monotonously, tediously. What I really want is to be left alone. To watch my phone and figure out what the hell is happening to me and who's responsible and why. Back and forth. The cops won't shut up.

"Since when are you such an expert, Hyde?"

"I'm just stating the facts of life."

"Look. With Amanda Gilbert on her way here? We'd better answer everything even if there's not a question. She probably knows all kinds of important people in high places who can cause us heartburn. For sure the media will be all over this if they don't already know about it."

"Wonder if she had life insurance, if Mama took out a policy on her unemployed druggie daughter."

"Like she needs the money? You got any idea what Amanda Gilbert is worth? According to Google about two hundred million."

"I don't like that the air-conditioning was turned off. That's not normal."

"Yeah and I make my case. That's exactly the sort of thing people do when they're stoners. They pour orange juice on their cereal and carry snowshoes to the tennis courts."

"What do snowshoes have to do with anything?"

"I'm just saying it's different from being drunk."

CHAPTER 3

THEY TALK TO EACH OTHER AS IF I'M NOT HERE, and I continue looking at the video playing on my phone. I continue waiting for something to happen.

I'm more than four minutes into it and can't pause or save it. Every key I touch, every icon and menu is nonfunctional and the recording rolls on but nothing changes. The only movement I've detected so far are the subtle shifts of light from the edges of the closed slatted blinds.

It was a sunny day but there must have been clouds or the light would be steady. It's as if the dorm room is on a dimmer switch, bright then not as bright. *Clouds moving across the sun* I deduce as Hyde and the trooper hover near the mahogany staircase, loudly voicing opinions, making comments and gossiping as if they think I'm obtuse or as dead as the woman on the floor.

"If she asks I don't think we tell her." Hyde has stayed on the subject of Amanda Gilbert's anticipated arrival in Boston. "The air being turned off is a detail we want to keep away from her and for sure keep out of the media."

"It's the only thing weird about this. You know that gives me a bad feeling."

It's certainly not the only thing weird about this, I think but don't verbalize.

"That's right and it starts a shit storm of rumors and conspiracy theories that end up all over the Internet."

"Except sometimes perps turn off the air-conditioning, turn on the heat, do whatever to make a place hot so they can speed up decomp. To disguise the correct time of death so they can create an alibi and screw up evidence, isn't that true, Doc?" The state trooper with his Massachusetts accent addresses me directly, his r's sounding like w's when he's not coughing.

"Heat escalates decomposition," I reply without looking up. "Cold slows it down," I add as I realize what it means that the dorm room walls in the video are eggshell white.

When Lucy first started staying at Washington Dorm the walls in her room were beige. Later they were repainted. I recalculate my timeline. The video was taken in 1996. Maybe 1997.

"Dunkin's got pretty good breakfast sandwiches. Would you like something to eat, ma'am?" The trooper in his blue and gray is talking to me again, sixtyish with a belly and he doesn't look well, his face wasted with dark circles under his eyes.

I have no idea what he's doing at the scene, what useful purpose he might possibly serve. Besides that he sounds quite ill. But it wasn't up to me who to invite, and I glance down at Chanel Gilbert's battered dead face, at her bloody nude body with its greenish discoloration and bloating in the abdominal area from bacteria and gases proliferating in her gut due to putrefaction.

The housekeeper told the police she didn't touch the body or even get close, and I don't doubt that Chanel Gilbert is exactly as she was found, her black silk bathrobe open, her breasts and genitals exposed. I've long since lost the impulse to cover a dead person's nudity unless the scene is in a public place. I won't change anything about the position of the body until I'm certain everyone is done with photographs and it's time to pouch it and transport it to the CFC. That will be soon enough. Very soon as a matter of fact.

I'm sorry, I wish I could say to her as I scan puddles of blood that are a viscous dark red and drying black around the edges. *Something urgent has come up. I have to leave but I'll be back,* I'd tell her if I could, and I'm vaguely aware of how loud the flies have gotten inside the foyer. With doors opening and shutting as cops come in and out of the house, flies have invaded, shimmering like drops of gasoline, alighting and crawling, looking for wounds and other orifices to lay their eggs.

My attention snaps back to the display of my phone. The image is the same. Lucy's empty dorm room as seconds tick by. Two hundred and eighty-nine. Three hundred and ten. Now almost six minutes and there must be something coming. Who sent this to me? Not my niece. There would be no reason on earth. And why would she do it now? Why after so many years? I have a feeling I know the answer. I don't want it to be true.

Dear God don't let me be right. But I am. I'd have to be in total denial not to put two and two together.

"They have vegetarian sandwiches if that's your thing," one of the cops is saying to me.

"No thanks." I keep waiting as I watch, and then I sense something else.

Hyde is pointing his phone at me. He's taking a photograph.

"You're not going to do something with that," I say without looking up.

"I thought I'd tweet it after I Facebook it and post it on Instagram. Just kidding. You checking out a movie on your phone?"

I glance up long enough to catch him staring at me. He has that glint in his eyes, the same mischievous gleam he gets when he's about to spitball another lamebrain quip.

"I don't blame you for entertaining yourself," he says. "It's kinda *dead* in here."

"I can't do that. I'm too old-school," the trooper says. "I need a decent size screen if I'm watching a movie."

"My wife reads books on her phone."

"Me too. But only when I'm driving."

"Ha-ha. You're a real comedian, Hyde."

"Do you think it's worth stringing in here? Hey Doc?"

I realize another Cambridge cop has appeared. He starts in about how to handle the blood evidence. I don't know his name. Thinning gray hair, a mustache, short and squat, what they call a fireplug build. He doesn't work for investigations but I've seen him on the Ivy League streets of Cambridge pulling people, writing tickets. One more nonessential who shouldn't be here but it's not for me to order cops off the scene. The body and any associated biological evidence are my jurisdiction but nothing else is. Technically.

Yes *technically.* Because in the main I decide what are my business and my responsibility. It's rare I get an argument. Overall my working relationship with law enforcement is collaborative and most times they're more than happy for me to take care of whatever I want. They almost never question me. Or at least they didn't used to second-guess hardly anything I decided. That might be different now. I might be getting a taste of how things have changed in two short months.

"In this blood spatter class I went to they said you should string everything because you're going to get asked in court," the cop with thinning gray hair is saying. "If you testify that you didn't bother with it? It looks bad to the jury. What they call the list of *NO questions*. The defense attorney goes through all these questions he's sure you'll answer *no* to, and it makes you look like you didn't do your job. It makes you look incompetent."

"Especially if the jurors watch *CSI*."

"No shit."

"What's wrong with *CSI*? You don't got a magic box in that field case of yours?"

This continues and I barely listen. I let them know that stringing would be a waste of time.

"I figured as much. Marino doesn't see the point," one of the cops replies.

I'm so glad Marino says it. That must make it true.

"We could bring in the total station if you want. Just reminding you we have that capability," the trooper says to me, and then he goes on to explain about TSTs, about electronic theodolites with electronic distance meters although he doesn't use words like that.

I know your capabilities better than you do and have handled more death scenes than you'll ever dream of.

"Thanks but it's not necessary," I answer without so much as a glance at the hieroglyphics of dark bloodstains under and around the body.

I've already translated what I'm seeing, and using segments of string or sophisticated surveying instruments to map and connect blood streaks, swipes, sprays, splashes and droplets would offer nothing new. The area of impact is the floor under and around the body plain and simple. Chanel Gilbert wasn't upright when she received her fatal head injuries plain and simple. She died where she is now plain and simple.

This doesn't mean there was no foul play, far from it. I haven't examined her for sexual assault. I haven't done a 3-D CT scan of her body or autopsied it yet, and I go through my differential about what I'm seeing as I ask what was in her bathroom, on her bedside table.

"I'm interested in any prescription bottles for drugs. Any drugs including medications such as lenalidomide, in other words long-term nonsteroidal therapy that is immunomodulatory," I explain. "A recent course of antibiotics also could have contributed to bacteria growth, and if it turns out she's positive for clostridium, for example, that could help explain a rapid onset of decomposition."

I inform them I've had several cases of that due to a gas-producing bacteria like clostridium where literally I saw postmortem artifacts similar to these at only twelve hours. All the while I'm going into this with the police I keep my eyes on the display of my phone.

"You talking about C. diff?" The trooper raises his voice and almost strangles on his next fit of coughing.

"It's on my list."

"She wouldn't have been in the hospital for that?"

"Not necessarily if she had a mild form. Did you see antibiotics, anything back in her bedroom or bathroom that might indicate she was having a problem with diarrhea, with an infection?" I ask them.

"Gee I'm not sure I saw any prescription bottles but I did see weed."

"What worries me is if she had something contagious," the gray-haired Cambridge cop offers reluctantly. "I sure as hell don't want C. diff."

"Can you catch it from a dead body?"

"I don't recommend contact with her feces," I reply.

"It's a good thing you told me." Sarcastically.

"Keep protective clothing on. I'll check for any meds myself and would rather see them in situ anyway. And when you get back from Dunkin' Donuts?" I add without looking up. "Remember we don't eat or drink in here."

"No worries about that."

"There's a table in the backyard," Hyde says. "I thought we could set up a break area out there as long as we do it before the rain comes. We got a couple of hours before the big storm they're predicting rolls in."

"And we know nothing happened in the backyard?" I ask him pointedly. "We know that's not part of the scene and therefore it's okay for us to eat and drink back there?"

"Come on, Doc. Don't you think it's pretty obvious she fell off a ladder here in the foyer and that's what killed her?"

"I don't arrive at a scene supposing anything is obvious." I barely glance up at the three of them.

"Well I think what happened here is obvious to be honest. Of course what killed her is your department and not ours, ma'am." The trooper chimes in like a defense attorney. Ma'am this and Mrs. that. So the jurors forget I'm a doctor, a lawyer, a chief.

"No eating, drinking, smoking or borrowing the bathrooms." I direct this at Hyde, and I'm giving him an order. "No dropping cigarette butts or gum wrappers or tossing fast-food bags, coffee cups, anything at all into the trash. Don't assume this isn't a crime scene."

"But you don't really think it is."

"I'm working it like one and so should you," I answer. "Because I won't know what really happened here until I have more information. There was a lot of tissue response, a lot of bleeding, several liters I estimate. Her scalp is boggy. There may be more than one fracture. She has postmortem changes that I wouldn't expect. I will tell you that much but I won't know for a fact what we've got here until I get her to my office. And the air-conditioning turned off during a heat wave in August? I definitely don't like that. Let's not be so quick to blame her death on marijuana. You know what they say."

"About what?" The trooper looks perplexed and worried, and he and the others have backed up several more steps.

"Better to be around potheads than drunks. Booze gives you dangerous impulses like climbing ladders or driving a car or getting into fights. Weed isn't quite so motivating. It isn't generally known for causing aggression or risk taking. Usually it's quite the opposite."

"It depends on the person and what they're smoking, right? And maybe what other meds they're on?"

"In general that's true."

"So let me ask you this. Would you expect someone who fell off a ladder to bleed this much?"

"It depends on what the injuries are," I reply.

"So if they're worse than you think and she's negative for drugs and alcohol, that might be a big problem is what you're saying."

"Whatever happened is already a big problem you ask me." It's the trooper again between coughs.

"Certainly it was for her. When's the last time you had a tetanus shot?" I ask him.

"Why?"

"Because a DTaP vaccination protects against tetanus but also pertussis. And I'm concerned you might have whooping cough."

"I thought only kids got that."

"Not true. How did your symptoms start?"

"Just a cold. Runny nose, sneezing about two weeks ago. Then this cough. I get fits and can hardly breathe. I don't remember the last time I had a tetanus shot to be honest."

"You need to see your doctor. I'd hate for you to get pneumonia or collapse a lung," I say to the trooper.

Then he and the other officers finally leave me alone.

CHAPTER 4

EIGHT MINUTES INTO THE VIDEO AND ALL I SEE is Lucy's empty dorm room. I again try to save the file or pause it. I can't. It just keeps playing like life passing by with nothing to show for it.

Now nine minutes into the clip and the dorm room is exactly the same, empty and quiet, but in the background the firing ranges are busy. Gunshots pop and I can see glaring light seeping around the edges of the white blinds closed the wrong way. The sun is directly in the windows and I remember Lucy's room faced west. It's late afternoon.

Pop-Pop. Pop-Pop.

I detect the rumbling noise of traffic driving by four floors below on J. Edgar Hoover Road, the main drag that runs through the middle of the FBI Academy. Rush hour. Classes ending for the day. Cops, agents coming in from the ranges. For an instant

I imagine I smell the sharp banana odor of isoamyl acetate, of Hoppe's gun-cleaning solvent. I smell burnt gunpowder as if it's all around me. I feel the sultry Virginia heat and hear the static of insects where cartridge cases shine silver and gold in the sun-warmed grass. It all comes back to me powerfully, and then at last something happens.

The video has a title sequence. It begins to roll by very slowly:

DEPRAVED HEART—SCENE 1
BY CARRIE GRETHEN
QUANTICO, VIRGINIA—JULY 11, 1997

The name is jolting. It's infuriating to see it in bold red type going by ever so slowly, languidly, dripping down the screen pixel-by-pixel like a slow-motion bleed. Music has been added. Karen Carpenter is singing "We've Only Just Begun." It's obnoxious to score the video to that angelic voice, to those gentle Paul Williams lyrics.

Such a sweet loving song permuted into a threat, a mockery, a promise of more injury to come, of misery, harassment and possibly death. Carrie Grethen is flaunting and taunting. She's giving me the finger. I haven't listened to the Carpenters in years but in the old days I wore out their cassettes and CDs. I wonder if Carrie knew that. She probably did. So this is the next installment of what she must have put into the works a long time ago.

I feel the challenge and my response bubbling up like molten lava, and I'm keenly aware of my rage, of my lust to destroy the most reprehensible and treacherous female offender I've ever come across. For the past thirteen years I hadn't given her a thought, not since I witnessed her die in a helicopter crash. Or I believed I did. But I was wrong. She was never in that flying machine, and when

I found that out it was one of the worst things I've ever had to accept. It's like being told your fatal disease is no longer in remission. Or that some horrific tragedy wasn't just a bad dream.

So now Carrie continues what she's started. Of course she would, and I remember my husband Benton's recent warnings about bonding with her, about talking to her in my mind and settling into the easy belief that she doesn't plan to finish what she started. She doesn't want to kill me because she's planned something worse. She doesn't want to rid the earth of me or she would have this past June. Benton is a criminal intelligence analyst for the FBI, what people still call a profiler. He thinks I've identified with the aggressor. He suggests I'm suffering from Stockholm syndrome. He's been suggesting it a lot of late. Every time he does we get into an argument.

"Doc? How we doing in here?" The approaching male voice is carried by the papery sounds of plasticized booties. "I'm ready to do the walk-through if you are."

"Not yet," I reply as Karen Carpenter continues to sing in my earpiece.

Workin' together day to day, together, together . . .

He lumbers into the foyer. Peter Rocco Marino. Or Marino as most people refer to him, including me. Or Pete although I've never called him that and I'm not sure why except we didn't start out as friends. Then there's *bastardo* when he's a jerk, and *asshole* when he's one of those. About six-foot-three, at least 250 pounds with tree trunk thighs and hands as big as hubcaps, he has a massive presence that confuses my metaphors.

His face is broad and weathered with strong white teeth, an action hero jaw, a bullish neck and a chest as wide as a door. He has on a gray Harley-Davidson polo shirt, Herman Munster–size sneakers, tube socks, and khaki shorts that are baggy with bulging cargo pockets. Clipped to his belt are his badge and pistol but he doesn't need credentials to do whatever he wants and get the respect he demands.

Marino is a cop without borders. His jurisdiction may be Cambridge but he finds ways to extend his legal reach far beyond the privileged boundaries of MIT and Harvard, beyond the luminaries who live here and the tourists who don't. He shows up anywhere he's invited and more often where he's not. He has a problem with boundaries. He's always had a problem with mine.

"Thought you'd want to know the marijuana is medical. I got no idea where she got it." His bloodshot eyes move over the body, the bloody marble floor, and then land on my chest, his favorite place to park his attention.

It doesn't matter if I have on scrubs, Tyvek, a surgical gown, a lab coat or am bundled up for a blizzard. Marino is going to help himself and openly stare.

"Bud, tinctures, what looks like foil-wrapped candies." He hunches a big shoulder to wipe sweat dripping off his chin.

"So I heard." I watch what's playing out in my phone's display, and I'm beginning to wonder if this is all there is, just Lucy's empty dorm room with the light caught in the slats of the blinds and Mister Pickle looking misunderstood and isolated on the bed.

"It's in a really old wooden box I found hidden under a bunch of shit in her bedroom closet," Marino says.

"I'll get there but not now. And why would she hide medical marijuana?"

"Because maybe she didn't get it legally. Maybe so the housekeeper wouldn't steal it. I don't know. But it will be interesting to see what her tox is, how high her THC is. That could explain why she decided to climb up a ladder and monkey with lightbulbs in the middle of the night."

"You've been talking to Hyde too much."

"Maybe she fell and that's really all that happened. It's a logical thing to consider," Marino says.

"Not in my opinion. And we don't know if it was the middle of the night. I frankly doubt it. If she died at midnight or later that would put her death at eight hours or less by the time she was found. And I'm certain she's been dead longer than that."

"With it so hot in here it isn't possible to know how long she's been dead."

"Almost true but not quite," I reply. "I'll figure it out as we get deeper into the investigation."

"But we can't this minute say exactly how long. And that's a big problem because her mother's going to demand answers. She's not someone you guess with."

"I don't guess. I estimate. In this case I'm estimating more than twelve hours and less than forty-eight," I reply. "That's as good as it's going to get right now."

"A powerhouse like her? A huge producer like Amanda Gilbert's not going to be happy with an answer like that."

"I'm not worried about the mother." I'm getting annoyed with Hollywood this, Hollywood that. "But I am worried about what really happened here because what I'm seeing doesn't add up. The time of death is a free-for-all. The details are arguing with each other. I'm not sure I've ever seen anything quite so confusing, and maybe that's the point."

"Whose point?"

"I don't know."

"The high yesterday was ninety-three. The low last night was eighty-two." I feel Marino's eyes on me as he adds, "The housekeeper swears she last saw Chanel Gilbert yesterday around four P.M."

"She swore that to Hyde before we got here. Then she left," I remind him of that.

It's not our habit to take another person's word for anything if we can help it. Marino should have talked to the housekeeper himself. I'm sure he will before the day is out.

"She said she saw Chanel pass her on the driveway, heading to the house in the red Range Rover that's out there now," Marino repeats what he's been told. "So assuming she died at some point after four o'clock yesterday afternoon and was already in bad shape this morning by quarter of eight? That works with what you estimate? Twelve hours or maybe longer."

"IT DOESN'T WORK," I say to him as I watch my phone. "And why do you continue to refer to her dying in the middle of the night?"

"The way she's dressed," Marino says. "Naked with nothing but a silk robe on. Like she was ready for bed."

"With no gown or pajamas on?"

"A lot of women sleep naked."

"They do?"

"Well maybe she did, and what the hell are you looking at on your phone?" He confronts me in his usual blunt way that more often than not is plain rude. "Since when are you glued to your phone at a scene? Is everything all right?"

"There may be a problem with Lucy."

"What's new?"

"I hope it's nothing."

"It usually is."

"I need to check on her."

"That's nothing new either."

"Please don't trivialize this." I look at my phone and not him.

"Thing is I don't know what *this* is. What the hell is going on?"

"I don't know yet. But something's wrong."

"Whatever you think." He says it as if he doesn't care about Lucy but that couldn't be further from the truth.

Marino was the closest thing she had to a father. He taught her how to drive, how to shoot, not to mention how to deal with bigoted rednecks because that's what Marino was when we first met in Virginia long ago. He was a chauvinistic homophobe who would try to steal Lucy's girlfriends until he finally saw the error in his ways. Now despite his disparagements and insults, despite how he might pretend otherwise, he is Lucy's biggest defender. In his own way he loves her.

"Do me a favor and tell Bryce I need Rusty and Harold here right away. Let's get the body to my office now." I tilt my phone so Marino can't see the video playing on it, so he can't see the empty FBI Academy dorm room with its small green stuffed bear that he's sure to recognize.

"But you got the truck." He has an accusing tone in his voice as if I'm keeping something from him, which I am.

"I want my transport team to handle this," I reply and it's not a request. "I'm not doing it or going to the office straight from here and neither are you. I need you to help me with Lucy."

Marino crouches close to the body, keeping clear of the dark sticky blood, swatting at flies, the droning of them constant and maddening. "As long as you're sure Lucy's more important than this case? As long as you're asking Luke to do the post?"

"Is this multiple choice?"

"I just don't understand what you're doing, Doc."

I inform him that either my deputy chief Luke Zenner will do the autopsy or I will when I finally get to the office. But that may not be until this afternoon, possibly midafternoon or the end of the day.

"What the hell?" Marino is getting louder. "I don't get it. Why aren't you transporting the body to the office yourself so we can know what the hell happened to her before her Hollywood mother shows up?"

"I have to leave and come back."

"I don't see why you can't take the body first."

"As I've already said my first stop won't be the CFC. We need to head to Concord and obviously I can't be driving around with a body in the back of the truck. It needs to go into the cooler right away." I make that point again. "And Harold and Rusty need to get here now."

"I don't get it," he says yet again, this time with a scowl. "You're rolling out of here in a freakin' double-wide and not going straight to the CFC? You got a hair appointment? Getting your nails done? You and Lucy are hitting the spa?"

"You didn't really just say that."

"I'm kidding. Anybody can look at you and know I was just kidding. You haven't bothered with shit for months." Marino's voice is flinty with anger, with judgment, and I feel it starting up again.

Blame the victim. Punish me for almost dying. Make it my fault.

"And what is that supposed to mean?" I ask him.

"It means you've sort of let yourself go. Not that I don't understand it. I'm sure it's not easy moving around, at least not as easy as it was. I'm sure it's hard to dress, to fix yourself up."

"Yes it's been a little difficult to *fix myself up,*" I reply dryly, and it's true that my hair could use styling and a trim.

My nails are short and unpolished. I didn't bother putting on makeup when I left the house earlier this morning. I'm a bit thinner than I was before I got shot. But this isn't the time or place to pick on me, and that has never stopped Marino, not in all the years I've known him. But he's sunk to an all-time low criticizing my appearance at a death scene while I'm worried sick about my niece. He should simply take my word for it when I say it's important we get to her right away. He doesn't trust me the way he once did. And that's the problem.

"Jesus. Where's your sense of humor?" he says after one of my long silences.

"I didn't bring it with me." I'm so on edge it's all I can do to control the level of my voice, and the marble floor seems to radiate through my boot, stiffening my right leg.

It aches and throbs like an abscessed tooth. I almost can't bend my knee, and the longer I stand here the worse everything gets.

"I'm sorry. I wasn't trying to piss you off but you're not making sense, Doc," Marino says. "I'm assuming you're doing her autopsy like right away? Before her mother gets here with a million questions and demands? Isn't that a little more important than dropping by Concord to check on Lucy? Unless she's sick or hurt or something? I mean do you know what's the matter?"

"I don't. That's why we need to check."

"We sure as hell don't want a problem with Amanda Gilbert and she's exactly the sort to give us one. And of all times? You don't need to be causing problems. I'll just say it because you don't need . . ."

"I'm well aware of what I don't need." I watch my phone and avoid looking at him.

Marino interrogates and lectures me like this because he can. At one time he was my chief investigator until he decided he didn't want to work for me anymore. He knows my office routines and protocols. He knows exactly how I think. He knows the way I do things and why. Yet suddenly I'm an enigma. I'm from another planet and this has been going on since June.

"I want her transported now and it can't be me doing it," I say to him. "I've got to get to Concord. We need to leave as soon as possible."

"Okay." He gets up and looks down at the body for a long moment as I stare at the display on my phone.

The title sequence is long gone. The music has stopped. I continue to be confronted with Lucy's empty dorm room from what seems half a life ago, and my tension and frustration build. I'm being teased, goaded, tortured, and it occurs to me that Carrie would be hugely amused if she could see me now, if she could spy on me the same way she did on Lucy.

"I admit she looks pretty damn bad for falling what? Not even six feet?" Marino says next. "Drugs and then she's got a lot of occult shit all over the place. So no telling the company she keeps. I agree with you this case has some aspects that don't add up in a good way."

"Please make the call now." I'm riveted to my phone.

I'm vaguely aware of the sound of him walking away, of him getting hold of my chief of staff Bryce Clark as I watch the seconds tick by. Ten minutes into Carrie Grethen's cinematic gift and already I know I'm being harassed and manipulated, that she's having sadistic fun at my expense. But I can't resist.

I don't know what else to do but watch, to give myself up to it as I linger inside the foyer feeling Chanel Gilbert's morbid presence and the pain in my leg. I look down at my phone, watching a segment of my niece's past go by in the palm of my ungloved hand. I smell decomposing flesh and blood breaking down. I'm sweating and chilled as I watch the video and think this can't be real.

But it is. There can be no question as I recognize the dorm room's blank walls, the two windows on either side of the bed, and of course Mister Pickle perched on the pillow. I can see the closed door that leads into the dormitory's fourth-floor hallway, the light shining in from the right where there's a bathroom. Only VIP guest quarters had private baths. Lucy was a VIP to me and that's how I mandated she would be treated by the Feds.

She occupied this room from 1995 through 1998, not constantly. But on and off while she finished the University of Virginia, working for the FBI's Engineering Research Facility (ERF) almost the entire time. Quantico was her home away from home. Carrie Grethen was her mentor. The FBI placed the niece I raised like a daughter into a psychopathic monster's care, and that decision changed the course of our lives. It has changed absolutely everything.

CHAPTER 5

CARRIE WALKS INTO THE ROOM, A SUBMACHINE GUN slung over her shoulder. The Heckler & Koch flat against her waist is an MP5K. *K* is for *kurz*, German for *short*.

The machine gun is designed to fit into a firing briefcase, and familiarity touches the back of my brain. I know this gun. I've seen it somewhere. I feel my chest tighten as Carrie leans close to a camera, stares directly into it with wide eyes as cold and bright as a winter sky. Her hair is a bleached silver buzz cut, her narrow fine-featured face compelling the way a machete is, and her tank top, gym shorts, shoes and socks are solid white.

In 1997 she was in her midtwenties although I wasn't sure of her age at the time. She could pass for much older or younger or ageless or ancient with her lean hard body and blue eyes that rapidly change shadings like a volatile ocean as her dangerous moods shift. She is very pale, as if the sun has never touched her. Her white skin seems to glow like a lampshade, contrasting sharply with the black sling loop around her neck, with the stubby black weapon that is close to the camera now.

An early model with a wooden foregrip, probably manufactured in the 1980s, possibly earlier but I'm uncertain why I know that. I can see the three modes of fire stamped in white over the thumb area. *E* for semiautomatic mode. *F* for full auto. The selector is set on *S* for safe. I know this gun somehow dammit. Where did I see it?

"Greetings from the past." Carrie's eyes are deep blue as she smiles, resting a forearm on the machine gun's receiver. "But you know what they say. The past is never over. It isn't even past. If you're viewing my cinematic masterpiece then congratulations are in order. You're still on this earth, Chief." The way she says *chief* sounds odd, possibly edited. "What you should conclude from that is I don't want you gone yet. Or you would be.

"By the time you watch this can you imagine how many chances I will have had to put a bullet in your head?" Carrie points the machine gun's short barrel at a camera. "Or better yet? Right here?" She touches the back of her neck at the base of her skull at the level of C2, and a transection of the spinal cord at that junction is instantly fatal.

As I watch her describe this I'm not surprised. It's the exact injury I encountered in recent sniper shootings that occurred in New Jersey, Massachusetts, and Florida when a stealth assassin the press calls Copperhead fired solid copper bullets into the necks of four victims. One of them was Bob Rosado, a United States congressman scuba diving off his yacht in Fort Lauderdale when he was murdered this past June. His teenage son Troy, a budding violent psychopath with a criminal history, vanished at the same time and might also be a casualty. We haven't found him. We don't know where he is. He was last seen with her, with Copperhead, with Carrie Grethen.

"There are many different ways to cause death if you're an expert." She talks slowly, deliberately in the recording. "And I'm not sure what would be best suited for you. Quick so you have no idea what's happening? Or drawn out and painful so you have full awareness? Do you want to know you're about to die or not? That is the question. Hmmm."

She looks up at the white acoustical tile ceiling with its grayish fluorescent tube lights that are turned off. "I'm probably still giving these options careful consideration. I wonder how close I will have come to ending you by the time you see this. But let's get started while we're alone. Lucy will be back soon. This is between you and me. Shhhh!" She holds a finger to her lips. "Our secret.

"I've written it all out in a narrative that explains what you're seeing and hearing." She holds up sheets of paper filled with typing in the format of a script.

She's showing off. She wants attention. But from whom? This video clip was sent to me. Yet my gut says I'm not the intended audience. *Maybe you can't be objective anymore.*

"There are six hidden cameras here inside *four-eleven,* Lucy's cozy little dorm room with all her juvenilia."

She points the machine gun at movie posters on the wall. *Silence of the Lambs* and *Sneakers*. She walks to another wall where a rampant *Tyrannosaurus rex* from *Jurassic Park* is a black silhouette against a blaze orange background. Lucy's favorite movies. I went to a lot of trouble to find the posters for her after she began her internship with the FBI.

Carrie walks to the bed and pokes the machine gun's barrel in Mister Pickle's forlorn fuzzy face. His wide glassy eyes seem panicked, as if he knows he's about to die, and I catch myself projecting emotions onto an inanimate object, onto a tiny toy bear.

"She's a child, you know." Carrie is in constant motion as she talks. "She may have an IQ that's two hundred and beyond, well into the uncharted airspace of super genius, but she's always had the emotional maturity of a toddler. Stunted. Lucy is hopelessly stunted. She has no idea what wizardry is in her room, covering every angle and completely out of sight.

"Imagine how I spend my spare time when she's not around? I'm always watching." She points two fingers at her eyes. "Like the billboard in *The Great Gatsby.* Dr. T. J. Eckleburg peering through glasses, watching over the Valley of Ashes, the moral wasteland of American society with its blind, greedy, lying government."

I glance up from my phone at Harold and Rusty. They look like Ghostbusters in hooded white Tyvek coveralls, their hands gloved in blue nitrile, respirators over their noses and mouths. They're debating with Marino how best to get the dead woman inside the pouch and whether it would be a good idea to place a bag over her head. Maybe there's important trace evidence in her hair. Brain tissue is oozing out of an open fracture in her skull. Some of her teeth may be loose. One was knocked out, a front tooth I recovered from blood on the floor.

"We don't want to displace anything. No telling what's sticking to the blood, especially in her hair," Marino is saying as Carrie's voice sounds in my ear.

"ONCE UPON A TIME there was a dorm room that was tiny and tidy," she reads from her script as Marino unfolds a stretcher and the aluminum legs clack. "It was dimly lit by a gooseneck lamp on the desk, which like the matching chair, the wardrobe, the dresser and twin bed was cheaply built of plywood with a fake wood-grain veneer."

Carrie walks around the room giving a tour, and I don't look up from my phone as I tell Marino, Rusty and Harold to bag Chanel Gilbert's head and also her hands and her feet. After that, wrap disposable sheets round her. I'm fairly certain I've collected everything that might not survive the trip to my office but let's be meticulous. Nothing left behind. Nothing lost. Not a hair. Not a tooth.

"Then you can pouch her and carry her out," I tell them as Carrie says in the recording: "On top of a hotel-size refrigerator were a Mr. Coffee maker, a jar of generic-brand creamer, a bag of Starbuck's House Blend, three FBI mugs, a chipped ceramic beer stein with the crest for the Richmond police department"—she picks it up, shows the chip—"a Swiss Army knife, and six boxes of Speer Gold Dot 9 mil ammo that went with the MP5K Lucy stole from Benton Wesley and kept hidden inside this room."

There's something strange about the way she said Benton's name. But I can't stop the recording. I can't replay it. If Carrie intended this recording for me then why would she say Benton's last name as if whoever is listening might not know it? I don't understand what's happening but I don't believe Lucy would steal a gun or anything else from him.

Carrie's lying about the MP5K and in the process she's creating a record that suggests both Benton and Lucy violated the National Firearms Act, a felony punishable with serious prison time. The statute of limitations should be up by now. But that depends. Everything depends. This is potentially very bad, and I'm aware of paper rattling less than ten feet away from me.

Harold opens what looks like a plain brown paper grocery bag with no handles. Wisely he decides against it. Chanel Gilbert's head is a gory mess. Plastic bags are better suited as long as the body is quickly refrigerated, and I say this without looking up.

"As long as she goes into the cooler the minute you get her inside the building," I emphasize because plastic and moisture are a bad combination, especially when decomposition is advancing.

"I agree," Harold says. "That's exactly what we'll do, Chief."

He used to work in a funeral home and I halfway wonder if he sleeps in a suit and tie, in dark socks and dress shoes. By his way of thinking he covers up in personal protective clothing anyway. So he may as well be dapper and properly attired underneath Tyvek.

"I think there's something in her hair. It might be glass." Light winks on his black-framed glasses, his brown eyes magnified and owlish through the prescription lenses.

"Well duh," Rusty says, and when he first got here he looked like he always does, a has-been Beach Boy, today in baggy flannel drawstring pants and a hoodie, his long graying hair tied back in a ponytail. "There's broken glass all over the place."

"I'm just being careful. It didn't look like lightbulb glass. But it was just a glance and now I don't see it."

"Wrap her up really well. Make sure we don't lose anything," I reply as Carrie walks into a small bland bathroom and flips on a light.

"Well I'm just not seeing it." Harold is looking at the bloody matted hair, walking his gloved fingers through it. "I saw something and now I don't."

"I'll look carefully again later. I didn't notice anything like glass in her hair," I reply.

"But wouldn't you think there might be?" Harold stares up at the light fixture in the ceiling, at the empty sockets where two lightbulbs had been screwed in.

He looks around at the broken glass all over the floor, and

then he acts out an imagined scenario at the same instant Carrie is acting out her drama on the video. Harold demonstrates someone changing lightbulbs and suddenly falling backward off the ladder.

"If she had lightbulbs, the chandelier's glass dome in her hands and they hit the floor at the same time she did it would be like a glass bomb going off. Wouldn't you expect glass all over her?" he asks as Carrie stares in the mirror over the bathroom sink and gives a big smile to her own reflection, then musses up her very short white-gold hair.

"Just cover her really well and she goes straight into the cooler, and I'll deal with her," I repeat my instructions.

I can't pause the video. It's as if Carrie has hijacked my phone at the worst possible time, in the middle of a suspicious death scene that should require my full attention.

CHAPTER 6

THE ONLY WAY I COULD STOP THE RECORDING IS TO power down my phone and turn it off. I'm not about to do that and it vaguely occurs to me that what's happening could come back to haunt me. If the police complain that I was on my phone, that I was watching a movie, texting or who knows what? It would be very bad.

"Off to one side of the only door that led in and out of Lucy's room is a private bath." Carrie sweeps her hand around it as if she's Vanna White on *Wheel of Fortune,* and Rusty shakes open plastic bags and begins covering Chanel Gilbert's bare feet.

"And the new agents in training didn't enjoy similar luxury." Carrie glances down at the script, then back into a hidden camera, and she does this repeatedly. "All of them had roommates. They shared toilets, vanities and showers at the far end of the hall. But young precocious Lucy didn't mingle with any of those lesser females, all of them older, some with law degrees and Ph.D.s. One was an ordained Presbyterian minister. Another was a former beauty queen.

"An unusual well-educated group with no common sense, no street smarts, and by the time you see this . . ." She ends the sentence abruptly, awkwardly, and there's no question the recording has been edited. "I wonder how many of them will be dead. Lucy and I used to make predictions. You see she'd gathered intelligence on every resident on her floor. But she didn't call anyone by name. She didn't speak to anyone in passing, and her reserve was correctly interpreted as entitlement and arrogance. Lucy was spoiled. Her Auntie Kay had managed to spoil her rotten."

Carrie refers to you as if she's talking to someone else.

She turns a page in her script. "A teenaged civilian with special gifts and special connections, Lucy enjoyed a special status at the FBI Academy that was on a par with a protected witness, a visiting chief of police, an agency director, a secretary-general or in other words a *very important person,* which Lucy is by merit of her associations and not her accomplishments.

"Her Auntie Kay mandated up front that during her precious niece's internship and until she turned twenty-one she would have her own room with a bath and a view and a curfew. She would have constant supervision, and she did ostensibly and officially. It was spelled out in her file, a thin unimportant file as I film this. But with time it likely would get much bigger as the federal government wises up to Lucy Farinelli and realizes she must be stopped."

Where is this file? The question floats up in my mind like a bubble in a cartoon strip. *Benton should know.*

"But on this bright July afternoon in 1997"—Carrie walks and talks somberly, pensively like the host of a true crime show—"the Academy faculty and staff had no idea that young Lucy's chaperone, yours truly, was a frequent sleepover and not the harmless eccentric geek who passed her extensive background check, interviews, and a polygraph with flying colors before she was hired to overhaul the FBI's computer and case management system.

"Even the psychological profilers in the Behavioral Science Unit including their legendary chief somehow missed that *I am a psychopath*." She says *legendary chief* weirdly. "Just as my father was and his father before him." Her eyes are cobalt in the camera. "I'm actually quite rare. Less than one percent of the female population is psychopathic. And you know the evolutionary purpose of psychopathy now don't you? We're the chosen ones who will survive.

"Remember that when you think I'm gone. And oops! I have to stop reading my wonderful little story for now. We have company."

THE WHISPER OF A LONG PLASTIC ZIPPER, and I glance at Marino as he stands up from a crouched position. The body is a black cocoon on the floor, and Marino, Rusty and Harold yank off their dirty gloves and drop them into the red biohazard bag.

They pull on fresh gloves. When they lift the body it is limp. Rigor mortis was fully developed and has passed, leaving her flaccid. That usually takes a minimum of eight hours, depending on other factors that include the environmental temperature, which is extremely hot, and the state of dress and body size, which are naked and slender with good musculature.

Chanel Gilbert is about five foot seven, maybe 130 pounds, and I suspect she was athletic and fit. She has tan lines from wearing a bathing suit but is pale from the waist down, her belly, hips and legs spared from exposure to the sun. Wearing a wet suit could leave a similar tan pattern, and I'm reminded of what Benton and I always do between scuba dives. We take off our dive socks and pull down our wet suits, tying the neoprene arms around our waists. Our faces, shoulders, chests, arms and the tops of our feet get sun exposure but not much else.

"Do we know if Chanel Gilbert was into sports?" I ask Marino, startled as it dawns on me that she and Carrie Grethen resemble each other physically. "She has well-developed shoulders and arms, and her legs look strong. Are we sure who this is?" I glance at him. "Has anybody talked to her neighbors?"

"What the hell?" He frowns at me as if I just said the world is flat. "What are you thinking?"

"I'm thinking she's not visually identifiable and we need to be careful."

"You mean because she's bloated and rotting with her face smashed in?"

"We should be sure we know who she is. We shouldn't assume it's the woman who lived in this house." I'm not going to mention that the dead woman on the floor could pass for Carrie Grethen's twin.

I think of my recent sighting of Carrie when she shot me in Florida, comparing that face with the photograph on Chanel's driver's license. The two women look eerily similar, and if I dared to suggest this I'll sound obsessed and irrational. Marino would want to know why the thought has occurred to me now, and I can't tell him I'm watching Carrie on my phone. Marino can't know that. No one can. I'm not sure what the legal implications might be but I'm worried the video is a trap.

"What makes you suspect she isn't the lady who lived here?" It's Harold who asks as he squats by his scene case, packing it up.

My answer is a question. "Do we have any reason to think she might have been a scuba diver?"

"I've not seen any dive gear anywhere," Marino says as Lucy appears in the video, unaware and casual. "But I noticed some underwater photographs in one of the rooms down the hall. I'll look around some more after we get her into the van."

I watch Lucy walking around her private space that Carrie has invaded and violated.

"I need a sample of Chanel Gilbert's DNA, maybe from a toothbrush, a hairbrush," I remind Marino but it's hard to focus as I watch the image of my niece. "And let's find out who her dentist is and get her charts. We're not releasing her identity to anyone including her mother until we're sure."

"Seems like there's a little problem with that," Marino says but I'm no longer looking at him. "Someone alerted her mother, remember? And she's on a plane headed here from L.A., remember? So if you've got any reason to think this isn't her daughter . . . Well that will be a real shit show when Mama shows up."

"Have you found out who might have notified her?" I ask.

"No."

"Because it wasn't us," I repeat what I've said before. "I explicitly instructed Bryce not to release anything until I say so."

"Someone sure as hell did," Marino says.

"The housekeeper might have after she found the body," Rusty suggests and it makes sense. "Maybe she notified the mother. That would be expected don't you think?"

"Yeah maybe," Marino answers. "Because let me guess. Mama probably paid for everything including the housekeeper. But we need to find out who got hold of her and told her the bad news."

"What we need to know first and for a fact is who this dead woman is." I glance up at Marino's bloodshot eyes, then I look back down at my phone, at Lucy, in workout clothes, her rose gold hair as short as a boy's.

She could pass for sixteen but was three years older than that when this was filmed, and watching her gives me an indescribable feeling. I feel enraged and sick. I keep reminding myself to feel nothing at all, and I barely glance at Rusty and Harold as they wheel the stretcher out the front door. I'm packing my scene case, tidying up as I watch the video playing on my phone and listen to it through my wireless earpiece.

Multitasking. I shouldn't be.

Marino has begun walking around the house checking windows and doors, making sure everything is secure before we close up and head out. I'm not done. But I'm not staying. I'll be back after I'm sure Lucy is safe—after I make damn sure she's not the one who sent this recording to me.

CHAPTER 7

I KNOW MY NIECE. I CAN TELL WHEN SHE TRUSTS that whatever she's saying and doing is private and unmonitored.

She believes her conversation with Carrie is between the two of them. It isn't. I can't imagine how Lucy would feel if she knew that in a sense I was inside that room with them. I may as well have been there then because I am now, and I feel disloyal. I feel I'm betraying my own flesh and blood.

"How was the gym?" Carrie's eyes move around the room, finding cameras Lucy can't see. "Crowded?"

"You should have done weights while you could."

"Like I told you, I had things to take care of including a surprise."

Carrie is in the same running clothes but there's no sign of the machine gun. There's no time stamp on the recording, only a run time of almost twenty minutes now, and I watch her open the small refrigerator.

"I brought you a present." She grabs two St. Pauli Girls, pops off the caps and hands one of the green bottles to Lucy.

She stares at it but doesn't take a sip. "I don't want it."

"We can have a drink together can't we?" Carrie brushes her fingers through her peroxided buzz-cut hair.

"You shouldn't have brought it here. And I didn't ask you to."

"You didn't need to ask. I'm very thoughtful." Carrie picks up the Swiss Army knife from the top of the refrigerator, resting the thick red handle in the palm of her hand, flipping open a blade with her thumbnail, and stainless steel flashes.

"You shouldn't have done it without asking." Lucy strips down to her sports bra and bikini briefs, and she's sweating and flushed from exertion. "I get caught with alcohol in my room and I'm fucked." She drops her clothing into a bamboo hamper I bought for her, grabs a towel and begins drying off.

"You'd better hope they don't find out you have a gun in here," Carrie says somberly and for the effect as she studies the knife blade shining thinly, sharply. "A very illegal one."

"It's not illegal."

"Maybe it's about to be."

"What have you done? You've done something."

"Well it would be a crime if it's missing. But what the hell is legal anyway? Arbitrary rules invented by flawed mortals. Benton's more or less your uncle. Maybe it's not stealing if you took it from your uncle."

Lucy walks over to the closet, opens the door, looks inside. "Where is it? What the hell did you do with it?"

"Have you learned nothing in the time we've been together? You can't stop anything I want to do and I don't need your permission." Carrie looks directly into a camera and smiles.

I watch Lucy sit on a corner of the desk inside her dorm room, her tan muscular legs dangling. She's getting visibly upset.

LIGHT SEEPING around the edges of the closed blinds is different, and just seconds ago Lucy had her running shoes and socks on. Now they're off. She's barefoot. The video has been edited heavily, skillfully, and I wonder what has been deleted and stitched together for purposes of Carrie's propaganda and manipulations.

"You always manage to take whatever you want," Lucy is saying to her. "You're always trying to make me do things that are wrong, that are bad for me."

"I don't make you do anything." Carrie walks close, strokes her hair, and Lucy jerks her head away. "Don't rebuff me." Carrie is inches from Lucy's face, almost nose to nose, staring into her eyes. "Do not rebuff me."

She kisses her and Lucy doesn't react. She sits stoically, stiffly like a statue.

"You know what happens when you act like this," Carrie says with an edge that hints of what she's capable of. "Nothing good and you really must stop blaming everybody for your behavior."

"Where's the fucking gun!" Lucy gets up from the desk. "You'd like to get me in trouble, wouldn't you? You'd like to deliberately set me up for it. Why? Because if you discredit me then no one will believe what I do or say. I won't get anything I've earned and deserve. Not ever. That would be a horrible way to live."

"How horrible? Do tell." Carrie's eyes are bright silvery blue.

"You're sick," Lucy says. "Go to hell."

"Don't worry. I'll hide the evidence, carry out the empty beer bottles and get rid of them." Carrie takes a swallow of the German lager. "So you don't get sent to the principal's office."

"I don't give a shit about the beer! Where's the gun? It doesn't belong to you."

"You know what they say about possession being nine-tenths of the law. It's fixable you know. That MP5K is going to shoot so sweet."

"Do you understand what could happen? Of course you do. And that's the point, isn't it? Everything you do in life is about creating leverage, finding dirt that can give you an advantage, and that's been your MO from the start. Give me the gun. Where is it?"

"In due time," Carrie says in a syrupy, patronizing tone. "I promise it will turn up when you least expect it. How about a massage? Let me dig my fingers into you. I know exactly how to cure what ails you."

"I'm not drinking this." Lucy retrieves the bottle of St. Pauli Girl from the desk.

She pads barefoot into the bathroom and there's a hidden camera in there too. I watch her on video pour out her beer. I hear it splashing into the sink, and when she glances into the mirror her keenly pretty face is a mixture of sad, hurt and angry but mostly sad and hurt. Lucy loved her. Carrie was her first love. In some ways she was Lucy's last.

"I don't trust anything you give me, anything you do." Lucy raises her voice as she turns on the water full blast, washing the beer away.

She looks in the mirror again and her face is so young, so child-like, and her eyes are teary. She's trying to be brave, to control her volatile emotions, and she splashes water on her face and dries off with a towel. She walks back into the bedroom as I realize that Carrie must have set up a network of motion-sensitive recording devices that she programmed to override each other when someone moved from room to room. I could see what Lucy was doing in the bathroom but I couldn't see Carrie. Now I can. I'm watching both of them again.

"That was wasteful. It was ungrateful." Carrie touches the tip of her tongue to the opening of her St. Pauli Girl bottle, lightly tracing the beveled rim.

She stares into a camera and slowly licks her bottom lip. Her eyes are glassy. They're almost Prussian blue, changing like her moods.

"Please leave," Lucy says. "I don't want to fight. We need to end this without a fucking war."

Carrie bends over to take off her running shoes and socks. "Can you hand me the lotion, please?" Her ankles are unnaturally pale with prominent blue veins, the skin almost translucent like beeswax.

"You're not showering here. You need to go. I have to get ready for dinner."

"A dinner I'm not invited to."

"You know exactly why that is." Lucy retrieves a camouflage toiletry bag from the top of the dresser.

Rummaging for an unlabeled plastic bottle, she tosses it to her. Carrie snatches it out of the air like a touchdown pass.

"Just keep it. I don't use it, no way I would." Lucy returns to her perch on top of the desk. "The long-term side effects of rubbing copper peptides and other metals and minerals into your skin is unknown. In other words fucking untested. Look it up. But what is known is that too much copper is toxic. Look that up too while you're fucking at it."

"You sound just like your annoying aunt." Carrie's eyes darken, and it continues to jar me when she refers to me as if I'm not the one watching this.

"I don't," Lucy says. "Aunt Kay doesn't say *fuck* nearly as often as I do. And while I appreciate you mixing up a batch of your bullshit collagen-producing vanishing cream for me . . ."

"Vanishing cream? Not hardly." Carrie's arrogance puffs her up like a Komodo dragon. "It's a skin regeneration preparation." She says it condescendingly. "Copper is essential to good health."

"It also encourages the production of red blood cells, and that's the last thing you need help with."

"How touching. You care about me."

"Right now I don't give a shit about you. But why the fuck would you rub copper into yourself? Did you ask a physician if someone with your disorder should apply a topical lotion with copper in it? You keep using shit like that and you'll have blood pudding sluggishly moving through your veins. You'll drop dead of a stroke."

"God you're becoming just like her. Little Kay Junior. Hello Kay Junior."

"Leave Aunt Kay out of it."

"It's really not possible to leave her out of anything, Lucy. Do you think if you weren't blood kin you might be lovers? Because I could understand it. I could go for her. Definitely. I would try it." Carrie touches her tongue to the beer bottle, inserts it into the opening. "She'd never go back. I can promise you that."

"Shut the fuck up."

"I'm just speaking the truth. I could make her feel so good. So *alive*."

"Shut up!"

Carrie sets down the beer as she unscrews the cap from the lotion, sniffs the fragrance, swooning. "Ohhhh soooo nice. You sure? Not even a little bit in those hard-to-reach places?"

"For the record?" Lucy swipes ChapStick on her lips. "I'm sorry I ever met you."

"All this because *Miss Beauty Queen* was running the Yellow Brick Road the same time we were. A coincidence. And you go nuclear."

"The hell it was a coincidence."

"It really was. I swear, Lucy."

"Bullshit!"

"I swear on the Bible I didn't tell Erin we'd be out there at three o'clock. And voilà." Carrie snaps her fingers. "She happens to show up."

"Running out there all by her lonesome and there we are and she joins us. Ignoring me like I wasn't there. Focused only on you. Right. What a coincidence."

"It wasn't my fault."

"Just like she's happened to show up everywhere else the two of you have fucked each other, Carrie."

"You want to talk a health threat?"

"You mean you?"

"Jealousy. It's toxic."

"How about lying, which is all you ever do. Over and over again."

"You need to start putting this on every time you go out, even on overcast days in the dead of winter." The viscous translucent lotion Carrie dribbles into her palm looks like semen. "And you say *fuck* too much. Vulgarity is inversely proportionate to intelligence and facility with languages. Profuse swearing is generally associated with a low IQ, a limited vocabulary and uncontrollable hostility."

"Are you listening to me? Because I'm not kidding." Lucy seems to vibrate with emotion, with fury and pain.

"How about a back rub? I promise you'll feel better."

"I'm done with your lying! Your cheating and stealing credit!" Lucy is crying. "Every shitty thing you do! You don't know what it is to love anybody. You aren't capable of it!"

Carrie is completely calm no matter what is happening or said, her attention flicking from one concealed camera to another like an exotic reptile reading the air with its forked tongue.

"You're a cheater-whore!"

"Someday I'll remind you what you said. And you might wish you hadn't." Carrie holds up her hand with a dollop of lotion, smiles brightly.

"I'm scared." Lucy glares at her, the veins standing out in her neck.

Carrie begins rubbing the lotion on herself, slowly, salaciously on her face, her neck. She clicks her tongue at Lucy as if she's a dog, waving the bottle of lotion at her as if it's a bone.

"Come. I'll put it on you. I'll rub it in the way you like." She rapidly rubs her palms together. "I'll warm my hands and drive my magic potion into your skin. Sort of an improvised nanotechnology."

"Stay away from me!" Lucy furiously wipes tears with the back of her hand, and suddenly the video stops.

I try to rewind it but I can't. I can't replay it. I can't do anything to it at all.

CHAPTER 8

THE ICONS ARE INERT. WHEN I CLICK ON THE LINK in my text messages nothing happens.

Then just as suddenly the link isn't there anymore, as if I deleted any trace of it from my messages. But I certainly didn't. The recording has vanished before my eyes like a disturbing dream. It's gone as if it was imagined, and I look around the foyer at the dark dried blood, the shattered glass, the gory area on the floor where the body had been. My attention stops on the upright ladder.

Fiberglass, rubber feet, four steps and a platform on top, perfectly centered, and that begins to bother me like many details in this case. The ladder is set up directly under the light fixture, which at some point shattered over the marble floor. If Chanel really lost her balance I would have expected the ladder to slide, possibly to tilt and tumble over as she fell. I scan feathery marks made by her bloody hair at the perimeter of the putrid crazed blackish mess where her upper body had been. It appears that at some point she moved her head.

Or someone moved it.

We've found no footprints, handprints, nothing that might suggest the presence of a second person including the housekeeper who discovered the body. I recall the bottoms of Chanel's bare feet were completely clean. Once she was down, she stayed down. She didn't step in her own blood. It doesn't appear anybody did, and then I begin looking harder at a scene that is increasingly suspicious as I listen for Marino, waiting for him to come back so we can check on Lucy. I halfway expect another alert tone on my phone, another video link to land, and I keep hoping Lucy will call me. I text her at the same time I carefully scan the foyer, focusing on areas of clean white marble, looking for any indication that someone may have washed the floor in an attempt to alter the scene, to stage it.

We haven't yet checked for latent blood, for a trace residue that might have been left if blood is washed away and we no longer can see it without chemical assistance. I'm not sure the police were going to bother since they seem convinced the death is an accident, and I crouch down by my scene case and open it again.

I find the bottle of reagent. I shake it and start spraying areas of the floor that appear clean. Instantly a rectangular shape and swipe marks fluoresce a vivid blue just inches from the decomposing blood where the body had been. The shape was made by something manufactured, possibly a bucket it occurs to me, and that and other shapes are eerily vivid on the white marble.

Darkness isn't required for this particular chemical, and sunlight coming through the transom and the ambient illumination don't interfere with the sapphire blue luminescence. I see it plainly as I notice a pattern of elongated droplets, some as small as a pinhead, what looks like back spatter that impacted at an acute angle. Medium velocity. What I associate with beatings.

I closely inspect a blue mist near where the head had been. Possibly expirated blood, and I think of the missing front tooth I recovered when I first got here. Chanel would have been bleeding inside her mouth, and when she was down on the floor, unconscious and dying, she was exhaling blood mixed with air. It appears someone wiped up this area of the floor, attempting to eradicate anything that might not be consistent with an accidental death.

That's what it's looking like but I need to be conservative and cautious. There could be other explanations such as a false positive chemical reaction to something other than blood. Or even if it is nonvisible blood it could have been on the floor for a while. It might be completely unrelated to Chanel Gilbert's death. But I don't believe it.

Next I conduct a quick and easy presumptive test, moistening a swab with distilled water, gently rubbing a small area of the rectangular shape that is fluorescing blue. Then I drip a phenolphthalein solution and hydrogen peroxide onto the swab and instantly it turns pink, which is positive for blood. Next I take photographs using a plastic ruler as a scale.

"Marino?" I look for him.

The house is empty except for the two of us. Hyde, the gray-haired Cambridge officer and the state trooper are en route to Dunkin' Donuts or headed who knows where. I detect sounds in the area of the kitchen. Then I hear a door shut, the thudding distant and muffled, possibly downstairs, and that's perplexing. I could have sworn everyone was gone, that no one is left on the property except Marino and me. Maybe I'm mistaken, and I listen. I detect more movement in the kitchen area.

"Marino?" I call out loudly. "Is that you?"

"No it's the boogeyman." I can't see him, only hear him, and now the sounds are coming from the hallway beyond the staircase.

"Are you sure there's nobody here besides us?" I ask the empty foul-smelling air.

"Why?" Slow heavy footsteps coming closer.

"I thought I heard a door shut. I heard something thud. It sounded like it came from the basement."

No answer.

"Marino?" I swab several other fluorescing stains and the presumptive test continues to be positive for blood. "Marino?"

Silence.

"Marino? Hello!"

I shout to him several more times but he doesn't answer, and I text Lucy again. Then I call her ICE number and it goes straight to voice mail, and next I try the cell phone line I usually reach her on. She doesn't answer that either. When I enter her unlisted unpublished home number I get an error tone and a recording.

The number you have reached is no longer in service . . .

The sound of a door shutting again, distant and muffled. It doesn't sound like a normal door. It's too heavy.

Like a vault door slamming.

"Hello?" I call out. "Hello!"

No one answers.

"Marino?"

I look around, standing perfectly still, listening. The house is silent, just the incessant noise of flies. They crawl over blood and circle sluggishly like tiny spotter planes looking for the putrefying wounds and orifices, the rotting flesh where they laid their eggs. Their buzzing sounds angry and predatory, as if they've been robbed of their unborn babies and denied a carcass, a food supply that was rightfully theirs. The flies seem louder even though there are fewer of them, and the stench seems just as strong with the body gone but that's not possible.

My senses are on high alert, in overdrive and the same sensation drifts over me like a noxious vapor. I feel a presence. I feel something evil and curdled inside this house and then I think about what Marino said. Chanel Gilbert was into *occult shit,* and I don't know what he meant. Maybe she consorted with the dark side, assuming there really is anything to that, and I remind myself it's understandable if I'm feeling spied on because Lucy was. I just witnessed it.

"Marino?" I try again. "Marino are you here? Hello?"

I ENVISION THE DOOR that leads down to a basement where I've not yet been.

I've not had the chance to search the house but I'm fairly sure that the door is off the kitchen, which is how I entered when I first got here. I came in the same way the housekeeper had earlier, and I remember noticing the closed door opposite the pantry. It occurred to me it led down into what likely was a laundry area, a cellar, possibly a kitchen for the household staff in centuries past.

I listen carefully and have waited long enough. I'm about to go look for Marino when I hear footsteps again, big heavy ones. I stay where I am and listen as they get closer. Then I see him near the staircase.

"Thank God," I mutter.

"What's the matter?" He walks into the foyer and his eyes instantly find the blue luminescent shapes on the floor. "What've we got here?"

"Someone may have tampered with the scene."

"Yeah I'm seeing something. I don't know what but something. Good idea to spray it down just to be on the safe side."

"I thought you'd vanished."

"I checked the basement and there's no sign of anybody," Marino says as he looks at the blue luminescence from different angles. "But the door that leads outside? It was unlocked and I know I locked it after I looked around earlier."

"Maybe one of the other cops did it?"

"Maybe. And let me guess who. See what the hell I deal with?" His thick thumbs are busy on his phone as he sends a text. "That would be stupid, careless as shit. Probably Vogel. I'm asking him. Let's see what he says."

"Who?"

"The trooper. You know Typhoid Mary? He's not thinking straight, probably got the *whoop* just like you said, should go home and stay home."

"Why was the state police here anyway?" I ask.

"Nothing better to do. Plus it turns out he's a buddy of Hyde's, who probably cued him in about the mother. Whenever Hollywood's involved you know how people get. Everybody wants to hop on the celebrity train. Well it's a good thing I tried the basement door. Someone breaks in here because we left a door unlocked and talk about hell to pay?" He checks his phone. "Okay here we go. Vogel's answered. And he says the door was locked for sure. He dead bolted it from inside. He says it should be dead bolted. It's not." Marino types a reply.

"Let's get out of here." I carry my scene case past the staircase, into a short hyphen of a dark paneled hallway, heading out the same way I came in. "As soon as we check on Lucy we'll be back. We'll look around carefully. Then we'll take care of the rest of it at my office. We'll do whatever we need to do."

"You've heard nothing from her?"

"No."

"I could send . . ." he starts to say but doesn't finish.

There's no point. Marino knows better than anybody that you don't send police to make a *wellness check* on Lucy. If she's home and okay she's not going to open her gate, and if the police get in without her assistance they'll set off an explosion of alarms. She also has a lot of guns.

"I'm sure she's fine," Marino says and now we're in the kitchen.

It's been remodeled in the past twenty years or so, the original woodwork replaced by a knotty pine that is lighter than the wide-board floor. I make mental notes of the white appliances, minimalist with hanging stainless steel lamps, and the Shaker-style oak table set with a single plate, a wineglass and silverware facing a window that overlooks the side of the house.

I walk closer to the table set for one, and I get the feeling again as I dig into a pocket for clean gloves and pull them on. I pick up the plate, dinner size with a colorful pattern that depicts King Arthur on a white horse draped in bloodred, surrounded by Knights of the Round Table riding after him, a castle in the background. I turn the plate over and stamped on the back is *Wedgwood Bone China, Made in England.* I scan the kitchen and spot an empty plate hanger to one side of the door that leads outside.

"This is peculiar." I return the plate to the table. "This is Wedgwood, in other words a collector's plate." I walk over to the empty plate hanger. "It appears this is where it was hanging." I open cupboards and survey shelves of simple white stoneware, practical, durable, dishwasher and microwave safe, no sign of Wedgwood or anything similar. "Why would you remove a decorative plate off the wall and set the table with it?"

Marino shrugs. "I don't know."

He moves to the sink where a cabinet is open underneath. Nearby on the black and white subway tile is a stainless steel trash can. He steps on the foot pedal and pops open the lid, peers inside and gets an astonished angry look on his face.

"What the hell?" he says under his breath.

"Now what?" I ask.

"That moron Hyde. He must have taken the trash when he left. The entire bag of trash without even going through it. What the hell is wrong with him? You don't dump entire bags of garbage on the labs, and last I checked he wasn't a detective. See what I mean about what I put up with?"

Marino gets on his phone as I open the door that leads outside, the same door I came in at 8:33 this morning. I know the exact time. I always make a point of knowing.

"What the hell did you do?" Marino is saying nastily, his earpiece winking blue as he holds up his phone so I can see Officer Hyde's name in the display. "What do you mean you didn't and you don't know?" Marino is loud and accusatory. "You telling me it's not with you or at the labs? That someone else made off with the kitchen trash and you got no idea? You realize what might be in that damn trash?

"Try this on for starters, asshole. It looks like she set the table for herself, meaning she was in here probably not all that long before she died and then something happened because she didn't get around to eating." Marino's face is deep red. "Plus the Doc's found an indication that someone may have tried to clean up blood in the foyer, maybe staging something. Meaning you need to get your ass back here and secure this place like a damn crime scene. I don't give a flying fuck what the neighbors think of our tying this place up in a big yellow bow. Do it!"

"Ask him what was in the trash as best he knows," I say as he continues to chew out Hyde over the phone.

"He doesn't know." Marino looks at me as he ends the call. "He says he didn't touch the trash yet. He didn't take it and has no idea what was in it. That's what he says."

"Well it appears someone took it."

"He says he'll find out. Either Vogel or Lapin must have it. Goddamn it!"

Vogel is the state trooper. Lapin must be the gray-haired Cambridge cop I've seen writing tickets around here, the one who went to a seminar and is now a bloodstain expert by his way of thinking.

"Maybe check with Lapin?" I ask. "Make sure he did something with the trash? Because this is disturbing."

"I can't imagine he would take it." But Marino calls him next.

He asks him about the kitchen trash. He meets my eyes and shakes his head as he slips a pair of sunglasses out of a pocket of his cargo pants. Vintage wire-rim military aviator Ray-Bans I got him for his birthday last month. He puts them on, blacking out his eyes. He ends the call.

"Nope," he says to me as he walks to the door that leads outside. "He says he's not aware of anybody doing anything with the trash yet, and he didn't touch it. Didn't see it even. And he sure as hell didn't take it with him. Well somebody did because it wasn't like this when I first got here."

We walk out into the sultry summer morning, the wind light and hot as it stirs the old trees in the side yard.

"Maybe the housekeeper took out the trash before she left." I suggest the only other possibility that comes to mind. "Did anybody actually see her leave and notice if she had anything in her hands?"

"That's a good question," he says as we go down three wooden steps that end on the old brick driveway.

To one side of them flush against the house are two supercans and Marino opens the heavy dark green plastic lids.

"Empty," he says.

"Garbage collection is weekly, probably Wednesdays here in mid-Cambridge, and today's Friday," I reply. "So Chanel Gilbert hasn't put anything in the cans in several days? That's a bit odd. Did you notice anything that might suggest she'd been out of town and just got back?"

"Not so far." Marino wipes his hands on his shorts. "Might make sense though. She comes home and notices a light or two out and decides to change the bulbs."

"Or that's not what happened at all. If we consider other evidence we're finding the story begins to change." I remind him of what I discovered when I sprayed a reagent in the foyer. "Let's make sure Lucy's okay and we'll get back here and finish up. If Hyde and others are going to secure the perimeter you might want to suggest they hold off searching the house any further until we return."

"Good thing I have you to tell me how to do my job."

"I've sent a message to my office. We'll get the CT scan going right away and see if it tells us anything helpful," I reply.

Parked on the brick driveway in front of my truck is the red Land Rover registered to Chanel Gilbert. I look through the driver's window without touching anything. On the backseat is a bag of empty glass bottles, all of them the same and unlabeled, and the dash is dusty, the SUV filthy with pollen and trash from trees. Leaves and pine needles clog the space between the hood and the windshield. Cars don't stay whistle clean around here. If people have garages they use them for storage.

"It looks like it's been sitting outside for a while. But that doesn't mean it hasn't been driven recently," I start to say as I detect a distant thudding that is rapidly coming closer.

"Yeah." Marino is distracted, staring at my right leg. "Just so you know you're walking a lot worse than you were earlier. Maybe the shittiest I've seen you walk in weeks."

"Good to know."

"I'm just saying."

"Thanks for pointing it out with your typical diplomacy."

"Don't get pissed at me, Doc."

"Why would I?"

The helicopter is a beefy black twin engine at about fifteen hundred feet and several miles west, flying along the Charles River. It's not Lucy's Agusta with its Ferrari blue and silver paint job. I dig my keys out of my shoulder bag and try to walk without a hitch, without stiffness or a limp as Marino's comments sting and make me self-conscious.

"Maybe I should drive." He watches me skeptically.

"Nope."

"You've been on your feet way too much today. You need to rest."

"That's not happening," I say to him.

CHAPTER 9

FIFTEEN MILES NORTHWEST OF CAMBRIDGE THE ROAD is barely wide enough for my big boxy truck.

White with dark tinted windows and built on a Chevy G 4500 chassis it's basically an ambulance with the caduceus and scales of justice in blue on the doors. But there are no flashing lights. There's no siren or PA system. I'm not in the business of offering emergency medical care. It's a little late by the time I'm called, and I'm not expected to engage in high-risk aggressive driving. Certainly not here in the nation's proud and proper birthplace where the shot was heard 'round the world during the Revolutionary War.

Concord, Massachusetts, is known for its famous former residents like Hawthorne, Thoreau and Emerson, and for hiking and horse trails and of course Walden Pond. The people here keep to themselves, often snobbishly so, and whelping horns, beacons, flashing red and blue strobes, and breaking the speed limit and outrunning traffic lights aren't normal or welcome. They're also not part of a medical examiner's SOP.

But if I had a siren right now it would be screaming. I'd be encouraging everyone on the road to stay out of my way. It's just a damn shame about the truck. I wish I were driving something inconspicuous. Even one of the CFC vans or SUVs. Anything but this. Everybody we pass is staring at the *Grim Reapermobile,* the *double-wide,* in Marino's words. It's about as common as a UFO in this low-crime part of the world where Lucy lives on her spectacular estate. Not that people don't die around here. They have accidents, sudden cardiac catastrophes and take their own lives like anybody else. But those types of cases rarely require a mobile crime scene unit, and I wouldn't be driving one if I weren't coming directly from Chanel Gilbert's house.

It would have made sense to swap out vehicles but there isn't time. I don't have the luxury of taking a shower and changing my clothes. I feel concern that's fast becoming raw fear, and it ratchets me into a higher gear. Already I'm mobilizing, getting a determined iron-hard attitude edged in stoicism that will break bones. I've tried Lucy repeatedly and she doesn't answer. I've tried her partner Janet. She's not answering either, and their main home number continues to seem out of order.

"I hate to tell you but I smell it." Marino cracks open his window and hot humid air seeps in.

"Smell what?" I pay attention to my driving.

"The stink you carried out of the house with you and trapped inside this damn truck." He waves his hand in front of his face.

"I don't smell anything."

"You know what they say. A fox can't smell its own." Marino routinely butchers clichés and thinks an idiom is a stupid person.

"The saying is *a fox smells its own hole first,*" I reply.

He rolls down his window the rest of the way, and the sound of blowing air is soft because we're moving slowly. I hear the helicopter. I've been hearing it ever since we left Cambridge and I've about decided we're being followed, possibly by a TV news crew. Possibly the media has found out who the dead woman's mother is, assuming the dead woman is really Chanel Gilbert.

"Can you tell if it's a news chopper? It would make sense but sounds bigger than that," I ask Marino.

"Can't tell." He's craning his neck, looking up as best he can, and sweat is like dew on top of his shiny shaved head. "I can't see it." He stares out his side window at big trees, an overgrown hedge, a dented mailbox going by.

A red-tailed hawk circles in the distance, and I've always considered birds of prey a good sign, a positive messenger. They remind me to keep above the fray, to have a keen eye and follow my instincts. Another stab of pain knifes through my thigh, and no matter how many times I've dissected what happened I can't figure out what I miscalculated, what I didn't notice or could have done differently. I was a hawk that got hunted down like a dove. In fact I was a sitting duck.

"The thing is it's not like her," Marino is saying, and I realize I didn't hear what he said right before it. "It's not like you either, Doc. And I feel a need to point that out."

"I'm sorry. Now what are we talking about?"

"Lucy and her so-called emergency. I keep wondering if you've misunderstood something. Because it doesn't sound like her. I don't like that we got up and walked out of a scene that may turn out not to be an accident."

"It's not like Lucy to have an emergency?" I glance over at him. "Anyone can have an emergency."

"But I'm not understanding this and I swear I'm trying to. She texts you from her emergency line and that's it? What did she say exactly? Hurry here now or something like that? Because like I said that doesn't sound like her."

I haven't told him what the text said. Which was nothing. It was a video link. That's all. Now it's gone without a trace and he has no idea about any of it.

"Let me see the text." He holds out a huge hand. "Let me see exactly what she said."

"Not while I'm driving." I dig myself deeper into what's becoming a pit of lies, and I don't like the feeling.

I resent the position I've been put in and I can't find my way out. But I'm protecting people or at least that's my intention.

"And she said what exactly? Tell me her exact words," Marino badgers me.

"There was an indication of a problem." I'm careful how I phrase it. "And now she's not answering any of her phones. Janet isn't either," I repeat myself.

"Like I said it doesn't sound like her. Lucy never acts like there's a problem or that she needs anyone," he says and it's true. "Maybe someone stole her phone. Maybe it wasn't her who sent the message. How do you know we're not being set up so we get to her property and find out it's an ambush?"

"Set up by whom?" I scrutinize my own voice.

I sound calm and in control. My tone doesn't begin to belie my feelings.

"You know damn well who. It's the kind of thing Carrie Grethen would do. So she can ambush us, lure us right where she wants us. If I see her I'm shooting on sight." Marino isn't making an empty threat. He means it 100 percent. "No questions asked."

"I didn't just hear you say that. You didn't say it and don't say it again," I reply, and the diesel engine seems unnaturally loud.

I'm a white elephant on this road. I shouldn't be on it, not driving a medical examiner's truck, and I imagine if I saw it and didn't know why it was headed to Lucy's neighborhood . . .

Why isn't she answering her phone? What has happened?

I won't think about it. I can't stand to think about it, and I'm bombarded by images I can't shake from a video I never should have seen. At the same time I wonder what I really watched. How much footage did Carrie take out of context? How could she have had me in mind as a future audience? Or did she?

How could Carrie have known then what she would do almost two decades later? I don't think it's possible. Or maybe I just don't want to believe she's capable of executing her schemes so far in advance. That would be scary and she's scary enough, and I obsessively sift through what's happened today. I work my own morning like a crime scene, detail by detail, second by second. I dig, excavate and reconstruct as I drive with both hands on the wheel.

The video link landed on my phone at exactly 9:33 A.M., a little more than an hour ago. I recognized the alert from Lucy's ICE line. It sounds like a C-sharp chord on an electric guitar, and immediately I pulled off my soiled gloves and stepped away from the body. I watched the recording and now it's gone. Irretrievably gone. That's what happened. That's what I want to tell Marino. But I can't and it's making matters more difficult with him than they already were.

He doesn't completely trust me. I've sensed it since my near miss in Florida.

Blame the victim.

Only I'm the victim this time, and in his mind it has to be my fault. That suggests I'm not who I used to be. At least not to him. He treats me differently. It's difficult to pinpoint and define, subtle like a shadow that didn't used to be there. I see it in front of me whenever he's around, like the changing shades of blue and gray on a heaving sea. He blocks my sun. He makes reality shift when he shows up.

Doubt.

I think that's mostly it. Marino doubts me. He hasn't always liked me and in the beginning of my career he might have hated me and then for the longest time he loved me too much. But throughout it all he didn't doubt my judgment. There's plenty he criticizes and harps on but being erratic, irrational or unreliable was never on the list. Not trusting me as a professional is new and it doesn't feel good. It feels damn terrible.

"The more I think about it the more I agree with you, Doc," Marino continues to talk as I drive my big truck. "She hadn't been dead all that long to be in such bad condition. I don't know how we're going to explain it to her mother. That and what lit up blue on the floor. A case that started out as no big deal and now there are questions, serious questions. And we can't answer them. And why? Because for one thing we're here in Concord and not in Cambridge getting to the bottom of things. How do I explain to Amanda Gilbert that you got a personal call and left her daughter's body on the floor and just walked out?"

"I didn't leave the body on the floor," I reply.

"I meant it figuratively."

"Literally the body is safely at my office and I didn't just walk out. There's nothing figurative about it. Everything has been left as is and we'll be back soon. And it's also not for you to explain, Marino, and at the moment I don't intend to discuss details with Amanda Gilbert. Not to mention we need to confirm the dead woman's identity first."

"For the sake of the argument," Marino replies, "let's assume it's Chanel Gilbert because who else would it be? Her mother is going to ask a shitload of questions."

"My answer is simple. I'll say we need to confirm identification. We need more details and reliable witness accounts. We need undisputed facts that tell us when her daughter was last seen alive, when she last e-mailed or made a phone call. That's the missing link. We find that out and I have a better chance of knowing when she died. The housekeeper is important. She's the one who may have the best information."

I hear myself using words such as *reliable, fact* and *undisputed*. I'm being defensive because of what I sense from him. I feel his doubt. I feel it like a glowering mountain looming over me.

"I'm suspicious of the housekeeper to tell you the truth," he says. "What if she's involved and is the one who turned off the air-conditioning?"

"Was she asked about it?"

"Hyde said it was already like that when he got to the house. She didn't seem to know anything about why it was so hot."

"We need to sit down with her. What's her name?"

"Elsa Mulligan, thirty years old, originally from New Jersey. Apparently she moved to this area when Chanel Gilbert offered her the job."

"Why New Jersey?"

"That's where they met."

"When?"

"Does it matter?"

"Right now we have so many questions everything matters," I reply.

"I got the impression Elsa Mulligan hadn't worked for Chanel all that long. A couple years? I'm not sure. That's about as much as I know since she wasn't still at the house when I got there. I'm passing on what Hyde said. She told him that when she let herself in through the kitchen door she could smell this horrible odor like something had died, and yep something sure had. The house was hot as shit and she got a whiff and followed it into the foyer."

"Did Hyde feel she was being truthful? What's your gut tell you?"

"I'm not sure of anything or anyone," Marino says. "Usually we can at least count on the dead body to tell us the truth. Dead people don't lie. Just living people do. But Chanel Gilbert's body isn't telling us shit because the heat escalated decomp, confusing things and I wonder if a housekeeper would know something like that."

"If she watches some of these crime shows she could."

"I guess so," he says. "And I don't trust her. And I'm getting an increasingly bad feeling about the case and wish to hell we hadn't walked out on it."

"We didn't walk out on it, and you'll be the problem if you keep saying that."

"Really?" He looks at me. "When's the last time you did something like this?"

The answer is never. I don't take personal calls in the middle of a scene and interrupt what I'm doing. But this was different. I heard an alert tone from Lucy's emergency line, and she's not the sort to overreact or cry wolf. I had no choice but to check on whether something terrible has happened.

"What about the burglar alarm being on when she arrived this morning?" I ask Marino. "You told me the housekeeper turned it off. Are we sure it was armed when she unlocked the door?"

"It was turned off at seven-forty-four, which is when she told Hyde she got there. Quarter of eight is exactly what she said." Marino takes off his sunglasses, starts cleaning them on the hem of his shirt. "The alarm company log verifies the alarm was turned off at that time this morning."

"What about last night?"

"It was set, disarmed and reset multiple times. The last time it was armed was close to ten P.M. The code was entered and after that none of the door contacts were broken. In other words it doesn't appear someone set the alarm and then left the house. It's like the person was in for the night. So maybe Chanel was still alive then."

"Assuming she's the one who reset the alarm. Does she have her own code that only she uses?"

"No. There's just one and it's shared. The housekeeper and Chanel used the same dumbass code. One-two-three-four. Sounds like Chanel wasn't particularly security conscious."

"With her Hollywood background that would surprise me. I wouldn't expect her to be trusting. And one-two-three-four is usually the default code when a security system is installed. The expectation is you'll change the code to something difficult to guess."

"Obviously she didn't bother."

"We need to find out how long she's lived there, how often she's in Cambridge. While I didn't have a chance to look around I can say the house didn't feel all that lived in." As I explain this I'm desperate to tell him the truth about why we're rushing to Lucy's house.

I want to show him the video but I can't. Even if I were able to I couldn't let him see it. Legally I wouldn't dare. I can't prove who sent it or why. The video could be a setup, a trap, maybe one cooked up by our own government. Lucy admits on film to being in possession of an illegal firearm, a fully automatic machine gun that Carrie accuses her of stealing from my husband Benton—an FBI agent. Any violation involving a Class III weapon is serious trouble, the very trouble Lucy doesn't need. Especially now.

Over recent months the police and the Feds have been watching her. I don't know how closely. Because of her prior relationship with Carrie almost everyone is concerned about what Lucy's involvement might be with her. Or is Carrie even still alive? That's the most inflammatory question I've been hearing this summer. Maybe Carrie really is dead. Maybe everything happening is being manufactured by my niece, and this thought leads back to Marino. If only I could show the video to him.

I continue arguing with myself that were it possible and prudent there would be no point. I know how he would react. He would be convinced that someone—probably Carrie—is harassing me. He would say she knows exactly how to push my buttons, to stick it to me, and the stupidest thing I could have done is what I'm doing now. I should have stayed put. I shouldn't have reacted. I've let her get the best of me and there must be other nasty tricks to follow.

Let the games begin, I imagine Marino commenting, and I wonder what he'd say if he knew the date it was filmed.

July 11, 1997. His birthday seventeen years ago.

CHAPTER 10

I DON'T REMEMBER IT. BUT BIRTHDAYS ARE A BIG deal and I would have cooked him dinner, one of his favorite dishes, whatever he wanted.

It also was long ago when Lucy was at the FBI Academy, inside her dorm room breaking up with Carrie. Assuming the date is correct on the video file, the two of them had run the FBI obstacle course known as the Yellow Brick Road. Then Lucy worked out in the gym. I have no idea where I was and I don't know where Marino might have been or what he was doing. So I ask him.

"That's sure as hell out of the blue," he replies. "Why do you want to know about my birthday in 1997?"

"Just tell me if you remember."

"Yeah I do." He looks over at me as I keep my eyes straight ahead. "I'm surprised you don't."

"Help me out. I have no clue."

"You and me drove to Quantico. We picked up Lucy and Benton and went to the Globe and Laurel."

The legendary Marine Corps hangout is suddenly vivid in my mind. I see the beer steins around the polished wooden bar, the ceiling covered with law enforcement and military patches from all over the world. Good food, good booze, and a huge seal over the door, the eagle, globe and anchor emblazoned with *semper fidelis*. We were part of the always faithful, the always loyal, and what went on in there stayed in there. I haven't been in years, and then I envision something else. Marino drunk. It was ugly. I see him wild eyed in the incomplete darkness of the parking lot yelling, swearing at Lucy, his arms rigidly by his sides, fists clenched as if he might hit her.

"Something was wrong with Lucy that night." I'm deliberately vague with him. "You two were having a bad time, got upset with each other. That much is coming back."

"Let me refresh your memory," he says. "She couldn't eat anything. She had belly pain. Me? I figured it was her period."

"Which you didn't mind saying to her in front of everyone."

"I thought she was having cramps and PMS. That's what I remember about my birthday in 1997. I was really looking forward to the Globe but she freakin' ruined it."

"I believe she said she'd pulled an abdominal muscle on the obstacle course." I know Lucy was in pain and I do recall that she wouldn't let me check her.

"She was weird as a shithouse rat, a real asshole. A worse one than usual," Marino says.

I remember the two of them shouting at each other by the car. She wouldn't get in. She threatened to walk back to her dorm, was angry and in tears and now I might know why. She and Carrie had gone out to run the Yellow Brick Road earlier that day and not so serendipitously encountered the new agent in training, a former beauty queen named Erin. Lucy believed Carrie was cheating on her with Erin and it's all there on film.

More pieces of a puzzle from the past, and I keep going back to my question. How could Carrie have known at the time that one day she would give me a ringside seat to what was going on in my niece's private life? And would Carrie also have anticipated that I would begin to interpret and in some ways embellish the video even as I watched? Each second of it brought back information I've buried and blocked. Other details are new and that's equally troubling. What else don't we know about Carrie Grethen?

I think about her obsession with the harmful effects of pollution and the sun. I had no idea about her magical beliefs and pathological vanity. To my knowledge no one has ever mentioned she has a blood disorder, and all of it will hold Lucy in very poor standing with the authorities. She knew these details. Obviously she did because she's talking about them in the recording I saw. But I'm not aware that she's ever passed the information along to anyone, and then my mood dips deeper into the dark trough of guilt.

I was the moving force behind Lucy's internship at Quantico. Carrie was telling the truth when she said I was instrumental in lining it up and had implemented strict guidelines for how the FBI was to deal with my teenaged niece. So I suppose it's fair to say that it's my fault Lucy ever met her mentor, her supervisor Carrie. The nightmare that would unfold is because of me. And now it's unfolding further. And I wasn't expecting this. And I honestly don't know what to do except to get to Lucy as fast as I can and make sure she's safe.

Marino pats his pockets for his cigarettes. This is the third time he's lit up since we left Cambridge. If there's a fourth time

I might have to give in. I could use a cigarette right now. Badly. I try to shut out images from the video. I try to get past what I felt, which was like a spy, a traitor, a terrible aunt as I watched Lucy and Carrie together intimately and barely dressed, as I listened to Carrie's disrespectful, disparaging comments about me. I wonder the same thing I always do. How much is deserved? How much is an accurate portrait of who and what I really am?

I'm so tense I might explode to the touch, and my right leg throbs, the ache spreading down my thigh to my calf muscle. Even the slightest adjustment of the accelerator is at a price. When I press the brake as I just did, I pay for it all right, and Marino hunches his shoulder and sniffs his shirt to make sure he doesn't smell bad.

"It's not me," he decides. "Sorry about that, Doc. You stink like a decomp and might want to stay away from Lucy's dog."

I DRIVE SLOWLY around blind curves where round convex mirrors are mounted on thick old trees. I look and listen for anything coming.

The sun shines through heavy canopies, painting dapples of light and shadow that reshape themselves like clouds. The wind blusters, ruffling leaves, shaking them like pompoms, and creosote-stained utility poles with sagging black power lines make me lonely for music. The faces of old homes we pass are tired, and New England pines and hardwoods grow chaotically, the earth a thick compost of tangled vines, dead weeds and rotting leaves.

Buildings are paint-peeled. They lean and sag. I'll never understand why scarcely anyone seems to care about how run-down and unhappy everything looks. Few Concord residents bother with landscaping or grass, and nothing is gated or fenced-in except

Lucy's estate. Dogs and cats wander at will and I have to look out for them when I drive here. In general that's once or twice a month for dinner, brunch, a hike, or if Benton is out of town I might spend the night in the guest suite Lucy designed and furnished for me.

Up ahead a green snake as bright as an emerald is stretched out on a sunny patch of pavement, its head raised, feeling the vibrations of our approach. I slow down as it begins to undulate across the road, vanishing into the greenness of dense summer foliage. I speed up. Then I slow down for a squirrel, a plump gray one that stands on his hind legs, its whiskers twitching as if it's scolding me before scampering off.

Next I come to a complete stop to let a panel-sided station wagon pass. It stops too and for an instant we're at a stalemate. But I'm not backing up. I can't possibly. It inches past with difficulty. I feel the driver's unhappy stare.

"I think you've just ruined everybody's day around here," Marino says. "They're wondering who got murdered."

"Let's hope the answer to that is nobody." I glance at my phone for another text from Lucy's ICE line, but there isn't one as I continue along the road, the road that leads to her, the road I know so well and have come to hate.

Grass and weeds are chest-high up to the edge of the pavement, and heavy tree branches hang low, making visibility even worse. There are few streetlights, and more often than not when I show up I find some poor creature in harm's way. I always stop. I'll hurry along a turtle, picking it up if need be and setting it safely in the woods. I routinely watch for rabbits, foxes, deer, escaped ornamental chickens.

I'm on notice for baby raccoons that waddle out of the woods and lounge in the middle of the sun-warmed road, as innocent and sweet as cartoons. The other day after a hard rain I encouraged an army of green frogs to abandon their post. They seemed to grumble as I prodded them. There wasn't the slightest gesture of gratitude for saving their lives. But then my patients don't thank me, either.

I rumble over asphalt cracked and crumbling at the edges like a stale brownie, avoiding potholes deep enough to blow out tires and damage wheels, and I envision the low-slung supercars Lucy drives. I marvel just as I always do over how she manages Ferraris and Aston Martins in conditions like this. But she's as nimble as a quarterback, streaking around anything that might hurt her or get in her way. Slaloming, fast cutting, my Artful Dodger stealthy niece.

Except something got her this time. I can see that instantly as a tight curve brings us to the entrance of her fifty-acre estate. The tall black iron gates are frozen open, and blocking her driveway is an unmarked white Ford SUV.

"Shit," Marino says. "Here we go."

I ease to a stop as an FBI agent in khaki pants and a dark polo shirt steps out of the SUV and approaches us. I don't know him. He doesn't look familiar. I reach inside my shoulder bag, my fingers brushing against the hard shape of my Rohrbaugh 9 mm in its pocket holster. I find the thin black leather wallet that holds my brass shield and credentials. I roll down my window and hear the loud thudding of the helicopter, a big one, probably the same twin engine I've been hearing only now it's lower and slower. It's much closer.

The agent is late twenties, early thirties, muscle-bound and poker-faced with veins roping his forearms and hands. He's possibly Hispanic and definitely not from around here. New England natives in general have a certain way about them that's typically low-key but observant. When they figure out you're not the enemy they try to be helpful. This man isn't going to be nice or accommodating, and he knows damn well who I am even if I don't know him.

I have no doubt he's aware that I'm married to Benton Wesley. My husband works out of the Boston Division. Probably this agent does too. The two of them probably are acquainted and may be friendly with each other. I'm supposed to think that none of it matters to the tough guy guarding my niece's property. But the message he sends is exactly the opposite of what he intends. Disrespect is a symptom of weakness, of smallness, of an existential problem. By acting rude to me he's showing me what he really thinks of himself.

I don't give him the chance to make the first move. I open my wallet and display what's inside. Kay Scarpetta, M.D., J.D. I'm duly appointed to the positions of chief medical examiner of Massachusetts and director of the Cambridge Forensic Center. I'm charged with the duty of investigating the cause of death pursuant to Chapter 38 of the General Laws of Massachusetts and in accordance with the Department of Defense Instruction 5154.30.

He doesn't bother to read all that. He barely glances at my creds before returning my wallet as he stares past me at Marino. Then he stares at me, not directly in my eyes but between them. The trick isn't original. I do the same thing in court when I'm faced with a hostile defense attorney. I'm quite skilled at looking at people without looking at them. This agent's not so good at it.

"Ma'am, you need to turn around," he says in a voice as flat as the expression on his face.

"I'm here to see my niece Lucy Farinelli," I reply calmly, pleasantly.

"This property is under the control of the FBI."

"The entire property?"

"You need to leave, ma'am."

"The entire property?" I repeat. "That's rather remarkable."

"Ma'am, you need to leave right now."

The more he says "ma'am" the more stubborn I get, and when he said "right now" he pushed me too far. There's no going back. But I won't show it and I avoid Marino's eyes. I feel his aggression and refuse to look at him. If I do he'll catapult out of the truck and get in the agent's face.

"Do you have a warrant to access this entire property and search it?" I ask. "If the answer's no and you don't have a warrant for *the entire property,* then you need to move your vehicle and let me through. If you refuse, I'm going to call the Attorney General and I don't mean of Massachusetts."

"We have a search warrant," he says with nothing in his tone, but his jaw muscles are flexing.

"A search warrant for fifty acres including the driveway, the woods, the shoreline, the dock and the water around it?" I know the FBI doesn't have any such thing.

He says nothing, and I call Lucy's ICE line again. I almost expect Carrie to answer but she doesn't, thank God, and I can't abide another possibility that is worse. What if Lucy sent the video to me? What on earth would that mean?

"You're here," Lucy surprises me by answering, and I'm reminded my techno wizard niece has surveillance cameras all over the place.

"Yes we're at your gate," I reply. "I've been trying you for the past hour. Are you all right?"

"I'm fine," Lucy says and it's definitely her voice.

She's quiet and subdued. I don't detect a note of fear. What I sense is combat calm. She's in a mode to defend herself, her family against the enemy, which in this case is the federal government.

"Yes we got here as quickly as we could. That's what you wanted." It's as much of an allusion as I plan to make about the video link that landed on my phone. "I'm glad you let me know."

"Excuse me?" It's as much as she'll say but the implication is loud and clear.

She doesn't know about the text. She didn't send it. She wasn't expecting us to show up like this.

"Marino's with me," I say plenty loud. "Does he have permission to be on your property, Lucy?"

"Yes."

"Very good. Lucy, you've just given Cambridge Police Investigator Pete Marino permission. You've given me, your aunt, the chief medical examiner permission. Both of us have your permission to be on your property," I reply. "Is the FBI inside your house?"

"Yes."

"Where are Janet and Desi?" I'm worried about Lucy's partner and their little boy. They've been through quite enough.

"They're here."

"The FBI probably isn't going to let us inside your house right now," I inform her of what I'm sure she already knows.

"I'm sorry."

"Don't be. They should be sorry. Not you." I stare at the agent, fixing on a point between his eyes and I'm further emboldened by my protectiveness of someone I love more than I can describe. "Meet us outside, Lucy."

"They won't like it."

"I don't care if they don't like it." I stare hard between the agent's eyes. "You're not under arrest. They haven't arrested you, correct?"

"They're looking for a reason. Obviously, they think they're going to get me on something, anything. Littering. Jaywalking. Disturbing the peace. Treason."

"Have they read you your rights?"

"We haven't gotten that far."

"They haven't gotten that far because there's no probable cause, and they can't detain you if you're not under arrest. Head out now. Meet us on the driveway," I tell her, and we end the call.

Next the game of chicken starts. I hold my ground, sitting in my medical examiner's monster white truck while the agent stands next to his dwarfed white Bureau SUV. He makes no move to get inside it. He intends to block the driveway, and I wait. I give him a minute, and I wait. Two minutes, three minutes and when nothing changes I shove the gear into drive.

"What are you doing?" Marino looks at me as if I might be a little crazy.

"Moving so traffic can get past." It isn't true. The truck is off the street by a good twenty feet.

Nosing forward, I cut the wheel at a tight angle. I park at a slant, almost perpendicular to the SUV, not even three inches from the rear bumper. If the agent backs up he's broadsiding me. If he pulls ahead and turns around he's no better off.

"Let's go." I cut the ignition.

Marino and I climb out and I lock the doors. Click. I drop the keys into my shoulder bag.

"Hey!" The agent is animated now, giving me direct eye contact, glaring like a vicious dog. "Hey! You've got me blocked in!"

"See how that feels?" I smile at him as we move past through the open gate, Lucy's house about a quarter of a mile from here.

CHAPTER 11

I CAN'T BELIEVE YOU DID THAT," MARINO SAYS.

"Why not?" The relentless churning of the helicopter is building on my nerves, and I'm struggling.

Lucy's house is on a rise high above the Sudbury River, and the driveway is steep in this direction. It's not an easy walk. It's not possible for me to keep up with Marino's thoughtless long stride. He seems to forget what happened not that long ago. Maybe because he wasn't there. Maybe because he's in denial. It would be like him to suppose he could have saved me, and for his focus to be that instead of what I'm left with and how I feel.

"Well one thing's for sure. There's not a single cop in Massachusetts who would tow a medical examiner's truck," he says next.

"It weighs almost five tons and could have dead bodies inside. So not a good idea." I've resorted to walking several yards behind him, forcing him to slow down and turn around to talk.

"Yeah no kidding." He looks back at me, then up at the helicopter. "What the hell? This is what we've been hearing since Cambridge? You think it's the same chopper?"

"Yes."

"It's no news crew, that's for sure. It's the damn Feds and they followed us from that scene to here. Why? What's their interest in Chanel Gilbert or us?" he asks.

"You tell me." Pain shoots through my thigh.

"Obviously they knew we were headed here."

"I don't know what they knew."

"It's like they escorted us to Lucy's property."

"I don't believe that's what they're doing. I got the distinct impression a minute ago that we're not welcome here. They may have followed us. But they're certainly not escorting us." I have to stop for a moment.

I rest my weight on my left leg, and the full symphony of pain in my right thigh subsides to a low drumroll, to the slow sawing of a cello. The high pitches are gone, and it's those that are intolerable. The rest I've learned to live with, the quieter, deeper rhythm of hurt.

"Geez Doc." Marino pauses. "You all right?"

"I'm the same."

He stares straight up, and we resume walking. "Something fucking weird is going on," he decides.

He has no idea how weird it is. "It's serious. That's for sure," I reply.

The chopper is a beefy twin-engine Bell 429. Completely blacked out, Apache-ominous, and I note the mounted gyro stabilized camera under the nose, the thermal imaging system or FLIR that looks like a radar dome on the belly. I recognize the special operations platforms known as *cargo racks* that are designed to move SWAT or members of the FBI's elitist Hostage Rescue Team (HRT). There are going to be at least half a dozen agents on bench seats inside the cabin, ready to rappel down and swarm the property on command.

"Maybe they're spying on you," Marino says, and his comment reminds me of other types of spying that I can't stop thinking about.

For an instant I see Carrie inside Lucy's dorm room. I see her piercing eyes and startlingly short bleached hair. I feel her cold-blooded aggression. I sense her as if she's within reach, and she might be.

"Then they should think of something a little less obvious than a tactical helicopter." I continue to say one thing while my mind is on another as we follow a circular driveway long enough to jog on.

In the center are acres of meadowland splashed with wildflowers where huge granite sculptures of fantastic creatures seem to wander and make themselves at home. We've already walked past a dragon, an elephant, a buffalo, a rhinoceros, and just now a mother bear with her cubs, sculpted from native stone out west somewhere and set in place by a crane. Lucy doesn't have to worry about anyone stealing her tons of art, and I watch for her as the monotonous noise continues overhead, rotor blades batting air. Thump-Thump-Thump-Thump.

I'm hot and sticky and hurting as I walk, and the sound is maddening. THUMP-THUMP-THUMP-THUMP! I love helicopters except for this one. I feel hateful as if it lives and breathes and we're personal enemies. Then I do a systems check of myself, concentrating on my hearing, my vision, my breathing, the pain jolting my leg with each step, with each shift of balance.

Focusing keeps me centered and calm, and I feel the hot pavement through the soles of my ankle-high boots, and the sunlight soaking into the soft fabric of my cotton tactical shirt. Sweat is cool as it trickles down my chest, my belly, my inner thighs. I'm conscious of the pull of gravity as I push my way uphill, and my body seems to weigh twice what it does. Moving around on land is heavy and slow, and when I was underwater I weighed nothing at all. I floated.

I floated and floated, drawn deeper into blackness, and it isn't true what they say about moving toward the light. I didn't see a light, not a bright one, not the smallest one. It's the darkness that seeks to claim us, to seduce us like a drugged sleep. I wanted to give in. It was the moment I've always waited for, the moment I've lived for and that more than anything else is what I can't get past.

I met death on the bottom of the sea as silt billowed in a cloud and a dark thread fled up from me, dissipating in my bubbles. I realized I was bleeding and had the irrational desire to take the regulator out of my mouth. Benton says I did, that as soon as he'd place the regulator back in I'd pull it out again and again. He had to hold it in place. He had to fight off my grabbing hands and force me to breathe, force me to live.

He's since explained that removing the regulator is a typical response when one panics underwater. But I don't remember panicking. I remember wanting to shed my buoyancy control device (BCD), my regulator and scuba tank, to free myself because I had a reason. I want to know what it was. It's on my mind constantly. Not a day goes by that I don't think about why dying seemed like the best idea I've ever had.

LUCY APPEARS around a bend.

She walks briskly toward us, and the thunderous noise seems suddenly louder. Of course it's my imagination. But what she's wearing isn't. The shapeless old gray gym shorts and T-shirt have the FBI ACADEMY boldly emblazoned on them, and it's as deliberate as waving a battle flag. It's like showing up in uniform after you've been court-martialed or wearing an Olympic medal after you've been stripped of it. She's flipping off the FBI, and maybe something else underlies her behavior.

I stare at her as if she's a ghost from the past. I was just watching her teenaged self inside her FBI Academy dorm room, and I almost wonder if my eyes are deceiving me. But the way she's dressed stays the same, and she could pass for being that young again. It's as if the Lucy in the videos is walking toward me in real time, a Lucy in her midthirties now. But she doesn't look it. I doubt she'll ever look her age.

Her energy is fiercely childlike, her body really hasn't changed, and her discipline about being fit and vital isn't vanity. Lucy lives like an endangered creature that twitches at the slightest movement or sound and hardly sleeps. She may be volatile but she's sensible. She's steely logical and rational, and as I step up my pace to meet her, the searing pain reminds me that I'm not dead.

"Your limping is worse." Her rose gold hair flares in the sun, and she's tan after a recent trip to Bermuda.

"I'm fine."

"No you're not."

The expression on her chiseled pretty face is difficult to read but I recognize tension in the firm set of her lips. I sense her dark mood. It sucks up the bright light around her. When I hug her, she's clammy.

"Are you all right? Are you really?" I hold on to her a second longer, relieved she's not injured or in handcuffs.

"What are you doing here, Aunt Kay?"

I smell her hair, her skin and detect the swampy salty odor of stress. I sense her state of high alert in the pressure of her fingers and her constant scan, her eyes moving everywhere. She's looking for Carrie. I know it. But we aren't going to discuss it. I can't ask if she's aware of the video link sent to my phone or tell her that it appears she was the one who sent it. I can't let on that I watched a film clip secretly recorded by Carrie. In other words, I'm now an accessory to Carrie Grethen's spying and who knows what else.

"Why is the FBI here?" I ask Lucy instead.

"Why are you?" She's going to push for an answer. "Did Benton drop a hint that this was going to happen? Nice of him. How the fuck does he look at himself in the mirror?"

"He didn't tell me anything at all. Not even by omission. And why all the swearing? Why must you and Marino swear so much?"

"What?"

"I'm just mindful of all the profanity. Every other word is *fuck,*" I reply as an emotional surge rolls over me.

It's as if the Lucy I'm facing is nineteen again, and I'm suddenly shaky inside, overwhelmed by the loss of time, by the betrayal of nature as it gives us life and instantly begins to take it back. Days become months. Years become a decade and longer, and here I am on my niece's driveway remembering myself at her age. As much as I knew about death I really didn't know that much about life.

I just thought I did, and I'm aware of how I must look as I limp along on Lucy's property as it's being raided by the FBI two months after I was shot with a spear gun. I'm thinner and my hair needs cutting. I'm slow and at war with inertia and gravity. I can't silence Carrie's voice in my mind and I don't want to hear it. I feel a stab of pain and suddenly I feel angry.

"Hey. You okay?" Lucy is watching me carefully.

"Yes. I'm sorry." I look up at the helicopter and take a deep breath, calm again. "I'm just trying to sort through what's going on."

"Why are you here? How did you know to be here?"

"Because you sent an urgent message?" It's Marino who answers. "How else would we know?"

"I have no idea what you're talking about."

"You know." His vintage Ray-Bans bore into her. "You let us know you have some sort of emergency and we dropped what we're doing. We literally left a damn dead body on the floor."

"Not exactly," I reply.

"What?" She seems genuinely amazed and baffled.

"A text message landed on my phone," I explain. "From your In Case of Emergency line."

"I promise it wasn't from me. Maybe from them." She means the FBI.

"How?"

"I'm telling you it wasn't from me. So you got a message? And that's why you suddenly decided to show up here in a crime scene truck?" She doesn't believe us. "Why the hell are you really here?"

"Let's focus on why they are." I glance up at the helicopter.

"Benton," she again accuses. "You're here because he tipped you off."

"No. I promise." I pause on the driveway, resting for a second. "He indicated nothing to either of us. He has nothing to do with why I decided to rush here, Lucy."

"What did you do?" Marino has a way of acting as if everybody is guilty of something.

"I'm not sure why they're here," Lucy replies. "I'm not sure of anything except I got suspicious early this morning that something was up."

"Based on?" Marino asks.

"Someone was on the property."

"Who?"

"I never saw whoever it was. There was nobody on the cameras. But motion sensors went off."

"Maybe a small animal." I start walking again very slowly.

"No. Nothing was there and yet something was. Plus someone's in my computer. That's been going on for about a week. Well I shouldn't say *someone*. I think we can figure out who it is."

"Let me guess. Considering who's dropped by for an unexpected visit." Marino doesn't disguise how much he hates the FBI.

"Programs opening and closing on their own and taking too long to load," she says. "The cursor moving when I'm not touching it. Plus my computer was running slow and the other day it crashed. No big deal. Everything is backed up. Everything vital is encrypted. It must be them. They're not particularly subtle."

"Anything leaked or corrupted?" I ask. "Anything at all?"

"There doesn't appear to be. An unauthorized user account was created by someone pretty savvy but no genius, and I'm on top of all that, monitoring unusual log-ins, all e-mails sent, trying to figure out what the hacker or hackers want. It's not a sophisticated attack or we wouldn't know about it until it's too late."

"But it's the FBI for sure?" Marino asks. "I mean it would make sense since here they just showed up with a warrant."

"I can't say with certainty who's rooting me. But it's probably them or related to them. The FBI often uses outside servers when they're investigating cybercrime. And alleged cybercrime is their excuse for snooping. You know for example if they have reason to suspect I'm laundering money or surfing kiddy porn sites, shit like that. So if it's them, they'll say they were investigating me for something totally trumped-up just so they can spy."

"What about my office?" I ask about the most problematic scenario. "Is it safe? Is there any chance our computers have been breached?"

Lucy is the systems manager and I.T. administrator for the CFC computer network. She does all the programming. She forensically examines all electronic and data storage devices turned in as evidence. While she may be the firewall that surrounds the most sensitive information associated with any death, she's also the biggest vulnerability.

Should the wrong person get past her, it would be catastrophic. Cases could be compromised before they ever reach court. Charges could be dropped. Verdicts could be overturned. Thousands of murderers, rapists, drug dealers and thieves could be released from prison in Massachusetts and elsewhere.

"Why all of a sudden?" I ask her. "Why the interest right now, assuming it's the FBI?"

"It started when I got back from Bermuda," she says.

"What the fuck did you do?" Marino demands with his usual tact.

"Nothing," she says. "But they're determined to fabricate a case that sticks."

"What case?"

"Something," she says. "Anything. I wouldn't be surprised if they've already convened a grand jury, in fact you can count on it. In fact I'm convinced. The Feds have the nasty little habit of raiding a place after they've already got a grand jury ready to indict you. They don't base a case on the evidence. They base the evidence on the case they're determined to make even if it's wrong. Even if it's a lie. Do you know how rare it is for a grand jury *not* to indict someone? Less than one percent of the time. They aim to please the prosecutor. They hear only one side of the story."

"Where can we talk?" I don't want to continue this conversation in her driveway.

"They can't hear us. I just knocked out the audio for that lamp and that one and the next one." She points at copper lampposts. "But let's go someplace we don't have to worry about it. My own personal Bermuda Triangle. They're watching and all of a sudden we vanish from their radar."

The agents searching her house are monitoring us on her security cameras, and I feel a rush of frustration. Lucy's battle with the Feds is as old as wars in the Middle East. It's a power struggle, a clash that's gone on so long I'm not sure anyone remembers exactly what started it. She was probably one of the most brilliant agents the Bureau ever hired, and when they eventually ran her off, that should have been the end of it. But it wasn't. It never will be.

"Follow me," she says.

CHAPTER 12

WE TRUDGE THROUGH BRIGHT GREEN GRASS SPATTERED with poppies as red as blood and brazen with gold sunflowers, white daisies, orange butterfly weed and purple aster.

It's as if I'm wading through a Monet painting, and beyond a shady fragrant stand of spruces we emerge into a low-lying area I've never seen before. It looks like a place of meditation or an outdoor church with stone slab benches and sculpted rock outcrops evocative of a pond filled by running water formed of river stones. I can't see the house or the driveway from here, nothing but rolling grass and flowers and trees and the constant whomping of the helicopter.

Lucy takes a seat on a boulder while I choose a stone bench in dapples of light shining through dogwoods. Hard unyielding surfaces aren't my first choice these days, and I sit down very carefully, doing what I can to diminish my discomfort.

"Has this always been here?" I ask, and the light moves on my face as branches move in the wind. "Because I've never seen it."

"It's recent," Lucy says and I don't ask how recent.

Since mid-June, I suspect. Since I almost died. I look around and don't see any sign of cameras, and guarding her rock garden is another sculpted dragon, this one small and comical lounging on a huge chunk of rose quartz. Its red garnet eyes stare right at me as Marino tries the bench across from mine, shifting his position several times.

"Shit," he says. "What are we? Cave people? How about wooden benches or chairs with cushions? Ever thought of that?" He's dripping sweat in the heat and humidity, and he flaps irritably at bugs and checks his socks for ticks. "Jesus! Did you forget to spray out here?" His dark glasses turn on Lucy. "There's damn mosquitoes everywhere."

"I use a garlic spray, pet and people safe. Mosquitoes hate it."

"Really? These must be friggin' Italian mosquitoes. Because they love it." He slaps at something.

"Steroids, cholesterol, large people who give off more carbon dioxide than the rest of us," Lucy says to him. "Plus you sweat a lot. Hanging garlic around your neck probably wouldn't help."

"What does the FBI want?" I look up at the helicopter hovering at no more than a thousand feet. "What exactly? We need to figure this out while we have a few minutes to talk privately."

"Their first stop was my gun vault," she replies. "So far they've packed all of my rifles and shotguns."

Carrie is suddenly in my mind again. I see her inside the dorm room, the MP5K strapped around her neck.

I ask Lucy, "Do they seem interested in any gun in particular?"

"No."

"They must be looking for something in particular."

"Everything I have is legal and has nothing to do with the Copperhead shootings," Lucy says, "which they damn well know were committed with the Precision Guided Firearm recovered from Bob Rosado's yacht. They confirmed it's the weapon two months ago so why are they still looking? If they're looking for anyone it should be his rotten little shit of a son, Troy. He's at large. Carrie's at large. He's probably the latest Clyde to her Bonnie, and where's the FBI? Here on my property. This is harassment. It's about something else."

"I got a couple shotguns you can borrow," Marino offers. "And a thumpin' four-fifty Bushmaster."

"That's all right. I've got more than they're bargaining for," she says. "They have no idea what they're missing, what they're walking right past."

"Please don't poke a stick at them," I warn her. "Don't give them cause to hurt you."

"Hurt? I think hurt is the point and it's already started." Her bright green eyes look at me. "They want me hurt. They intend to leave me unprotected so I can't take care of my family, my home. They're hoping all of us will end up defeated, annihilated, at each other's throats. Better yet, dead. They want all of us murdered."

"You need something all you gotta do is ask," Marino says. "With the likes of Carrie on the loose you should have more firepower than just your handguns."

"They'll take those next if they haven't already," she replies, and it really is outrageous that they listed handguns on the warrant. "Plus they're bagging up all of my kitchen cutlery, the Shun Fuji santoku knives you gave to us," she says to me, adding yet another outrage.

As far as we know, Carrie Grethen's recent deadly rampage includes a stabbing with a tactical knife. There's no evidence, not even a hint that Lucy had anything to do with it, and her guns and the cutlery are completely inconsistent with the characteristics of the murder weapons. To clean out her gun vault, her kitchen is absurd.

For an instant Carrie's recent victims parade through my mind, seemingly random people until I realized each of them had a connection to me, even if remotely. They never knew what hit them, except for Rand Bloom, the sleazy insurance investigator she stabbed and left on the bottom of a swimming pool. He would have had a moment if not several of terror, panic and pain.

But Julie Eastman, Jack Segal, Jamal Nari and Congressman Rosado didn't suffer. They were going about their business one second and then nothingness, annihilation, and I envision the Carrie I saw on video touching the back of her neck between the first and second cervical vertebrae. Even then she knew about the sweet spot for a hangman's fracture and that such a catastrophic injury literally causes instant death.

She's back. She's alive and more dangerous than she ever was and even as I'm thinking this I'm washed over by doubt. What if all of us are being tricked? I can't prove I've seen or heard from Carrie Grethen since the 1990s. She's left no real evidence that connects her with a crime spree that began late last year. What if it's not her who sent the video to me from Lucy's phone?

I look at my niece.

"From the beginning," I say to her. "What happened?"

LUCY SITS on her big rock and explains that this morning at exactly 9:05 her house phone rang.

The number is unlisted and unpublished but that wouldn't stop the FBI from getting it, and it doesn't stop her from foiling their efforts and then some. She has communication technology that can easily outsmart anyone attempting to catch her by surprise, and in a matter of seconds she knew the identity of the caller was Special Agent Erin Loria, a recent transfer to the FBI's Boston Division, thirty-eight years old, born in Nashville, Tennessee, black hair, brown eyes, five-ten, 139 pounds—and as I hear Lucy say this I don't show my shock.

I don't let on that I know who Erin Loria is. I don't react as Lucy goes on to explain that when Erin was in range of the security cameras, facial recognition software verified that she is indeed Erin Loria, a former beauty queen, a graduate of Duke University and its law school before she signed on with the Bureau in 1997. She was a street agent for a while, married to a hostage negotiator who left the Bureau and joined a law firm. They lived in Northern Virginia, had no kids, divorced in 2010, and soon after she married a federal judge twenty-one years her senior.

"Which one?" Marino asks.

"Zeb Chase," Lucy says.

"No way. Judge NoDoz?"

He's called that for the opposite reason people might expect, and I remember his small predatory eyes beneath heavy lids as he slumped on the bench, his chin almost on his chest like a black-robed vulture waiting for something to die. It was easy to misconstrue his posture as relaxed or half asleep when in fact he couldn't have been more alert or aggressive, waiting for attorneys, for expert witnesses to make a miscalculated move. Then he would dive-bomb, snatching them up to swallow alive.

In my earliest years in Virginia when he was still a U.S. attorney, we worked many cases together. Even though my findings usually supported the prosecution, Zeb Chase and I often clashed. I seemed to annoy him and he got only more hostile once he was on the bench. To this day I have no idea why, and I distantly recall that he might just hold the record for the judge who most frequently threatened to hold me in contempt. Now he's married to Erin Loria who has her own history with Lucy and therefore de facto has one with me. My internal weather vane moves. It points. I can't tell at what. Maybe I don't want to know.

"So Special Agent Loria moved to Boston and her husband the judge is still in Virginia," Marino assumes.

"It's not like he can pick up and come after her," Lucy replies and she's right.

Judge Chase's duty station would be the Eastern District of Virginia, where he will hold his seat until he resigns, dies or is removed from office. He can't pick up and relocate to Massachusetts even though his wife did. At least I can be grateful for that.

"Are you certain of the year Erin Loria started with the FBI?" I ask Lucy. "Nineteen-ninety-seven? As in the year you were there?"

"Not the only year I was there," she says as I think about Erin Loria being married to a federal official who was appointed by the White House.

That's not good. It's not good at all. She'll claim that he has no more influence in her cases than Benton has in mine. She'll swear His Honor has no professional involvement with her, that both of them stay completely within the legal boundaries and guidelines. Of course it isn't true. It never is.

"I realize you were at Quantico before and after 1997," I'm commenting to Lucy as my thoughts continue to slam into each other like billiard balls. "That once you got started with the FBI you never really left."

"Until they ran me out of Dodge," she says as if it's nothing that for all practical intents and purposes she was fired. "Even before I was an agent I was there summers, holidays, most weekends, every spare minute I had. You probably remember. I'd start arranging my classes so I could leave Charlottesville early Thursday morning and not come back until late Sunday. I was at Quantico more than I was in college."

"Jesus," Marino mutters. "Erin Loria was there when you were. And it's not exactly a big place."

"That's right," Lucy says.

"Another blast from the past just like Carrie. What did you step in during that informative time in your life, huh? Some Super Glue–like dog shit that you can't clean off?"

He means *formative,* but Lucy and I ignore it. We don't crack a smile. Not now as we perch on our hard, unforgiving seats in Lucy's place of meditation, her church, her Stonehenge.

"You step in some special brand of it?" he's saying. "And you not only still have it on your damn shoes but you're tracking it everywhere for the rest of us to step in."

"Which session?" I can't believe this is happening.

"We overlapped," she says. "Erin was at Quantico while I was an intern at ERF, while Carrie was there, yes. That's true. And they were familiar with each other."

"How familiar?" I ask it blandly.

"Familiar enough." Lucy doesn't flinch. "They got pretty friendly."

"Jesus Christ." Marino reaches around to his back and scratches another itch, real or perceived. "It's hard to imagine that's a coincidence in light of everything else. Whatever you sprayed out here doesn't work, just so you know. I've got bites, big ones. You can see them from friggin' outer space."

"Erin and I were on the same floor in Washington Dorm but I don't remember her very well except she was dismissive of me." Lucy is talking as Marino continues to claw and swat and bitch.

"I didn't know her firsthand. I didn't make friends with any of the new agents in training, not in that session, only in my own, which wasn't until two years later. Mostly I recall that she was Miss Tennessee. It's as far as she got in her beauty queen career, totally bombed the talent portion of the Miss America pageant, then went to law school, then applied to the FBI Academy. Great for undercover when you look like a Barbie doll, I guess. Well, hey. It gets you married to a judge, I guess. It gets you invitations to White House Christmas parties."

"You were at Quantico at the same time. Meaning Erin would be familiar with your background beyond what would be in your personnel file." I allude to the specter of Carrie.

Lucy doesn't say a word.

"Carrie Grethen," I'm out with it. "Erin would know about her for a number of reasons. Erin would know exactly who and what Carrie is."

"Now she would," Lucy says. "That's for sure. But in 1997 no one had any idea what they were dealing with. Including me."

As far as we know, Carrie hadn't committed murder back then. She wasn't a Ten Most Wanted criminal. She wasn't locked up in a forensic psychiatric facility for the criminally insane and hadn't escaped from it yet, and she hadn't allegedly been killed in a helicopter crash off the coast of North Carolina. Certainly when she worked at the ERF she wasn't a known felon or presumed dead, and she and Erin Loria might have been allies. They might have been friends. They might have had an affair and still be in communication, and what a bizarre notion that is to contemplate.

One of the most dangerous fugitives on the planet might be on amicable terms with an FBI agent married to a federal judge who was appointed by the president of the United States. My mind speeds through possible connections, adding two plus two and maybe getting four. Maybe getting five or some other wrong answer. Or maybe there's no answer period.

But it bothers me considerably that even as Erin Loria was making her way to Lucy's property barely two hours ago, I was sent a text message that included a link to a covert video recording Carrie made in Lucy's dorm room while the former Miss Tennessee–turned-FBI-agent was living right down the hall. Worse, Carrie and Lucy argued about her in the recording.

"Hold up a second," Marino says to Lucy. "Before we drink the Kool-Aid and start imagining all sorts of crazy crap let's go back to when your house phone rang. Your software collected data on who it was. You discovered Special Agent Loria was leading the charge and then what?"

"Literally?"

"Blow by blow."

"I knew she was in a vehicle moving fourteen miles per hour along the same road you were just on." Lucy pulls up her legs, planting her feet on the boulder, wrapping her arms around her bent knees.

None of us can get comfortable in her outdoor church. Except the sun feels good even if the humidity is oppressive, and the stirring air is sluggish but pleasant when it touches my damp skin. It's the kind of hot heavy weather that promises a violent storm, and one is predicted for this afternoon. I look up at thick dark clouds advancing from the south, and I fix on the helicopter loudly hovering near the water, hanging in the air like a huge black Orca float in a Macy's parade.

"I knew when she placed the call she was about fifty yards from my gate," Lucy describes, "and when I asked her what I could help her with she informed me the FBI had a warrant to search my house and any outbuildings associated with it. She ordered me to open the gate and leave it open, and within minutes five Bureau cars including a K-nine were in front of the house."

"What time did you notice the helicopter?" I continue to watch it hover rock solid, now over dense woods to the left of Lucy's house, which we can't see from where we're sitting.

"About the same time you rolled up."

"Let me get this straight." Marino frowns. "For some reason an FBI chopper just happened to be in Cambridge where we were working a case? And next it just happened to follow us here? Okay. Now I'm getting really hinky, you know, one of those really bad feelings that makes my hair stand up . . ."

"You don't have any hair," Lucy says.

"What bullshit are they pulling?" Marino glares up at the sky as if the FBI is God.

"Well they sure as hell aren't going to tell me," she says. "I don't know where they've been flying or for what reason, and there hasn't been time for me to check. After their cars showed up I no longer had privacy. It wasn't a smart idea for me to check with ATC or tune into their freq to hear who was buzzing around and maybe why. Plus I had a lot of other things to attend to. The K-nine in particular is upsetting—intentionally. What I call being a real asshole."

"Who?"

"Erin, I can only conclude. If she's gathered any information about me she realizes that I have an English bulldog named Jet Ranger who's so old he can hardly walk or see, and to have a Belgian Malinois searching the house would scare the hell out of him. Not to mention scaring Desi. Not to mention hassling Janet to the point she was about to deck someone. This is personal."

Her green eyes are intense. She holds my stare.

"I wouldn't be so quick to assume that." I'm cautious about

what I say. “I wouldn’t take any of this personally,” I advise my niece even as I wonder about her. “All of us need to be coldly objective and think clearly right now.”

“It feels like someone is settling a score.”

“I admit I’m wondering the same thing,” Marino says.

“This is planned.” Lucy seems convinced. “It’s been planned for a while.”

“What score and who?” I inquire. “Not Carrie.”

“Not Carrie my ass,” Marino snarls.

“I’ll just come right out and say it.” I keep going but I’m careful. “Carrie isn’t giving orders to the FBI even if she might have known Erin Loria while all of you were at Quantico together.”

“The two of them weren’t exactly strangers.” Lucy stretches out her lean strong legs, starts doing lifts for her abs, her eyes fixed on her blaze orange running shoes moving up and down. “Not hardly,” she adds.

“Oh hell. Don’t tell me they were sleeping with each other too.” Marino shifts his position on the hard bench, massaging the small of his back. “Does the judge know?”

“I don’t know how much sleeping went on,” Lucy says, as if it no longer bothers her, and I don’t believe that.

“Well one thing we know about Carrie is she’s an equal opportunity employer,” Marino says. “Age, race, gender, nothing holds her back. This story’s only getting worse.”

“I remember walking into the cafeteria one time and noticing them eating at the same table,” Lucy says to me and not him. “Now and then I saw them talking in the gym, and there was the rainy morning when Carrie ran the Yellow Brick Road and slipped when she was scaling down a rock face. She got a really bad rope burn and told me one of the new agents helped her, cleaned up the wound and dressed it. It was Erin Loria. I do remember that and suspecting the reason Erin might have helped her wasn't because they happened to be in the same place at the same time. They weren't just bumping into each other. They were running the obstacle course together. But beyond that?" Lucy shrugs, lifting her face to the sun, shutting her eyes. "Carrie was a lot more outgoing than I was. If you know what I mean."

"You ever hear her talk about Erin, specifically discuss her?" Marino asks.

"Not really. But Carrie's a master manipulator. She's a politician. She's a lot better with people than I'll ever be and can get almost anyone to cross the line with her."

"Exactly. And we don't know who she might be in communication with," Marino retorts. "And we don't know who the FBI might be talking to. Bottom feeders will get information any way and from any source they can. They make deals with the devil all the time."

"I agree," Lucy says. "She's fed them something. Even if it's indirectly."

CHAPTER 13

AS SHE TALKS SHE TRIGGERS MORE IMAGES FROM the video she doesn't know about. Or I assume she doesn't know about it and then I entertain another unsavory possibility.

If Carrie is in fact the person who texted the video link to me then she might also be sending things like that to the FBI. She might have sent the same recording to Erin Loria, and I don't want to think about what the Feds could do with it. How embarrassing for Lucy. How dangerous. And then I think of the illegal machine gun again.

It might be why they're here right now.

"Only thing about Carrie feeding the FBI information or having anything to do with anything?" Marino adds. "I doubt they believe she exists. Seriously. They genuinely might believe she's dead, just like we did until two months ago. Forget the judge.

Forget your Quantico past. Forget everything except that there's no proof Carrie's alive. Doesn't matter our opinion."

"Our *opinion*?" I look at him. "Is it merely an opinion that she shot me with a spear gun and it's a miracle I didn't hemorrhage to death or drown?"

"That's her favorite thing. Making you think she doesn't exist," Lucy says with her eyes shut, her face peaceful in the bright light.

She's calm but beneath it all she can't be. I don't know of anyone more private than my niece. The idea of agents going through every inch of her personal life is unimaginable. It occurs to me that I might be next, and I wonder what Benton would do if a squadron of his colleagues showed up at our picture-perfect antique Cambridge home.

"Let's stick with what's under our nose." Marino gives up on his slab bench, standing and stretching. "What are they saying you did, Lucy?"

"You know the Feds." She shrugs from her perch on her rock. "They don't say what they think you're guilty of and they don't ask. They throw things up against the wall until they find something that sticks. Like maybe you don't remember a detail exactly right. Maybe you say you went to the store on Saturday and it was really Sunday, so now they get you for a false statement, a felony."

"I don't suppose you've called Jill Donoghue." I'm sure I know the answer.

She's one of the most highly regarded criminal defense attorneys in the United States, and a brilliant dirty fighter. That's exactly what we need right now. It doesn't mean I like her.

"I haven't contacted her or anyone." Lucy confirms what I suspect.

"Why not?" I ask. "She should have been your first call."

"Come on Lucy. You know better than that," Marino says.

"You can't be dealing with them and not have a lawyer. What's wrong with you?"

"I used to be them. I know how to think like them," she says. "I wanted to cooperate with them long enough to gather intelligence on what exactly it is they're so hot and bothered about. Or what they're pretending they're so hot and bothered about."

"And?" I ask.

She shrugs again. I can't tell if she doesn't have an answer or refuses to say.

"I'm going to wander up to the house to see what the hell they're doing," Marino decides. "Don't worry. I won't go inside. But I'll make sure they see me. Fuck 'em."

"Janet, Desi and Jet Ranger are in the boathouse," Lucy says to him. "Maybe you can check on them. Make sure they stay there. They need to stay in the boathouse, and remember Jet Ranger can't swim. *Do not* let him near the edge of the dock," she adds emphatically. "*Not anywhere near it. They aren't to let him out of their sight,*" she says, and it's then I see it.

I catch the twitch on her face, an involuntary muscle reaction to an intensely unpleasant thought.

"And tell them I'll be right there," Lucy says, and I detect her murderous anger.

Just as quickly it's hidden under her many layers, down deep in a space that's not reachable. Like a diver breaking the surface, and then dropping down and gone. Nothing there but the rocking sea and the light caught by the water, and the flatness of an empty horizon.

I don't remember. I just know it happened. It's what I imagine it must be like to be born, to be warm and submerged, then suddenly, violently forced through the birth canal, and shocked and manhandled into breathing, into living this life. I have no memory of Benton helping me to the surface. I can't recall reaching the stern of the boat or how I got up on it. I couldn't have climbed the ladder.

My first real memory is someone holding a mask over my face, giving me oxygen, and how dry my mouth was. It felt as if my right thigh was in a vise that was clamped so tight it was crushing my femur. It was the worst pain I've ever experienced, at least that's my impression of it now. The black carbon fiber spear had entered through the quadriceps, perforating the vastus medialis and in the process grazing the bone before protruding from the other side of my leg. When I saw it, I didn't understand.

For a bizarre instant I thought I'd been involved in a construction accident and my thigh was impaled by rebar. Then I didn't believe what I was seeing was reality until I touched the tip of the spear and pain reverberated along the shaft. I saw blood on my hands, and smears of blood on the fiberglass flooring of the boat. I kept feeling for my inner thigh, making sure the spear was nowhere near my femoral artery.

Dear God please don't let me bleed to death. You're going to bleed to death. No, if you were going to you already would have. I remember what was going through my mind. The thoughts were splinters piercing my awareness, disconnected bits and pieces, and then blackness, and then I would drift back. I'd have a vague awareness of lying on the floor of the boat. I remember blood and a lot of towels, and Benton leaning close to me.

"Benton? Benton? Where am I? What's happened?"

He gently kept my leg still, and as he made me breathe he talked to me. He explained everything. He says he did but I can't replay it, not a word of it now. It's all so hazy. It's so strangely out of reach.

"Does Desi have any idea what's going on?" I ask Lucy, focusing on her, realizing she's not sitting anymore.

"Are you okay?" She stands over me. "Where were you just then?"

I don't tell her that when I go *there* wherever *there* is, it's like disjointed fragments of a dreadful illusion. It constantly enters my mind that I died and came back, and I won't share such thoughts. I won't mention the intrusions, the sensations and images that suddenly seize me when I least expect it. The cues are imperceptible. The spitting of a cigarette lighter, of a hose spraying. A movement in the corner of my eye.

Then out of nowhere, suddenly, violently like a seizure, the tugging, the screaming pain reverberate inside my brain. It was as if my leg was in the jaws of a shark, yanking, swimming away with me. I accepted my fate. I was about to drown. Then everything went empty and dark like a power outage. And suddenly, crazily, I hear it again.

The C-sharp cord of an electric guitar.

My eyes land on my phone absently gripped in one hand, at the message at the top of the display:

LucyICE Message.

I enter my password and go to my messages, and this one is just like the other. A link and nothing more. But it can't be from Lucy. How can it be? There's no way. She's standing not even six feet from me. She recognizes the alert tone that she knows so well, and meets my eyes.

Next she looks at her own phone, then at me. "I didn't just text you," she says.

"I know. Better put I didn't see you do it."

"You didn't see me? I just heard the alert tone for my ICE line, my second line on this phone." She holds it up and looks baffled and wary. "And I didn't send you anything."

"Yes. I'm aware I didn't see you touch your phone."

"Why are you talking like this?"

"I'm just commenting on what I did and didn't see," I reply.

"Have you assigned that tone to anyone else?"

"You customized my ringtones, created this one for me because it's unique, Lucy. No other caller in my contacts list has . . ."

"Okay," she interrupts impatiently. "What number is showing up?"

"There isn't one. It just says *LucyICE*, which is how I have the number labeled in my contacts list. And if I go to contacts now and look? There." I hold up my phone but don't let her get close. "It looks exactly as it always has. LucyICE." I recite the phone number. "And that's yours." I look her in the eye. "Is it possible someone's hijacked it? Specifically is it possible someone has found a way to hijack your In Case of Emergency line so it appears you're calling or texting urgently when in fact you're not?"

"A great way to get your attention. To make you stop everything you're doing—just like you are right now. A great way to manipulate you to respond as directed at a precise time for a certain reason." Lucy looks around as if someone might be watching, then walks over and holds out her hand. "Let me see."

I'm not about to give her my phone, and I get up from my chair. I step back from her.

"I need to take a look." She continues to hold out her hand for my phone. "I promise whatever you just got isn't from me. Let me see what it is."

"I'm not going to do that."

"Why not?"

"Legally I can't. Legally I won't be that reckless. I don't know for a fact who's doing this, Lucy."

"Doing what?"

"Sending me things as if they're from you."

"And you worry it might really be me doing it." She looks hurt, then stung.

"I don't know for a fact who it is," I repeat.

"What do you mean by *legally*?" She begins to react angrily and so do I. "You're just like them. You think I did something. The FBI's all over my property so that makes me guilty of something?"

"We're not discussing this. You didn't overhear anything, not even a ringtone, dammit, and you need to step back." I'm dismayed by the tone in my voice, and Lucy is about to lose her temper.

"I can't help if you withhold things from me, Aunt Kay!"

"You can help by answering my very simple question, Lucy. Could someone be spoofing your number? Could someone have hijacked it?"

"You know better than anyone that I don't give out my phone numbers." Her arms are defiantly crossed. "I almost never call anybody from my emergency line, anyway. And nobody has that number except you. And Benton, Marino and Janet of course."

"Well it seems somebody has it. I'm wondering how that could happen. Especially to you."

"I don't know how. I don't know enough yet."

"I almost never hear you say you don't know." I carefully, painfully get up from my stone slab. "I need a few minutes of privacy, please."

I dig into a pocket for my wireless earpiece. I put it on as I click on the link and immediately text rolls by, bloodred like before:

DEPRAVED HEART—VIDEO 2

BY CARRIE GRETHEN

JULY 11, 1997

I feel the stone dragon watching from his rose quartz perch. His glinting red garnet eyes seem to follow me as I move as far from Lucy as I can.

CARRIE'S FACE looms large and porpoise-like as she peers into a microcamera disguised as a battery-operated beige plastic pencil sharpener shaped like a brick.

She picks it up and films herself from different angles, then directs the tiny lens inside the dark pink cavern of her mouth. She wags her tongue and it moves hugely, fatly in different tempos like an obscene metronome. Slowly up and down. Side to side very fast. She rapidly touches her pink lips together and they make musical popping sounds. Then she holds up the pencil sharpener like the skull in *Hamlet* and talks directly to it.

"To be or not to be God? That is the question. Whether 'tis nobler to suffer the abstinence of putting off pleasure or should I give in to instant gratification? The answer is no. I must not give in. I must be patient, as patient as required no matter how difficult or demanding. God plans events millions of years in advance. And so can I, Chief," she says and I hear it again, a sentence that has been edited.

Who is she talking to when she says Chief?

"Howdy. Welcome back." Carrie walks over to the computer on the desk, sets down the pencil sharpener, pulls out the chair and sits.

Reaching for the mouse, she clicks on it and a paused image of Lucy and me fills the screen. In it I'm gesturing midsentence while Lucy sits on top of a wooden picnic table, listening, smiling. I recognize the pearl gray silk suit I had on, long since given away. Carrie must have had a zoom lens. She must have been out of sight, and I instantly recognize the perspective, the weather, the foliage.

The ERF's parking lot. Hot and sunny. Late in the day.

The canopies of the hardwood trees are densely green and mature. There is no sign of the leaves turning, not the slightest hint of gold or red. It's summertime. July or August. It could be the second half of June, but not the first half. No earlier than mid- to late June. Carrie might have been inside a car filming Lucy and me at the picnic tables in the wooded area flanking the employee parking lot, and I see it, feel it, smell it as if I'm there.

I have on the elegant silk suit that Benton gave me for my birthday, June 12, almost exactly one month before Marino's. In 1995 I'm pretty sure, and I know for a fact I wore the suit only once to court because it wrinkled terribly. By the time I was called to the stand the skirt looked like it had been balled up in a drawer before I put it on, the wrinkles radiating from under the arms of the jacket are huge crow's-feet. I see the suit clearly. I remember making a joke about it to Lucy.

It was a Northern Virginia case, not far from Quantico, and I stopped by after court and had lunch with her in the picnic area. Not in 1997. Definitely not. She was just starting her internship and I was laughing about my suit. I said it showed sweat stains too, and that Benton was a typical man who didn't think of things like that. He may be sensitive and hyperintuitive and have exquisite taste, but he shouldn't be picking out clothes for me.

I don't work for the Bureau, I remember saying to Lucy, or words to that effect. *I don't dress for meetings in war rooms, I dress for a landfill. Wash and wear, that's me.*

As early as 1995 and already Carrie was spying. She may have been covertly recording Lucy and even me soon after she met us, and I look at my phone display and watch Carrie get up from the desk two years later, in July 1997. I watch her walk across the dorm room. Pay attention. Don't let your memories distract you from her manipulations.

"Are you having a nice trip down memory lane, Chief? Because I have a feeling you're having a nice long leisurely stroll remembering all sorts of things you've not thought about in the longest time." Carrie finds another camera, talks directly into it. "I wish I knew what stardate you're in at this very moment. I'm here inside Lucy's cramped unimaginative boudoir in this land of walking dicks who wear guns and flash their badges."

Carrie is barefoot and in the same white running clothes, and the light seeping around the outer edges of the slatted blinds isn't as intense as earlier. It's later in the day.

"Lucy just stepped out for a few minutes to be domestic. Surprised? I imagine you are scratching your head. And I wonder? Okay tell me the truth." Carrie leans toward the camera conspiratorially. "Does she help out around her Auntie Kay's house? Does she do dishes or clean toilets or take out the trash or even offer? If not you should work with her on that particular aspect of her considerable immaturity and spoiledness. Because I have no problem getting her to be responsible. I simply tell her, 'Lucy, do this or do that. And snap to it!' " Carrie laughs as she snaps her fingers. "Right now she's taking care of our dirty laundry.

"So while we have a second alone I'm going to tell you a little bit about what to expect. By the time you see this months and years will have passed. I don't know how many. It could be five. It could be thirty. They will pass in the twinkling of an eye and the older we get the faster time will speed on, carrying us closer to dilapidation and physical nonexistence.

"Already the days seem to go more quickly for me than they do for Lucy, and your days must go much faster than either of ours because the brain's biological clock, the suprachiasmatic nucleus in the hypothalamus"—she taps her forehead—"ages just like the rest of us. What changes isn't time but our perception of it as the instruments inside our biological vessel are subject to stress, fatigue and wear and tear. They become less accurate like a precessing directional gyro or a wet compass out of calibration, and what you perceive isn't accurate anymore.

"Already your memory-bumps should be moving you back in time like an assembly line. Already the past is being reconstructed and restored rapidly and miraculously as you relive what you see, and what a wonderful ride that will be. Consider it my gift to you. A bit of immortality, a spritz from the Fountain of Youth. But as I continue to emphasize by way of an apology *I can't say when*.

"At this juncture in time and space I honestly can't predict when I will decide the history of the world is perfectly poised and suited for you to be properly and at long last enlightened about the meaning of your life and death, and the beginnings and ends of all the people on earth who matter to you. Including me. Yes me. We've never had an opportunity to be friends. We've never had a substantive conversation. Not even a cordial one. And that's shocking when one considers what you could learn from me. Let me fill you in on a few facts about Carrie Grethen."

Another hidden camera picks her up as she walks across the room to an Army green canvas backpack on the floor. She crouches and digs inside it. She finds a manila envelope that isn't sealed and slides out folded sheets of paper, more pages of a script.

"Did you know I'm a writer, a raconteur, an artiste? That I'm a devotee of Hemingway, Dostoyevsky, Salinger, Kerouac, Capote? Of course not. You wouldn't want to humanize me. You wouldn't want to assign anything positive or noteworthy—no pun intended—such as an appreciation for poetry and prose. Or that I have a very wicked sense of humor.

"I offer a brief character sketch that will give you a few clues, and you go right ahead and share them with whoever you like. Put them in one of your boring technical books. Now there's an idea. Please excuse that I prefer the third person when I talk about myself. I don't talk about *me*. I talk about *her*. Are you ready? Are you sure?"

CHAPTER 14

ONCE UPON A TIME THERE WAS AN ALCHEMIST WHO prepared her own special protective potions that kept her forever young."

Carrie holds up the bottle of lotion as she reads from her script.

"With her very fair skin"—she touches her pale cheek—"and very fair hair"—she touches her platinum hair—"she blended like a moth inside the bland off-white FBI dorm room as if natural selection was the explanation for what she'd become. But it wasn't. Something else had leached the color out of her soul, mutating it and creating paranormal cravings and behaviors that made her seek out lightlessness and gloom.

"As a young child Carrie knew she wasn't good. When people at church talked about good stewards, good Samaritans, good believers pure of heart she knew she wasn't one of them. From the earliest age she knew she wasn't like anyone at school or inside her own home. She wasn't like anyone at all and while this was confusing it also pleased her greatly that she had been unusually blessed. Such a rare gift not to mind extreme temperatures, to scarcely feel heat or cold and to see in the dark like a cat. What a treat to leave her body during sleep and travel to distant lands and into the past, to speak languages she'd never learned and remember places she'd never been. Carrie's IQ was too high to measure.

"But to whom much is given much also can be taken, and one day her mother uttered the terrible words that no child should ever hear. Little Carrie's destiny was to die young. She was so special that Jesus couldn't bear to be without her long and would take her back to heaven early.

" 'Think of it as a Holy layaway plan,' Carrie's mother explained. 'Jesus was shopping, and as He browsed through all the millions of new babies about to be born, He picked you out and set you aside. Very soon He'll return to pick you up and take you home with Him forever.'

" 'Then He has to get the money to pay for me?' Carrie inquired.

" 'Jesus doesn't need money. Jesus can do whatever He wants. He's perfect and all-powerful.'

" 'Then why didn't He just pay for me when He found me and take me home with Him?'

" 'It's not for us to question Jesus.'

" 'But it sounds like He's poor and not very powerful after all, Mommy. It sounds like He couldn't afford me the same way you can't afford things you put on layaway.'

" 'You must never say anything disrespectful about our Lord and Savior.'

" 'But I didn't, Mommy. You did. You said He can't afford me right now or else I'd be gone from here and in heaven with Him. And then I wouldn't be a burden for you anymore. You don't want me and wish I was dead.'

"Carrie's mother responded by washing her young daughter's mouth out with a bar of Ivory soap, twisting it so hard that the bright white cake turned red from her bleeding gums. After that her mother gave up on the layaway analogy, realizing it was close to what she meant but not quite right. Instead she took to reminding Carrie that she should live an exemplary pure-hearted life and to thank God for it while she could because none of us knows how long we'll be here anyway.

"She explained that what she really meant when she brought up the metaphor of a layaway plan was that life on earth is like being in the back room of a department store. Some of us will be in that back room a shorter time than others, depending on 'what we came equipped with before we were put in storage on this earth, waiting for Jesus.'

"In other words, what her mother really was referring to when she used that corny layaway analogy was the family flaw, a potentially fatal one that Carrie had inherited. This wasn't made up. It was an unfortunate fact, and by Carrie's fourteenth year she'd lost both her maternal grandmother and her mother to a thromboembolism caused by the bone marrow abnormality polycythemia vera. Carrie made a pact with God that she wouldn't suffer a similar fate, and like clockwork every two months she underwent phlebotomy, removing as much as a pint of blood that she would retain for her own personal use. It wasn't the only interesting ritual that would follow her well into adulthood."

Carrie walks around the dorm room, gesturing, looking into the camera. She's enjoying herself. She's loving this.

"Eventually odd rumors about her would circulate at the FBI's Engineering Research Facility," she continues, "where it would have been a civil rights violation to question their most senior civilian computer savant about her health, about her personal beliefs and how they were manifested. It was nobody's business if she saved or drank her own blood or was poly-sexual or communed with the Other World. Her appetites and fantasies were of no concern as long as she kept them to herself.

"How long she lived wasn't relevant either, only that she finished the important job the federal government had recruited her to do, a technical feat that didn't call for an FBI special agent, and Carrie wasn't one. Professionally she was classified as a non–law enforcement, non-military independent contractor with special security clearances. Personally she was considered a nerd, a weirdo, a nobody who was called derisive and crude nicknames behind her back."

Her eyes are dark and cold as they bore into the camera. "Sexist, vulgar names and snipes that the FBI didn't think Carrie overheard. But she did, and her upbringing had prepared her well for not reacting to taunts or retaliating or doing anything that gave the enemy any power.

"Punishment isn't punishment if you don't feel punished, if you don't experience the suffering that's intended. It's all about perception. It's all about the way you react to something and that reaction is the real weapon. The weapon is what injures, and in your case I'm banking on you being injured by your own self, by your own reactions because you've yet to learn a lesson no one had to teach me: If you feel no pain and show no injury then there was no weapon, only a weak attempt . . ."

Her mellow, pleasant voice with its subtle Virginia lilt suddenly stops and the frame goes black. It's the same as before. The link is disabled. Instantly it's gone like the first one.

JILL DONOGHUE is unavailable, and I insist that her secretary interrupt her. I don't give orders unless I mean it, and right now

I feel like an engine about to overtorque. I know I don't sound particularly nice but I can't help it.

"I'm sorry Doctor Scarpetta. But it's a deposition," the secretary tries to plead with me. "They're supposed to break at noon."

"Noon won't work. I need her now and I'm very sorry. I'm sure whatever she's doing is important. But it's not as important as this. Please get her for me," I reply, and I think about patience, about whether I'm a patient person because I certainly don't sound like it.

I don't for a very good reason, I decide. Not this morning, and Carrie knew what she was doing. She's giving me clues, and as much as I can't stand to think about how manipulated I feel it would be reckless and foolish to wear blinders. She's made it clear that everything is about timing. Therefore it stands to reason that the timing of the texts landing in my phone isn't random.

I wonder if she's spying even as I stand in Lucy's rock garden, the sun moving in and out of white clouds that are ruffled like a washboard underneath, the tops of them building vertically. The storm is coming, a whopper summer thunder cell and I smell its ozone approach as I begin to wander well beyond Lucy's outdoor sanctuary, thick green grass springy beneath my boots. I move into the partial shade of a dogwood tree, waiting for my pulse to slow down. The Muzak on Donoghue's office line is awful and I feel a flare of irritation. My face feels angry hot.

I've always considered myself a disciplined deliberate person, a long-suffering, patient, logical, unemotional scientist but obviously I'm not patient enough, nowhere near patient enough, and my thoughts race as images flash. I keep seeing Carrie Grethen's face, the stoniness of her skin as pale as paper, and the way her eyes changed color and shading during her lecture, her soliloquy. Deep blue then aqua then icy pale like a Siberian husky and next her irises were so dark they looked almost black. I was seeing what was going on in her psyche, the shadings of her monster, of her spiritual malignancy, and I take another deep breath and blow out slowly.

The video and its abrupt ending had the effect of a triple shot of espresso or maybe a large dose of digitalis. My heart is about to beat its way out of my chest. I feel poisoned. I feel so many things I can't begin to describe them, and I take deep slow breaths. I open up my lungs and breathe in and out deeply, very slowly and quietly as I wait for Donoghue. Finally I hear a click on the line and the Muzak stops.

"What's happening, Kay?" Jill Donoghue gets right to it.

"Nothing good or I wouldn't be calling like this. I apologize for interrupting." I move a few steps, and my right thigh reminds me it's there.

"What can I do for you? And what's the noise? Is that a helicopter? Where are you?"

"It's an FBI helicopter most likely," I reply.

"I take it you're at a crime scene . . ."

"I'm on Lucy's property which is being treated like a crime scene. I would like to retain you as my attorney, Jill. I'd like to do so immediately." I watch Lucy sitting some distance away on a bench pretending she isn't interested in my conversation.

"Certainly we can talk about that later but what's happening . . . ?" Donoghue starts to say.

"For the record we're talking about it now," I interrupt her. "Please make a note of it. On August fifteenth at ten minutes past eleven A.M., I hired you as my attorney and asked you to represent Lucy, too. Assuming you're amenable."

"So the three of us are protected by attorney-client privilege," she considers. "Except you aren't protected if you talk to Lucy without me present."

"I understand. I'm about to believe nothing is privileged or private anyway."

"That's probably a smart attitude to adopt this day and age. For now the answer is yes about representation. But if there's a conflict I'll have to withdraw from representing one of you."

"Fair enough."

"Can you talk now?"

"Lucy says where I am right this minute is safe. My guess is most of her property isn't, and the same may be true of my phone if they've wiretapped into it. It may be true of my office e-mail. I have no idea what's safe to be honest."

"Has Lucy talked to the FBI? Has she so much as said *good morning*?"

"She's been cooperating with them to a degree. I'm afraid she's too comfortable." I look up at the helicopter and imagine the agents inside looking back. "I'm not happy that she didn't call you right away."

"That wasn't a good idea. But I know her. It's her nature to underestimate them. She absolutely shouldn't."

Lucy is now pacing, looking at her phone, texting, and she must not have serious worries about the FBI accessing her e-mail or anything else. I suppose I shouldn't be surprised, and I don't envy anybody who decides to intrude upon her privacy. She'll treat it as a challenge, as a competition. She's happy to return the favor. I can only imagine the cyber mischief and destruction she's capable of if she puts her mind to it, and I remember the look in Carrie's eyes as she said how spoiled Lucy was. The video clip I just watched continues playing in my mind. I can't make it stop.

I can't shake Carrie's mockery, her grandiose self-absorption and bottomless pit of hate, and it's outrageous and wrong that I'm subjected to any of it. I feel saddened, angered and undone in a way that's hard to define. I wonder if that's the real point in subjecting me to this, and then I have another thought. If I tell anyone—including Jill Donoghue—there will be the problem of credibility.

No one will believe me, and for good reason. The links texted to me are dead. It's impossible to prove they were ever connected to recordings made by Carrie Grethen or anyone else.

"Who besides you is on the property?" Donoghue continues to ask me questions, to prep herself before she heads out the door.

"Marino. Janet and their adopted son, Desi," I reply. "Well he's not officially adopted yet. His mother, Janet's sister, died of pancreatic cancer three weeks ago."

Donoghue says she's deeply sorry to hear it, and whenever she attempts to show empathy or kindness she gets a certain tone in her voice. It reminds me of a piano key that's a little flat or the dull clink of cheap glass. Her walking around in another person's moccasins is a well-oiled act. Unfortunately she doesn't mean it, and I go out of my way never to forget that her charisma, her alleged empathy are a rubber chicken. You hungrily sink your teeth into it and discover it's fake.

"What about Janet and Lucy?" Donoghue asks. "Are they married?"

I'm caught by surprise and feel another wave of misgiving and maybe shame as I reply, "Actually I don't know."

"You don't know if the niece you've raised like a daughter is married?"

"They've never said anything. Not to me."

"But you would know if they are."

"Not necessarily. It wouldn't be unlike Lucy to get married in secret. But I'd be surprised," I explain. "It wasn't all that long ago that she told Janet to move out."

"Why?"

"Lucy fears for Janet's safety, for Desi's safety." I glance at Lucy, making sure she can't hear me.

She's standing with her back to me as she looks at something on her phone.

"Aren't they safer with her?" Donoghue asks.

"It doesn't seem Lucy thought so several months ago."

"Married people can kick each other out of the house. You don't have to be unmarried to have that happen."

"Which brings me back to the same thing. I don't know what they are. I don't know if they're protected by spousal privilege. You'll have to ask them."

"Does Janet know she shouldn't say a word to the FBI?" Donoghue asks. "Because they'll try to trick her into chatting, into anything they possibly can. If they ask her what time it is or what she ate for breakfast, she's not to tell them."

"Janet is former FBI. She's an attorney. She's knows how to handle them."

"Yes, yes I know. Both she and Lucy are former FBI, meaning they're overly confident about their ability to handle the FBI. Does Benton know what's happening? I'm assuming he must."

"I have no idea." I don't want to.

It's yet one more unthinkable possibility. A strong possibility. In fact it's hard to imagine Benton didn't know his own family was about to be raided. How could he not have known? This isn't a spontaneous event. The Feds planned it.

"I saw him in court early this morning at a status hearing," Donoghue adds. "I started to say he acted as if everything is fine. But he always acts like that."

"Yes he does." I don't recall Benton telling me he had court this morning.

"And you haven't told him where you are right now and what's happening," Donoghue makes sure. "And he's given you no reason to suspect he knows?"

Benton and I had coffee together. We spent a few quiet minutes on our sunporch before both of us got ready for work, and I envision his handsome face, conjuring it up from hours earlier.

"He didn't," I reply.

I didn't detect the faintest shadow of anything that might have been bothering him. But Benton is stoical. He's one of the most unreadable people I've ever met.

"What's the likelihood he doesn't know, Kay?"

There's no likelihood, and that's probably the dismal truth because how could he not have had a clue that his colleagues were about to raid Lucy's property and seize her belongings? Of course he knew, and how could he not be bothered by that fact? How could he sleep in the same bed and make love to me while knowing such a thing was about to happen? I feel a twinge of anger, of betrayal, and then I feel nothing. This is our life together. We have more nonconversations than any two people I know.

We routinely keep secrets from each other. At times we lie. It might be by omission but we deliberately mislead each other and misrepresent the truth because that's what our jobs require. At moments like this as an FBI helicopter beats overhead and agents raid my niece's property I wonder if it's worth it. Benton and I answer to a higher power that's actually a lower one. We faithfully serve a criminal justice system that's flawed and compromised on its way to being broken.

"I've not talked to him since we left the house this morning," I summarize to Donoghue. "I've told him nothing."

"Let's leave it like that for now," she says, and after a weighty beat she adds, "I have a question for you, Kay, while we're on the subject. Have you ever heard the term *data fiction*?"

"Data fiction?" I repeat, and Lucy turns around and stares in my direction as if she heard what I just said. "No I haven't. Why?"

"It's a term that's central to a case I was just in court about this morning. Not a case that has any direct relevance to you per se. Well we'll talk when I see you. I'm on my way."

CHAPTER 15

I END THE CALL AND LEAN AGAINST THE DOGWOOD tree, thinking. The helicopter is a huge menacing black hornet. It's been nosing low and loud over the river, going up and down, then cutting hard left or right, flying a grid pattern as if searching for someone.

I feel sunlight on the back of my neck as I look around at the freshly mown grass and lush trees. The meadow beyond the rock garden is a paint-spattered canvas in bold primary colors and electric mixtures of them. It's breathtakingly beautiful in this spot. It's supposed to be peaceful but the FBI has turned it into a war zone and I realize how alone I am. I can't confide in anyone, not really, and especially not Benton.

Jill Donoghue was in a status hearing early this morning and ran into him. What business took him to the federal courthouse in Boston and why didn't he mention it before we both left for work? What really gnaws at me is that Donoghue brought up something called data fiction in the context of why I just called her. What does it have to do with Lucy or me or any of us? Or was she simply referencing something that was on her mind? I twist around and look up at the helicopter banking east, swooping around, thundering over Lucy's house directly toward us.

"Are we ready?" Lucy's face is stone.

I can't be sure that she didn't overhear my conversation. I have no idea what she really knows.

"Yes we should go," I reply, and we set out for the house together. "Before we say another word to each other let me remind you that whatever is communicated between the two of us isn't privileged."

"That's nothing new, Aunt Kay."

"So I want to be very careful what I ask or tell you, Lucy. I just want to make sure you understand that." Thick grass makes a brushing sound against my boots, and the humidity is fast approaching the dew point.

In another hour or so we're going to have a Noah's Ark downpour.

"I know all about privilege." She glances over at me. "What do you want to know? Ask me while you can. In a few minutes it won't be safe to have this conversation."

"Jill Donoghue mentioned something about a case involving data fiction. I'm curious if you have any idea what she might have been referring to because I'm not familiar with the term."

"Data fiction is a trending concept on the Undernet, the underground of the Internet."

"The Undernet where most of what goes on is illegal?"

"Depends on who you're talking to. For me it's just an extreme frontier of cyberspace like the wild wild west, just another place to data mine and send my search engines loose."

"Tell me about data fiction."

"It's what can happen if we're so reliant on technology that we become completely dependent on things we can't see. Therefore we can no longer judge for ourselves what's true, what's false, what's accurate, what isn't. In other words if reality is defined by software that does all the work for us then what if this software lies? What if everything we believe isn't true but is a facade, a mirage? What if we go to war, pull the plug, make life-and-death decisions based on data fiction?"

"I'd say that happens more than we'd like to imagine," I reply. "It's certainly something I worry about every time we generate our annual crime statistics and the government makes decisions based on our data."

"Imagine armed drones controlled by unreliable software. A click of the mouse and you blow up the wrong person's house."

"I don't have to imagine it," I reply. "I'm afraid it's happened."

"Or how about financial misinformation and manipulation, something far worse than a Ponzi scheme? Think about all those online transactions and digital reads of what you have in your bank accounts. You believe you have a certain amount of cash, assets or debt because it says so right there on your computer screen or in your quarterly report that was generated by software. What if this software creates data that accounts for every penny but in fact it's false? What if it's a front for fraud? Then you have data fiction."

"And right now there's a case in federal court involving that." I'm walking slowly and uphill again. "Apparently Jill Donoghue has something to do with it. Benton might have something to do with it too."

"Do you need to stop for a minute, Aunt Kay?" Lucy pauses to wait up for me.

"We need to work on what you call me. You can't keep calling me Aunt Kay."

"Then what?"

"Kay."

"Feels strange."

"Doctor Scarpetta. Chief. Hey you. Something besides Aunt Kay. You're not a kid. Both of us are adults."

"You seem to be hurting a lot," Lucy says. "We need to get you someplace where you can sit down."

"Don't worry about me. I'm all right."

"You're hurting. You're not all right."

"Sorry I'm so damn slow."

The pain in my leg is a radiating throb that I've gotten used to for the most part. Each week I'm better but I can't move fast. Stairs are difficult. Standing on the hard tile in the autopsy room hours on end is miserable. But vigorous activity such as trudging uphill in extreme heat and humidity would be considered off-limits so soon. I'm not supposed to get my blood pressure up.

When I do I'm reminded that bone is living tissue, and the longest heaviest bone in the human body is the femur. It has two super-nerves, the femoral and the sciatic, that run from the lower back to the knee like high-speed trains carrying pain along their tracks. I stop walking for a moment and rub my thigh, gently massaging the muscles.

"You should use a cane," Lucy says.

"God no."

"I'm serious." She glances at me, at my leg as I resume walking stiffly. "You're at a disadvantage. You can't outrun anyone and at least if you had a sturdy walking stick, a cane, you could use it as a weapon."

"That sounds like the logic of a seven-year-old, like something Desi would say."

"Looking so obviously wounded and vulnerable makes you an easy target. Bad people smell your weakness like a shark smells blood. Metaphorically it's the wrong message."

"I've already been an easy target once this summer for a shark of sorts. It won't happen again. And I have a pistol in my bag." I sound a little winded.

"Don't let them see it. They'd love an excuse to shoot us."

"That's not funny."

"Do I look like I'm laughing?"

Her house comes into view, timber and glass with a copper roof on a rise overlooking a part of the river as wide as a bay. The helicopter is over the woods again, very low this time and treetops churn in the downwash.

"What the hell are they looking for?" I ask.

"They want the recording." Lucy says it matter-of-factly, and I'm shocked.

I stop on the driveway and stare at her. "What recording?"

"They think I have it hidden somewhere, maybe buried like treasure, maybe in some secret bunker. I mean really?" she says derisively. "They think I'm going to tuck the camera into a little metal box and dig a hole and whoaaa it's safe? If I don't want them to find something they won't in a million years."

"What recording?"

"I can guarantee you they're using ground-penetrating radar, looking for geologic parameters that might tell them I have something hidden belowground." Lucy's attention is fixed on the helicopter, so loud and close we're having to shout. "Next they'll probably show up with fucking backhoes just so they can have the pleasure of destroying my landscaping. Because more than anything this is revenge, this is putting me in my place."

"What recording?" I expect her next to admit that the *Depraved Heart* video clips were sent to her too.

"The one from Florida."

She means the recording of my being shot while diving a shipwreck off the coast of Fort Lauderdale two months ago.

"There's nothing helpful in it but I guess they don't know that. It depends on what they're really looking for," she says as I realize she's been lying to me, to everyone. "Or better yet what they're not looking for, which is the more likely story. And I can't give them that bonus. I'm pretty sure I know what it is and they won't get it courtesy of me."

MY SCUBA MASK with its embedded mini-recorder is missing. Or I thought it was. It was never recovered after Carrie tried to kill me. Or that's what I've been led to believe.

The explanation I've been given is that finding it wasn't the top priority. Saving my life was. By the time divers searched for the mask the current had moved it and possibly covered it with silt.

"They wanted that recording two months ago." I'm careful what I say. "Why is this coming up now?"

"Before now it was theoretical. They're convinced I have it."

"The FBI is convinced," I reply and she nods. "Based on what? How can you know what they're convinced of?"

"When I flew back from Bermuda recently I landed at Logan and within minutes Customs police were all over my plane."

"Stop." I hold up my hand and pause on the driveway again. "Before you continue, why would the Feds care if you were in Bermuda? Why would they be monitoring you there?"

"Maybe because of who they suspected I was seeing."

I think of Carrie as I ask, "And who was that?"

"I was seeing a friend of Janet's. No one you need to concern yourself with."

"I'd say there's a need for me to concern myself since it would seem this person is someone the FBI is interested in."

"And they'll just keep on snooping around in case Carrie really does exist."

"If she doesn't then who did this to my leg?" I tamp down a flare of anger.

"Long story short, the FBI sicced Customs on me. They went through everything on my plane and asked me a long list of questions about my trip, about why I was traveling and had I been scuba diving. They held me for well over an hour and I have no doubt about the point of it. They were instructed to look for the mask, for recording devices, in other words for items the FBI had interest in but didn't want to tip their hand about with me. The FBI couldn't crawl all over my plane and go through my luggage to their hearts content without drawing huge attention. But Customs could."

I don't know how Lucy could have gotten hold of my scuba mask, and next I think of Benton. If he found it and never turned it in he would be guilty of tampering with evidence, obstruction of justice, anything his FBI compatriots might hurl at him.

"Should we be . . . ?" I don't finish the question as I make a point of looking at lampposts, at the cameras mounted on them.

"I've been knocking out the audio of every camera we pass. I'm sure they know I'm doing it. As soon as I get inside they'll take my phone so I can't tamper with my own security system," Lucy says. "They were going through my scuba gear earlier."

"But you weren't diving with me when it happened."

"They'll make a case that I was."

"That's ridiculous. You weren't even in Florida."

"Prove it."

"They're making a case that you were with me when I was

shot? You were on that dive? How could they possibly make a case for that? You weren't with us."

"Who will irrefutably prove I wasn't?" She continues to push her point. "Benton and you? Because everyone else isn't talking."

What she means is the two police divers who had gone down to the wrecked barge first were murdered. I'm not aware of any witnesses to my being shot except Benton and the one who did it, Carrie.

"They believe I have your dive mask," Lucy says.

"Do you?"

"Not exactly."

"Not exactly?"

"The instant you activated the camera on your mask," she says, "it began to live stream to a designated site."

I think of Bermuda again. I think of Janet's friend whom Lucy supposedly was seeing.

"What site?" I ask.

"We won't get into that."

"Now we're up to two things you won't tell me. The person you met in Bermuda and where the video was live streamed."

"That's right."

"Well I'm not aware that anybody has my mask," I add, and her answer is silence, and her house is very close now. "To my knowledge it's never been found. The first priority of course was keeping me alive when they got me into the boat. Plus there was an underwater crime scene to work, a double homicide."

I envision the two speared bodies in the hatch of the sunken barge, the police divers killed just moments before Benton and I took our giant stride off the boat. When I found them I knew I was next, and then Carrie appeared around a section of the rusting hulk. I hear the faint buzzing sound of her being propelled through the water toward me, and the clink of the first spear hitting my tank, then the shock when the second one impaled my thigh.

"There were bodies to recover in addition to any gear I might have lost after I was shot," I remind Lucy. "It was hours before the sunken barge and the area around it were thoroughly searched, and I've always been told my mask was never found." I keep saying that.

"But they know it existed," Lucy replies. "They know about the mask you had on when Carrie supposedly attacked you. And that's the problem. They were told about it."

"Supposedly attacked?"

"That's the way they look at it. Yes," Lucy says. "They know there was a mini-recorder attached to your mask and that it might stand to reason the video captured on that dive was live streamed. Possibly to me. They would assume I was sitting somewhere with a device that was capturing everything happening to you."

"Why would they assume such a thing?"

"Because they would."

"There must be more of a reason than that." I get an increasingly unsettled feeling. "Tell me what it is," I say as the feeling is stronger, fluttering through my chest.

"The reason is you," Lucy says and now I remember. "You mentioned the mask in interviews. You told the FBI that I'd installed a mini-recorder on the mask you had on when Carrie shot you, so there should be an irrefutable record of exactly what happened. Except there isn't."

"What do you mean there isn't?"

"Do you remember telling me about it after they talked to you in the hospital?"

"Barely."

"Do you remember telling the FBI about the mask and its capabilities?"

"Barely."

I don't really recall what I said to Lucy, to the Feds, to anyone. Those initial conversations are disjointed and dreamlike, and I can't retrieve the questions or my answers word for word. But I know I would have told the truth if asked, especially if I were injured and medicated, if I were as out of it as I must have been.

I would have had no reason to feel it was unsafe to relay precisely what I knew or thought I did, never imagining the information would be used against us. I couldn't have anticipated that two months later the FBI would be crawling all over Lucy's property and searching it from the air.

"I'm sorry if I've caused you trouble. In fact not *if*. Clearly I have," I say to her.

"You haven't."

"It would appear that I have made things worse somehow," I reply and we're almost to her sidewalk. "I'm very sorry, Lucy, because it certainly wasn't my intention."

"You have nothing to be sorry about and now we stop talking. Three-two-one and the audio is back on." She touches an app on her phone, looks at me and nods.

Our privacy is gone just like that.

CHAPTER 16

AS IF ON CUE A WOMAN IN KHAKI CARGO PANTS AND a dark polo shirt opens the front door. She could see us on the surveillance cameras even if she couldn't hear what we were saying.

The .40 caliber Glock and the shiny brass badge on Erin Loria's belt overwhelm her thin frame, and I do an instant inventory. Shoulders slightly rounded on their way to hunched. Teeth straight and natural with no discoloration due to enamel loss. Arms covered with lanugo, fine dark hair. Anorexic versus bulimic. She'll have early osteoporosis and cardiac problems if she's not careful. She doesn't look familiar. I don't think I've ever seen her before. But I know who she is all right.

The special agent in charge who may have had an affair with Carrie Grethen watches us reach the stone sidewalk. We follow it as she looks on silently, her face framed by long black hair that is thinning prematurely at the temples and on the crown. She has a cockeyed smile that on her best day is insincere and on her worst is condescending like it is right now, and I have to scrutinize closely to detect the scaffolding of a former beauty queen. I have to look carefully for the fine bone structure beneath sunbaked skin, the curves that have been replaced by raw bones and flat buttocks and sagging breasts. Her dark eyes are widely spaced with bags underneath, and her pouty mouth has puppet lines.

The remnants of her Barbie doll prettiness are rapidly eroding, and if I met her at Quantico when Lucy was there I can't tell and I'm pretty good at remembering people. There's no spark of recognition and there would be had we been introduced, had I ever chatted with her. At most we might have passed in a hallway. We may have been on the elevator at the same time. I don't know, and I don't care if she really was involved with Carrie sexually. What matters is what Lucy believed at the time, and it's stunningly inappropriate that Erin Loria has led the raid on Lucy's property, that Erin has anything at all to do with my niece.

"A curious conflict of interest comes to mind." I don't greet her in a friendly manner.

"Excuse me?"

"Give it careful thought and you might know what I'm talking about." I don't offer to shake her hand.

It's impossible not to think about what I witnessed on film, and I envision Lucy beside herself with hurt and jealousy after Erin showed up on the Yellow Brick Road obstacle course. It wasn't a coincidence. It would seem Carrie and Erin were having a relationship right under Lucy's nose, and I can't imagine what must have gone through Lucy's mind when seventeen years later Erin shows up on her private property with a warrant.

"I'm Kay Scarpetta, the chief medical examiner."

"Yes I know."

"I'm just making sure you do. I can show you identification if need be," I say as she blocks the doorway, not budging an inch in any direction. "I believe you and Lucy have already met," I add a sting of irony.

"I know who you are. And I know your niece. I'm sure you're aware we go back a long way." That maddening smile again as she stares at Lucy. "It's nice to see you didn't run off."

"I'm sure that's the real reason you have the helicopter up. In case I try to escape from my own property. That sounds like the FBI's brilliant thinking." Lucy has a way of sounding bored when she's contemptuous.

"A glib remark. I said it lightly. Tongue in cheek." Erin's clever humor comes across as haughty. "Of course you wouldn't be so silly as to run off. I was teasing."

"Let me guess who's flying." Lucy looks up at the military black twin-engine bird. "John, six-five with a three-ten steroid body. Big John who has the light touch of a Mack truck. You should have seen him setting down on the dolly the other day at that hangar your people use at Hanscom. Oh I'm sorry. Did you not know it's common knowledge the FBI has a secret special ops hangar at Hanscom Air Force Base? That big tax-dollar-subsidized recently refurbished hangar next to MedFlight?

"Anyway"—Lucy continues to needle her about the FBI's not-so-secret hangar just outside of Boston—"it took Big John three tries to get your bird centered on the dolly, skids all whack-adoo, one of them touching down and bouncing off like a wobbly puppy feeling for the next step when it's learning to do the stairs. I can always tell when it's Big John on the stick. I could give him some pointers about overcontrolling. You know, think-it-don't-touch-it. That sort of thing."

I can see thoughts racing behind Erin's eyes. She's incensed and trying to figure out her best comeback. I don't give her the chance.

"I'd like to enter my niece's house." I look past her into a vast open space of timber and glass soaring over the water.

"Perfect," Erin says without stepping aside. "Because I need to ask you a few questions."

I TAKE IN the dusty footprints all over the deep red cherry floors, the stacks of white Banker Boxes against a wall.

Inside the living room the lamps are missing their mica shades, and the mission-style furniture has been carelessly rearranged, the cushions sloppily replaced. I notice the take-out coffee cups and crumpled food bags on top of tables and scattered over the hand-carved African mahogany fireplace mantel. Empty sugar packets and stirring sticks fill an art glass bowl I bought for Lucy in Murano. In the space of two short hours it looks as if a small army has been tromping through her *Architectural Digest* spread. The FBI is giving her the finger back. More precisely her former dorm mate is.

"You can save any questions for Jill Donoghue," I let Erin know. "She'll be here soon. And in the world I come from?" I meet her cool customer stare. "We don't eat or drink at scenes. We don't bring in coffee, help ourselves to water or the bathroom. We certainly don't leave our detritus. It looks like you've forgotten basic crime scene training, which is surprising since you're married to a judge. You should know better than most that lapses in protocol can come back to haunt you in court."

"Please come in," Erin says as if she lives here and I didn't just say what I did.

"I'm going to check on everyone." Lucy starts to walk away.

"Not so fast." Erin lightly grips her arm.

"You need to get your hands off me," Lucy says quietly.

"How's your leg?" Erin asks me as she continues to hold on to Lucy's arm only harder. "When I heard about it my first thought was how did you manage not to drown? And by the way, Zeb sends his regards."

I'm sure Judge NoDoz misses me like a hole in the head. What I say is, "And please give him mine."

"I'm asking you politely to get your hands off me," Lucy says, and Erin realizes the wisdom of letting her go.

"It looks like walking is pretty hard for you these days." Erin turns her attention to me. "You were what? Some ninety feet, a hundred feet down and lost consciousness? If someone shot me with a spear gun I'm sure I'd pass out."

"It will be a while before my leg is back to normal. But I'm expecting a full recovery." It sounds stilted and it's supposed to when I recite what I scripted long painful weeks ago. "That's the only question I'm going to answer before Jill Donoghue gets here."

"Sure. Have it your way but I don't see anyone here trying to Mirandize you, Doctor Scarpetta. We're not interrogating you, just asking for a little helpful guidance." Then she says to Lucy, "And I'm afraid I'm going to have to take your phone. I've been nice about it. I could have taken it when I got here but I didn't. I gave you the benefit of the doubt and what do you do? You tamper with the security system."

"It's not *the* security system," Lucy says. "It's *my* security system. I can do whatever I want with it."

"I gave you the benefit of the doubt," Erin repeats, "and the thanks I get is you interfere with our investigation." She takes the phone from Lucy. "Now I'm not nice about it anymore."

"Your *benefit of the doubt* was to let me keep it long enough to see who I might contact and what else I might do as you tap into everything you think I have," Lucy says. "And I thank you for that. It was helpful to me to see what you're interested in but not so helpful to you. What you really want is usernames and passwords, and getting those hasn't happened, has it? And guess what? It never will. The NSA, the CIA couldn't break through my firewalls."

But someone did.

It appears someone, most likely Carrie, is spoofing Lucy's cell phone and has gotten into her computer system, her wireless network, and that in turn would compromise her home security system. Everything in Lucy's world is part of a web too complex for me to comprehend. Her networks have networks, her servers have servers, and her proxies have proxies.

The fact is that no one really knows what she does and just how extensive her range might be, and if someone is hacking into her privacy, even if Carrie is? Then I have to wonder if Lucy has allowed it. She may have invited it. If offered a cyber challenge her reaction is to bring it on. She believes she'll win.

"We can get into anything we want," Erin boasts to her. "But if you're smart you'll decide to cooperate. You'll give us whatever we need, including passwords. The more difficult you make this, the worse off you're going to be."

"Now I'm really scared." Lucy's tone has a dry ice bite and I'm reminded of her in the video sarcastically saying to Carrie, *I'm scared.*

Lucy wasn't. Not the way anybody else would be.

"You always were too sure of yourself." Erin bars the doorway with her arm, and I'm deciding what she's doing right now is for my benefit.

It's amazing. She's showing off. I would smile if anything right now were funny.

"It's what got you into trouble the first time," Erin says to Lucy.

"The first time?" Lucy watches the helicopter circle her property again. "Let me try to figure out when that was. Let's see. When did I get in trouble the first time? I was probably two or three or maybe hadn't been born yet."

"I can see you're determined to make this as difficult as possible."

"Six, seven hundred feet in this heat and humidity with what I'm sure is a heavy payload?" Lucy hasn't taken her eyes off the helicopter now hovering low over the woods next to the house. "Let me guess. At least six people in back. Probably muscle-head guys with a lot of gear. But I wouldn't be hanging out in the dead man's curve if I were Big John. Good luck auto-rotating in an emergency. And if I were him I'd already be back on the ground with this weather rolling in. You might want to radio Big John and tell him that and also remind him he's got maybe thirty minutes of decent viz left before it rapidly deteriorates to special VFR on its way to nothing. He might want to get the hell back to Hanscom while the getting's good and tuck your expensive custom bird into its custom hangar because there's a chance of hail."

"You've not changed. You're the same arrogant . . ." Erin starts to say something vulgar and stops herself.

"Arrogant what?" Lucy meets her eyes.

"You're the same as you always were." Erin glares at her and then says to me, "Your niece and I were at Quantico at the same time."

"Funny I don't remember you," Lucy lies easily, convincingly. "Maybe you can show me an old class photo, point yourself out."

"You remember me well enough."

"I don't." Lucy looks innocent.

"You do. And I remember you."

"And from that I'm supposed to assume you know me?"

"I know enough." Erin says it to her while she looks at me.

"The fact is you don't know me," Lucy says. "You don't know shit about me."

Now isn't the time for me to give Lucy a lecture. But if I could I'd tell her how unsafe it is to talk this way. Her anger has blown her cover. Her anger has asserted itself and given the FBI further incentive to clip her wings or cage her.

"I'd like to see the warrant," I say to Erin.

"This isn't your property."

"Some of my personal possessions including possible case-related materials are inside this house. You might want to be careful about compromising something that could cause you a problem."

"Start with this. You're only here because I'm allowing it." Erin has decided to turn this into a competition. "Because I'm being friendly and inclusive."

I dig inside my shoulder bag and pull out a pen and legal pad. "I'm just doing the same thing you are. Making notes."

"I'm not writing anything." She holds up her empty hands.

"But you will." I glance at my watch. "It's twenty-five minutes past eleven on Friday morning, August fifteenth. We are in the foyer of Lucy's house in Concord." I write it down. "And I've just asked Special Agent Erin Loria for the warrant because I also am an occupant of this house. Not full-time but I have an apartment here that contains personal possessions and confidential information. So I'd like to see the warrant."

"It's not your house."

"To quote the Fourth Amendment in the Bill of Rights," I reply, "people have a right to be 'secure in their persons, houses, papers, and effects against unreasonable searches and seizures.' I'd like to see the warrant to make sure it's properly signed by a judge, and that the judge doesn't happen to be Special Agent Erin Loria's husband the honorable Zeb Chase."

"That's ridiculous!" she interrupts me. "He's in Virginia."

"He's a federal judge and theoretically could sign off on any federal court order you request. Of course it would be unethical." I'm jotting notes. "I'd like to see the warrant. I've asked you three times." I underline it for emphasis.

CHAPTER 17

IT'S THE USUAL DOCUMENT, NOTHING CLEVER OR UNexpected. The search-and-seizure warrant lists everything but the kitchen sink, including secret hatches, doors, rooms and egresses that may or may not be attached to the main residence and its outbuildings.

The inventory of what the FBI has nabbed so far includes long guns, handguns, ammunition and reloading tools, and knives and cutting/stabbing instruments of all descriptions, dive and boat gear, electronic recording equipment, computers, external hard drives and any other form of electronic storage. The legal wish list also includes possible sources of biological evidence, specifically DNA, and I find that odd. Not that anything this day is even close to normal.

It's on my mind that the FBI has Lucy's DNA. She used to work for them. They have her DNA profile and fingerprints on file and also Janet's, Marino's and mine for exclusionary purposes. I assume they have no interest in seven-year-old Desi. He has nothing to do with anything, and I don't understand exactly what the agents are hoping for. But clearly they aren't done yet, and because they're hell-bent to help themselves to every computer and whatever's on them I'm forced to consider another grim scenario. What if the Feds are looking for a way to access confidential information at my headquarters, the Cambridge Forensic Center?

Lucy is the skeleton key to everything we do at the CFC. She's the keeper of my electronic kingdom, and therefore potentially a portal for the Feds. They could attempt to use her to gain access to office e-mail accounts and case records that go back many decades, and next I start wondering why they might care. I wonder why the helicopter followed me here. Did it really? Or did it just seem like it? Is the FBI only after Lucy? Are they after her at all or is it me they want?

"The CFC's cases and all investigative and laboratory documents related are classified." I hand the warrant back to Erin Loria. "They're protected by state and federal law, and you can't exploit Lucy's position on my staff and use it as a means to access the CFC's proprietary information. You know how improper that would be."

I don't say *illegal* because the FBI would make sure it isn't. They would twist and permute the truth to justify their every move. Going up against them is worse than David and Goliath. It's David without a rock and Goliath with an assault rifle. But knowing that never scares me from a fight with government officials. I don't forget they're supposed to work for the people and aren't a law unto themselves even if they act like it. I'm always outnumbered and I never forget that either.

"You realize how seriously such a violation could impact every criminal case the CFC works," I add. "I would be unable to ensure the integrity of any of our records, including thousands of those pertaining to federal cases, FBI cases. I think you're quite aware of the potential consequences. I also would venture a guess that the Department of Justice doesn't need more news stories about privacy violations, about spying and screwed-up investigations."

"Are you threatening me with bad press?"

"I'm reminding you of certain consequences of your potential actions," I repeat my careful phrasing as I follow her down a hallway of rich cherry paneling hung with Miró paintings and lithographs. "Your warrant to search my niece's property in no way grants you any rights to access the CFC. Or to me personally for that matter."

"Because if you do go to the press with anything about this," Loria says as we reach the master suite, "I'll charge you with obstruction of justice."

"I've not threatened you in any way." I write it down. "I'm the one feeling threatened." I write that too. "Why are you threatening me?" I underline it.

"I'm not."

"It feels like it."

"And I respect your feelings." She has a notebook out now and is writing down what I'm saying, maybe out of self-defense.

I never forget the Bureau is sly like a fox in its insistence on using primitive paper and pen to record what agents supposedly witness. They take notes. That way it's easier to misrepresent what a suspect or a witness did or said.

"It's not enough for you to respect what I feel," I reply, and it's difficult to watch what's happening inside the master bedroom. "You have no probable cause, no justification whatsoever to go through confidential medical examiner records or communications associated with them, some of which includes classified materials relating to our troops, our men and women in the military. You have no right to the e-mails and other communications of my staff or me."

"I understand your position," Erin says.

"You'll understand it better if you place any of my cases in jeopardy," I reply not so politely. "And it's not a threat. It's a promise."

"I'll make a note you said that."

THANK GOD Lucy isn't here to see the two female agents inside her walk-in closet, their gloved hands going through the pockets of everything she's ever worn, her jeans, her flight suits, her dress clothes.

They're looking at her shoes, her boots, and riffling through briefcases and built-in drawers while on the other side of the room a male agent roots through Janet's closet and another removes artwork from the walls, spectacular canvases and photographs of African wildlife. He props them up, pounds on paneling with the flat of his palm, looking for secret compartments I can only guess, and I feel a knot in my stomach the size of a softball.

"This can be made so much easier if we have honest communication," Erin is saying as I move to a window and open the shade. "So much can be prevented if we get the truth about what happened."

"About what happened?" I don't turn around.

"In Florida," she says. "We need the truth."

"You're implying that those of us involved are lying, as if it's your default position that everybody lies." I look out the window at the late morning because I'm not going to look at her. "And you might be right. In your world everybody probably does lie, including the organization you work for. In your world the end justifies the means. You can do whatever you want and truth is incidental. Assuming you even recognize it."

"When you were injured in June . . . ?"

"You mean when I was attacked." I scan the spacious backyard that drops off precipitously into a steep hillside thick with trees.

"When you were shot. I stipulate that there's ample evidence you were shot."

"You stipulate? Sounds like you're making a court case . . ."

"Let me ask you," she interrupts. "Have you ever owned a spear gun?"

"You can ask me that when Jill Donoghue gets here."

"What about Lucy? She's obviously into weapons. Do you know how many firearms she stores in her vault? Would it surprise you if I told you almost a hundred? Why does she need so many guns?"

The answer were I inclined to give it is Lucy collects what she calls handcrafted small-batch weapons. She loves intricate technology, the art and science of every fine innovation including those that kill. She's drawn to symbols of power whether they're guns or cars or flying machines, and she collects because she can. There isn't much she can't afford. If she wants a Zev customized Glock or a 1911 hand-fitted for a lefty and exquisitely beautiful she doesn't care what it costs.

I don't answer Erin's questions but that doesn't stop her from asking them as I look out at light flickering on the water, at the gentle current and the hundred-foot cypress dock with the teak and glass boathouse at the end. Lucy left to check on Janet, Desi, and Jet Ranger, and I encouraged her not to come back to the main house until Donoghue arrives. I hope it's soon. I look for Marino but don't see any sign of him.

"I'm not going to mince words with you, Kay. And I assume you don't mind my calling you that."

I say nothing. I do mind.

"All we have to go on is what you claim happened, and what Benton claimed to have observed. You claim Carrie Grethen shot you . . ."

"It's not what I claim or what Benton claims. It's what is factual and true." I turn around and look at her.

"Your claim that Carrie Grethen shot you is based solely on your visual recognition of her. A woman you'd not seen in what? Thirteen, fourteen years at least? A woman whose death was witnessed."

"It wasn't exactly." I'll sure as hell tell her this much. "Her death was assumed. We never actually saw her in the helicopter that crashed. Her remains were never found. There's no proof she died. In fact there's proof to the contrary, and the FBI knows all this. I don't need to tell you . . ."

"Your proof. Your speculative and fanciful proof," Erin interrupts me again. "You catch a glimpse of a person in a camouflage dive skin and somehow you instantly knew who it was."

"A camouflage dive skin?" I ask. "That's an interesting detail."

"One you gave us."

I don't say anything. I offer her an uncomfortable silence to fill.

"Maybe you don't remember. There's probably a lot you don't remember after a trauma like that," she says. "How's your memory now by the way? I've wondered if you went for a while underwater without breathing."

I remain silent.

"That can have serious consequences for memory."

I don't react.

"You claimed the person who shot you had on a camo dive skin," she then says. "The detail came from you."

"I don't recall saying that but I might have because it's true."

"Of course you don't remember." Her voice oozes condescension.

"I don't remember telling your agents this," I reply. "But I remember what I saw."

"Somehow you recognized this person presumed dead." She rephrases her argument about Carrie. "Even though you'd not laid eyes on her or seen a photograph of her in more than a decade you're positive in your identification of her. And I'm loosely quoting from your own sworn statement that you gave to our agents in Miami on June seventeenth while you were still in the hospital."

"A statement that wasn't recorded," I remind her. "Only written. What agents write down and what was actually said can be difficult to prove since there's no unimpeachable record. And I'm just wondering how can we be sure my statement was *sworn*?"

"You're saying if you didn't swear under oath to tell the truth you might not . . . ?"

She's cut off by a familiar voice in the corridor. "Hello! Hello! That's enough! It's bad manners to start without me!"

Jill Donoghue walks in smiling, typically chic in one of her designer suits, this one midnight blue. Her wavy dark hair is shorter than when I saw her last. Other than that she looks the same, perpetually energetic and fresh, permanently somewhere between thirty-five and fifty.

"I don't believe we've met." She introduces herself to Erin, and a brief turf war ensues that the FBI isn't going to win. "Then you're new to the Boston area," Donoghue summarizes. "So let me tell you how things work. When my client says she won't talk to you until I show up? You stop talking."

"We were having a casual discussion about her recognizing Carrie Grethen . . ."

"See? Now that sounds like talking."

" . . . And how she could have recognized her or anyone for that matter, considering how fast it happened, considering the extreme duress of the alleged situation."

"Alleged?" Donoghue almost laughs. "Have you seen Doctor Scarpetta's leg?"

"Show me." Erin's eyes dancing with defiance, with her certainty I'm not about to undress.

But she couldn't be more mistaken. I unzip my cargo pants.

CHAPTER 18

THAT'S OKAY," SHE QUICKLY SAYS. "YOU DON'T NEED to prove anything."

"In my profession you give up modesty rather quickly." I ease the right pants leg down to my knee. "When you've just finished working a decomp, a floater, you really don't care who's in the shower next to you. The entrance and exit scars are right here."

I point to them, round and angry red and smaller than a dime.

"The spear skewered my quadriceps muscles," I explain. "Entering here almost midthigh and exiting just above my patella, my kneecap. The tip protruded about four inches from my skin. Obviously the significant damage was to muscle and bone, which were further injured because of the rope. One end was attached to the spear and the other to a float on the surface. You can imagine the tugging and pulling."

"An awful thought. Very painful." Erin pauses for effect. "But it's within the realm of possibility the wound could have been self-inflicted, prompting you to make up some imaginary story about some phantom in camouflage."

I hold an imaginary spear gun and try to line up the tip with the entrance wound on my thigh. "Difficult but not impossible. What would be my motivation?"

"You would do anything for your niece, wouldn't you?"

"You don't have to answer that," Donoghue says.

"I wouldn't," I reply. "And I didn't shoot myself. And I don't know anything about a camo dive skin but that doesn't mean Carrie wasn't wearing one."

"What if it meant saving Lucy's life? Would you lie?"

"You don't have to answer that," Donoghue says.

"Would you lie to cover the shameful fact that you were suicidal?"

"It would be my nature to shoot the source of the threat," I reply.

"You aren't required to explain," Donoghue says to me.

"Shooting myself, which I certainly didn't do, would make no sense," I add. "And which is it? Because I'm confused. I'm lying to cover for Lucy? Or I'm lying about attempting to kill myself? Maybe you have another theory to add to the mix?"

"Did you feel you panicked?" Erin is having a harder time keeping her composure. "When you realized you were shot? Did you feel panic?"

"You don't have to answer that," Donoghue says.

"Have you ever entertained even the slightest doubt that the person who shot you was Carrie Grethen?" Erin tastes blood.

"You don't have to answer that."

"Has it ever occurred to you, Doctor Scarpetta, that in your panic you thought it was her but you were mistaken?"

"You don't have to answer that."

"That's fine because I really didn't understand the question. I'm confused by yet another theory." My attention is on the river beyond the window, on the slow eddies and ruffles.

The water is the greenish color of old bottle glass as it languidly bends around the point of land Lucy owns. An image flashes in my mind. I see my face through a fogged-up dive mask in murky muddy water. I see myself dead.

"I'm sorry," Erin says with a chilliness that's about to freeze over. "Let me try again. Has it ever entered your mind that the person you saw might have been someone else?"

"You don't have to answer that."

"Oh I see. We're off the suicide theory and back to my being shot by someone," I reply.

"Isn't it more likely"—Erin continues her disjointed line of questioning—"that during the nanosecond you saw this person you made an instant assumption it was Carrie Grethen? You didn't know it, you assumed it. And why wouldn't you? Certainly she was on your mind."

"You don't have to answer that either," Donoghue says.

"You were justified in fearing her, looking over your shoulder every minute." Erin is baiting me, trying to make me react. "Therefore wouldn't it be fair to conclude that if you were *looking* for her, then that's who you imagined you saw in the nanosecond we're talking about?"

She's going to persist in using the word *nanosecond*. She's practicing for a jury, making the case that the encounter happened so fast I didn't really see anything. Therefore I didn't see who shot me. I simply feared who it might be and made an assumption that I won't back down from. Or if that story doesn't work then I suppose she can resort to painting me as a crazy person who speared herself for God knows what reason. After several more minutes of this, Donoghue says she needs to talk privately with her client.

"I've never been here before," she says to me for Erin's benefit. "Do you mind showing me around, Kay? It looks absolutely breathtaking."

We walk out into the corridor and follow red jarrah wood flooring slowly, quietly, beneath mica lamps that glow a pleasant coppery yellow. I'm aware of Lucy's security system, of every keypad, camera and motion sensor we pass. I'm mindful that there can be no assumption of privacy.

"Is there anything in particular you'd like to see?" I ask Donoghue a seemingly innocuous question as I'm mindful of cameras all over Lucy's house.

"I noticed when I first walked in that if I'd taken a right instead of a left there seemed to be an area of interest at the end of that hallway." Her casual comment points out a serious problem.

What she's referring to is the guest suite Lucy renovated for me. It's my bedroom, my private space when I stay here. As we get closer to the entranceway I can see what Donoghue is talking about. Beyond is another hallway. At the far end of it the door to my suite is open. As we get closer a man in a cheap khaki suit emerges with a large sealed brown paper package that he carries in both arms. Strong and sinewy, he's dark with glittering brown eyes, his hair cropped close to his scalp on the sides and a buzz cut on top. He looks military.

"Afternoon," he says as if we're on the same team. "Can I help you with something?"

"Where are you taking that and why?" Donoghue indicates the brown paper package he clutches.

"Oh now I wouldn't want to bog you down in every little thing we're doing here. But you can't go in right now. I'm Doug Wade. And you're?"

"Jill Donoghue. May I see your badge?"

"I'd be happy to if I had one," he says. "But I'm just a revenue officer for the IRS. We don't get badges, guns, nothing fun like that."

WHEN I REACH MY ROOM I don't step inside. But I make my presence known.

I stand in the open doorway watching two agents strip my queen-size bed, flipping the mattress over and halfway off the frame, piling the honey-colored Egyptian cotton linens on the floor. Their gloved hands feel carefully for any hint of a hiding place. They aren't IRS unless they're looking for a mattress full of untaxed money. They're looking for something else. But what?

More rifles? A spear gun? My dive mask? Drugs?

Through the open closet door I can see my clothing, my shoes sloppily returned to shelves that were riffled through. I confirm that my iMac computer is missing from the desk inside my country office with its river view. Lucy worked hard to make my guest quarters exactly what she thought I'd like, a lot of glass, a colorful silk rug on the shiny cherry floor, copper light fixtures, a coffee bar, a gas fireplace and large photographs of Venice.

I've enjoyed many contented cozy times here, innocent gentle hiatuses that I may never have again. I feel my anger picking up steam as I think of the large brown-wrapped package I just watched go by. My mind races through what might be on the desktop or stored in documents. What might the IRS or FBI or some other agency see that could be a problem?

I'm diligent about dumping files and emptying the trash but

that won't stop government labs from recovering everything that was on my computer. Lucy could have scrubbed the hard drive and ensured that nothing deleted could be restored. But I assume she didn't have time. She claims she didn't know her property was being raided until Erin Loria called the house phone and announced her presence, and that would have given Lucy only minutes to take care of any security concerns. But I don't know what's true. She can be as manipulative and untruthful as the FBI. Maybe that's where she learned it.

"Good morning," I say and both agents look up at me, neither of them a day over forty, typically well groomed and buff in their cargo pants and polo shirts. "Am I being audited?"

"I sure hope not because that's no fun," one of them says cheerfully.

"I'm just wondering if I'm being audited and if that's the explanation for why an IRS revenue agent just walked off with my computer, which by the way I don't believe is proper. It's my understanding that revenue agents can't just enter a private residence without permission. Did Lucy give the IRS permission?"

No answer.

"Did her partner Janet?"

Nothing.

"Well for sure I know I didn't," I say to them. "So I'm wondering who gave the IRS permission to search this house and remove personal property from it? Not just my niece's personal property but also mine."

"We're really not at liberty to discuss an active investigation, ma'am," the other agent says curtly, loudly.

"If I'm the target of an active investigation and am being audited I have a right to know. Isn't that true?" I ask Donoghue but I don't need her to answer. "And I'm confused and find it necessary to continue to point out that revenue agents aren't allowed to simply help themselves to whatever they decide to carry off-site."

I'm playing them and they know it. The smiles are gone.

"You'll have to take it up with them, ma'am," the loud curt agent says and his tone is sharper. "We don't work for the IRS."

I'm not certain the man in the khaki suit who just walked out with the iMac works for the IRS either. He didn't look like the type, not like any auditor I've ever met. Also he introduced himself as a revenue officer and not a revenue agent, and officers are usually assigned to cases that involve unpaid tax debts while agents conduct audits. I don't know why either type of IRS employee would be inside Lucy's house.

"This is my attorney and I'm glad she's a witness to your active investigation," I then say. "A picture's worth a thousand words. You gentlemen have a nice day."

"How did they know this is your room?" Donoghue asks me as we walk away.

"How did *you* know it's my room?" I ask her back.

"Because I overheard someone make a reference when I first walked into the house. I caught words to the effect that what they'd just packed up was the *Doc's* computer and to make sure it's clear the contents of that room are yours," she explains. "They had no doubt about it. Any reason to think you might have a problem with the IRS?"

"No more reason than anybody else that I'm aware of."

"And Lucy?"

"I have nothing to do with her finances. She doesn't discuss them with me. I do assume she pays her taxes," I reply.

"Why might the IRS investigate her for tax crimes?"

"There's no reason I'm aware of." I don't add that Doug Wade in his khaki suit isn't that kind of IRS employee.

If he were empowered to investigate suspected criminal tax offenses he would have a gun and a badge. Special agents for the IRS also usually travel in pairs. I don't say there's something fishy about who Doug Wade is and why he's here. But I'm quite sure it's not for reasons that meet the eye. The FBI has an agenda. It won't be one that's palatable or in this case even justified.

"More to the point?" I'm saying to Donoghue loud enough for everyone to hear. "The Feds have a right to anything that's mine? Just because it happens to be inside Lucy's house?" I already know what she'll say but that doesn't stop me from hoping for a loophole, and I'm in a mood to remind the FBI that I won't be bullied.

"Anything on the premises they have a warrant to search and it's open season," she says. "They would argue that they have no way of knowing whether laptops all over the place are Lucy's or belong to someone else such as Janet or yourself. They would argue that the only way to be certain is to examine the contents."

"In other words they get to do what they want."

"In other words yes," she says. "They pretty much do."

Outside the house in the stifling heat I don't see any agents walking about, and I look at the vehicles parked in front, a caravan of four white Tahoes. Behind them is a black Ford sedan and I wonder who it belongs to. Maybe the phony IRS agent.

The helicopter is gone, and I hear the wind in the trees and the distant kettledrums of thunder. Clouds to the south are rising like the Great Wall of China, building formidably like an edifice you can see from outer space. The air is humid and ominous.

"Why?" Donoghue looks up at the threatening sky.

"Why what?"

"Why did they have a helicopter here? What the hell was it doing? It circled for how long?"

"The better part of an hour."

"Maybe they're filming everything that goes on down here."

"For what reason?"

"Political caution," Donoghue decides, and what she means is public embarrassment or looking bad.

"I suggest we head down to the dock." I point out every lamppost and some of the trees that have cameras with audio.

I'm slow picking my way down wooden steps that lead from the backyard to the water's edge. It's low tide and I smell the swampy odor of decomposing vegetation, and the hot flat air has gotten still, simmering with violent promise. To the south threatening clouds are building rapidly. We're about to get a severe thunderstorm and I don't want the damn FBI here when it hits. I don't want them tracking water and mud in and out. They've done enough damage.

Our footsteps are hollow thuds on the weathered gray wooden dock. The boathouse is built on pilings, and underneath are colorful kayaks that are rarely used. Lucy has little interest in any mode of transportation that doesn't include an engine. I suspect that anything requiring a paddle was Janet's idea.

"How was your status conference this morning?" I lead us around to the front of the boathouse as I think about data fiction, about a case Donoghue apparently was discussing in federal court this morning.

Benton was there. Does data fiction have anything to do with why the FBI is here now? I don't ask directly and Donoghue isn't saying anything.

"I was just wondering because you brought it up." I don't say what she brought up but she understands what I'm suggesting.

"Yes I did," she finally answers me. "There was a motion made that the case be dismissed because the evidence can't be trusted."

"Based on?"

"I think it's the nature of digital media that we should assume it can be corrupted," she replies, and as she continues to talk cautiously and shrewdly it dawns on me that she was the attorney who requested this dismissal.

Donoghue is a powerful, skilled attorney who wouldn't miss the slightest opportunity to make a jury question the integrity of every aspect of the prosecution's case. For her data fiction would be a dream come true. But I have to wonder about the timing. Why today? Why was Benton there? Why is the FBI on Lucy's property?

"It's all connected," I say under my breath, and then I hear it again.

The C-sharp cord on an electric guitar. I look at the message that's just landed on my phone and Donoghue can tell by my face that I'm upset.

"Is everything all right?" She stares pointedly at my phone and says very quietly, barely moving her lips, "Use extreme caution. I'm sure they've seized her networks."

I stop walking. "I need a minute."

"Is it anything I can help you with?" She continues her careful conversation.

"It's quite a view Lucy has here." I look out at the water and Donoghue knows not to question me further.

I've been sent a communication she shouldn't see, and if what I'm about to find relates to criminal activity then she doesn't need the exposure. It's bad enough that I have it, and I watch her walk ahead of me as I stand alone on the pier and put on my earpiece again. I face the river and hold my phone close, protecting any sliver of privacy I might have, calculating the most likely location for Lucy's cameras and keeping my back to them, tucking myself in, preparing for something else that will be difficult for me to watch.

Like the other two messages this one appears to have been sent from Lucy's ICE line, and there's no text, nothing but a link. I click on it and without delay the video starts inside Lucy's dorm room again. Then the credits begin to roll by, dripping down slowly in bloodred type:

DEPRAVED HEART—VIDEO III
BY CARRIE GRETHEN
JULY 11, 1997

CHAPTER 19

SHE STOPS READING AND HER NIMBLE PALE FINGERS quickly fold the sheets of white unlined paper with their script format.

Carrie tucks the envelope into the Army green backpack as a door closes in the background, and the camera picks up Lucy walking into the dorm room. It appears she has showered since the last video I watched, and this reinforces my growing conviction that the recordings were knitted together to convey a message. I need to pay close attention no matter how manipulative and uncomfortable. It's crucial I remember everything I'm hearing and seeing because the video likely will self-destruct when it's finished playing.

Lucy's hair is damp. She has on faded jeans, a green FBI polo shirt and flip-flops. Carrying an armful of folded underwear, shorts, shirts, and socks tucked into balls, she drops everything on the foot of the bed as Mister Pickle's amber eyes watch glassily.

"Yours is on top," she says coldly to Carrie without looking at her. "Pretty much everything that's white is yours. Funny but I usually don't associate *all white* with bad guys. I thought I asked you to leave. Why the fuck are you still here?"

"It's subjective who's bad and who's good. And you don't really want me to leave."

"It's not subjective and you need to get the hell out."

"I wear white for the same reason you should. Chronic exposure to chemical dyes is toxic." Carrie tucks her white clothes into the backpack. "I know you don't pay attention to such mundane minutiae because you think you'll never have to worry about anything aging you. Or God forbid giving you a neurological disorder or cancer or destroying your immune system so your own body is chronically attacking itself. Not a good way to die."

"There's no good way to die."

"There are plenty of bad ones though," Carrie says. "Better to be shot. Better to be killed in a plane crash. You don't want to be sick or poisoned. You don't want to linger and lose your functionality. Imagine brain damage. Or being old and that's the worst offender and biggest enemy and what I intend to defeat."

"You mean with your stupid creams that have copper in them?"

"Someday you'll think back on this moment and wish you'd done everything differently. I mean absolutely everything." Her stare is unwavering. She doesn't blink. "Very nice of you to do the laundry. Was it busy?"

"I had to wait forever for a dryer. I hate sharing." Lucy is in a withdrawn leaden mood, and she won't look at her.

"My, my how entitled we are. You should hear yourself. Have we forgotten that you're the only elitist on this floor who doesn't have a roommate or share a bathroom?"

"Shut up, Carrie."

"You're nineteen, Lucy."

"Shut the hell up."

"You're a child. You shouldn't even be here."

"I want the MP5K back. Where is it?"

"It's safe."

"It's not yours."

"It's not yours either. We're so much alike. Are you aware of that?"

"We aren't anything alike." Lucy puts away clothes, yanking open drawers and slamming them shut.

"But we're exactly alike," Carrie says. "We're different sides of the same ice cube."

"What the fuck does that even mean?"

Carrie pulls her tank top, her sports bra off over her head, and half-naked she faces Lucy. "I don't believe what you said. You didn't mean it. You love me. You can't live without me. I know you didn't mean it."

Lucy stares at her, then shoves shut another drawer while Carrie leaves her sweaty clothing on the floor where it fell. I notice there's no visible line of demarcation on her exposed flesh, no variations in pigmentation. Her breasts, belly, her back and neck, all of her is the same opaque milky white.

"It's not like Benton won't eventually figure out it's missing," Lucy says. "Where the hell is it? This isn't funny. Just give it back and leave me alone."

"I can't wait to restore it to its proper condition and do some test fires when it's all packed up in its fancy briefcase. Just imagine it? You're standing on a busy sidewalk holding your briefcase as the motorcade goes by."

"Whose motorcade?" Lucy stares at her.

"There are so many choices."

"You're sicker than I ever imagined."

"Don't be so dramatic." Carrie retrieves the St. Pauli Girl from the desk and takes a swallow of it inches from Lucy's face. "I know you didn't mean what you said earlier." She leans against her drinking the beer, sliding a hand under Lucy's shirt.

"Don't." She pulls Carrie's hand away. "And water doesn't have sides, and an ice cube is water so as usual you're full of shit."

"Am I?" Carrie kisses her, and their faces disconcertingly mirror each other.

"Don't," Lucy says.

Both of them have sharp features, keen eyes, strong jaws, straight white teeth and extreme agility and gracefulness. It's not surprising. Benton says Carrie is the classic narcissist who falls in love with herself, moving from one image of herself to the next. The world is a mirrored room filled with her own projections, and she met her match with Lucy. Benton describes Carrie as Lucy's doppelgänger, her evil double.

"Don't, Carrie. No."

They're both exquisitely toned like Olympic runners, five-foot-eight with ample breasts, narrow hips, six-pack abs, and chiseled arms, quads and calves. They easily could pass for sisters.

"No!" Lucy pulls back from her. "Stop!"

"Why did you say it?" Carrie doesn't take her eyes off her. "You know you can't possibly leave me."

"I'm going to dinner and when I come back you'd better not be here." Lucy's voice trembles, and she sits on the edge of the desk and starts putting on socks and black leather trainers.

"Tell Marino happy birthday." Carrie stands aggressively close to her. "I hope you have fun at the Globe and Laurel. Be sure to tell him why I'm not there."

"You're not invited. You never were and shouldn't have expected otherwise. And you wouldn't have wanted to go anyway."

"I wouldn't have missed it but I understand. He should be surrounded by his favorite people at his favorite hangout." Carrie's eyes are cold blue steel. "I'll give you money to buy him a round of drinks or a special dessert with a candle on it."

"He doesn't want you there and he doesn't want your money."

"It's not nice though. Not inviting me to the big birthday party," Carrie says. "Watch out. A poison apple may follow."

"You know damn well you can't have dinner with us."

"Let me guess whose idea it was to exclude me tonight. Not Marino's. It was your precious Auntie Kay."

"It's true she has the lowest opinion of you that she could possibly have of any human being I've ever been with, will ever be with."

"Don't be so boring."

"You're really pathologically controlling and competitive." Lucy is pacing the room, getting increasingly agitated.

"And you're immature and tedious, and when you're like that you're boring." Carrie says it in a dead voice as she stands perfectly still, perfectly calm near the desk. "I hate being bored. I might just hate it more than anything. Except I wouldn't want to lose my freedom. Which would you hate more, Lucy Boo? Being dead or being in prison?"

LUCY WALKS INTO THE BATHROOM. She fills a glass with water from the sink and returns to the bedroom where Carrie is near the desk, playing with the Swiss Army knife.

"Why did you say it? You haven't before," Carrie perseverates with no inflection in her voice.

Lucy clears her throat and averts her eyes. "Don't make this harder than it already is."

"You're being petulant." Carrie watches her with reptilian steadiness.

"I'm not." Lucy clears her throat again as she drinks water.

"Of course this is you acting out," Carrie is saying. "Because you couldn't possibly leave me. You can't really act on your threat and never have been able to. Just look at you. You're about to cry. You're about to completely disintegrate at the mere thought of not being with me. You love me more than you've ever loved anyone in your life. You loved me first. I'm your first love. And you know how that works? Actually you don't. You're a child compared to me. But file this away." Carrie's index finger tap-tap-taps her temple.

"You never forget your first," she says slowly and with emphasis. "You never get over it because it will always be the most intense thing you ever felt, your most unbearable desire and lust. The crush. The blushing. The thumping in the chest. The rushing and roaring of blood up your neck to your brain that lifts the top of your skull. You can't think. You can't talk. All you want to do is touch. You want to touch the person so badly you would kill to do it. Is there anything better than lust?"

"You're fucking around with the beauty queen. So I guess you should know all about lust.

"We're done."

"You sure?" Carrie stares at the bulky red Swiss Army knife in the palm of her hand. "Because you'd better mean it. Words can change everything. Be careful what you mean or don't."

"I should have known from the first time we met." Lucy paces faster, gesturing furiously. "When they escorted me into the ERF and turned me over to you, my supervisor, my mentor, my personal plague."

"That wasn't the first time I met you, Lucy. It was just the first time you met me." Carrie rubs the knife with her thumb, testing its sharpness. "Come here. You need to take it easy."

"You're a cheat and a fake, a fraud, an intellectual thief, and that's the worst kind because you're stealing someone's soul. I created CAIN and that's what you can't stand. All along you've taken the credit for what I in fact did. You trick people out of whatever it is you decide you want."

"Oh my God we're back to that." Carrie laughs.

"The Criminal Artificial Intelligence Network and who should get all the thanks? Who would get it if you're truthful?" Lucy's eyes blaze and she gets in Carrie's face. "Who invented the name, the acronym CAIN? Who wrote all of the code that really matters? I can't believe how much I've allowed you to use me. You'll probably hurt me worse before it's over."

"Before what's over?"

"Everything."

"If I plan to hurt you? You won't know about it until I decide," Carrie says as gunshots sound like faraway fireworks from a celebration about to end.

She grabs Lucy, kissing her hard, and Lucy cries out in shocked pain. I see the Swiss Army knife in Carrie's hand, the small shiny steel blade. I watch blood darkening Lucy's green shirt, staining her fingers bright red as she clutches her abdomen, staring at Carrie dazed, enraged, disbelieving and devastated.

"What did you do?" Lucy screams at her. "What the hell did you just do you fucking lunatic!"

"The mark of the beast." Carrie grabs a towel and lifts Lucy's shirt, dabbing blood flowing from a horizontal incision in the lower left quadrant of her belly. "In case you forget who you really belong to."

"Jesus Christ. Holy fucking shit! What have you done?" Lucy jerks the towel away from her, and then nothingness.

The display on my phone goes black.

CHAPTER 20

THE FRONT PORCH IS ARRANGED WITH TEAKWOOD lounge chairs that have bright green cushions and matching ottomans.

Water laps against the pilings, the river a quarter of a mile wide here with uninhabited forests on the other side. I watch a pair of bald eagles soar high over the leafy canopy of hardwoods and evergreens. I'm reminded that there are a lot of nests around here, and I'm annoyed all over again about the FBI helicopter thundering over this quiet conservation land, unsettling the wildlife, upsetting everything imaginable.

Under different circumstances the boathouse would be a perfect spot to sit and have a drink at the end of an awful day like this, and I wonder why Lucy hasn't stepped outside to meet us. She should have noticed our approach. She probably has fifty security cameras on her property, and as we've made our way here we're being monitored. It's strange she hasn't walked out to greet us, and I knock on the front door. I hear laughter, music, people speaking Japanese. A television playing.

The sound of the lock and Lucy opens up, and my eyes involuntarily drop down to her gray T-shirt as if I expect to see blood, as if Carrie just cut her with the small blade of a Swiss Army knife that Marino gave to her. I remember it was after he'd begun taking her to deserted parking lots, teaching her to ride his Harley, and he told her she should never be without tools. Always have money in your pocket and some sort of blade handy, I remember him advising her in the early years.

Carrie picked that knife, Marino's knife. She used it to mark Lucy, to hurt her, and I envision the delicate colorful dragonfly tattoo on the left lower quadrant of Lucy's abdomen. The first time I saw it she explained that dragonflies are the helicopters of the insect world and that was the inspiration. It wasn't. The inspiration was a scar she'd never want anybody to know about. It would shame her. She especially didn't want me to learn the truth.

"Hi." Lucy holds the door.

"You didn't see us?" I ask.

"I'm not watching who's on my property because I already know," Lucy replies as Donoghue and I walk in. "And more importantly I know what they don't."

"Which is?" Donoghue asks her.

"What I know as opposed to what they know? It's a very long list. I'm about to tell you some of what's on it."

"Only if it's safe to talk," Donoghue says.

"I'm going to get into that too." Lucy shuts the door.

"This stinks." Marino is seated on the couch and careful with his language.

What he really wants to say is this is fucked-up or it sucks. But he has a seven-year-old sitting next to him.

"Can't you do something?" he asks Donoghue. "This is ridiculous. What about unlawful search and seizure? What about malicious prosecution?"

"Legally I can't do anything. Not yet."

"What damn judge would sign a court order allowing all this?" Marino reaches for a mug on the end table, and I spot the Keurig in the kitchen.

"One who probably knows Erin Loria's federal judge husband," I suggest. "Does anybody need coffee?"

"Well it's not right. It's like where the hell are we? Russia? North Korea?" Marino complains.

"I don't disagree that this seems pretty extreme and outrageous. A coffee would be nice," Donoghue says to me.

"Yeah. It's totally f-ed up, that's what it is," Marino adds from his end of the couch.

In the middle is Desi, and next to him is Janet, and I hear Jet Ranger before I spot him under the breakfast table snoring. I bend down to pet his head and silky ears, and he licks my hand and wags his stump of a tail as I walk to the kitchen counter. I make coffees as I take an inventory of my surroundings, starting with the sixty-inch flat screen on the wall.

It's been switched from security to TV mode, and a Japanese sitcom is playing softly on the Tokyo Broadcasting System. No one is remotely interested. That's not why the show is on. The flat screen is more than a TV or a monitor I decide as coffee streams loudly into a mug. What Lucy has in here is a device such as a base station that scrambles mobile phone communications, and whoever intercepts the encrypted data stream will hear nothing but static.

I look around at built-in speakers, at the thick cypress walls and triple-glazed glass that's reflective from the outside so people can't see in. I've been in here before, not often but on occasion and this is the first time it's occurred to me that the boathouse isn't merely a boathouse. Lucy has set up a sound-masking system, and I wonder if it's a new addition like her rock garden. She's anticipated for a while that she was going to be visited by the Feds. Since mid-June at least. Since I was shot. That's my guess.

"They've not been in here?" I ask Lucy as I hand a coffee to Donoghue.

"They did a sweep. I told them they had to do it first and get out because we needed a quiet place for Desi and Jet Ranger."

"How nice of them to accommodate," Donoghue says wryly.

"I demanded a quiet safe place for them."

"Yes how very kind and sensitive of the FBI to comply with your wishes," I say pointedly because the FBI isn't kind or sensitive and they don't care about Lucy's wishes. "Rather unusual, don't you think?" I look around at the built-in speakers and up at the ceiling tiles. "They didn't fight you on it or insist on having an agent in here with you?"

"No."

"You're saying they have no concern about your home improvements." I speak euphemistically, still unconvinced that our conversation is safe.

"There's nothing they can do about how I've chosen to construct my house and any associated outbuildings. A search warrant doesn't grant them permission to destroy someone's property," Lucy says and she's right but in theory only.

FBI agents aren't supposed to damage belongings or disable someone's residential infrastructure or deliberately create a security liability. But that doesn't mean they won't. It doesn't mean they'll have any problem trumping up a justification for their actions. I wonder if they recognized the sound-masking system in here, and if so why they didn't insist that the boathouse is off-limits.

Why really?

What is the actual reason they're permitting us to hole up in here and is there any way at all they could have us under surveillance despite Lucy's protestations that it's not possible? She swears we're safe when I ask about it again just now. She swears everything we're discussing is private. But I continue to have my doubts no matter what she swears. I don't trust a damn thing.

"I hope you're right and we're okay." I hold Lucy's gaze. "How about everybody else? Is everyone okay?" I direct this at Janet as I walk to the couch. "How are you and Desi doing?"

I GIVE THEM A HUG, and Janet is cool and composed. It's her nature, her personality to be that way, and my attention lingers on her youthful attractive face.

She's not wearing makeup. Her short blond hair is messy as if she's been running her fingers through it, and her nails are dirty. She's wearing scrubs and I happen to know she sleeps in scrubs. But she doesn't lounge in them. I've never seen her wear them around the house except right before bed or when she first gets up. It's lunchtime and she's unkempt and in scrubs, and it means something I need to figure out.

If the FBI got here midmorning then what were Lucy and Janet doing before that? I'm quite certain they weren't relaxing. When I hugged Janet just now and kissed her cheek, I tasted salt. I picked up the loamy pungent odors of soil mingled with the vague musky scent of sweat. Lucy was sweaty too. Perhaps they were doing some type of yard work earlier today.

They don't do yard work. They have a lawn service and a landscaper.

I look around at built-in bookshelves, the exposed beams, the gray slate floor, the kitchenette with its gas stovetop and stainless steel sinks and appliances, and the backsplash of Venetian glass tiles the color of smoke. The boathouse is bright and simple, a small living area and a bath. It's clean but has the empty patina of places rarely used. Maybe only when Lucy needs to scramble conversations. Or when she's feeling hunted. And possibly she feels that way more than I've realized.

"We're safe in here." Lucy watches me taking in everything around us. "It's the only place on the property that's completely safe right now. They can't hear us. I promise. They can't see us. As long as we stay inside."

"And they're permitting this?" Donoghue asks dubiously and Lucy laughs.

"They are but they don't have a clue what they're permitting. The boathouse is on a secure wireless network that suffice it to say is hidden." She is suddenly smug and mirthful and just as quickly she ducks back behind her somberness.

But I saw it. She has the FBI outsmarted or at least she believes she does. Nothing would amuse her more.

"There are other features that make this foolproof. I'm not going to go into it." She looks at Donoghue, then back at me. "You don't need to know anything more than that we're safe in here right this minute."

"Are you sure?" I sip my coffee and realize how much I need it. "Absolutely sure?"

"Yes."

"Then I'm going to talk freely."

CHAPTER 21

"GO AHEAD," LUCY SAYS.

"You think they're after the dive mask I was wearing." I don't ask. I tell. "You think they're on your property because of the video captured by the mini-recorder mounted on my mask—a mask I've been led to believe was never recovered."

"I don't really know why they're here. It could be about that," Lucy says. "It could also be about more than one thing," she adds, as if that's what she really thinks.

"I've not heard anything about a missing mask or a mini-recorder." Donoghue has moved to a mission-style chair across from the couch, and she has a yellow legal pad and pen out.

"There's been no mention of them in the news," I reply.

"Well there's plenty else about what happened in Florida including the two police divers murdered and you being almost murdered." Donoghue directs this at me.

"But let me guess," Lucy says. "You don't recall seeing the name Carrie Grethen anywhere."

"No I haven't."

"And you won't." It's Janet who says this. "The FBI will deny her existence. They're denying it and will continue to do so."

"How can you be sure of this?" Donoghue asks her.

"Because I know them."

"Clearly there's a lot you need to brief me about, Kay." Donoghue writes down the name Carrie Grethen in capital letters and circles it.

"I realize that."

"They didn't want to alert anybody that the mask is missing," Lucy says. "Or is believed to be missing. It's stupid. It's not even logical."

"*They* being the FBI," Donoghue assumes.

"Yes," Lucy says. "They've been managing the press releases about what happened in Fort Lauderdale."

"How could you know about it?" I ask. "Why would you know anything about how they're handling the media?"

"My search engines. I see everything that goes out."

She's hacking.

"There's been no mention of the missing mask, which is dumb as hell since the person they're trying to keep that detail from is the person who shot you," she's saying to me. "That person is Carrie and she knows damn well the mask you had on is missing because she's the reason it's missing."

"And on the video you can see this. You can see her take my mask." I hope it's true but don't understand how it can be. "When I realized my mask was missing it made sense that Carrie might have ripped it off my face as a parting gesture. She would have recognized the camera embedded above the nosepiece. I can imagine her wanting the recording."

"She didn't rip off your mask," Lucy says. "But she definitely would want the recording."

"Then how did my mask come off? I understand I was spitting out the regulator. Benton says I was but he never mentioned I took my mask off too. Certainly he wouldn't have done it." I'm feeling more uncertain as I say all this. "And he wouldn't have allowed her to get close enough to me to rip off my mask." I'm becoming less sure of everything with each minute that passes. "I can't imagine it happening like that."

"She didn't get any closer, Aunt Kay. She shot you and then was out of sight."

"Out of sight? She wasn't caught on camera?" I begin to get a cold feeling, a terrible one that clenches my gut.

"Your mask got knocked off when you were struggling, when you were being pulled around by the rope attached to the spear and the surface buoy," Lucy says, and I try to stay positive as I feel the boom about to drop.

"Good. Fine. So we have documentation." I'm deluding myself now but can't seem to stop. "So we're beginning to put the pieces together to show exactly what happened and who's responsible." My spirits lift even as I fail to comprehend how any of this makes sense.

"I wish it were that simple." Lucy begins her windup for the bad news that will follow. "Carrie doesn't need to find out from the media that this critical piece of evidence is lost, missing, stolen, whatever." She says it sarcastically, and my mood sinks lower, back to the dark space where it has been for weeks.

"How the hell does it matter what's in the news?" Marino retorts.

"The FBI thinks it does," Janet says quietly, seriously. "Not for the right reason, and that's the problem. It's always the problem."

"You're presenting information as if it's an undisputed fact,"

Donoghue says to Lucy. "You're basically stating irrefutably that Carrie has something to do with Kay's missing dive mask. And what I keep asking myself is why do you know anything about it?"

"I think what she's trying to say is Carrie may not have ripped my mask off but she recovered it and now Lucy has the recording." I look squarely at my niece to see if she's going to deny this, and instantly I know she won't.

Dear God. What have you done?

"I'll explain." Lucy stares out a window at the darkening sky.

"Holy shit. Please tell me you're kidding." Marino's eyes seem to bug out of his head.

"I don't understand how you got it from her," I say to Lucy as my inner alarm hammers.

"Dammit!" Marino says loudly. "Sorry," he apologizes to Desi.

"I didn't say I got the mask from her," Lucy replies. "Or anything directly from her."

"Don't copy the way I talk, dude. Got it?" Marino puts his arm around Desi, pulls him close and vigorously knuckles his scalp.

"Ouch!" Desi yells and giggles.

"You know what that's called? It's called a noogie."

"Which is what school yard bullies do," Janet says.

"Mom makes me pay when I use swear words. A quarter for *damn,* and fifty cents for *shit* and a dollar if I say the *f*-word. You're up to at least a dollar and twenty-five cents so far," Desi lets Marino know, and he continues to refer to his mother in the present tense.

"Did you have contact with Carrie? Did you see her?" I ask Lucy as calmly as I can muster.

"It's not what you might assume," Janet says, and I can't stop thinking of Lucy's recent trip to Bermuda.

I know she went but I didn't know that she was going. She never mentioned it. Then days ago I found out she'd been there, and Janet and Desi didn't go with her. Lucy doesn't seem inclined to explain herself beyond what she's already told me. She was on a dive trip. It wasn't a vacation. She was meeting a friend of Janet's. I have a feeling this person wasn't merely a social acquaintance.

"What are we supposed to assume?" Donoghue asks Lucy.

"Nothing. Don't assume anything."

"I need you to tell me everything."

"I never tell everything. Not to anyone."

"You're going to have to with me if I'm going to represent you."

"I'm not at liberty to reveal certain details, and it's up to you how you deal with that." Lucy is getting combative with her.

"I'm not sure I can be of much use to you then."

"I'm not the one who called you," Lucy says to her as she looks at me.

"Don't go," I say to Donoghue as she gathers her belongings and gets up from her chair.

"YOU NEED TO STAY," I say to her. "You're representing me too."

"I worried this might not work." Donoghue picks up her pocketbook.

"Lucy, please." I give my niece a warning look, and she shrugs.

"You should stay." The way Lucy says it isn't very convincing but it's enough.

"Okay then." Donoghue sits down, and Desi is looking back and forth at whoever is talking.

He's a wise old soul, small for his age with a mop of pale brown hair and huge blue eyes. He shows no distress or angst but he shouldn't be sitting here listening to this, and Marino can tell what I'm thinking.

"I'll take him outside for a walk," he offers, clawing at mosquito bites that are angry wheals on his legs.

"That sounds fun doesn't it, Desi?" Lucy moves chairs from a small table off the kitchenette, arranges them near the couch.

I've been standing all this time because I've gotten stubborn about being the first one to sit. People assume I need to because of my leg so I stand longer than I should even if I'm miserable.

"How about a walk with Marino?" Lucy encourages Desi.

"No. I don't want to." He shakes his head, and Janet puts her arm around him, hugs him close.

"Yeah you do." Marino picks up a tube of After Bite from the kitchen counter.

"Tell me about the mini-recorder." Donoghue directs this at me. "Give me any details you can."

But it's Lucy who answers her. She explains that U.S. Congressman Bob Rosado was shot to death June 14 two months ago while diving off his yacht in South Florida. His scuba tank and part of his skull weren't found, and since it's a federal case and I have federal jurisdiction through my military affiliation, I decided to meet Benton's tactical team in Fort Lauderdale. I showed up the next day, June 15, to help with their search and recovery efforts.

"Is it routine for you to attach a mini-recorder to your dive mask whenever you're doing an underwater recovery?" Donoghue asks me.

"I wouldn't put it that way because the camera is permanently mounted." I smell ammonia and tea tree oil as Marino slathers gel over his mosquito bites.

"But you turn the camera on and off. You do that manually and deliberately." She slowly turns her coffee mug on the armrest of her chair as if to imply we're talking in circles.

"Yes," I answer. "If for no other reason than to prevent questions about the procedures I used, about the veracity of my testimony. I like jurors to see where I found evidence. It's helpful if they can witness for themselves that it was properly handled and preserved, and in dive search and recoveries it's especially important because there's no talking, no narrative, no explanation. You can't hear much underwater except bubbles."

"So when you saw who you believe was Carrie Grethen, the camera on your mask was recording the entire time," Donoghue says to me. "And that's because you had turned it on."

"That's correct."

"Then Carrie should be on film."

I start to answer that of course she will be but the look in Lucy's eyes stops me. Something is wrong.

"Wherever my face was directed, the camera was recording it," I explain to Donoghue as uncertainty stirs inside me. "And there are no assumptions involved. It's not what I believe. It's about what's true. I know who I saw."

"I have no doubt you believe you do."

"It's not merely what I believe."

"But it is exactly that," Donoghue says. "It's what you believe, Kay, which isn't necessarily what's true. It happened fast. Out of nowhere. The blink of an eye. You had Carrie Grethen on the brain and then someone confronted you in not exactly optimal conditions. You'd just had the shock of discovering the two divers had been murdered by someone . . ."

"By her."

"I know that's what you believe. I'm sure you're sincere. The visibility had to be pretty bad. Do you wear contact lens when you dive? Is your mask prescription?"

"I know who I saw."

"Let's hope we can prove it," she says, and Lucy has the same look in her eyes.

Something is wrong.

"This is what you really think?" I'm getting angry. "You think I was in shock, couldn't see, was confused, and misidentified whoever was down there with a spear gun?"

"We have to prove it," Donoghue repeats. "I'm giving you a dose of what the opposition will say."

"And the opposition is the FBI," I reply. "What a sad thing to contemplate and it seems I contemplate it all too often these days. When I was getting started I was told that law enforcement was a public service. We're supposed to help people not host inquisitions and persecute."

"We absolutely view the FBI as the opposition," Donoghue confirms. "And I'm warming you up to what they'll say, what they're already saying I'm willing to bet. We have to prove it absolutely was Carrie Grethen, that she absolutely isn't dead, that she absolutely is the one shooting people, including you. We have to demonstrate that she absolutely is . . . What are they calling the sniper?"

"Copperhead."

"Yes. That she's Copperhead."

My eyes are on Lucy's face as she stares stonily at the Japanese sitcom no one is watching. Then she looks at me and I don't like what I'm seeing. I feel iced water around my heart. I hear a whisper of doom.

Something is wrong!

"I watched Carrie point a spear gun at me and pull the trigger." I feel as if I'm defending myself to Donoghue, and I don't like it.

"She looked right at me from no more than twenty feet away and I watched her shoot me. I heard the first spear hit my tank and then the second spear hit. Except I didn't hear that one. I felt it. I felt it like a cement truck slamming into my thigh."

"It must have hurt so bad!" Desi exclaims, as if what I've said is new information.

It's not. We've had many conversations about my being shot and what it means and did it hurt and was I afraid of dying? He wants to know all about death as he struggles to understand how it's possible that he'll never see his mother again. It's not been easy for me to handle his questions.

I understand biological death. It's provable. A dead organism isn't going to limber up and get warm again. It's not going to move or speak or suddenly walk into a room. But I'm not going to talk to Desi about the clinical finality of nonlife, of physical nonexistence. I'm not going to instill fear and fatalism into the mind of a little boy who just lost his mother.

It would be selfish and unkind of me not to use a metaphor, an analogy or two that might offer hope and comfort. *Death is like a trip to a place that has no e-mail or phone. Or maybe think of it as time travel. Or something you can't touch like the moon.* I've gotten rather good at giving Desi unsound pathological explanations that I halfway believe.

Marino drops the tube of anti-itch gel on the kitchen counter. "Come on, big buddy."

Janet is rubbing Desi's back. "You must be getting stir-crazy. How 'bout a little fresh air before it rains?"

"No." He shakes his head.

"Marino's really good at fishing," Lucy says. "He's so good the fish have his picture up in the post office to warn everybody. Grab this man! Watch out! Reward offered!"

"Fish don't have a post office!"

"How do you know that, huh? See you can't unless you get some direct experience." Marino picks up Desi and holds him high in the air as he shrieks in delight. "You want to know what kind of fish are in the water around here? You want to know what huge fish we could catch if we had poles right now?"

Desi decides he does, and Marino takes him out. I hear them on the dock. Then I don't.

CHAPTER 22

I DON'T HAVE THE MASK," LUCY SAYS. "BUT I'VE got access to the recording."

"You didn't recover my mask yourself." I have to be sure she wasn't anywhere near me when I lost it and almost died.

"Of course not."

"You couldn't have recovered it unless you were there when I was shot." I'd be devastated if I found out she was.

It would change the history of my life and my entire worldview if I found out she was there. It's one of those things that I honestly might not want to know because the consequences would be irreversibly awful.

"I wasn't in Florida. Why would I shoot you?" Lucy is saying. "Why would I hurt you? Why would I allow anybody to hurt you? Why do you ask me? How could you think for even a minute . . . ?"

"It's not Kay thinking it," Donoghue interrupts her. "And this may be what they intend to prove. This may be the case they present to a grand jury." She directs this at me. "That Lucy was in Florida and was present when you were shot because she's an accomplice to Carrie Grethen. Or worse? Lucy's the one who did it and there is no Carrie Grethen."

"Maybe the FBI's position is that she really did die in a helicopter crash thirteen years ago." Janet says this and it sounds like more than a suggestion, and she looks at Lucy. "And that you've fabricated everything about her."

"Exactly." Donoghue is nodding. "It's the scenario all of us should be worried about. But I'm curious," she says to me, "what about Benton? He witnessed what happened. He saved your life. He must have looked right at the person who shot you. He must have been very close to this person."

"He didn't see her." I've asked Benton this many times and his answer is always the same. "When he realized I was in distress that was it. He was completely preoccupied with me and she must have fled."

"More likely she hung back out of sight and watched," Lucy counters.

"So it sounds to me that if asked Benton will say he can't swear Carrie Grethen shot you and the two police divers," Donoghue decides. "Specifically I'm anticipating what he's said to his FBI colleagues because you can rest assured they have questioned him ad nauseam."

"If Benton says to them what he's continued to say to me in private," I reply, "then he wouldn't swear to anything except that it happened. He knows what happened to me. He knows Lucy wasn't with us."

"In my opinion the Bureau wants to pin everything on her," Janet says, and it's more than opinion.

She's stating what she believes.

"I think they intend to show that Carrie Grethen is a ruse, a ghost Lucy has conjured up as an alibi," Janet adds.

"But what I don't understand is why they would want to show such a thing," I say to them as I consider the *Depraved Heart* videos and whether they're evidence that Carrie is alive.

They're not. I'm forced to admit it to myself as much as I can't stand the thought. I know damn well the videos don't mean what I wish they did. The recordings were made seventeen years ago. All they really show is that Carrie was alive then, and besides that I don't have these videos or even the links texted to me. I can't prove a goddamn thing.

"Payback," Lucy says.

"I doubt the FBI has the time or energy to get a warrant and do all this simply because they're vindictive." Donoghue tap-tap-taps the tip of her pen on the legal pad.

"You'd be surprised by the government's capacity for pettiness and wasting money and time." Lucy's sarcasm is biting, her hostility simmering.

"Payback might be the icing on the cake. A little bit of icing on a very little cake." Janet is always the voice of reason and if anything tends to understate. "But certainly not the whole of it, maybe not even a significant part. Of greater importance is the FBI has reason to want Carrie dead. They want it badly. That's more important to them than paying you back, Lucy. Again it's just my opinion but an educated one. I know the Feds. I used to be the Feds."

"They want Carrie dead now? Or they want her to stay dead?" I ask.

"That's my question too," Donoghue says, and I wish she'd stop tapping her pen.

Everything is plucking my nerves right now.

"Do they want her dead?" Donoghue poses. "Or is it that they don't want anyone to think she wasn't dead after all?"

"They want her to stay dead," Janet replies. "They don't want anyone to find out she was never gone."

"What reason besides the obvious embarrassment?" I inquire.

"That's what I want to know," Janet answers. "But the obvious reason is a bad enough one for them. It would be like finding out Bin Laden is still out there somewhere after our government has reassured us that he's buried at sea. Just as Carrie supposedly was buried at sea when the helicopter went down."

"I can see why everybody might want her dead," Donoghue comments. "Certainly what she did to you"—she looks at me—"demonstrates her callous indifference to human life, her depravity. You could have died. You could have been permanently maimed. You could have lost your leg at the very least."

"True," I reply. "All of the above."

"If Carrie's still alive you can imagine the black eye the Bureau gets." Janet pushes the point.

"WHAT DO YOU MEAN *if*?" Lucy says to her.

"I didn't mean to imply . . . ," Janet starts to say.

"But you did imply it. You said *if*," Lucy confronts her.

"Well it's hard," Janet says as I envision the recording I watched moments ago, a recording that is gone. "I've not seen Carrie. I've not seen a recent picture or a video. I've seen absolutely nothing that would prove she's alive. Only what you've said. Only what Kay says she saw."

I look at Lucy sprawled in a chair, a sliver of her flat belly showing between the hem of her shirt and the waistband of her gym shorts. I think of her dragonfly and what it covers, and then

I think about the FBI and other possible motives it might have to raid Lucy's property, seizing her weapons and electronics.

"Let's talk about motivation. Is it possible that what they're really after is access to the CFC database, to all of our records?" I voice that concern, and Donoghue stops tapping her pen. She starts writing again. "Lucy is certainly a conduit into every state and federal case I've ever worked."

"What might they be after that they couldn't get in a less convoluted fashion?" Donoghue is jotting notes in her loopy scrawl.

"There could be a lot of things."

"And how do you know the FBI isn't already in your database?"

"I would know," Lucy says, and I'm struck by her nonanswer.

Saying she would know if someone has violated our database isn't the same thing as saying it hasn't happened.

"Something's going on with my e-mail. There's been snooping," she adds.

"Snooping? That's a mild way to put it," Donoghue says.

"I know that some of the time it's Carrie."

"And you've condoned it?" Donoghue's tone turns sharp.

"She can't go anyplace I don't let her. Think of it as a rat in a cyber maze. She just keeps running into my firewalls. And so what if she sees e-mails I want her to see? But the CFC electronic case records are a different story." Lucy doesn't answer that question either.

She continues to speak ambiguously when asked if the security of the CFC database has been breached. She's simply saying she would know if it were true. She's not saying it isn't.

"And the FBI?" Donoghue taps her pen for emphasis. "Could they get into the CFC database, into its sensitive records through the networks here on your property?"

"I'm sure they believe they can." Lucy continues to be cryptic.

"Then that might be the real reason they're here. They want to use you as a portal."

"They may think that's what they're going to do."

"But they can't?" Donoghue watches Lucy carefully.

"I have no automatic log-ons, nothing that's going to help them look at anything important. But I wouldn't be surprised if this is part of their motivation. They want to use my personal technology, my personal communication software as a gateway."

"It's important to accept that they don't want just one thing." Janet's repeated comment is making me curious.

"What could they want?" Donoghue again asks me. "One thing, two things, however many things? What might they want that's in your database for example?"

"They may not know what they're looking for," I decide. "It may be something they don't know enough about to list on a warrant."

"A fishing expedition in other words."

"They may be casting a net for something they don't want to draw attention to or have no authority to request. Or they may not even know how to request it or what or why, and mind you I'm coming up with any imaginable bonuses that might entice them to go after Lucy," I explain. "For sure she's a path that leads to me. For sure she's a means of getting to me, for acquiring extremely confidential information that relates to both local and federal law enforcement and also in some instances to the military and other government agencies including the intelligence community."

"You have CIA, NSA cases in your computer system?" This piques Donoghue's attention.

"We have data that are of interest to our State Department. That's as much as I'm going to say about it."

"Have you had any recent cases of that nature?" she asks.

"I can't discuss it." I'm thinking about Joel Fagano, a New York forensic accountant found dead in a Boston hotel room last month.

The door was bolted from the inside with a DO NOT DISTURB sign turned on, and what appeared an obvious suicide by hanging wouldn't have aroused my suspicion had the federal government not showed up for the autopsy. The two FBI agents turned out to be a stalking horse for the CIA, and it wasn't the first time this has happened and it won't be the last. Spies die in car and plane crashes. They kill themselves and get murdered like other people but there's a big difference.

When it's a government operative the assumption has to be foul play. But in Fagano's case there wasn't any. Every finding was consistent with him looping a belt around his neck and cutting off the oxygen to his brain, and I remember Benton's cryptic comment that Fagano took the only power he had when he took his own life—that he must have feared something much more than death. And it lands hard on me.

Data fiction.

Joel Fagano's body came to us with a thumb drive in his pocket, and on it was financial software Lucy claimed was capable of fraud massive enough to undermine the entire U.S. banking system. I remember her saying the point was to make it appear money was present or accounted for, and then one day you wake up and realize you have nothing left. You're told you spent it all and to prove it you're shown a general ledger also generated by the fraudulent software.

What if we go to war, pull the plug, make life-and-death decisions based on data fiction?

Lucy said the term is trending on the Undernet where users

are chatting about whether it's possible anymore to be sure what's real. How do we know what to trust in this day and age? It's not a new concern for me. I never accept anything as reliable unless I have empirical proof. This is my nature and it's also my training. The Greek root of the word *autopsy* is *autopsiā*, which means to see for oneself, to look, to touch, hear and smell. I can't exactly do that in cyberspace, and when every detail of our lives and businesses is turned into an electronic symbol it's both convenient and extremely dangerous.

Technology made everything better for a while and now it seems life is circling back around to the dark ages. Digital communication has begun to make me feel I'm moving faster than ever even as I lose the trusted navigational equipment I was born with. My own eyes. My own ears. My own sense of touch. I miss paper and pen. I miss face-to-face conversations. I worry we're on a collision course with doubt and delusion on a galactic scale.

What if we are finally put in a position of distrusting everything managed by computers? That would include medical charts, emergency services, blood types, health histories, professional directories, fingerprints, DNA, money wires, financial information, background checks and even personal text messages and e-mails. What if we can't believe anything anymore?

"Where were you at the exact time your aunt was shot on June fifteenth?" Donoghue relentlessly questions Lucy.

"I was flying my helicopter from Morris County, New Jersey. Headed back here," she says.

"The attack occurred at what time?" Donoghue asks me.

"About two-forty-five in the afternoon."

"You were in the air at that exact time?" She directs this at Lucy.

"By then the helicopter was back in the hangar. I was in my car."

"Which car?"

"I think I was in my Ferrari FF that day. I may have run a few errands on my way home. I don't remember what I did every minute."

"It's the *I don't remember* part that's a problem," Donoghue says. "Janet? Do you know what Lucy was doing on that day?"

"I didn't see her. Things weren't so good with us then. She'd asked me to move out and I'd left town to spend time with my sister in Virginia." Janet's eyes are on Lucy. "Natalie was in really bad shape. She was in pain. And she was scared. So it was a good time for me to relocate there and as it turned out she didn't last long." She looks away from us, her eyes bright with tears. "But I wasn't happy about the reason I left home. Suffice it to say it was a rough time."

"I didn't want Carrie to hurt you," Lucy says quietly.

"She has anyway."

"Your problems with Janet and the fact that she'd left town aren't good for you either," Donoghue says to Lucy. "You don't have a witness. Domestic difficulties point to personal instability, which also isn't helpful. And with your resources you could have climbed out of your helicopter and straight onto a private jet and been in Fort Lauderdale in two and a half to three hours." She plays the bad guy as if she enjoys it. "Tell me that wasn't physically possible."

"It was more than possible in a Citation-Ten. With the winds that day I could have made it to Fort Lauderdale in two hours."

"So that's a vulnerability they'll exploit," Donoghue informs me. "They'll poke big holes in the alibi that she wasn't in Florida when you were attacked. They'll say she could have been."

"What about other proof?" I ask Lucy. "I.P. addresses, telephone logs, recordings on your security cameras? Is there anything that would place you here in Concord, for example, here at your house? I realize Janet wasn't home. But what about anything else that might place you here?"

"You know how good I am at making my life untraceable."

"You're so good at it that you sacrifice the chance of ever having an alibi if you need one," Donoghue says.

"I don't make it a habit to think in terms of alibis."

"In this instance that's too bad."

"I don't live a life that requires alibis."

"But you live a life that seems to require you to cover your tracks, to make sure no one knows where you are or when or why." Donoghue is sparring with her now.

"Are you asking if there are people out to get me?"

"I'm not asking that," Donoghue says. "It's obvious you think so."

"I know so."

"What's important right now is your own relentless privacy measures that make my job difficult."

"I'm sure there isn't much about me that wouldn't make your job difficult."

"Your electronic communications never come back to a real location and you don't use your real name if you decide to jet somewhere and don't want anybody to know. Am I right?"

"Close enough."

"It's very hard for spies to have alibis," Donoghue says to her. "I hope you thought of that when you started living your so-called untraceable life."

CHAPTER 23

"I'M NOT A SPY." LUCY BEGINS THE NEXT ROUND OF verbal volleys.

"You live like one," Donoghue says.

"I learned to a long time ago."

"Did Carrie teach you?"

"I was a college intern, a teenager when I first met her. She taught me a lot of things but nowhere near as much as she takes credit for. When I interned at the ERF . . ."

"What is that?" Donoghue asks.

"The FBI's Toyland where the latest greatest technologies are developed for surveillance, biometrics and obviously data management that includes their artificial intelligence network I created in the late nineties. CAIN. That was all mine and Carrie took credit for it. She stole my work."

"Meaning both of you might be capable of getting into the FBI database. Since both of you created it."

"Hypothetically," Lucy says. "But I did most of the creating despite her lies about it."

"The two of you were close friends for a while." Donoghue isn't interested in any credit that might have been stolen. "Until eventually you realized who and what she is."

"That's fair to say," Lucy agrees, and I look at Janet.

I wonder how hard it is for her to be reminded that Carrie was Lucy's first love. What Carrie says in the videos is true, and I'm not sure Lucy has ever loved anyone else as much. It's understandable. The first fall is the most intense, the hardest, and when Lucy began as an intern at ERF she was emotionally immature. She was more like a twelve-year-old, and it will forever be her misfortune that the supervisor she was assigned to would end up on the FBI's Ten Most Wanted list. It occurs to me to inquire if Carrie is back on it.

"That's one way to know if the Bureau takes her existence seriously," I explain.

"Well too bad. Because she didn't make the list." It's Janet who answers. "They've known for more than two months that she was in Russia and Ukraine for the past ten years and now is back in the U.S. And she's not officially wanted. She's not been added back to any list anywhere."

"They've *known*?" Donoghue says pointedly.

"For months at least that she's now back in the U.S."

"They've *known*?"

"They know she's tied to serial murders and that she tried to kill Doctor Scarpetta." Janet powers forward with her argument, and it's as if a dim light flicks on in a distant part of my psyche.

I look at Janet carefully, at her rumpled faded scrubs, at her dirty nails and sleep-deprived face. Her eyes burn hard and bright, and I'm reminded of how private and stoical she can be. And strong. Janet is very strong. She's quietly dangerous like an undertow if you plunge into an area where you don't belong or dare to threaten anyone she loves.

She's not telling us something.

"Yes, yes, the FBI knows what they've been told," Donoghue argues. "But that doesn't mean they accept or believe it, as we've been pointing out. Frankly it's most likely that they don't accept Carrie is responsible for anything. In other words she's been dead for years and that's the explanation for why she isn't back on the Most Wanted list or possibly any lists."

"I agree," I reply. "That's the explanation for why she isn't *wanted*. The Bureau hasn't listed her as a fugitive. They haven't asked Interpol to amend her from a black to a red notice, from a dead fugitive to an active extremely dangerous one. I know. I've periodically been checking Interpol's website and her status hasn't changed. It won't unless the FBI changes it."

"In other words the FBI is still treating her as if she's deceased," Donoghue says.

"Yes," I reply. "Adding to the theory that they're refusing to acknowledge her existence because the consequences will be significant, perhaps ones we have no idea about."

"And the last time you saw her was thirteen years ago when you thought you witnessed her die in a helicopter crash." Donoghue directs this at both Lucy and me.

"It was the last time I thought I saw her." I sip my coffee. "As it turned out I didn't see her at all on that occasion."

"What we literally saw was a helicopter crash into the ocean," Lucy says more precisely.

"We? Both of you witnessed it independently?"

"Yes," I reply. "I was in the left seat. Lucy was in the right seat flying. We were in her helicopter when we saw the other one, a white Schweizer, crash into the Atlantic Ocean off the coast of North Carolina."

"When I caused it to go down," Lucy qualifies. "The pilot was shooting at me. I shot back and his helicopter blew up. Aunt Kay and I thought Carrie was on it."

"I'll trust you that she wasn't." Donoghue doesn't take her eyes off Lucy now, and I can't tell if she believes her or any of us.

"As I've mentioned," I reply, "no remains we recovered were identified as hers or possibly hers. The only body parts and other personal effects found were the pilot's, a fugitive named Newton Joyce."

"The video recording of when you were shot with the spear gun? Is there any possibility the FBI has seen it?" Donoghue directs this at me but it's Lucy who answers.

"I don't know how. They've never been in possession of the recorder. They couldn't have seen the video unless someone turned it over to them."

"The same way this recording was turned over to you?" Donoghue asks. "I need to know exactly how you got it but I don't want to hear about it with Janet in the room. She's not protected."

"I could leave," Janet offers.

"Stay," Lucy says to her. "The recording wasn't *turned over* to me," she says to Donoghue.

"Please explain."

"Suffice it to say I have access to it and the FBI couldn't unless they have the mask. And they don't."

"I don't see how they could," I agree with Lucy. "By the time the FBI showed up on the scene the mask was long gone. Other responding police divers had looked and had no luck based on what Benton's told me. It's probably safe to assume that Carrie might have gotten her hands on the mask. She would have recognized the embedded mini-recorder. If nothing else she might have expected I would have one."

"If Carrie has the mask," Donoghue says, "then she's seen the recording."

"Yes," Lucy says, nodding. "You should assume she has."

"And she couldn't have tampered with the recording you have?"

"No. When the camera was running it live streamed to a device. I won't say what or where," she says and I again think of her sudden trip to Bermuda. "But the instant Aunt Kay turned the camera on it began to live stream the video to a designated device. That link has been deactivated and the device is untraceable with more firewalls around it than the Pentagon. May I see your phone please?" she asks Donoghue.

"Might I ask why?"

"Please," Lucy says, and Donoghue hands the phone to her. "What's your password? I can figure it out but it would be quicker if you give it to me."

Donoghue does as she asks. "Is this a test to see if I really trust you?"

"I don't have time for tests." Lucy enters the password and starts typing in the glass display. "I'm assuming you'd like to see what was recorded." She looks at us. "I've kept it out of e-mail, basically off the Internet with the exception of my transmitting the data over a secure wireless network they'll never trace to me as I just explained. In summary the Feds do not have this. I've made sure they will never ever have this."

"*This?*" I ask.

"What the camera on your mask recorded when Carrie shot you," Janet says and she's obviously watched it, and that dismays me.

NOT EVEN FIFTEEN MINUTES AGO she said she hadn't seen a photo or a video that could convince her Carrie is alive. Then who or what did Janet see in the recording Lucy is talking about? My misgivings about the video intensify.

"Do you know where Carrie is?" I come right out and ask Lucy.

"Don't answer that," Donoghue tells her in no uncertain terms. "Not unless you and Janet are married."

"We're not," Janet says.

"Then it's as I've been warning you. And you're not listening. There's no spousal privilege. Whatever you and Lucy discuss or witness isn't protected." Donoghue continues to make this point but it's as if Lucy and Janet don't hear her or care.

"You're about to see how Carrie always manages to land on her feet. You're about to see why the Feds can't have this." Lucy touches Donoghue's phone on the table. "It will prove a fatal error if we're not careful. It will only help them and hurt us."

"Let me ask you this point-blank," Donoghue says. "Is the actual recording of your aunt being shot in your physical possession?"

"No," Lucy says. "It never has been. Not completely. Only nine-tenths."

"It's nine-tenths in your possession," Donoghue says. "That's your definition of ownership."

"You know what they say. If you have it, you've got it. If you've got it, you have it."

"I don't know who says that but I understand what you're implying." Donoghue is getting unhappier. "I think we get the drift loud and clear." She looks at me.

But she doesn't understand and I'm not going to help her. Lucy is saying that she has the recording because she managed to get it.

She's not saying how and she won't, and that can mean only one thing at least to me. Lucy doesn't have the mask or the recorder in her possession. She never has and doesn't need them. I'm betting the live-streaming went to a device that isn't in this country, and I keep thinking about Bermuda. Why did she go there recently? Who was she meeting?

"You installed the camera on my mask about a year ago," I say to her. "I'd only done two dives with it. The dive in Fort Lauderdale was my third one."

"Can you describe what would happen when Kay turned the camera on?" Donoghue asks Lucy.

"It would send me an e-mail that the recorder had been activated. Sort of the same principle as a nanny cam. Only in those cases the cameras are motion sensitive. With a dive mask that wouldn't make sense. If you have the mask on and have activated the camera, well obviously you want to start recording and will continue to do so until you're out of the water with your mask off. In other words," Lucy says to me, "your mask wasn't motion sensitive. It was on-off sensitive, so to speak. It was either recording or it wasn't."

"When she turned the camera on at the beginning of the dive exactly two months ago," Donoghue says, "did you get an e-mail prompting you to watch what was being recorded in real time?"

"I didn't," Lucy says.

"You didn't?"

Lucy shakes her head no.

"Why not?" Donoghue asks.

"Because the message got diverted." Lucy is cryptic again, and then she falls silent for a long uncomfortable pause.

"If you don't have the recording legally," I finally say to her quietly, somberly, "then let me suggest that we be exceedingly cautious about what we discuss." I look at Janet.

"I think I should step out now." She abruptly gets up from the couch.

"A picture's worth a thousand words." Lucy slides the phone closer to me as Janet leaves the boathouse. "Unedited, uncut. I did try to sharpen the images as best I could."

"How could you do that if you don't have the actual recording?" Donoghue asks.

"Not in my physical possession, I don't," Lucy replies as I keep thinking of her recent trip and her story about Customs agents crawling all over her plane. "What you see is as good as it's going to get."

"You don't say that in a way that instills confidence." I pick up the phone and press PLAY.

CHAPTER 24

THE RECORDING STARTS SEVERAL FEET BENEATH THE surface of the Atlantic Ocean.

I remember my giant stride off the stern of the boat. I relive the sensation of water splashing, and the cold salty chop against my chin as I floated, easing my way to the mooring line, breathing through my snorkel with the sun glaring in my eyes. It seemed like a routine dive. Underwater missions like this aren't new to me. I distinctly remember feeling there was nothing to worry about.

I had a false sense of safety, and I hit PAUSE. I have to think about this long and hard.

"What is it?" Donoghue's breath touches my hair as she looks on.

"I felt safe and I shouldn't have. I'm trying to figure out why."

The previous night I'd seen images of Bob Rosado's murder

at a dive site called the *Mercedes*. The congressman's wife was on the stern of their yacht, drinking a martini, filming him, joking with him as he floated on the surface. He was waiting to make his descent when a bullet struck the back of his neck and a second one pierced his tank, sending him pirouetting into the air. Copperhead.

There was every reason to suspect that Carrie was in the Fort Lauderdale area. She'd flown there under an assumed name with her partner in crime at the time, Rosado's sadistic son, nineteen-year-old Troy, a sex offender, a pyromaniac, Carrie's latest monster boy toy. I knew this and yet I wasn't worried.

Why?

Most importantly it didn't seem to penetrate my conscious mind that she might be thinking about me.

Why?

I'm anything but a careless, unobservant person.

Why did you feel safe?

Maybe I was simply in shock. The night before I flew to Florida I was sitting in New Jersey, having just found out from Lucy that Carrie isn't dead, that she's been living in Russia and Ukraine for at least the past decade. After the pro-Russian President Viktor Yanukovych was ousted, Carrie fled and returned to the United States. Using the name Sasha Sarin she began doing dirty work for Congressman Rosado and chaperoned his troubled, increasingly violent son, Troy. So I was astonished and maybe I was in denial when I found out all this. Maybe that's why I wasn't worried. I don't know and I think back, conjuring up every detail I possibly can.

I remember floating in the bright blue water on the bright sunny afternoon, bobbing, waiting for Benton. I envision him striding off the dive platform, splashing, floating, smiling, giving me the okay sign and I gave it back. I placed the regulator into my mouth, bled the air out of my BCD, and reached up to turn on my mask's mini-recorder. I wasn't afraid. I wasn't wary. Carrie had just murdered Bob Rosado. Or maybe Troy was to blame. Or maybe Carrie had murdered Troy too, possibly in this very spot barely a mile offshore, and yet I wasn't worried.

What were you thinking?

I hit PLAY again and resume watching the video on the small display, the volume turned up as high as it will go. Bubbles blast up past my mask, and the sound of them is loud as I touch the mooring line, following it down, pinching my nose to clear my ears, down and down. Glimpses of my legs, my fins, my gloved hands, and the water is a darker blue as I descend deeper. Benton is above me and I don't look up at him. My attention is directed down, looking straight down through bubbles.

Down and darker, and I remember the cooling of the water the deeper we went. I could feel the chill through my three-millimeter wet suit. I could feel the pressure of the heavy water weighing on us, and I watch myself on the video as I continuously lift my left hand to my nose, clearing my ears, the sound of my breathing artificial and loud. The shape is vague when it first comes into frame, and then it becomes the wrecked barge, a twisted, broken, rusting carcass.

My attention is fixed on it in the surrounding darkness, getting closer and closer, and the images bring back sensations, the flutter of unsettledness when I didn't see any sign of the two police divers who had gone down minutes before us. I'm looking for them. I'm scanning the surroundings for them as I puzzle over where they are. Now Benton and I are almost a hundred feet deep where the sunken German freighter called the *Mercedes* is nestled in the silt. We move away from the mooring line and turn on our small flashlights attached by lanyards to our wrists.

Fish swim by, magnified by the water, and Benton hovers inches above the ocean floor, horizontal, his buoyancy perfectly controlled. He shines his light over a fishing lure, the antenna of a spiny lobster hiding in the rocks, the old tires that are supposed to help build an artificial reef. A small shark leisurely snuffles past, skimming the silt and stirring it up, and I use gentle movements of my fins to propel myself to the barge. I sweep my light into gaping holes in the corroded metal.

Disturbed fish dart off, a barracuda big and silvery, and then I'm suspended above the deck, dropping lower into an opening, what used to be a hatch, and as I watch the recording I vividly remember not understanding what I was seeing at first. A man's neoprene-covered back. The hoses hanging down. The absence of bubbles, and when I moved him I could see the spear embedded in his chest. Then below him my light finds the second body, two dead police divers inside the freighter's hull. I bolt out of there with powerful kicks.

I dart to Benton and tap my knife against his tank. Clink, clink! I'm pointing my light up at the barge, and suddenly I'm looking around. I remember hearing a faint vibration, like a distant power tool, and I see my fins kicking up into the camera as I try to back up and twist away. She's there. Pointing a spear gun at me. Pandemonium. The blast of my bubbles and the clank of something hitting my tank as the camera jerks crazily. A second spear, and the line attached to it leads tautly to the surface where it's tethered to a float that moves with the strong current, tugging my impaled leg. Thrashing crazily. Thundering bubbles.

This goes on for several seconds, and I get the impression of another diver, someone's lower body and arms. A flash of a double white stripe around a leg, a chest zipper with a long pull tag, and black neoprene gloved hands near my face. Benton. It must be Benton but it enters my mind crazily that I don't remember his wet suit having a double white stripe. Then the only image is water, then nothing. My mask had come off. I back up the recording and replay it again and again as my disappointment grows. This isn't helpful. In fact it's worse than not helpful. It's extremely harmful.

Carrie would have recognized the mini-recorder built into my mask. She knew she was being recorded. I'm sure she knows by now that she's not identifiable. The lighting is poor, and I'm seeing her through bubbles streaming up from my regulator. I'm seeing my own movements as I reach around, frantically feeling the right side of my BCD, and then I'm slashing at someone I can't see, madly slashing my dive knife at empty murky water.

"Please tell me this isn't all there is." I nudge the phone back in Donoghue's direction, and I feel sick.

"I'm sorry," Lucy says.

"Then how do we know it's her? We can't see who it is." Donoghue is so close to me now our shoulders are touching. "And you were sure at the time it was her?"

"Yes. I'm completely sure." I feel emptied of any hope I might have had. "What is this?" I say to Lucy. "What the hell am I looking at? I cut her with the knife. I cut her face."

"I know you believed you did," she says. "But based on this recording it doesn't look like it."

"A recording you got from who?" I can't keep an accusatory tone out of my voice.

"What matters is who doesn't have it." Lucy's demeanor is steady and still. "And I can promise the FBI doesn't. My initial hope was we'd get to rub their noses in it but that's not possible. Because all it would do is make things a thousand times worse. I'm sorry, Aunt Kay."

"I remember cutting her," I insist.

"I know you believe you did."

"You sure she couldn't have somehow Photoshopped it out?"

"I'm sure," Lucy says. "I won't explain why I know that."

"I don't want a technical hypothetical explanation. And just because it's not on the recording doesn't mean it didn't happen." Now I sound argumentative.

I sound ridiculous.

"It didn't happen." Lucy locks eyes with me as the boathouse door opens.

Lucy doesn't look at Janet as she walks back in, quietly shutting the door behind her.

"Is this okay?" she asks Donoghue. "Am I allowed back?"

"It probably isn't okay."

"It's always polite to ask. I'm staying anyway." She sits back on the couch, and I get the same sensation again.

There's a calm about Janet that goes beyond her usual disposition. It's as if she's made up her mind about something and is simply going through the motions with us.

"Desi has a new talent," she's saying lightly and with a smile. "Throwing rocks. Marino is teaching him to skip them across the water."

"If the FBI gets hold of this, it will undermine everything you've said in your statements to them, to the police." Lucy is going to lecture me now. "Do you see that? Because it's the most important point I'm making and the real reason for showing this to you."

"Lucy's right I'm afraid," Donoghue agrees. "No matter how we got the recording or who might have had it first, what's on it now is a problem for you, Kay. Let's play through it again, paying close attention to the moment when you were attacked. Tell me everything you remember."

"I saw her bleeding into the water." I know I did. "I saw it after I swung the knife at her."

"You saw your own blood," Lucy replies. "When you swung at her, you jerked the spear in your thigh and you bled more."

"It wasn't my blood. I know what I saw."

"I'm going to show you what happened," she says. "Watch very closely."

A SUDDEN MOVEMENT around the hulk of the wreck, and a shape becomes a sleek person in a hooded camouflage dive skin the tawny colors of a reef, moving aerodynamically like a squid.

That's what I see in my mind but it's not what's in the video. Carrie Grethen isn't recognizable in what I'm watching. It's not possible to tell if the murky figure is male or female or what type of dive skin he or she has on. Lucy hits PAUSE.

"What do you see?" she asks me.

I stare for the longest time, touching the display to enlarge the image, then making it small again to sharpen the poor resolution. I lean back in my chair and close my eyes, groping for the slightest additional detail of what I remember or thought I did.

"Admittedly it's poor quality because there was so little light—so little that there was no color, just murky shades of brown and black. Admittedly I can't tell who it is and it could be a male for that matter." My face is turned up toward the ceiling, my eyes still shut.

"Troy Rosado," Lucy says to Donoghue. "I just want to toss that out there because someone will suggest he could be who Aunt Kay was seeing. Nineteen years old, five-nine, a hundred and forty pounds. He'd disappeared with Carrie, was definitely in Florida, was definitely in the area and probably was complicit in the murder of his own father and on the family yacht when it happened. Then he and Carrie vanished."

"That's not who shot me. It wasn't Troy Rosado," I reply.

"You would swear to that under oath?" Donoghue asks.

"I'm positive the person I saw wasn't him."

"You'd met him before?" Donoghue asks.

"No. But I'd seen photographs and it doesn't matter because I recognized Carrie. But I wish what I remember is clearer. What I see in my mind now isn't as distinct as it was at first. The images have been overlaid by what I've found out since, and by the trauma."

"Do you think being shot and its aftermath changed what you remember about your encounter?" Janet asks.

"I don't know because I've never been shot before," I reply.

"I have," she says. "When I was just getting started with the Bureau and hadn't been out of the Academy even a year. One night I walked into a 7-Eleven to buy a soda. I have the cooler door open, figuring out what I want. I bent down to reach for a Diet Dr Pepper when this guy comes in with a gun and proceeds to rob the place. I took care of it but got wounded. Nothing serious. Except later when I saw the security video, the kid in it didn't look like the one I saw."

"You're suggesting that trauma changes your perceived reality," Donoghue says.

"It did for me. I knew the guy I killed was the one who robbed the store and shot me, but it's really weird that what I remember I saw and what I really saw weren't the same thing. I swore his eyes were dark when in fact they were blue. I remembered his skin as light brown with pimples when in fact it was white with peach fuzz. I described a teardrop tattoo on his face and in fact it was a mole. I thought he was in his twenties and it turned out he was thirteen."

"That had to be hard," Donoghue says.

"Not really. He might have been a kid but he had a very grown-up Taurus nine mil and two extra magazines in his pocket."

"Would you have picked him in a lineup?" Donoghue asks.

"Fortunately I didn't have to since his body was right there on the floor."

"But would you have?"

"Honestly I don't know. It depends on who else was in it."

"What about a photograph of Carrie? Is there a way for me to see what she looks like? Or what she used to look like?" Donoghue asks.

Lucy reaches across the table and retrieves the phone. She types on it for a moment, hands it back to Donoghue.

"When she supposedly was killed in the chopper crash this was the photo on file, her mug shot from when she'd been arrested the year before and locked up in Kirby on Wards Island. Wikipedia, by the way. This photo's on Wikipedia. Carrie Grethen has her own Wikipedia page."

"Why?" I ask. "Why would she have a Wikipedia page now, and when did it happen?"

"Recently," Lucy answers. "You can look at the history and see the first version of her page was posted six weeks ago. Since then the same person appears to be revising it, and I have no doubt it's her. Carrie. I'm sure she's the one who posted her old mug shot and the aerial photo of Kirby Psychiatric Center."

"Which as you know is on an island in the East River. She's the only patient in history to escape from the maximum security forensic unit for the criminally insane," Janet tells Donoghue. "Somehow she'd managed to hook up on the outside with the psycho we mentioned earlier, Newton Joyce. Turned out he was a serial killer who liked to cut off his victims' faces to remember them by, and had a big stash in his freezer. He was a pilot, had his own helicopter and landed it on Wards Island and flew off with Carrie. The rest of his story didn't end so well, at least not for him."

"She had herself airlifted out by a serial killer? How could she manage something like that?" Donoghue is impressed.

"The question is always how she does things," Lucy says. "And there's always a long and involved story. Carrie is extremely smart and resourceful. She's patient. She knows she'll get what she wants if she takes her time and doesn't give in to impulses, to cravings and rages."

"So this is what she used to look like." Donoghue moves the phone closer to both of us.

CHAPTER 25

THE FACE IS YOUNG AND STRONGLY PRETTY, BUT IT was always the eyes that gave her away. They remind me of pinwheels. They seem to spin as her aberrant thoughts surge behind them, fueling the evil entity that inhabits her soul.

Carrie Grethen is a cancer. I realize that's an overused pathological metaphor but it's the truth in her case. There's no healthy tissue left, just the malignancy that has consumed her life and completely taken over her psyche. I barely view her as human, and in a way she's not because she's missing the major traits that qualify her to be a member of the same race as the rest of us.

"Well?" Donoghue says to me. "Is that who you saw?"

"Yes and no," I reply as my mood sinks deeper to what feels like the bottom of the sea, as deep and dark as where I almost died. "I couldn't swear to it in court. Not based on this."

The person I observed a hundred feet under the water looks

like an older Carrie, but the fact is I can't be positive and probably no jury would convict her based on this recording or what I claim occurred. I don't know what I expected but I thought the video would be of a higher resolution, a better quality. I thought I'd see my knife cut through the side of her face. It was so real.

I could have sworn I injured her badly. No one questioned me at the time, not even Benton. The FBI checked local hospitals and doctors based on my certainty that Carrie had a serious wound to her face that would require plastic surgery. Even so she likely would be disfigured for life, and that would be a terrible fate for her based on what I've learned today about her vanity, her fears of becoming old and unattractive. But I don't see anything to support what I felt sure happened. I'm increasingly frustrated and dejected, and Lucy can tell.

"It was dark down there and you didn't have your flashlight directed at what you were filming," she says to me. "And you were moving a lot. That's the tough part. You were moving."

"What about forensic image processing?" Donoghue asks her.

"What do you think you're looking at?" Lucy replies. "I've spent a lot of time on this." *She doesn't say when or where.*

"And as I've said, what you see is as good as it's going to get," she adds. "The camera I installed in her mask was for the purposes of recording evidence recovery, and in those instances Aunt Kay would have her light shining on what she was collecting. I didn't install a camera thinking she was going to be attacked underwater, that something like this was going to happen."

"Do you think Carrie anticipated that Kay might be recording the dive and the attack could end up filmed?"

"That's the point of the camouflage, the hood, the gloves," Lucy says. "She blends with her surroundings in poor visibility and to answer your question, yes. Carrie knew exactly what she was doing and would have recognized the camera mounted on the mask. Carrie for sure would have anticipated that someone might be filming that dive. She knows us."

"Maybe better than we know ourselves," Janet adds.

"What else?" Donoghue gives me her complete attention again.

"I remember rapidly backing away from the bodies, from the two dead divers inside the hull." I pick up the story where I left off. "Obviously someone had just been there with a spear gun, and this person intended to kill all of us. That was my instant reaction. Benton was searching the ocean floor with a light maybe fifty feet from me, and I swam to him and tapped his tank with my dive knife to get his attention. Then I saw her come around the side of the wreck."

"You saw *someone* come around the side of the wreck," Donoghue corrects me.

"I saw her pointing the spear gun at me," I repeat adamantly. "I spun around, giving her my back as I heard a spitting sound, then a clank."

"Your spinning around to protect yourself is why the first spear hit your tank," Donoghue infers.

"No," Lucy answers for me. "The first spear hit her tank because that was Carrie's intention."

"Why do you say that?" I ask. "How can you possibly know her intention?"

"You saw what happened when Rosado's tank was hit while he was waiting on the surface as his wife filmed him from the stern of their yacht," Lucy replies. "Compressed air blasted out like a rocket, propelling him into the air and spinning him around, and it's all on film. If he hadn't already been dead, he probably would have died of a broken neck or drowned."

"His tank was struck by a bullet not a spear," I reply.

"This is psychological," Lucy says. "Carrie would know you saw the video of Rosado spinning in the air. Clank! She hits your tank and you're going to make the connection. Maybe the same thing could happen to you. Only worse. You're a hundred feet down and your tank gets perforated and compressed air blasts out?"

"A spear couldn't have perforated my steel tank."

"Did you know that the second it happened?"

"That wouldn't have been possible," I reply. "I didn't really know anything when it happened."

"Did you even know it was a spear?"

"What I recall is an overwhelming impulse to take off my BCD, to get out of it as fast as I could." I remember that vividly. "Maybe that's why. Maybe after watching Rosado's murder on video I was afraid my tank was going to explode the same way his did."

"Then the second shot hits you in the leg," Lucy says. "And that too was an intentional target. Just as it was intentional that the spear was attached to a float. Carrie rigged it up so the float was going to start pulling you along with the current. She was treating you like a speared fish."

I think back to what Benton said after it happened. Carrie loves to degrade and humiliate. She batted me around like a catnip mouse and is probably still laughing about it. He explains when she looks at me what she really sees is herself and her eventual response. Will she run? Or will she rip me open? Was the plan to weaken me first? And finish me off later?

"What I want you to look at carefully is the image of her when you could see her pointing the spear gun." Lucy reaches for the phone. "I'm sorry I can't put this up on a big screen. But you're going to see what I'm talking about. A very important detail that's not noticeable in the video before I cleaned it up."

She returns the phone to us, and in the display is the blurry shape of Carrie when I first saw her come around the side of the wreck. I remember her looking me in the eye as she lifted the spear gun and fired. SPIT. And then a CLANK as I whirred around and the spear hit my tank. Lucy looks over my shoulder and points.

"There. Take a good look at the spear gun. Do you see what I do?" she asks me.

"I don't know. It just looks like a spear gun."

"It's actually a railgun, a long one, at least three and a half feet and intended for big game." She touches the screen with two fingers, enlarging the image. "But look what else. Watch her cock the gun. You can barely make it out but watch her arms, her hands pulling back toward her chest."

She replays several seconds of the video to show us. And it's murky and blurry but I see what she means.

"There. She has two rubber power bands but is using only one," Lucy explains. "That makes it easier and quicker to reload. But for a gun this big it's not enough firepower if she wants the necessary velocity, and you can bet when she shot the two police divers she used both rubber bands. But not with you," she says to me.

"She could have killed you and Benton," Donoghue decides. "She was fast and armed and the two of you were neither. But for some reason she allowed you to live. Is it possible, Kay, that you've assumed she won't kill you? Knowing what you do about her? And after a spate of her horrific murders? And yet you felt it was fine to go diving in that location?"

"I was simply doing my job." It's the only answer I have, and yet I realize it's not an honest one.

I wasn't scared and I should have been. I'm still not scared. Maybe it's because there's no point in it. Being afraid of Carrie Grethen serves no useful purpose. It's possible I gave up that normal human response long years ago and wasn't really aware of it until now.

"It's so frustrating that the figure you're pointing out isn't identifiable," Donoghue is saying. "I can't even tell it's a woman. But whoever it was this person allowed you to live."

"I wouldn't say she allowed me to live," I reply hotly.

"But she did." Lucy pauses the video, looking at me. "Whether you like it or not. That's what happened. Carrie didn't want you or Benton dead. At least at that very moment she didn't because it's not part of her long-term plan."

"Be careful saying things like that," Donoghue reprimands her. "You need to avoid any appearance that you can think Carrie Grethen's thoughts or predict her behavior."

"Well I can," Lucy says. "I can think like her and predict what she'll do, and I promise that whatever she's set in motion is just starting. That's not speculation. It's a fact you're about to witness because it's already unrolling even as we speak."

"Do you think Carrie has something to do with why the FBI is on your property?" Donoghue asks.

"What do you think." It's not a question, and Lucy resumes the video and then backs it up.

We again watch the hooded figure emerge from around the hulk of the barge, and Lucy explains that clamped to Carrie's tank is a diver propulsion vehicle (DPV), a small black plastic cylinder that's difficult to see. It's hands free, making it possible for Carrie to maneuver nimbly and quickly underwater while managing a railgun and spears. The sound I heard was the quiet vibration of the battery-powered motor, Lucy says, and it's the first time I've known this. I always thought I heard something strange but I never knew what it was or if I might have imagined it.

The whining power tool sound came from the sort of underwater scooter Navy SEALs use, Lucy points out, adding that none of us was any match for Carrie Grethen. Not the two divers she murdered. Not Benton. Not me. We didn't arm ourselves. We didn't have the advantage of a DPV propelling us at 170 feet per minute. We couldn't have caught her. We couldn't have gotten away from her either.

IT'S PAST NOON when Marino returns with Desi. I hear their feet on the dock. Then they're walking through the door and shutting it behind them.

"I've been asked to pass it along that you need to move your truck," Marino says to me. "The K-nine and another unit tried to leave but you've got the driveway blocked. They're waiting by the gate and I'm just warning you they're pissed."

"They were really mad!" Desi says excitedly. "And they had on guns too!"

"Ohhhhhh no. I'm so scared." Lucy picks him up and swings him around as he laughs hilariously.

"I suspect I've added to the problem," Donoghue says to Marino. "I had to leave my car down there for the same reason. I'm sure it must be blocking people."

"Yep," he says. "You're blocking the truck and the truck's blocking a couple of assholes."

"If you give me your keys I'll take care of it," Lucy says to her.

Donoghue digs them out and hands them over. "Not one word to the FBI, the police, not to anyone. No joking. No deliberately aggravating them. No obscene gestures." She's firm with Lucy.

But it won't do any good. I can already tell, and I know my niece. I know what enrages her. I know when there will be hell to pay.

"I'm going to insist that all further communications must go through me. Are you all right with that?" Donoghue asks.

"I don't care," Lucy says.

"I need you to care."

"It's better not to."

"I don't need you to be afraid but I do need you to care."

"I'm not afraid and I don't care. Not the way they want me to."

"I need you to care the way I want you to," Donoghue says, and she gives more instructions. "Don't return to the main house until they're gone. If they want to interview you, well I shouldn't indicate that they might not . . ."

"Sure you should indicate it," Lucy rudely cuts her off. "That's exactly right because the bigger worry is they don't want to question me, interview me, hear my side of anything, that it was never their intention. They don't care what I have to say. All they care about is making some case that fits with their petty politics."

"I'm assuming they want to ask you questions. I'll insist that we set up a formal time and they can do it at my firm." Donoghue's not an alarmist and she doesn't accept what Lucy just said.

In Jill Donoghue's playbook everybody wants to ask questions. The FBI wouldn't turn down the chance to interrogate Lucy, especially if they thought they could trip her up or corner her into a lie. If they can't send her to prison for crimes she didn't commit, maybe they can manipulate her into making false statements. It's what I call playing the legal lottery. My answer is don't let them put a nickel in your slot machine. Don't ever give them a chance to get lucky.

"What are you going to do about a phone?" Donoghue is asking my niece.

"It's been returned to the factory settings." What Lucy is saying is that she's made sure her phone self-destructed after Erin Loria took it from her. "It's in the exact condition it would be if they bought it brand-new in a store," she adds. "By the end of the day I'll have a different number for you to reach me on securely, privately."

"And they won't know what you've done? That you've acquired another device? Another phone?"

"Acquiring another phone isn't against the law. I can do it all day long and whatever they find out?" Lucy stares defiantly at her. "I'll just continue to defeat them. This is war. They've invaded my property and my life, and I'm not going to let it go. They want to spy on me? They want to take me on? They think they're going to leave me defenseless on my own property with Carrie Grethen on the loose? Really? Let's see what happens."

"Be careful. They can arrest you." Donoghue is blunt with her. "They have the power of the justice system on their side and you have nothing but your vigilantism and anger."

"Vigilantism and anger. An eloquent way to describe it. And you should be careful too, especially about trivializing what you don't completely understand."

"I intend to understand everything. But you need to do as I say."

"Gee that's the one thing I'm not good at." Lucy touches my arm. "Come on," she says to me. "Let's go unblock the driveway."

CHAPTER 26

OUTSIDE ON THE DOCK THE AIR IS STEAMY AND thick. I feel electricity. I smell the rain as veins of lightning shimmer in a black sky that soon will have its way with us.

I know an advancing big storm when I see one, and we're going to get a whopper. I hope there's no hail. This summer there have been violent late-afternoon thunderstorms, and hail as big as marbles has beaten the hell out of my yard. It's knocked several slate tiles loose from the roof and dented the new drainpipes I recently installed.

"We're going to be slammed but good." I look up and realize how quiet it's gotten, and I remember the helicopter is gone. "At least there's something positive to come from nasty weather. Listen. You can hear the peaceful sounds of the countryside again."

You can't really and I'm being just a little sarcastic. What I hear is the wind gusting through trees and our footsteps on the wooden dock and the plashing of the river against its pilings. But I say whatever I want because at this stage Lucy and I are no longer having an honest conversation. We're manipulating. But not in the same way. Not hardly.

Lucy is angrily and aggressively acting out while my every word is calculated with a very decided impression in mind. I imagine Erin Loria watching and listening. She won't get anything helpful from me. Mostly I intend to load her up with what I call *dead wood* that's too flimsy to build anything from and too green to burn.

"One big fishing expedition." Lucy walks slowly, considerately so I can keep up with her.

"I'm sure Desi loved the idea of fishing with Marino one of these days." I try to deflect what I already know Lucy will do next.

She's going to dish on the FBI. She's going to have her brand of fun. She's homicidally angry and this is what she does. She flaunts and taunts. She goads and inflames. She does it recklessly and with no regard for consequences. It's who my niece is. She's grown up and she's not and never will be.

"To catch me at whatever they miscalculate I might do," she says loudly. "For what they foolishly hope I've been up to when no one's looking such as . . . Let me see. Oh I know. Digging a hole to China. That must be it. Thus the aerial search. That tactical bird of theirs is equipped from soup to nuts including GPR, ground-penetrating radar. I'm sure they were hoping to detect underground safe bunkers or secret rooms or wormholes."

She boldly, loudly and in a hostile voice recites the exact wording in the warrant: "*Any hidden doors, egresses including but not limited to structures, dwellings, elevators or passageways which are partly or wholly belowground or separate from the main residence.*"

"Yes," I answer with more platitudes and vagueness. "It's what I call the kitchen sink scenario. Ask for everything."

"Precedents," Lucy announces as we reach the driveway. "Never forget the way their robotic rigid minds work. They think in precedents that have nothing to do with relevance or truth. It has to do with whatever else has been done, as opposed to what should be or could be done. What we think of as a *cover your ass* way of life. If you're never an original thinker how can you possibly get in trouble? If you're banal and unoriginal enough you'll get promoted."

We walk past surveillance equipment attached to lampposts and in trees. She doesn't care in the appropriate prudent way she should. In fact she's looking directly into the cameras.

"If a hidden safe room has been found in some other case then they're going to list it no matter how ridiculous." Lucy talks much too openly and snidely, and no signal I send her is going to do any good. "A couple years ago there was a drug bust in Florida that became a huge mess on appeal and was all over the news. The Feds were executing a routine search and found an escape tunnel and other hidden surprises they weren't looking for and hadn't included on the warrant. More recently there was a case involving an escape hatch. The popular thing to look for these days are secret rooms and tunnels. Especially in the drug business. You may also recall that tunnel dug from San Diego to Mexico. It even had train tracks."

"The drug business?" I'm breathing hard from exertion, and the dew point and humidity must be almost the same. The air is saturated. It feels like a steam room. "Since when has that subject come up?" I ask. "Who thinks that?"

"They're not thinking. What they do is harass and bully," Lucy almost shouts, and I imagine Erin Loria watching and getting incensed. "They're looking for anything that might give me the ability to disappear from here right under their nose. POOF! Because we all know I have a looking glass like Alice. I have a Bat Cave like Bruce Wayne and a phone booth like Clark Kent. The Fucking Bureau of Investigation is looking for anything that might give me the ability to make my getaway or hide something from them."

The walk in this direction is downhill and that's not easy for me either. I watch what I'm doing. I'm cautious about my body language and what I might say, and I wish Lucy would be the same way. She's taken off like a bomber jet and I'm not going to stop her. Lucy has a point to make. Or maybe it's more of a threat.

"You should try Benton," she says. "It will be interesting to see if you get him."

I wish she wouldn't act like this, and of course she knows me far too well. She knows I'm thinking about him, wondering what he's been doing while his employer pillages his family's privacy and possessions. While the FBI eviscerates the lives of the people he loves. While we are out here miserable and about to get rained on, and I'm hurt in a way I won't say. Right this moment I'm unhappy with him. I feel abandoned by him, possibly betrayed. I feel I might yell at him if I got him on the phone, and the wind gusts hard, sending pollen, dirt and leaves skittering over the blacktop.

"Are you crying?" Lucy looks over at me.

"It's all this stuff blowing around out here," I explain as I wipe my eyes with my shirtsleeve.

"Go ahead and call him," she encourages, and I don't respond. "Really. Go ahead. You might not have gotten him a half hour ago but I'll bet you will now."

"As if you have reason to know."

"Go on. I'll bet you twenty bucks you get him."

I try Benton's cell phone and he answers.

I DON'T SAY HELLO. I tell him I'm on Lucy's property. I've been here for the past hour and a half, and will be heading back to Cambridge shortly.

"I know where you are, Kay." Benton's mild baritone voice is quiet and friendly but I know when he's not alone. "I'm well aware of what you've been doing. Are you all right?"

"Where are you?"

"We landed at Hanscom. We were forced to with this weather moving in. Conditions have deteriorated extremely fast and you shouldn't be out in it either."

Benton was up in the helicopter, and Lucy suspected or knew it for some reason. It explains her cryptic comment to me about his ability to answer the phone right now when he might not have been able to a while ago. He's with his FBI colleagues, the same agents who followed Marino and me from Chanel Gilbert's house in Cambridge.

"Yes I'm aware of the chopper," I say next, and I'm answered with silence. "Can you offer an explanation?" I ask and he says nothing.

When Benton is like this there's no point in my probing because he's not going to respond in a helpful way, not over the phone, not with other agents within earshot. What I generally resort to is making statements. Now and then he'll address those, and my thought process picks up speed and I concentrate more intensely. I have to worry about what both of us say because people are listening.

"You're not going to tell me what's going on," I try again.

"No."

"You're not alone."

"I'm not."

"Is there interest in my Cambridge case from this morning?

Because unless I was looking at the wrong helicopter, you were in the area while we were there." I go ahead and say that much and instantly I sense he won't answer, and he doesn't.

"I'm sorry. You're breaking up," Benton says instead.

I'm probably not. But next I pose the same information as a statement, summarizing, "You're interested in my Cambridge case, the house on Brattle Street." I avoid mentioning the suspected name of the dead woman or any other details.

"I agree it's interesting."

"I'm not aware that it's a federal concern."

"It makes sense that you're not aware of it," he says in a pleasant voice.

"I don't have answers yet. A lot of questions but no answers yet," I repeat.

"I see. For example?"

"Suffice it to say there are a number of things, and I'm concerned about confidentiality, Benton." What I mean is I don't have privacy.

He doesn't ask me to elaborate.

I do anyway but I'm appropriately understated. "I haven't autopsied her and I need to do a second walk-through of the scene as soon as I'm done here. I was interrupted earlier."

"I understand."

But he can't really understand, and then it enters my mind again. Does he know about the *Depraved Heart* videos? I continue to wonder if Carrie Grethen has sent them to anyone else including the FBI.

"Will I see you tonight?" I ask.

"I'll call you later," he says and then he's gone, and I study an angry sky that looks punishing.

Lucy and I have reached her open gate. Parked in front of it are two white SUVs, engines idling as their FBI drivers wait for us. I recognize one of them as the agent I had words with earlier, and I don't smile or nod. He glares at me, his polo shirt sweat stained, his angry face shiny, and I unlock my truck and climb inside.

I crank the engine and it rumbles loudly to life as I call my forensic radiologist Anne. I want to know if anything unusual has turned up on Chanel Gilbert's CT scan because now I'm suspicious. The FBI is interested in her and I want to figure out why, and I can't be overheard inside my truck with its rolled-up windows and loud engine. I can talk freely.

"I need to make this quick," I say to Anne as I check my mirrors. "In a few minutes we're heading back to the Gilbert house. Is there anything I should know?"

"It's not up to me to decide the manner of death," she says. "But I'm voting for homicide."

"Tell me why." I back up so I can maneuver off to the side, leaving room for cars to pass in and out of the gate.

"I don't see how it's possible she fell from a ladder, Doctor Scarpetta. Not unless she fell from it three or four times. She has multiple depressed skull fractures that extend into the paranasal sinuses, the structures of the middle ear. Plus underlying areas of hematoma."

"How are we doing with her identification?"

"Dental charts are on the way. It's her. I mean who else would it be?"

"Let's get it confirmed."

"I'll let you know the instant we do."

"Has Luke started her post?"

"He's in the middle of it."

I open the screen of the laptop built into the console between the two front seats, and in a moment I'm logged into the CFC's closed camera system, a network of fish-eye panoramic domes in the ceiling of every room of the intake and examination areas. It allows me to monitor what my doctors and forensic investigators are doing at any given time. I type in my password and the computer screen splits into quadrants that cover each workstation in Autopsy Room A, which is where Luke and I work.

I hear the whine of the Stryker saw inside a vast space of bright overhead lights, glass observation galleries, and stainless steel. I see Luke at his station suited up in a teal green gown, an apron, a face shield and surgical cap. Our two medical residents are across the table from him, and Harold is sawing open Chanel Gilbert's skull, the oscillating blade grinding as he cuts through thick bone.

"It's Doctor Scarpetta. I've got you up on my screen," I say as if I'm talking to people inside the truck.

"Hello." Luke looks up at the camera in the high ceiling, and the glare of the face shield makes it hard to see his handsome face and vivid blue eyes.

The body has been opened from the clavicles to the pubic bone, the bloc of organs on a cutting board, and Luke is snipping open the stomach with a pair of surgical scissors. He pours the contents into a plasticized paper carton. I tell him I'm checking on how the case is going and explain that I'll be returning to the scene shortly, and is there anything I should know? Is there anything special I should look for?

"You definitely should check for multiple impact areas." His voice with its heavy German accent sounds from the laptop inside the truck. "I'm assuming you've seen the images on CT?"

"Anne has given me a quick summary." The diesel engine rumbles in my bones as I talk to the laptop's screen. "But I haven't viewed the actual scans yet. She doesn't think Chanel Gilbert is an accident."

"She has contusions and abrasions of the scalp which you can clearly see in areas where I've shaved her hair." He rests his bloody gloved hands on the edge of the table as he talks to me. "Posteriorally, temporally. Obviously I've not looked at her brain yet but on CT there's subgaleal hematomas of the left parietal-temporal and right occipital areas, and a coup contusion in addition to diffuse subarachnoid hemorrhage. Her fractures are complex, suggesting a lot of force, a high velocity and multiple impact points."

"Consistent with hard impacts such as someone beating her head against a marble floor."

"Yes. And what I'm just now seeing might be helpful." He holds up the carton of gastric contents.

"I'm zooming in." It's as if I'm inches away, and I can make out approximately 200 milliliters of what looks like a lumpy vegetable soup.

"What appears to be seafood, possibly shrimp, and greenish peppers, onions, some rice." He pokes through it with a scalpel. "Something she must have eaten not long before she died. It's barely begun to digest."

"What about a STAT alcohol?"

"Nothing much. Point oh-three. Maybe she had a glass of wine with dinner. Or it could be from decomposition."

"She certainly wasn't impaired, at least not by booze. I'll check to see what's in her refrigerator. I'm on my way back there." I log off the computer, cut the engine and climb out of the truck.

Lucy has parked Donoghue's big Mercedes sedan out of the way, and she trots over to me.

"Come on," she says. "I want to show you something."

CHAPTER 27

WE WALK AROUND THE SOUTH WING OF THE HOUSE where a narrow grassy strip of yard gives way to dense woods.

A ten-foot-high chain-link fence is coated in dark green PVC and anchored by heavy steel poles driven deep into the earth. Lucy unlocks a gate as another FBI SUV disappears down the driveway. There are only two government vehicles still parked in front of the house. One of them must belong to Erin Loria. I've been watching for her. I'm sure she's still here. She wouldn't miss it.

"Be careful," Lucy says. "There's plenty to trip over. The landscapers never come in here so it's really overgrown."

I follow her through the gate and then we're in the woods. There's no gradual transition. Her yard ends at the fence, and on the other side of it are acres dense with rhododendron, mountain laurel and old trees. Trails winding through were cleared long years ago and are mostly overgrown. I move very carefully, slowly along a vague scar of a path as Lucy leads us through ferns, birches and dogwoods. Then she stops.

"There." She points at a holly tree, at a white pine with motion sensor cameras and lights on them. "Several times now they've been activated by movement but there's nothing there. The cameras aren't picking up anything."

"I'll ask what I have before," I reply, and I realize why she's brought me here. "Couldn't an animal be to blame?"

"I have the sensors set to react to anything moving that's at least three feet off the ground like a deer, a bear, a bobcat," she says as I stand very still, bearing most of my weight on my left leg. "Something that size and the cameras would pick it up. But they didn't."

Lucy is putting on a show. Whatever she has in mind is the *go screw yourself* grand finale, and any minute now the fireworks will begin. She deliberately dressed in FBI sweats and if that wasn't enough she's about to do more. But it doesn't explain the strange object I'm noticing so close to her feet she's about to step on it. At a glance it could be a tiny raindrop on top of brown leaves beneath a mountain laurel. But it's not raining yet.

"Don't move," I say under my breath.

I hold her stare, making sure she understands and she does. I steady myself next to a clump of sassafras trees, grabbing on to a smooth trunk. Mitten-shaped pale green leaves brush against me, and I casually comment that in another month or so they will turn yellow, coral and orange. Lucy's property will be fiery with fall colors, I say good-naturedly for the benefit of eavesdroppers, and then the snows will come, and there can be no invisible intruders because they'll leave tracks.

"Unlike whoever has been here," I say not just to Lucy but to the FBI. "And I know someone was," I continue to announce as I dig in the pockets of my cargo pants and find a pair of fresh gloves.

Pulling them on I steady my balance as I bend over, moving as little as possible so I don't disturb the underbrush or leaves and lose what I'm trying to collect. The small bit of what looks like quartz sticks to my gloved index finger, and I cup my other hand under it to make sure it doesn't fall or sail off on a gust of wind. I can't help but think it miraculous that something no bigger than a grain of rice was plainly visible, and I suspect it hasn't been out here long.

"Unless you're the source," I say to Lucy, "then someone has been in this spot. Probably very recently."

The tiny flat hexagon is dull and opaque, and I hold it in my palm to show Lucy. It's not polished and looks industrial, bringing to mind a mineral or other material used in manufacturing or engineering.

"Do you have any idea?" I ask.

"I didn't notice it when I was out here looking around." She stares as if it's poison. "I didn't see it until you did just now. I'm surprised it's here." She says it oddly. "Maybe it's supposed to be. That's my first thought. We're supposed to find it." She says it slowly, loudly, making sure the FBI doesn't miss a word.

"It couldn't come from anything you own." I move it to the palm of my hand so she can get a closer look. "You sure it's not from you or something you've installed? What about your surveillance system? It was very close to several cameras."

"This isn't from anything of mine. It's certainly not from me because I wouldn't be so careless and stupid as to leave it out here." She's careful not to touch it or get too close.

But she's not careful about much else. Lucy is glancing around at the cameras in the trees. She's boisterous and cheerful as if we're having a happy nature hike or a picnic.

"It doesn't look like anything from normal clothing." I stay on subject. "Not from anything decorative either."

"It's been micromachined into this size and shape, and there's a tiny hole through it. Possibly something was threaded through it. She's been here."

"Carrie Grethen has been," I confirm who she means, and Lucy nods.

"This is from something she's doing. I'm not sure what but I have an idea what this relates to," Lucy says. "Carrie was always chasing after invisibility."

LUCY SUSPECTS that what I've found is a metamaterial possibly used in creating objects that bend and diffuse light.

"Let's see what it is after the labs do their thing but I'm guessing it's laser-quality quartz, in other words calcite," Lucy says.

"Then you've seen something similar before."

"I'm well aware of what's out there. She's always been obsessed with invisibility technology, what's known as augmented reality or optical camouflage." Lucy looks around, as if she's talking to the trees. "These idiots are so hell-bent on going after me they aren't paying any attention to the real danger. Carrie may have figured out how to cloak herself with the goal in mind that she can take out anyone she wants. I mean *anyone*. And she's a damn terrorist so that could concern the damn FBI." Lucy has no concern about being even moderately discreet.

In fact she's not really talking to me anymore. She's talking to them. She's talking to Erin Loria.

"This is where the motion sensors went off yesterday about four A.M. and then again this morning at the same time." She projects her voice, and her tone is peppered with mockery and beneath that is rage. "When the sun was up I did a walk around. Everything looked normal."

"Could she have been here in this spot and you didn't see her?"

"She could have been. Especially if she's rigged up something Harry Potterish. But it's not fantasy. They're engineering all sorts of materials these days that can change reality as we know it."

"I think reality's already been changed." I don't have my scene case with me so I improvise. "Possibly for good."

Finding another clean glove, I drop the metamaterial inside and shake it down into one of the fingers. I tightly roll up the purple nitrile and tuck it into my pocket, noticing that directly ahead through the fence are the south windows of Lucy's master suite. If someone had binoculars with night vision capabilities it could be a problem.

"Is that the way they usually are?" I point at her bedroom and what I'm asking is if she always keeps the shades down.

"It doesn't matter. A scope with ultrasonic sensors can basically see through walls," she replies in the same stage voice. "The purpose of a system like that is to continue to track targets after they duck behind cover . . ."

"Who would have such a thing?" I interrupt her as I feel a wave of impatience.

I'm tempted to tell her to keep her voice down but I won't. It's unwise for me to give any sign that I suspect the FBI is watching and listening. I know better than to behave as if I feel guilty and have things to hide so I continue to talk thoughtfully, what sounds like openly and comfortably. But I'm careful and deliberate and Lucy isn't. She doesn't have a *flight* switch only a *fight* one, and that's what I'm witnessing and can't begin to control.

"She's been here. I can promise you that." She says it with certainty and audacity, and I see the aggression in her intense green eyes. "Somehow she's been right here using some sort of technology for a specific reason. Maybe to spy. I don't know but it's not the Feds. They aren't that smart. It's Carrie. She might be somewhere out here right this minute but they'll never believe it. Maybe no one believes it's her because why would anyone want to? Even my own partner isn't sure."

I understand how painful this must be for Janet but I don't say it out loud. It's not necessary for me to remind Lucy of her history with Carrie, of all the years that have passed with us feeling safe because we were certain she wasn't a danger to us or anyone anymore.

"We need to go." Lucy looks up at storm clouds that have rolled in like a charcoal tarp, hanging low with tatters reaching down, a total gloom descending. "Okay we're leaving," she says loudly and not to me but to whoever is listening.

We head back carefully, not talking now. The wind gusts harder and the smell of rain is so strong I can taste it as I think about everything I need to do. I'll get the metamaterial to my labs later today. At the very least I'll confirm what it's made of but already there are problems. I didn't collect evidence according to my own unforgiving protocols. My DNA might be on the metamaterial or possibly Lucy's could be. If nothing else a competent defense attorney will claim that what I just collected is contaminated because it was improperly handled. The jury won't trust it or me.

The first drops of rain smack the trees as we emerge from them back onto the grass. In the distance, building thunderheads flash with lightning, flickering purplish-black like something shorting out, like something wounded. I smell ozone and feel the dropping barometric pressure pressing down heavily, and I'm startled by what I don't understand at first. Music explodes out of the audio surveillance microphones all over the property. Hozier's "Take Me to Church" is as loud as an air raid in the woods, around the house, over the water.

I look at Lucy and she's smiling as if we're out on a happy stroll. She doesn't have her phone. She's not at the controls anymore. Janet must be responsible, and I step up my pace as the music rocks fifty acres of conservation land. Pain screams in my leg and I accept that I'm going to get soaked. I tell Lucy to run ahead out of the downpour but she mimics my pace.

She stays with me and in a matter of seconds the bottom of the universe seems to burst in an explosion of thunder that sounds like gunfire. Rain pours down in the blasting wind. The temperature has dropped at least ten degrees, and Hozier is all around us as if God is enjoying a concert at the FBI's expense.

We were born sick, you heard them say it . . .

"I'm not the only one they have to worry about." Lucy raises her voice over the music throbbing in the rain, in the trees. "Don't fuck with us!" she shouts up to a rabid sky, and I imagine the FBI agents inside her house where Hozier must be deafening.

I was born sick, but I love it . . .

Then Lucy's palatial timber home instantly goes dark. I can't see a single light on. Her *smart house* is computerized. There are no switches in the walls. The FBI isn't controlling the audio system. Or the lights. Janet is. Of that I have no doubt, and Lucy is laughing in the hammering rain and music as if this is the funniest day of her life.

Amen. Amen. Amen. Amen . . .

"Tell Marino to meet me at the truck." I head toward the driveway, my wet shirt coldly plastered to my back. "You can't stay here. For a lot of reasons you, Janet and Desi absolutely can't." I talk over splashing water and Hozier worshipping *like a dog at the shrine of your lies*. "You need to move in with us for a while," I yell back at Lucy. "I don't want to argue about it."

CHAPTER 28

RAIN POUNDS THE METAL ROOF AS IF A MAD DRUMmer is on top of us. The early afternoon is dark. It feels like dawn or dusk. It feels like the world is about to end.

I'm coming out of my skin. Something is sliding, rolling around in the back of my big white truck as I drive in the monsoon. The object is hard and metallic. It moves a short distance, hits something then stops and rolls again depending on which way I turn or if I slow down or speed up. I can hear it clearly through the partition that separates the cab from the boxy body, and there was no such noise this morning before I parked by Lucy's gate. It started minutes ago as we lumbered around a hairpin curve.

CLANK CLANK CLANK.

"We need to see what the hell that is." Marino has said this several times but there's nothing I can do.

There was no place to pull over earlier and we're on Route 2 now in heavy rain and Friday traffic. The visibility is abysmal. Everybody has their lights on as if it's night, and even if I wanted to detour there's nothing here. Just the highway and a big mud hole of a construction site on my right and three lanes of cars and trucks on my left. I'm mindful of the day slipping away. I seem to have very little control over anything including my time.

"I can't pull over right now." I tell Marino the same thing I did when he first suggested it.

"It sounds like rebar rolling around."

"It can't be."

"Maybe a tool like a screwdriver or something that rolls around, gets caught on something, then rolls around some more."

"I don't see how," I reply and the noise suddenly stops again.

"Well it's giving me a creepy feeling and fraying my last nerve."

He cracks open his window to smoke, to calm his creepy feeling and soothe his fraying last nerve, and water spatters the inside of the door and the dash. I tell him I don't mind his cigarettes but I don't want the windows fogging up. I adjust the fan and that helps some but I can take only so much frigid air, and Marino complains about that too. He's hot and sweating and I don't want to get chilled. I'm keeping the temperature barely above tepid. I make constant adjustments, clearing the glass and getting cold, then warming up and unable to see.

This is stressful and uncomfortable, and it's almost impossible not to be edgy and rather frantic. My clothes are wet. I'm sticky and wilted. My leg aches miserably. I feel sick about Lucy, sick about the secrets I keep, and the debate inside me rages nonstop. Should I tell Marino about the *Depraved Heart* videos? I honestly don't know what to do, and as we drive farther away from Concord past flooded road construction and soupy woods shrouded in mist I force myself to concentrate on my new rule:

Pay attention even when you think you already are.

It's a new rule that used to be an old one but I got lax. I got lulled into a false sense of safety, and as I try to retrace my steps I see the pattern. I see it plainly, and a part of me is unforgiving while another part understands how it happened. No one can be vigilant every minute of every day. Time passes and some things get harder. I'm relentless about keeping up my scan for enemies but the ones from the past are the most treacherous. We know too much about them. We start re-creating them in our own image, assigning attributes and motivations they don't have. We form relationships with them. We delude ourselves into believing they don't want to kill us.

The same thought continues to nag at me. If I hadn't assumed that Carrie Grethen was no longer on this planet would I have stopped looking for her anyway? I worry that I might have. It's the path of least resistance to relegate nightmarish people to a cold file, to tuck them so far back in your mind that you don't think about them. You expect nothing from them. You don't fear them or anticipate or predict or worry. I dismissed Carrie long ago. I didn't do it simply because I was convinced she'd died in a helicopter crash. I couldn't stand to live with her anymore.

For years she'd invaded my psyche. She was a shadow cast by something I couldn't see, an inexplicable shift of air, a sound that made no sense. I lived with the constant expectation that my phone was going to ring and I'd get the next bad news. I waited for her to torture and murder someone else, to partner with another deviant and go on another spree. I constantly looked for her when I was with Lucy and when I wasn't. Then I stopped.

"You want a hit?" Marino offers me his cigarette. "You look like you sure as hell could use it, Doc."

"No thanks."

"I wonder if the music's still playing and what the Feds are doing about it because you can bet they aren't laughing." He inhales a lungful of smoke and blows it out the side of his mouth.

"Lucy and Janet didn't blast music and turn off the lights because they wanted to amuse anyone except themselves," I reply.

Lakes and forests spread out on either side of us as we pass the town of Lexington now.

"You sure it was them who did it?" Marino asks.

"Well it wasn't Desi."

"You'd be surprised what little kids can do with computers. It wasn't all that long ago that one hacked into the FBI database. I think the kid was like four or something."

"Desi had nothing to do with what we just witnessed. It probably was Lucy's idea. It's the sort of thing she'd find funny." Even as I say this I think of video links I'm supposed to believe were sent by her ICE number.

I'm convinced Carrie is spoofing Lucy's phone. There's no telling what else Carrie may have hijacked, broken into and appropriated as if our lives are hers to manipulate, trifle with, damage and destroy. I'm reminded of how skilled she is at creating implosions, internal failures, strife and catastrophes. If she can cause us to self-destruct what could be more gratifying to her than that?

She's trying to script our behavior, and that's how it starts.

"I'll never get over them hiring her." Marino is talking about Carrie with no prompting from me. "When you really think about it the Feds created Carrie Grethen like Frankenstein," he adds and he's right in a sense.

In some ways she was conceived, nurtured and transformed into an amoral monster by our own government. Then she decided to turn on what took care of her, to demolish any fairness and safety she'd been entrusted to ensure in this world. She'll take any side that suits her at any given time because she has no loyalty or love for anything or anyone except herself.

"A computer engineer for the Department of Justice," Marino is saying, "assigned to Quantico? And the FBI had no clue they'd placed a friggin' psychopath in charge of their computer and case management overhaul?"

"What became an unfixable failure," I add.

THE CRIMINAL ARTIFICIAL Intelligence Network known as CAIN morphed into the Trilogy program, a massive effort on the part of the FBI to modernize its outdated information technology.

The project was finally abandoned about a decade ago after wasting hundreds of millions of taxpayer dollars, and I can't help but wonder how much of this was Carrie's fault.

"More precisely," I'm saying to Marino, "I wonder how much was of her divining because nothing would suit her better than to be pitted against inadequate software and data management that she in fact may have manipulated and sabotaged during its inception."

"You got that right and exactly my point. A genius mad scientist like her?" Marino says. "You really think she couldn't wreak havoc on anything she wants? Especially if it's got to do with communication technology or computers?"

"So could Lucy," I remind him. "And I'll just keep emphasizing that unfortunate truth. She created CAIN, and virtually anything Carrie can do? So can Lucy. That's the way the FBI would think about it. That would be their justification for going after Lucy. They can blame her and assign means and motives to anything they want because she's capable. It's believable. And it suits them, let's be honest."

"Then maybe Carrie turned on the music to piss them off and get Lucy into trouble. Double the pleasure, double the fun," Marino says. "Screwing with the sound system is like waving a red flag in front of a bull. It's not against the law but it's stupid. We don't know that Carrie didn't do it to entertain herself."

"I'm not saying she isn't capable," I reply. "But I'm betting it was Janet and Lucy deciding to treat Erin Loria and her compatriots to a concert."

"They shouldn't be doing shit like that. They're playing right into Carrie's hands."

"We can't let anyone determine how we act. That's true. Specifically it's true that Carrie wants to control and change us. That's always been what she wants."

"And here I thought what she wanted was all of us dead."

"One way or another and eventually that's the plan I'm sure," I reply.

"Lucy needs to be careful about getting in people's faces right now. Maybe you can talk to her when things calm down. She doesn't need to be making things worse than they already are."

"How could they be worse, Marino? The FBI showed up with a warrant. Agents have been walking out the door with her belongings, violating her entire existence." I turn up the wipers as high as they'll go and they sound like an angry metronome throwing a tantrum.

"What could be worse is they arrest her and lock her up without bail." Marino smokes the cigarette down to the filter. "And don't think they can't do it. She owns a helicopter and a jet. She's a pilot. She has a ton of money. They'll argue she's a flight risk and the judge will rule in the FBI's favor. Especially if there's a judge behind the scenes who has an agenda—a federal judge like Erin Loria's husband. The first thing we should be asking is the timing for the sting operation. Why strike now?"

Today's date enters my mind again. August 15. The two-month anniversary of when Carrie shot me.

What I say is "You're right. Why today? Or is the timing random?"

"I don't know about random but I also can't think of anything important."

"Exactly two months ago Carrie attacked me." I shouldn't have to remind him.

"But how would that be important to the FBI? Why would that date motivate them? I don't see how it would matter."

"It's more likely to matter to Carrie."

"Well we can be sure they're looking for probable cause to get Lucy indicted for something. I don't know what but I think we can make an educated guess about who it relates to," Marino says. "Prison would be the end of Lucy. She wouldn't survive, and Carrie would love that . . ."

"Let's stay out of such a fatalistic airspace." I don't want to hear his Doomsday predictions, and I can barely restrain myself from admitting the truth to him.

I want to tell him about the videos even as I continue to entertain the same troubling questions. What if the FBI has seen them? What if the FBI texted them to entrap me and anybody else I might involve? I don't know who to trust, not even my own attorney Jill Donoghue the more I think about it, and when I'm this unsure of anything I'm careful. I'm deliberate and calculating.

"The problem is once an investigation gets in gear good luck stopping it." Marino is painting more fear-inducing scenarios. "The Feds don't let something go unless they got no choice, unless the grand jury comes back with a *no bill* and that almost never happens. Lucy's goose would be cooked. No grand jury is going to have any sympathy for a fired federal agent who's filthy rich and comes across the way she does . . ."

"I suggest we keep our attention on what we're doing." I absolutely can't stand to hear his dire projections about her, and I don't need him to tell me that she doesn't inspire empathy or even the benefit of the doubt.

"I'm just telling you the facts, Doc." He pinches out the cigarette, drops it in an empty water bottle and lights up another one, offering it to me. "Here. You need it."

I think what the hell. I take the Marlboro from him, and there are some things I've never stopped being good at. Smoking is one of them. I inhale slowly, deeply and my emotional elevator goes up to a floor I forgot I had. It's nice, a lot of light and a view, and for an instant I let go of gravity and it lets go of me.

I hold the cigarette in Marino's direction, giving it back and our fingers brush. I'm always surprised that his sun-weathered skin with its thick coppery hair is soft and silky. I detect his aftershave, spicy and overlaid with a patina of sweat and tobacco smoke. I smell the wet cotton fabric of his cargo shorts and polo shirt.

"You ever try weed when you were young?" He takes another drag, holding the cigarette as if it's a joint.

"You mean when I was *younger*?"

"Seriously? I'm betting when you were in law school, tell the truth? All you Ivy Leaguers hanging out smoking weed, arguing about interpretations and precedents and who's gonna make law review."

"That wasn't my experience at Georgetown. But maybe it should have been." My tone sounds somber and distracted as I continue checking my mirrors.

I stare through thudding wipers at misty lanes of traffic, water spewing from tires ahead and to the left of us. I don't go above the speed limit. I'm tense, my eyes constantly in my mirrors looking for Carrie. We sweep around the Fresh Pond reservoir and the pockmarked surging water is the color of lead. The noise of something metal rolling in back starts again and stops, and I can't get Carrie out of my thoughts.

CLANK CLANK CLANK.

"What the hell?" Marino says in a cloud of smoke. "That's just freakin' strange."

"Everything is inside storage lockers and containers." I go through every possibility I can think of that might account for the noise. "The folded-up stretchers are strapped in. There shouldn't be anything loose."

"Maybe one of your scene cases came open. Maybe it's an evidence bottle, a flashlight, something like that rolling around."

"I seriously doubt it." Carrie appears in my mind.

I see her face. I see her wide crazed eyes and the lust smoldering in them as she cut Lucy with the Swiss Army knife. It was the same way Carrie looked at me when she fired the spear gun, and the clattering and clanging in the back of the truck continues. Marino is making the point that the noise wasn't there earlier.

"And no one has been inside," he's saying. "I mean there's no way anyone went inside it while we were at Lucy's? You sure? You positive the truck was locked while you were blocking that FBI asshole's car? Did one of them go inside the truck? Maybe looking for an extra key so they could move it? Did someone try to force open a door and broke something and that's what we hear rolling around?"

"I'm sure it was locked." I think I am but now that he's mentioned it I can't swear to it.

Uncertainty begins to pick at me. When I packed up my equipment midmorning it was right after I got the first *Depraved Heart* video clip. Maybe I was distracted as I arranged the large plastic cases in the back of the truck. Maybe I forgot to lock the tailgate doors. It's something I do automatically with a key that also sets and unsets the alarm.

I never leave the back, the cab or any of the access panels unlocked for a number of reasons. Defense attorneys, for example. They'd harangue me about it on the witness stand. They'd have jurors doubting the integrity of any evidence I collected including the dead body itself.

"Jesus," Marino mutters as whatever is loose in back rolls again and stops with a clank.

"We're almost there," I reply. "I'm going to look."

CHAPTER 29

CARS IN CAMBRIDGE ARE FEW. THEY MOVE SLOWLY with their lights on as we drive near the Harvard campus, headed back to Brattle Street, one of the most prestigious addresses in the United States.

Former residents include George Washington and Longfellow, and the handsome timber-frame two-story house where Chanel Gilbert died was built in the late 1600s. Painted a dusky blue, it's symmetrical with black shutters, a gray slate roof and a central chimney. Over the centuries most of the original estate was subdivided and sold off, and the only way to reach it is a shared driveway of old interlocking brick pavers in a herringbone pattern.

I carefully bump along in my big truck and park in front, listening to rain pummel and splatter. As I look around I get an uneasy feeling. I get more than one of them. They're coming in waves as trees rock and thrash in the wind and rain, and I turn off the wipers and the headlights, and the glass is flooded. Ours is the only vehicle in the driveway and that's not right.

"Where is everyone?" I ask and it sounds like we're inside a car wash. "Where's your backup?"

"Damn good question." Marino is on high alert as he scans the long narrow driveway, the front of the house, the dense old trees shaking and losing leaves in a battering wind.

"I thought you instructed that the property was to be secured."

"I did."

"There's not a police car in sight and where's the red Range Rover?"

"No kidding. This is fucked up." Marino releases the thumb snap of the black leather holster on his hip, and thunder rumbles and cracks.

"Did you instruct Vogel, Lapin, maybe Hyde to have it towed to the labs?"

"There was no reason to do that. We weren't really thinking foul play until now. Maybe Bryce took it upon himself to get it towed after you talked to Anne and Luke and decided this is a homicide." Marino is scrolling through the contact list on his phone, glancing up every other second, his eyes moving constantly.

"I talked to them not even half an hour ago," I remind him. "There's not been time for the Range Rover to have been towed, and certainly I didn't request it and there's no way Bryce would have."

"I sure as hell didn't tell anybody to tow it." He wipes condensation off the side window as he stares out, checking the big mirror for the empty stretch of rain-swept driveway behind us. "The Range Rover key was on the kitchen counter and Hyde took a quick look inside it. He said he didn't see anything interesting. In fact there wasn't much in it at all and it was his impression maybe it hadn't been driven in a while. That was what he said, and we didn't do anything else because we were operating under the assumption there was no crime involved, just an accident. At that time there was no point in thinking about processing her car."

"What happened to the key after that?"

"I have it and the house key."

"Obviously there's a spare unless the Range Rover was hot-wired or gotten out of here some other way." I look around to see if anything else might be missing or altered since we were here midmorning.

The centuries-old house is shrouded in a gray mist that rises up from the rain-splashed earth, and my attention fixes on the solitary strip of crime scene tape barricading the brick front steps. The flimsy yellow plastic tape shivers in the wind and rain, and it wasn't there earlier. More importantly I notice the absence of scene tape anywhere else. It's not barricading the kitchen door we used this morning. It's not wrapped around trees or across the driveway.

Then I spot a fat roll of bright yellow tape abandoned in a flower bed next to wooden bulkhead doors that I assume lead down into the cellar. Apparently someone began securing the perimeter and stopped, leaving the roll where I see it now in a flower bed of purple asters and brown-eyed Susans that are rain-beaten and trampled. I think back to when I was alone in the entranceway and everyone was supposed to be gone except Marino and me.

I inexplicably heard what sounded like a heavy door thudding shut. The one in the basement that led out to the backyard was mysteriously unlocked even though Trooper Vogel claimed to have dead bolted it. Next the kitchen trash was missing and the table was oddly set with a decorative plate taken off the wall. Now the Range Rover is gone. I stare at the old house with its dark windows of wavy glass. Maybe it's haunted but not by a ghost. Someone has been on the property since we were here last.

"Didn't I hear you tell your guys to wrap this place in a big yellow bow?" I say to Marino. "Because the only tape I'm seeing is there." I point at the front of the house. "One strip tied to the railings doesn't exactly serve the purpose of keeping people out of the house or off the property. Do you know who did it and why the tape roll is over there? It's as if the person was interrupted and decided to walk around to the side of the house and left the roll in the flower bed before driving off. I can see from here that a lot of the plants near the bulkhead doors have been stepped on or crushed."

"Hyde or Lapin must have come back after you and me left for Lucy's place."

"And then what?"

"Damned if I know." Marino is looking at his phone. "I texted Hyde when we headed here and he's not answered. Nothing from Lapin either."

"When was the last time you heard from either one of them?"

"I talked to Hyde when I called him about the kitchen trash maybe three hours ago. I'm trying him again." He blows out a breath in loud frustration when the call goes straight to voice mail. "Dammit!"

"They haven't shown up and you've not heard from them. Are we worried?"

"I'm not ready to go there yet. If I instigate a search for either one of them there could be hell to pay. You want to get people into trouble and have them hate you then that's the way to do it."

"What about the state police?" I think of Trooper Vogel again. "Is it possible they've been here? Could they have towed her Range Rover?"

"Hell no."

"And the FBI?"

"They better not have been here without telling me. They better not have touched or towed anything."

"But is that possible? Could the Feds have taken over the investigation and we don't know? It certainly seems they're interested."

"If this was their investigation? By now they'd be crawling all over the place the same way they are Lucy's property. We wouldn't be sitting here by our lonesome. We probably couldn't get back on the driveway much less inside the house."

"They were in this area earlier up in the helicopter . . ."

"With Benton." Marino can't resist reminding me uncharitably. "He was flying right over us when we were here and then more or less followed us to Lucy's. So who are they really watching? Who's he really watching?"

"It's probably a good idea to assume the FBI is watching all of us." I kill the engine, and nor'easter-force winds shake the truck as rain floods the front windshield. "Let's just assume the Feds believe Lucy may be implicated in what's been happening and that I'm in collusion with her. Maybe you are too. Maybe they have all of us on their radar."

"In other words Lucy's a serial killer? Or she and Carrie both are, and we know it but are protecting them? And Lucy shot you in the leg and swam off with your dive mask? Or maybe you shot yourself? Or maybe Benton did? Or maybe Moby Dick or a fish called Wanda are to blame? What a crock of crap and how the hell can you be married to someone who's spying on you, treating you like a fugitive?"

"Benton doesn't spy on me any more than I spy on him. Both of us have our jobs to do." That's as much as I'm going to explain, and I stare out at the centuries-old property in the pounding rain.

THE HOUSE looks dead and lonely, and I'm feeling the same thing I did when we were here earlier. It's hard to describe. Like a coldness in my diaphragm that causes me to breathe shallowly, very quietly. My stomach is clenched like a fist. My mouth is dry. My pulse is rapid.

I'm questioning myself, and it's not that I never did before but I seem to do it constantly of late. Am I picking up on real danger? Is it my imagination because I've been traumatized? But no matter what I silently analyze or debate as I sit inside the truck I can't dispel my unsettledness. It's getting stronger with every moment that passes. I sense a malignant presence. I feel we're being watched. I think of the pistol in my shoulder bag as I keep up my scan and Marino scrolls through his recent calls.

He presses SEND and says, "Lapin's phone is going straight to voice mail too." He leaves a message for him to call right away, and then he says to me, "What the hell? They get beamed up by aliens?"

"If they're out in the middle of this weather they may have their phones tucked away so they don't get soaked. Or maybe they can't hear them ring. Sometimes the cell phone service is disrupted when we have storms like this." I watch large maple trees whipped and raked by the wind, the underside of their leaves flashing pale green. "But should we be worried, Marino? I don't want to get them into trouble but I'd like it a whole lot less if they're not all right."

"It's always the same damn no-win situation," he says. "You can't get hold of a cop and finally instigate a search? Then it turns out he's watching TV somewhere and eating a Big Mac. Or he's gotten drunk at lunch and is screwing his girlfriend."

"We can only hope that's what it is." I look out at the rain, at the roll of yellow tape in the flower bed.

"You and me both." Marino's jaw muscles are flexing.

"Maybe one of them was securing the property when the skies opened up and that's why only the front steps have tape across them and the roll was left where it is. Maybe the person got out of here in a hurry. This is a very bad storm."

"Yeah it's bad. But something's not right." Marino makes the understatement of the year. "First we think she's an obvious accident. Now she's a homicide and we can't find her Range Rover and I don't know where the hell my backup is. There should be two cruisers parked out here keeping an eye on the place. Hold on a second."

He tries another number.

"Hey it's me again back at the same address," he says to whoever answers, a female I suspect based on his flirty tone. "Have any units been dispatched to the house here on Brattle since I left around ten-thirty hours? Specifically two-thirty-seven and one-ten? Anything from them?"

Units 237 and 110 are Hyde and Lapin, I presume, and Marino meets my eyes and shakes his head.

"Really? No contact at all? They haven't responded to any radio calls in almost three hours? And they haven't marked out of service or anything like that? Because that's screwed up. They were coming back here from Dunkin', were supposed to secure the perimeter and watch the place . . . Well the point being I need to talk to them, and I need to know who's been on the property since I left. Okay? Get back to me as fast as you can."

I watch water boil on bricks. The billowing rain is almost horizontal.

"You could ping their phones," I suggest to him.

"That requires a warrant."

"Not the way I've seen you do it."

"Let me see what Helen finds out."

"I don't know who that is."

"The dispatcher I was just talking to. Me and her have gone out a few times."

"I'm glad you have helpful friends. We need assurance that Hype and Lapin are safe."

"What I don't want is to get them into trouble, Doc. And I could. Big trouble if they're out of service without telling anyone and we ping on their phones and figure out where they are and it's not related to their jobs."

"I don't want any chance that they're unsafe," I repeat.

"You think I do?"

"Don't take any risks, Marino. Not with her on the loose." I don't need to say Carrie Grethen's name. He knows who I mean.

"I get that and don't think it's not entering my mind. But it's serious shit when you sound the alert and every cop in northeastern Massachusetts starts looking for someone. I'm not ready to do that yet," he says. "There's not enough of a reason. Some cops are bad about the radio and don't always answer their phones or get back to you right away and there could be a lot of reasons why. But you don't call out the troops unless you're sure. And I'm not. There's probably a good explanation."

"I'm sure there is. But don't assume it's good. Do we have reason to think someone else might have had access to the Range Rover?" I ask. "What about the housekeeper? Elsa Mulligan I believe you said is her name? Is it possible she moved it for some reason?"

"She'd better not have."

"Does she impress you as someone who might do something like that? Based on what you've been told?"

"Hyde talked to her for only a few minutes, and I didn't talk to him long when you and me first got there. But I remember he said right off she was really upset and he told her to go on home and we'd sit down with her later. He felt bad for her. Probably because she's nice-looking."

I remember Marino in the kitchen with Hyde after we first got here early this morning. I couldn't hear what they were saying. I was in the foyer with the body. I was busy.

"He said she's nice-looking?"

"Nice body. Pretty face with funky short black hair and big dark-framed glasses. He said she looked very Hollywood."

"I thought you said she's from New Jersey."

"It was Hyde's opinion that she looked *Hollywood*. That's what he said."

"Did she understand she wasn't to touch or disturb anything or return here until you said it was all right?" I then ask.

"What's the matter? You think I forgot how to do my job?" He stares straight ahead as rain slaps the windshield.

"You know I don't think that."

"I made it clear to her not to touch anything or step foot here until I told her otherwise." He's busy with his phone again, his thumbs typing fast.

"That doesn't mean she obeyed your directive," I reply. "Maybe there were items inside the house that she wanted to retrieve or tuck out of sight. Or she might have feared that once the mother gets here there's no chance of getting back inside. People do all sorts of seemingly irrational or unwise things when there's a sudden death. Most of the time they don't mean to make our jobs harder. They don't mean to cause trouble."

"Why do I feel like you're lecturing me right now?"

"You feel that way because you're frustrated. You feel powerless and that makes you angry and impatient. Understandably."

"It's not understandable because I don't feel that way. I'm sure as hell not powerless. The other day at my gym I deadlifted three-fifty. That's not exactly powerless."

"Of course that's not what I'm talking about." I don't react to his rudeness and silly macho boasts. "I have no question about how physically strong you are. This isn't about how much iron you can lift."

I open my door and the sound of splashing water is much louder.

CHAPTER 30

COLD RAIN LASHES MY FACE AND SOAKS MY HAIR and clothes as I step out of the truck.

My attention returns to the flower bed, to the roll of bright yellow tape. I head there automatically like a divining rod, and the wind rushing around the eaves makes a whistling howl that is unearthly and foreboding.

I crouch down by the wooden bulkhead doors, painted the same dusky blue as the house, pitched at a steep angle and bordered in old bricks. Rain coldly smacks the top of my head and back. What feels like buckets of water splash around my soaked black nylon boots as I look around at broken purple asters, at brown-eyed Susans that have been flattened and bruised. My opinion doesn't change.

Someone began securing the perimeter and got as far as the front railing and then stopped. For some reason this person left the roll of tape in the flower bed next to the bulkhead doors. They're closed tightly but I can't tell if they're locked. I contemplate my next move as the wind moans in a lower octave.

I don't want to nudge or touch the doors with my boots or bare hands, and I pick up a branch snapped off by the storm. I hold it by its broken end, poking the tip through the steel handles. I try lifting. The doors don't budge. I shout this to Marino as he slogs toward me in the deluge.

"A key lock versus a padlock," I explain over the driving rain. "Someone may have been using these doors to enter the lower area of the house. The flowers have been crushed and gouged as if someone was stepping on them. When you were in the basement earlier did you notice if these doors might have been accessed recently?"

"Nothing much down there and nothing caught my eye." He looms over me, his hands on his hips. Water streams down his shaved head, and his shoes are beginning to squish. "If it was Hyde who came back here with the tape? What made him walk over here and step all over a bunch of flowers?"

"It would seem that someone did. That much we can say." I return to the back of the truck, and the water is already inches deep in low-lying areas of the lawn and walkway.

"And then he got interrupted?" Marino squishes and splashes after me. "Now nobody can find him or his police car?"

"As I've suggested maybe you should ping his phone." I try the tailgate's double doors.

They're locked just as I thought they would be. I find the right key, and my fingers are wet and slick. I open up the back. Lights automatically blink on and I smell the fresh citrus scents of the disinfectant and bleach we use to wash our transport vehicles. I mandate that we scrub and decontaminate them until they're clean enough to eat in although I don't mean it literally. I scan for the source of the mysterious clanking.

I don't see anything that could account for it. The diamond-plate steel floor is empty and spotless, shining like a new dime. The scene cases, the storage chests and cabinets are tightly buttoned exactly as I left them. Fire extinguishers, chemical cabinets and large tools such as rakes, shovels, an axe and bolt cutters are bracketed to the sides. Nothing is loose, not the laptops, not the camera and forensic light equipment, not the remote controls for the multiple flat-screen displays that constitute what I consider my mobile office. I have everything I need in here including communication technology that allows me to work while away from the CFC for the better part of a day as I am right now.

I climb up on the tailgate slowly, awkwardly, careful with my leg, dripping water as I walk around inside making a hollow thudding sound on the steel flooring. I search the rear area where the noise seemed to come from while I was driving, my attention fixing on the built-in workstation and a swivel chair secured to the floor with fasteners. On top of the desk are a computer tower and flat-panel monitors with tough polyurethane covers and screen protectors. On either side are watertight rustproof storage cabinets.

I open the one on my right. Nothing unusual, just a printer in the pull-out tray and under it reams of paper. I pause for a moment when Marino's phone rings. It's the dispatcher, the one named Helen.

"Okay. Like we thought. That's too bad. Nope. Me too. Still waiting," Marino says to her. "If I don't hear anything soon I'll let you know. Thanks again."

His phone is in a waterproof tactical case that he clips to the waistband of his soaking wet cargo shorts.

"No luck," he says to me. "No earlier radio traffic about any units responding here after you and me left midmorning. And nothing about the Range Rover. If we don't get some sort of idea of what's happened to Lapin and Hyde we'll put it out over the air."

"She's trying to raise them on the radio and neither of them are answering." I summarize as I find what I'm looking for in the cabinet on my left.

"Another few minutes and nothing from them? And we pull the trigger."

"You might want to pull it now," I tell him.

THE POLISHED COPPER ROD is approximately three feet long and the thickness of a pencil.

It rests against stacks of blue towels, and an alarm is sounding in a remote part of my brain. I notice a stiff yellowish fringe on one end and what looks like a claw of bent razor blades on the other. I bend down to get a better look and detect the acrid pungent stench of decomposing flesh. I begin opening drawers until I find a box of gloves.

"What is it?" Marino watches from outside the open tailgate as he's blasted by rain and wind. "What did you find?"

"Give me a minute." I put on gloves and a face shield. "There's something here that certainly shouldn't be."

"I'm coming up."

"No. It's best you stay where you are."

I print a label for the white plastic ruler I'll use as a scale, and I take photographs without touching or disturbing anything. Then I reach inside the cabinet and pick up an arrow that's unlike one I've ever seen before. It isn't functional. I can't imagine how it can be. What bow could fire a solid copper arrow that weighs as much as a pound? Were it even possible what would be the reason?

I hold it up in my gloved hands and inspect reddish-brown stains on the damaged three-bladed broadhead tip and the elaborately engraved polished shaft. I turn the arrow in my fingertips. The stench is from the fletching, which isn't made of feathers.

"What the hell?" Marino is about to climb inside anyway and I again tell him no.

"The back of this truck has just become part of a crime scene," I say to him. "We're going to have to treat it like that at any rate."

"What crime scene?" The look on his face is fierce. "Jesus Christ."

"I don't know yet," I reply as I watch it settle over him, one thing turning into another and going from ugly to unthinkable.

"Copperhead." He repeats the nickname that has stuck in the media, the nickname of a monster we know is Carrie. "Copper bullets. Now a copper arrow."

The splashing, the constant drumming on the metal roof are very loud and I have to yell when I explain that the arrow's broadhead tip is a mechanical game point. It expands on contact rather much the way a hollowpoint bullet does. The goal is to inflict catastrophic injuries, to kill quickly, mercifully.

"Except as you well know bow hunting arrows typically are constructed of extremely lightweight carbon fiber," I add. "The fletching or vanes meant to stabilize the arrow in flight are usually real feathers, occasionally synthetic. But not whatever this bristly material is."

It's about an inch long, pale blond and toothbrush-firm as if it's been varnished. I find a hand lens and a flashlight to get a better look at what could be pieces of a pelt. Not animal but human, and in bright light and magnification I see dirt, fibers and other debris including granules of what looks like black sugar.

I see remnants of glue where the three thin strips of leathery backing have been attached to notches machined into the copper shaft. I think of mummified human scalps, and I have a strong suspicion about what this is as I cover a countertop with blue towels. I place the arrow on them. The razor-sharp broadhead has been deployed. The reddish-stained blades are bent backward, as if the arrow penetrated a target and was forcibly pulled out. Carrie has hurt or killed someone else. I can't possibly know this for a fact. Yet I have no doubt and it's not coincidental that I can't conduct a simple and quick presumptive test for hemoglobin. Copper is an impossible problem and very little is random with Carrie.

I remember the way she used to look at me coldly and with calculation during our encounters at Quantico. No matter what I said about science, medicine, law or anything at all she always acted as if she were better informed on the subject. I felt she was judging me, looking for anything that might verify her superiority. She was competitive. She was jealous and impossibly arrogant. She was extraordinarily knowledgeable, charming when she chose to be, and one of the brightest people I've ever met. I know her patterns. I know them as well as she knows mine.

She's creating situations and then sabotaging any effort I might expend in response, and copper is part of her plan. I saw in the videos that she believes copper has healing if not magical properties. She would also be aware that it creates chaos at crime scenes. The reagent phenolphthalein plus a drop or two of hydrogen peroxide will instantly turn a swab bright pink no matter what chemical or material is present. In the typical presumptive blood test, copper tops the list of substances that react with a false positive.

In other words I'll definitely get a confirmation. It could be correct. It could be misleading, and that's Carrie's unique gift. She creates confusion, false hope, wrong turns, seeming impossibilities, and is supremely skilled at curdling one's deductive skills, of foiling science and procedures. She revels in upending our routines and training on their heads, and I feel as if she's inside the truck with me. I know without empirical proof that what I'm thinking will be validated soon enough. There's no point in denying that the disasters of the day all come from the same single source.

Carrie has been here. She might be here right now for all we know, and I explain this to Marino as he waits in the downpour, standing there stoically because he has no place else to go unless he sits inside the cab. He won't. He'll wait. I feel him watching me cut and fold heavy white paper. He can't be as certain as I am because he hasn't seen the videos and doesn't know about them. But I can imagine his thoughts as I seal my package with red evidence tape that I initial and date. He stares mutely at me with his head bent in the heavy rain. His darkening mood is palpable.

"Are you sure it couldn't have been in there for a while?" he finally asks. "Maybe from some other case and it got left in there somehow. Or maybe it's a joke. Someone's sick joke."

"You're not serious."

"As a heart attack."

"It's not from some other case and it's certainly not a joke. At least not something a normal person would consider a joke." I dig into my pants pocket for the nitrile-cocooned metamaterial I found on Lucy's property.

"I'm grasping at straws because I don't want to believe it," he says.

"I don't want to believe it either," I agree.

"How the hell did it get inside the truck?"

"I don't know but that's where it was."

"And you're thinking it's her."

"What do you think, Marino?"

"Jesus. How the hell could she get inside your truck? Let's start with that. One thing at a time."

"Someone put the arrow inside the cabinet to the left of the desk. It's a fact. It didn't get there on its own. That's what I can tell you without reservation." I label a plastic evidence bag with the time and location of when and where I found the tiny quartz-like hexagon that I tucked inside the finger of a glove.

"What are we talking about? A fucking Houdini?" Marino is angry and foul because he's unnerved, and his eyes are everywhere, his right hand down by the holstered .40 caliber Glock on his hip.

"My biggest concern is that someone else might be dead." Gloves and face shield off, and I place my packages inside a steel evidence locker, shut the door and scan my thumb to set the biometric lock. "If the stains and fletching are what I think they are then we have another problem. Where did this biological material come from? Who or what did it come from?"

"Could it be from her?" He means Chanel Gilbert.

"She's not missing any of her scalp and her hair isn't short and dyed light blond. If what I'm seeing is human blood and tissue they won't be hers."

I'm sure of that, and I go on to tell him I feel set up. I push two black plastic scene cases closer to him, and they scrape over the diamond-plate steel floor. I explain it would be tough to prove I didn't place the arrow in here myself.

"I witnessed you finding it. I know you didn't put it there." Marino lifts the cases and sets them on the flooded driveway.

"You really can't know that for a fact. It was inside my truck," I repeat, and I'm going to have to tell him about the videos because now the stakes have changed.

Carrie has just made her presence known. That transforms everything instantly and completely.

"But I certainly didn't put a copper arrow in here. I've never seen it before. I promise you that," I'm saying to Marino.

"I witnessed you take photographs and they'll have a date and time stamp. You've got proof that it was already inside the truck. That you found it because it started making noise."

"Say what you want. Whether I have proof or not, I'm being set up. This is deliberate," I repeat as he takes the truck keys from me. "Lucy feels set up and now I do," I add and I'm going to have to tell him the truth, the whole truth. "All of us are being set up and we'd better think long and hard and in different ways about everything we do. Starting right this minute."

He begins a slow walk around the truck while I wait inside the back of it and think about how he'll react to what I confess. He'll say I should have told him hours ago. He'll say I shouldn't have watched the videos unless he was watching them with me, and I hear him checking every access door, unlocking each and banging it shut in the relentless rain.

I argue with myself that it doesn't matter how he'll feel or react because in light of what's happening it would be irresponsible not to tell him, and I wait for him to return to the open tailgate. When he does he announces that every panel, every storage compartment is locked with no sign of tampering. Then I start in with him.

"Marino, I need you to listen carefully. You won't like what you're about to hear me say."

"What?" He's getting more out of sorts, and if this is a mistake there's no going back.

I really don't know what else to do, and that's the vortex we're caught in and it's precisely where Carrie has put us and wants us to stay. Our usual habits, protocols and procedures for handling the smallest tasks get turned inside out, upside down and are shattered and sucked away into another dimension. She's done it before. She's doing it again, and I remember what my boss General John Briggs, the chief of Armed Forces Medical Examiners, often preaches:

When terrorists find something that works they keep on doing it. It's predictable.

Carrie Grethen is a terrorist. She's doing what she knows works. Creating havoc and confusion. Until we lose direction and judgment. Until we hurt ourselves and each other.

Think!

"We're going to have to make things up as we go along," I tell Marino.

"I don't know what the hell you're talking about."

Think about what she'd predict you'd do right now.

"The usual way we do things isn't necessarily relevant and workable, and we're going to have to be flexible and extremely attentive, as if we're starting out all over, as if we're having to re-create the wheel. Because we are in a sense. She knows our playbook, Marino. She knows our cookbook. She knows every handbook we've ever read for everything we do. We have to be open to change and mindful of any assumptions she might make based on her knowing us so well."

She assumes you won't tell anyone.

"I wasn't going to tell you but now I've changed my mind because to keep it a secret is what I anticipate she expects me to do. I've been sent three video clips so far today." I speak loudly, slowly and in a calm manner that belies what churns inside of me. "Surveillance recordings taken by Carrie it would seem. Apparently they were filmed covertly in Lucy's dorm room when she was at Quantico in 1997."

"Carrie sent you videos that are seventeen years old?" Marino is incredulous and enraged. "Are you sure they aren't faked?"

"They weren't."

"What do you mean *weren't*?"

"As in the past tense."

"Let me see them."

"I can't. That's what I mean by past tense. The instant I finished watching them they were gone and the links were dead. Then the messages themselves disappeared as if I never got them."

"E-mailed?" Marino's wet face is pale and stony, his bloodshot eyes glaring.

"Texted. Supposedly from Lucy's In Case of Emergency cell phone line."

"That figures. That sucks. The FBI has her phone. They'll see what she sent. They'll think she sent the videos to you. It will be more of the same—her getting blamed for what Carrie does."

"Let's hope nothing shows up. It shouldn't because I'm fairly certain Carrie is spoofing the ICE line. The texts aren't really from Lucy or any device she owns."

"You should give me your phone." Marino holds out his hand. "I need to take out the SIM card and the battery if you want any proof you ever got what you're saying. We need to be able to show Lucy had nothing to do with it."

"No."

"Your SIM card may be the only record you've got . . ."

"No."

"The longer you wait— "

"I'm not disabling my phone," I interrupt him. "If I do that I can't see anything else she decides to send."

"Do you hear yourself?"

"The video links are the real reason I rushed out of here this morning. I was afraid Carrie had Lucy's phone and what it would mean if that were true. I have to keep my phone."

Marino bends over to look at something below me at the back of the truck. He's interested in a taillight.

"When I tell you more about the videos you'll understand my concern," I continue to explain, "and Lucy wasn't answering when I tried to reach her. Janet wasn't either. Now we know it was because the FBI was herding them around and seizing their possessions. What is it? What have you found?"

Marino has gotten interested in one of the truck's white high-intensity LEDs.

"Shit," he says in an ominous tone. "I don't believe it."

"Now what?"

"Right under our nose. What they mean by *in plain view*." He hovers over the left taillight, his hands clasped behind his back the way he does when he wants to make sure he doesn't touch something. "Can you hand me some clean gloves?"

I snatch a pair out of the box for him. I stick my head out of the back of the truck to see what he's found as I'm battered by heavy rain. It runs down my face and the back of my neck as I count the screws missing from the left taillight's chrome mount. Five are gone. The one that remains is scratched and gouged.

CHAPTER 31

THUNDER CLAPS. WATER HISSES AND SPLASHES AROUND his big black leather sneakers.

Marino talks on his phone to Al Jacks or Ajax as he's called. I piece together the gist of what the former Navy SEAL is asking about the house itself. He wants to know what makes Marino think someone could be inside. Is there any chance Hyde is in there? Maybe he's injured or a hostage? I watch all this from the back of the truck as Marino formally requests the assistance of SWAT, his earpiece flashing blue in the wet din. I'm well aware of the risk he's taking.

If a special ops team rolls out on this high-profile property it will be extremely embarrassing and difficult to justify if it's discovered there was no need. Furthermore such a dramatic display will be one more thing to explain to Chanel Gilbert's wealthy Hollywood mother. She's already going to be a force to reckon with. I'm sure of that.

"The rear lens assembly is fastened with stainless number one size Phillips screws but it looks like someone used a regular or number two size screwdriver," Marino describes over the phone as he looks at the damaged left taillight. "Or maybe a knife or who knows what? Because of the one screw left. The head's all buggered up like someone used the wrong tool."

I imagine Carrie Grethen. Would she use the wrong tool? It doesn't sound like her but who else would leave me such a grisly gift, and what's the rest of the story?

"I realize it's not likely but yeah I think we have to entertain the possibility he could be inside." Marino is talking on the phone about Hyde again as he stares at the dark silent house. "But how would he have gotten in on his own? I didn't leave him a key. And if he's incapacitated inside, for example, what happened to his car? Yeah, yeah. Exactly. That's all I'm asking. Let's clear the house but we do it on the lowdown. I want to be real careful what goes out over the air. I don't want a freakin' carnival at a multimillion-dollar house by the Harvard campus."

Marino tells him to bring several sets of dry clothes, and he describes my size as men's medium before I can tell him that will be a tent on me. He ends that call and makes another one. I realize he's talking to his contact at the phone company, probably the same technical operations manager he always gets hold of when he needs a warrant or wishes to bypass waiting for one. Marino recites two cell phone numbers that I assume belong to Hyde and Lapin. He wants to ping locations. Then we wait.

"It's going to take fifteen or twenty before we know anything, Doc." Marino struggles to pull gloves over his wet hands. "And I already feel like crap. I hope like hell I didn't just make a bad mistake. It's kind of like nothing we do this minute is right. If we leave it's wrong. If we stay out here on the driveway it's wrong. If we go inside the house it's wrong. If we ask for help it's wrong and if we don't it's wrong. There's not a damn thing we can do that even makes sense except to wait for Ajax and his guys to roll up."

He removes the taillight mount and sets it on the bumper, and I'm aware of how isolated and vulnerable we are. If someone wanted to take us out it would already have happened. If Carrie wanted to kill us this very second she would. I've never really believed we could stop her. When we thought she'd died years ago we didn't feel responsible or give ourselves the credit. We simply felt lucky. We felt blessed.

"Holy shit," Marino says. "The bulb's missing. And behind where it was screwed in is a decent-size wire routing hole that I'm guessing the arrow was shoved through. That would put it exactly where you found it on the floor inside the desk cabinet."

"I've been driving around with a taillight out? Well that verifies that the truck couldn't have been like this for very long."

"Exactly. The question is when was the damage done? Because someone couldn't have removed the screws, the bulb while the truck was parked on Lucy's driveway. Unless the FBI did it."

"Planting evidence, tampering with state and federal property? Let's hope the FBI wouldn't be that unethical or stupid." I crouch on the shiny steel floor near the open cabinet where I found the arrow as I remember what Lucy said about Carrie's obsession with invisibility technology.

I look around as if she's ubiquitous and transparent like air, and the wind buffets the truck and rain thrums it in varying intensities. Beating then thrashing then pouring, and Marino is hunched against the weather while I'm spared for the moment. I shine the flashlight inside the cabinet, painting the intense beam over the routing hole, over stacks of cheap blue towels tied with string, the steel floor mirror bright in the light. I notice something else.

THE CLUMP OF DUST is what people often refer to as a dust bunny or dust ball. It's about the size of a martini olive, fluffy like lint from the dryer.

Another pair of clean gloves and I use the adhesive back of a Post-it to collect a sample that I'm sure will prove a treasure trove, a microscopic landfill of debris. Fibers, hairs, insect pieces and parts, and particulates that could be anything I imagine. But I'm certain the origin can't be one of my CFC trucks. It can't be the labs or the parking lot surrounded by its high black fence that's supposed to be impossible to climb. Next I seal the dust bunny inside a plastic bag and it goes into the same locker where I placed the arrow and the metamaterial. I call my chief of staff.

For an entire minute Bryce and I have a useless conversation about chain of evidence, and I don't have the patience for his incessant chatter. I continue interrupting him. The CFC isn't even ten minutes from here and I want the truck swapped out immediately for an SUV. Get Harold or Rusty to take care of it right away. I apologize about the inconvenience but I need this truck out of here now. The chain of evidence must be preserved. Not just the evidence packaged inside but also the truck itself.

"I don't understand." Bryce has said this several times. "Because like you just pointed out you're ten minutes from here. You sure you and Marino can't drop it off yourselves when you're done, Doctor Scarpetta? I mean you're coming here anyway? I'm not trying to be a pain but we're kind of up to our eyeballs? We've had quite the full house this morning with you not here, and Luke's only just now starting his third case while Harold and Rusty clean workstations and suture up bodies for the other docs. And two of them decided to pull out that box from the skeleton closet so to speak? Remember the one from the other week . . . ?"

"Bryce . . ."

"The remains that washed up on Revere Beach? The anthropologists just got the DNA results and it's for sure the girl who vanished from her houseboat near the aquarium last year? They have the bones all spread out like a jigsaw puzzle, and . . ."

"Bryce, please be quiet and listen. It appears the truck has been vandalized. I want it to go straight into the evidence bay for processing, and I have additional evidence in a locker that needs to go to the labs ASAP."

I give him a list of what I want the scientists to look for first.

"There appears to be biological materials such as blood and tissue, and I want DNA as fast as we can get it," I add as I stand inside the truck and Marino is hunched against the relentless rain like Eeyore in *Winnie-the-Pooh*. "And trace evidence because I'm seeing dirt, fibers and an unknown material that looks like quartz. Plus tool marks on a screw."

"Quartz and a screw? Oh my God that sounds exciting."

"Let's get Ernie on it right away."

Ernie Koppel is my senior trace evidence examiner. He's a superb microscopist, one of the best.

"Texting him as we speak," Bryce says in my earpiece. "And B-T-W? What's all that racket in the background? It sounds like someone is beating an oil drum with a stick."

"Have you looked out your window?"

A pause and I imagine him looking, then his surprised voice, "Well hello! The acoustics are so amazing in this building? I couldn't hear an earthquake, and then I had my blinds closed because it's so depressing out. And whoops! I forgot we're having a flood. And I'm sending a note to Jen now about swapping out the truck if that's all right with you."

It isn't really. Jen Garate is the forensic investigator I hired last year after Marino walked off the job at the CFC and signed on with the Cambridge Police Department. She can't begin to take his place and never will. She wasn't a good choice with her tight clothes and bling and insatiable craving for attention. I can't stomach her flirting and flippancy. I've been meaning to begin the process of letting her go but the summer has raced away from me.

"All right," I concede to Bryce. "Tell her a response team is headed here as we speak and she's not to interfere or get in the way of their vehicle."

"A response team as in SWAT?"

"Please just listen, Bryce. I'll pull my truck over as far as I can so she can go around it and park the SUV in front of it. Then she can get out and so can I. She's not to come inside the house. She's to call me the instant she arrives and I'll meet her at the kitchen door and we'll exchange keys."

"Got it. I've just told her to head toward you in one of those amphibious boats they use for the Duck Tours and I'm kidding." He doesn't seem to breathe while he talks incessantly. "But it's so unfair. I just had everything washed the other day. Our entire fleet was all shiny and white and perfect, and now this?"

"Yes you do a great job keeping our vehicles clean which is exactly why I'm fairly sure the dust sample I collected came from somewhere else and was transferred to the inside of the truck. It's important to tell Ernie that."

"I love dust bunnies." Bryce says it as if he's talking about his favorite pet. "Well I mean as long as they're not inside my house. But they wouldn't be. Anyway who knows what story your little dust bunny will have to tell. Hair, fur, skin cells, fibers and all sorts of ticky tacky frick and frack that people track in and out of everywhere."

I ask him to explain to Ernie that an unusual projectile, an arrow was also left inside the truck, and under a lens I can see dirt, debris and glue.

"It's on the arrow and possibly in the dust bunny, and if so that suggests they may have come from the same source," I add. "They may have been in the same location at some point. We should be able to tell microscopically and by using X-ray spectroscopy to give us chemical and elemental information as well."

"Got it. I'll explain it to Ernie word for word. I know Anne's already sent him something. Well she didn't *send* it per se. Since we're on the subject of chain of evidence? She did it the right way, walked it up there and receipted it etcetera etcetera so if anyone tries to nail her in court? All to say we're holding down the ship here."

My compulsive talking chief of staff for whom so much ends in question marks is well known for his malapropisms. I have a diplomatic way of correcting him that he never notices. I simply repeat what he said and do a word substitution or two.

"I appreciate your holding down the fort," I say to him. "While you're at it I'd like the CFC security recordings checked for anybody who might have been in our parking lot tampering with the truck or anything else."

"But how would they get over the fence or through the gate?"

"Good question but where else would the tampering have been done? What day did you say the vehicles were washed and detailed?"

"Let me think. Today's Friday. So day before yesterday. Wednesday."

"I think we can safely conclude that the damage was done during or after the truck was washed. Otherwise a chrome mount barely attached by one screw would have been noticed. What did Anne receipt to Ernie? Did she find something important?"

"I can't wait to dash to his lab and ask."

I end the call and say to Marino, "We don't get dust bunnies inside our trucks." I climb out and it's like walking into a waterfall. "You know better than anybody how meticulously we wash and decon them inside and out. It's not possible for dust bunnies, dust balls, cobwebs or any such thing to form inside any of our vehicles."

"What the hell are you talking about?" he asks, and the taillight's chrome mount, gasket, outer lens, foam seal and housing are all the way off but still connected to the pigtail harness.

"Did you hear what I just told Bryce?"

"I can't hear a damn thing out here. I feel like I'm in a washing machine. This definitely has been messed with and for the obvious reason of planting something inside the truck. So the person had to have mechanical know-how and be familiar with trucks like this."

"Or specifically with this one." It's as if I'm standing under a shower.

"That's what I'm thinking. When you want a big transport vehicle that you use as a mobile office and command post it's always going to be forty-four-ten." He refers to the last four numbers of the truck's license tag. "Assuming it's available for deployment and in good repair with plenty of gas. Anyone who knows much about you knows that your first choice is forty-four-ten if you're driving yourself to a complicated scene."

"And I specifically requested this truck this morning because I knew Chanel Gilbert would be an involved time-consuming case. Even if it was nothing more than a random accident we have a bloody scene with a lot of questions. We have a high-profile victim and a high-profile neighborhood in Cambridge. We have potential political complications."

"It was a safe bet that this was the vehicle to tamper with," Marino says, and I step closer to him.

I'm up to my bootlaces in a puddle as I examine the rectangular outline on the white metal chassis where the mount was attached. I look at the hole with the plastic-coated wires threaded through it, and he's right. The arrow would have fit with room to spare.

"If this is the point of entry and I believe it is," I decide, "that's important because it suggests that whoever is responsible . . ."

"We know who." Marino blurts it out. "Why not just act like we know it's her. Who else would it be?"

"I'm trying to be objective."

"Don't bother."

"What I was about to say is she didn't necessarily access the inside of the truck. So she didn't need a key."

"Exactly. What she did was remove the lens and the entire housing, exposing the hole in the cab and the grommet the wiring runs through," he explains. "Now you have a breach, a way to get something inside the truck without opening it up. That made it a cinch when it was time to drop the arrow in. All she had to do was move the housing, swivel it to one side until the hole was exposed, drop the arrow in and straighten the mount again." He demonstrates. "It would take all of three seconds."

"And this was done while we were parked on Lucy's driveway."

"I'm thinking the taillight was sabotaged earlier, maybe when the truck was in the CFC parking lot. But I doubt the arrow was put in there at the same time or we would have heard it rolling around. We've been riding in this damn thing since we met at your office early this morning. We didn't hear anything clanking until we were headed back here a few minutes ago."

"You want to package this now?" I ask.

Marino says yes. There will be tool marks. We should have Ernie make comparisons of them with ones we found on other gifts from Carrie. Copper bullets. Cartridge cases. Pennies she polished in a tumbler and left in my yard on my birthday, June 12. The spears she shot the police divers and me with three days later. I climb back up on the tailgate, back into the truck. I put on clean gloves and Marino hands the taillight components to me. I tear off more sections of white butcher paper from the roll on a counter as I drip water on the floor.

"You probably wouldn't notice there's only one screw left unless you thought to look." He talks loudly as I begin wrapping. "But the mount would have come off soon enough if you hit a bad enough bump or pothole. Jesus!" He looks up at the swirling dark sky, at the blowing sheets of water spattering his face. "This is the kind of weather chickens drown in."

CHAPTER 32

I SLAM SHUT THE DOUBLE DOORS AND RELOCK THEM. I look around the rain-swept property as I walk through the downpour to the cab of the truck.

In the distance cars move slowly along Brattle Street. Their headlights burn through the fog. I watch for the tactical team. It will be here any minute. But everything seems like an endless wait as hard rain boils on brick. The wind shrieks and groans around the house and through the trees as if we've violated a spirit world, and Marino and I climb back into the truck's cab. Both of us are so drenched it no longer matters and I'm not reassured because a backup is on the way. I don't feel safe.

I don't care who or what is on the way—patrol units or SWAT. Nothing would give me peace of mind right now because we don't seem to be in charge. We're not the ones making choices. Even when we think something is our idea we discover maybe it's not.

We're being outmaneuvered and outsmarted, and Marino is feeling the same way. Since I told him about the videos he's accepted that when we got up this morning we didn't know the day belonged to Carrie Grethen. But it does and she must be getting high on her diabolical drama.

"How's this for screwed up," Marino says as we shut our doors and the downpour beats the metal roof. "We can't go anywhere including inside the house. We can't wait out on the driveway unless we want to drown or be a sitting duck. So we're stuck inside your damn truck. We've been stuck inside your truck the whole damn day. I feel we're going to be stuck inside it the rest of our lives."

"She must have placed the arrow inside before the storm hit. With the FBI right there?" I'm not interested in hearing him complain.

I'm interested in how what I just suggested is possible. What did she do? Is she invisible? Is it what Lucy suggested and Carrie has new tricks she's learned since she almost murdered me in Florida?

"Exactly. With the friggin' FBI right there." Marino lights a cigarette, and I crank the engine so he can open his window a little. "But no one could do that on Lucy's property without being picked up by the cameras."

"I'm not sure that's true if one knew exactly where the cameras are and how much they cover. Or if the person has a way of hacking into the system and foiling it somehow. Or maybe there's some other explanation." I think of the metamaterial again.

"Well I guess the way you parked might have partially blocked the view of the back of the truck because that asshole FBI agent's SUV was in the way," Marino says. "But we'll have to ask Lucy and see if she can help us. Or Janet."

"Supposedly yesterday and today the motion sensors detected

something but the cameras didn't," I inform him. "Lucy says this was at around four o'clock both mornings."

"Maybe a squirrel, a rabbit, something low to the ground." He flicks an ash out the top of the window.

"That wouldn't set off the motion sensors. Something was there but wasn't. She says she can't figure it out."

"I never believe it when Lucy says she can't figure something out. Erin Loria should know if anything's been picked up by the cameras."

"I'm sure she may know quite a lot." I feel a rush of hostility and realize how much I resent and blame her.

"You can bet she's been watching the monitors and looking at the recordings," he says as I turn on the defog and wipers to clear the glass. "Maybe she saw something that could help us."

"I'm not asking her a damn thing." I wonder how much he remembers from Lucy's FBI Academy days, and I prod him. "At one point she was a new agent in Lucy's dorm," I remind him. "Washington Dorm and they were on the same floor."

"When I saw her this morning she wasn't familiar, and I'm also not sure why I would have run into her back then," he says. "The only time I really came to Quantico was if we were working a case or I was meeting you. Why would I have known Erin Loria?"

"You wouldn't have necessarily. But based on what I saw in the videos she may have been romantically involved with Carrie." I go on to say that Carrie and Lucy had one of their worst fights and may have broken up because of the former beauty queen from Tennessee who has just raided Lucy's property and is now married to a federal judge.

"Agents climbing all over the place and with a chopper up?" Marino is busy picking off dirt and bits of wet grass and leaves stuck to his bare wet lower legs. "And we were walking around too? And she puts a possible murder weapon inside your crime scene truck?" He's not talking about Erin Loria anymore. He's talking about Carrie. "What for? To help us out? To help us work some other scene we don't even know about yet?"

"Even if she figured that I might be driving this today? We have to ask what scene might she have known about in advance." I shove the gearshift into reverse and check my mirrors. "And I'm voting for this one."

I back up and pull forward, maneuvering as far off the driveway as I can without running over shrubs or hitting trees. I suggest we should consider that she has planned and concocted everything we're experiencing including the homicide scene we're on right now. She knew I'd respond to it personally and which vehicle I'd choose.

"I'm in town," I continue to explain. "Anybody watching me would know that I'm not traveling. I'm here. I'm back to working cases like usual and that wouldn't have been true even a couple of weeks ago."

"She'd know all that if she's hacked into the CFC computer."

"Lucy says she hasn't."

"I don't care what Lucy says. That doesn't mean it's true. Not when you consider who we're talking about."

"If the CFC database has been hacked and the hacker is Carrie?" I reply. "Then yes. She could know everything about where I am and when and why."

"Your calendar, everything is electronic."

"That's right. But Lucy says the CFC database is safe." I check the mirrors and am startled by the blacked-out Suburban with glass tinted as dark as Darth Vader.

It seems the ominous SUV has appeared out of nowhere and is parked behind us with no lights or siren on. Its engine is drowned out by the storm and the diesel rumble of my truck.

"I'm going to have to let them in the house and you need to

stay put," Marino says to me as the Suburban's doors open simultaneously.

He opens his door and holds the cigarette out in the rain to extinguish it. He drops the wet butt into the water bottle.

"I'm not sitting in here by myself." I open my door too. "I'm not staying out here alone while you're inside."

"No wandering off anywhere," Marino says.

He climbs out to greet four SWAT operators in full tactical gear. Their binocular night vision goggles are flipped up from battlewear helmets. Slung across their chests are M-4 assault rifles fitted with green lasers that are visible only in the infrared spectral range of light.

"Stick with me at all times," Marino tosses back at me.

The team leader nicknamed Ajax is young and massively built. He's attractive in a scary way, square jawed with cool gray eyes and short dark hair. I recognize the roundish patch on his right cheek, a healed penetrating wound possibly from frag or a bullet. He hardly looks at me as he hands Marino a black trash bag that has something thick inside it. There are none of the usual quips, none of the typical teasing and banter.

No one is smiling and the plan is simple. His team will clear the house making sure it's safe while we hang back. This should take fifteen minutes depending on what they find, and we follow them to the entrance. We step over the single ribbon of yellow crime scene tape, and on the front porch Marino digs into a pocket for a key tagged as evidence. The security system begins to beep the instant he opens the door.

"That's good at least," he comments as the foul odor welcomes us back. "It doesn't appear someone entered the house since we were last here unless the person has the alarm code."

He shuts the front door behind us and it echoes solidly in a cool stillness punctuated by the tick tock of clocks. The four officers are nimble and light on their booted feet as they head down the central hallway and up the staircase, spreading out in pairs with weapons tucked in close and at the ready, leaving Marino and me alone. He sets down our scene cases. He opens the black plastic trash bag. He slides out folded tactical clothing that he stacks on the floor.

WATER SLOWLY DRIPS. Puddles begin to form around my sopping wet boots as I hover near the shut door. When we were here this morning I didn't hear the clocks.

TICK TOCK TICK TOCK

I scan the upright stepladder, the dark dried blood we mapped with orange evidence flags that flutter slightly in chilled air blowing through vents. I listen to the dull patter of rain on the slate roof. I'm keenly aware of the clocks.

TICK TOCK TICK TOCK

They're loud and disconcerting. I scan the shards of glass from the lightbulbs and antique crystal fixture we're supposed to believe Chanel Gilbert broke when she lost her balance and fell. That's what we're meant to accept. Or is it really? Are we supposed to be tricked? Are we supposed to figure out that we're being tricked? Possibly the answer is both. It's all of the above and nothing, and I look up at the silver base of the chandelier with its two empty light sockets. I'm reminded of the bulb missing from my truck's taillight. I'm reminded of Carrie. It's as if I've been infected by her. As if she's taken over my life. And my pulse kicks up another notch. I listen to the clocks.

TICK TOCK TICK TOCK TICK TOCK

Glassy splinters glitter, and the spooky blue glow of the reagent I sprayed this morning has faded entirely. The area of white marble is blank again as if nothing is there. Marino turned on the air-conditioning before we left this morning, and I'm cold on the way to shivering in my soaking wet clothes. I begin to pace and almost don't recognize myself in the Baroque mirror to the right of the front door. I look at the woman looking back at me in the corroded silvered glass in its chipped gilt frame of acanthus leaves.

I stare at my reflection as if it's someone I don't know, my short blond hair dripping wet and plastered to my head making my strong features seem more pronounced and dominant than I imagine them. My eyes are a deeper blue, a bruised blue that hints of my dark intense mood, and I can see the tension in muscles of my forehead and around my firmly set mouth. My navy blue field clothes with their embroidered CFC crest are dripping wet and clinging to me. I look like a waif, like an apparition, and I move away from the mirror.

My attention wanders past the staircase and into the living room, and I see what Marino meant when he was talking about Chanel Gilbert or someone having unusual interests. On both sides of a deep stone fireplace are antique spinning wheels, three-legged with wooden seats, and I spot another one next to the couch. I notice the hourglasses and thick candles on the mantel and tables, and I count the clocks. At least six of them. Wall clocks, tall case clocks, shelf clocks. From where I stand near the door I can see that their pale moon faces and ornate hands all show the same time of 1:20.

"Did you notice the clocks this morning?" I ask Marino as I listen for other sounds in the house.

I don't hear the tactical team. The men are so quiet it's as if they aren't here. All I detect is blowing air and the clocks.

TICK TOCK TICK TOCK

"Did you notice them?" I persist. "Because I didn't and I would have."

"I don't remember. But there was a lot going on." Marino has stationed himself between the staircase and the door under it that leads down into the cellar.

"I'm quite certain I would have noticed. I'm surprised you didn't."

Marino's answer is to look up at the ceiling, his head cocked as he listens, his right hand by his gun. I can tell he's thinking what I am. Ajax and his team are quiet. They're too quiet. If something has happened we'll be next. I feel a certain resignation about it, a deeply stored feeling I don't pull out and look at often. But it's there. It's familiar. It's not an acutely sad or unpleasant feeling but more of an acquiescence, a tacit consent that I can hold fate in my hands like a skull and unflinchingly look it in the eye.

You can't destroy me if I don't care.

This day could be our last and if it's in the cards then so be it. I'll prevent any bad thing I can. That's my life's mission. I also know how to accept finality, to give myself up to what I can't begin to change. I don't want to die. But I refuse to fear it. I wait for it without dread because there's no logic in living a tragedy before it's happened.

"Truth is," Marino says as I wait and listen, "I don't remember hearing any clocks but I saw them when I walked through. I'm pretty sure they all told a different time," he explains and my expectation intensifies as I wait for what's about to happen.

Something will. Or it already has.

"I did notice that when I was in the living room," Marino continues. "I couldn't believe all the weird shit in there, the spinning wheels, the little crosses made out of iron nails and red thread, the hourglasses. The more I think about it, Doc? I can't swear the clocks were working."

"They are now and antique clocks have to be wound manually. They have to be constantly adjusted if they're to be in sync." I listen to everything going on around us and hear blowing air and the clocks.

"Someone's been in here," Marino says.

"That's my point."

"Someone who has a key and the alarm code."

"Possibly."

"Not possibly. Absolutely unless you're talking about a ghost who can pass through walls." He's agitated and edgy as he looks at his phone, finding a number.

CHAPTER 33

WE SHOULD LEAVE. I HOVER NEAR THE FRONT DOOR and listen for the response team. I don't detect voices or doors opening and shutting, not so much as a floorboard creaking. Just the wind and the rain and the clocks. I glance at my watch. SWAT has been clearing the house for exactly six minutes. It's as if the men have vanished.

TICK TOCK TICK TOCK . . .

All Marino and I have to do is walk back outside into the storm. It's safer than being in here or at least that's the way I feel as I look at him, at his wide back turned to me. He has one of his contacts on the line, another female I can tell, and I realize he's talking to Chanel Gilbert's alarm company.

"I'm going to repeat this," Marino says, "and we're going to write it down."

He means I'm going to, and I get a notepad and pen out of my shoulder bag, reminded of my gun again. I slip it out and place it on top of a scene case.

"It was reset at ten-twenty-eight this morning," he's saying to a contact he calls *sweetheart,* "and there was no activity until twenty-five minutes past one P.M., which is when I disarmed the system."

I listen for another moment, and then he ends the call and says to me, "How are we supposed to explain something like that? I set the alarm when we left the first time at ten-twenty-eight, then unset it now. In other words no one's touched the alarm system in the past three hours except me. So how the hell did someone come in here and wind the clocks? It's a damn good thing you were with me the entire time or they'd say I did it."

"You couldn't have and that's ridiculous," I reply.

"You positive there's no other explanation for why we're hearing the clocks now but we didn't earlier?"

"What other explanation could there be?"

"But the alarm system had to be armed and disarmed. And it wasn't. So how were the clocks wound?"

"I can only tell you that they have been since we were here last."

"Maybe there's another way to get in that bypasses the alarm system." Marino is restless, looking and listening as I think of the locked bulkhead doors outside in the flower bed.

I'm reminded of the rusting hulk of the *Mercedes* on the bottom of the sea. It seems the broken-up shipwreck and the bulkhead are somehow the same. Portals to an evil place. Portals to destruction and death. Portals to our ultimate destiny, and I wonder if the bulkhead doors have alarm contacts and are wired to the system. If not, one could access the house that way. No code would be needed and there would be no record of someone coming in and out.

"As long as you have a key." I'm describing this to Marino. "You could get in through the bulkhead doors and at the very least be in the basement I'm assuming."

"Well if you have a damn key wouldn't you also have the alarm code and not need to enter the house that way?"

"Not necessarily."

He unclips his holstered Glock from the waistband of his soaked shorts and says, "I wonder if there was some way the housekeeper could have come back in here to poke around. Maybe she knows a way to do that without touching the alarm system. So she snuck in and while she was at it she wound the clocks."

"Why bother?"

"Habit. People do weird things when they're upset. Or maybe she's crazy." His eyes are wide, his holstered pistol pointed down by his side. "You look at all this stuff everywhere and I'm thinking somebody's a mental case or into bad juju."

None of it caught my attention when I was here this morning. I left too abruptly, and I can't stop thinking about the *Depraved Heart* videos and how they've made me feel and act. Stunned. Threatened. Angry. Sad. Most of all I was overwhelmed by a sense of urgency. I was too quick to race out of here.

If I'd had a chance to look around I would have wondered if Chanel Gilbert had psychiatric problems or was involved in pagan religions. Either could have made her vulnerable to a predator like Carrie, and I listen for the response team clearing the house. I hear nothing. Then Marino's phone rings, a birdsong ringtone that for an instant confuses both of us.

"What the hell is going on, Lapin?" he angrily blurts out the instant he realizes who it is. "Yeah well sorry to hear that but I don't give a shit if you're really sick or not. I sound like I'm in a tomb? Well guess why. It's because I am. I'm back in the foyer where a lady was found dead this morning, remember? And the Doc and I just got back here to finish up the scene of what's turned out to be a homicide and guess what? The perimeter hadn't been secured and my backup was nowhere in sight. And guess what else? Chanel Gilbert's Range Rover isn't at the house anymore. You heard me. Nope, I'm not being funny. It's not in the driveway where we saw it three hours ago. It appears someone went inside the house while we were gone. Maybe the same person who took her car . . . Hell no that couldn't be Hyde. He has no way to get in."

Marino looks at me as he listens. The conversation didn't start well and it only gets worse. I can see his internal struggle. I can see it in his eyes, in the set of his heavy jaw, and I'm convinced that Carrie is playing us for Keystone Cops, for fools, and I imagine her amusement, her smug smile and laughter. We're in the midst of a nightmare of her making because that's what she does while decent people try to live their lives and do their jobs. We're here according to plan. Not our plan. Her plan.

"And you got no clue," Marino is saying to Lapin over the phone. "You haven't talked to him, and when you saw him last he didn't give you any reason to think he had something to do, someplace to go? Any reason you can think of he'd quit answering his radio and phone? Yeah like you did. And you're home? Well it's a damn good thing because any minute we're going to see the exact GPS coordinates of where your phone is as we speak. Yeah you heard me right. Sorry, buddy. But that's what happens when you disappear off the radar."

It isn't really. Marino is exaggerating. Using cell towers to determine someone's exact location isn't foolproof. It can be off by twenty miles or more depending on the software, topography, the weather and how much signal traffic is handled by regional switching centers at any given moment. But that doesn't stop Marino from trying. If nothing else cell phone pinging is the stuff of bluffs if he wants to scare a suspect into a confession.

"Here's what we know." Marino is talking to me now as he bends down to remove his sopping wet sneakers. "Lapin claims he and Hyde pulled out of here in their respective vehicles while we were still inside the house. This would have been at about ten-fifteen." His ankles are white and imprinted with the pattern of his socks as he peels them off.

"I saw them leave." I'm so cold I'm beginning to shiver as we stand near the front door dripping. "The two of them and also Trooper Vogel. About fifteen minutes before you and I headed out."

I listen to him and I also listen for the tactical team. How can big men with all that gear be so damn quiet? The warnings are fast and strong. We shouldn't be inside this house. But we've walked in and here we are. We're safe. I keep telling myself we couldn't be safer. There are special ops cops in here, and I continue to wonder how it's possible they don't make a sound. They're silent like cats. I can't hear anything, not their feet or their voices, and my heart is beating harder.

SOMETHING HAS HAPPENED. Suddenly the two police divers are before me vividly, horribly, suspended facedown inside the hull of the sunken barge.

Their names were Rick and Sam and I envision their dead young faces, their hoses dangling, their hair floating up in the brownish murky water as their eyes stared unblinking behind their masks. There were no bubbles. The regulators weren't in their mouths.

I remember my disbelief, my electrifying explosion of adrenaline as I realized what I was seeing were spears sticking out of their black neoprene-covered torsos. It had been only minutes earlier that the men were alive and well, cheerfully checking each other's dive gear, taking their giant strides off the stern of the boat and disappearing below the surface. I was joking with Benton about them flashing their badges underwater, making sure nobody bothered us or interfered with our mission. We had an underwater escort. We had underwater security.

Then they were dead on the bottom of the sea, ambushed, trapped, and I've never figured out what drew them into the hatch and down into the lightless hull. Why did they go in there? Carrie must have lured them somehow. Maybe she was inside waiting with the spear gun, blending with the rusty metal when she struck out of the abyss, and I hope what I always do. I hope they didn't suffer as they hemorrhaged internally and drowned, and I feel conflicted. My thoughts are louder and more adamant as they argue in rhythm to the clocks.

GO STAY! GO STAY! GO STAY! GO STAY!

"Lapin supposedly started feeling bad, got a headache, a tickle in his throat," Marino is saying as I will myself to listen.

Pay attention!

"He swung by his house for cold medicine and didn't bother notifying the radio. At least that's what he claims, and a few minutes ago he finally marked out sick."

My intuition says we should leave and yet I can't. I need to finish what I started. I'll be damned if I'll allow Carrie Grethen to interfere with how I handle a scene.

GO STAY! GO STAY! GO STAY! GO STAY!

"What exactly was Lapin's understanding when he and Hyde left here this morning?" I ask Marino.

"That Hyde was going to grab coffee, borrow the john and

then return here to secure the perimeter with crime scene tape like I told him to. Supposedly he was in a hurry because he wanted to do it before the rain started."

"Unless someone else strung the tape across the front steps it would appear he did just that. He got started and then abruptly left. Look the other way please," I tell Marino, and of course he looks right at me. "Turn around. Don't look in this direction." I begin to unbutton my shirt.

I take it off and then my soggy boots, my soaked socks and cargo pants, leaving my clothing on the floor a safe distance from blood and broken glass. The tactical pants SWAT picked out are so big I could pull them on without unzipping them, and I fold over the waistband to tighten it a little. I put on the black shirt, and it's huge in the shoulders and waist, and the buttonholes are stubborn, the cotton fabric new and stiff. At least I have plenty of pockets for pistol magazines, pens, flashlights, knives, whatever one might need, I think ironically. I glance at myself in the mirror, and my tactical attire looks baggy and borrowed.

I don't exactly look menacing without ballistic armor, helmet, night vision goggles or the smallest caliber assault rifle or even a pistol that holds more than six rounds. I can only hope that if the wrong person sees me I don't get shot because it's assumed I'm dangerous, and I am dangerous. But not the way I'd like to be right this minute.

"Well Lapin is suddenly sick thanks to you." Marino is standing with his back to me, scrolling through his phone.

"Why thanks to me?" I sit down on the cool marble and put my wet boots back on without socks, and over them disposable shoe covers that will prevent me from tracking water in the house.

"You said something about Vogel not having a tetanus shot and maybe what he's really got is the whooping cough. Lapin's right there listening, and it's what I call power of suggestion. Suddenly he started feeling sick." Marino puts soaked sneakers back on as his phone rings again.

I gather from what he says that it's his contact at the phone company. For a long moment Marino listens. He says very little. I can tell that what he's being told isn't helpful. Or maybe he doesn't understand how it's helpful or even plausible.

"This is nuts," he exclaims to me when he ends the call. "We pinged his phone . . ."

"Hyde's phone."

"Yeah we don't care about Lapin. We know where he is, at home playing hooky. The last call Hyde made was at nine-forty-nine this morning while he was still inside this house," Marino says. "The phone records show that the call connected to a cell tower that has the exact same GPS coordinates as this house."

"I don't understand," I start to say.

"Yeah you don't understand because obviously there's no cell tower at this location. It doesn't exist." Marino raises his voice in frustration. "In other words Hyde's call connected to a fake tower, probably one of these cell site simulators, a phone tracker, something like a stingray. They're so compact these days you can carry one in your car, in a briefcase, or maybe there's one hidden inside this house somewhere."

"Bad people use equipment like that." I think about Lucy and how much I wish I could talk to her.

She would know about such surveillance devices. She probably could tell me exactly what's been happening on this property and who's spying or intercepting communications and why.

"But law enforcement uses it too," I'm saying to Marino. "There's been a lot of controversy about cops relying on such devices to capture content, to track people or in some instances to jam radio signals."

"That's right. It works both ways. Spying and counterspying," Marino says. "You can track someone and intercept content or use the same device to prevent yourself from being tracked. Benton would know if the FBI's been spying on this property."

"If you say so."

"But he's not going to tell you my guess is."

"He probably wouldn't." I hand Marino a dry set of clothing, size double X. "Get changed." I toss him a pair of blue Tyvek shoe covers.

CHAPTER 34

I POLITELY AVERT MY GAZE AS HE DROPS SOPPING wet garments to the floor in a pile near mine, and I'm again reminded of how uncharitable crime scenes are. We can't help ourselves to privacy, a drink of water or a toilet. I can't borrow the clothes dryer, a bath towel or even sit in a chair.

"May as well get started while we wait." Marino zips up his borrowed black tactical pants and they fit him just fine.

"I don't think that's wise." I roll up my cuffs so I don't trip on them. "Surprising SWAT is a good way to get shot. I suggest we stay put until they say otherwise."

"We're fine as long as we restrict ourselves to rooms they already cleared. We don't go upstairs yet or in the basement." Marino hops on one foot then the other, tugging the blue booties over his wet sneakers. "Not until they've been there first."

He clips his holstered Glock to his waistband and tucks his

radio into one back pocket, his phone in the other and picks up a scene case. We walk out of the foyer, past the stairs, into a living room crowded with formidable antiques and silk rugs in bright patterns on the heart of pine floors, and something rolls through me like a seismic tremor.

My attention locks on the six white votive candles in simple glass holders on the red lacquer coffee table. They've never been lit. They aren't dusty and look new. I lean close to them, isolating the familiar scents of jasmine, tuberose and sandalwood. I recognize musk and vanilla, the rich erotic fragrance of Amorvero, Italian for *true love,* the signature perfume of the Hotel Hassler at the top of the Spanish Steps in Rome where Benton proposed to me eight years ago.

I have Amorvero perfume, bath oil and body lotion at home. He always buys it for my birthday and now I smell it here inside this house. I sniff my wrists to make sure it isn't me even though I know it can't be. I didn't put it on this morning.

"What do you smell?" I ask Marino.

He sniffs, shrugs. "An old house, maybe flowers. But my nose is stuffed up because of all the dust in this place. It's like it's been closed up for a long time. Have you noticed?"

"Do you recognize anything?"

"Like what?"

"What you described as a flowery fragrance. Is it familiar?"

"Yeah. It smells sort of like what you wear now that you mention it." He walks closer to me, sniffs a few more times.

"That's because it's the same fragrance but I don't have it on right now. It's also uncommon and I rarely run into it anywhere. Benton has to order it from Italy."

"You're saying it's your special scent." Sweat is popping out on top of Marino's shaved head. "And people close to you would know it."

"That's what I'm saying," I reply and he's thinking the same thing I am.

"It's like the clocks," Marino says. "I walked through this room this morning and I know the clocks weren't working. I didn't hear them. I don't remember seeing these little white candles or smelling anything in here except dust."

"The candles haven't been used." I point a gloved finger at one on a side table. "And if I pick one up"—I do it as I say it—"there's no sparing, no round shape in the dust on the tabletop. It appears the candles were placed in here recently and the room hasn't been cleaned in a while."

Marino's eyes dart around as the clocks tick tock tick tock, and the rain drums the roof louder, softer, then in a hard roll. The wind rushes and moans as I listen for the tactical team. I turn on alabaster sconces and a chandelier, and they glow wanly. The centuries-old oil paintings of landscapes, the stern portraits on the oak-paneled walls are just as dark, the room just as gloomy.

An elaborately embroidered screen blocks off the deep brick fireplace, and I don't see any indication it's ever used. I don't smell the stale acrid odor of old burned wood and soot. I don't see sawdust, firewood or firelogs, and I think how dreary. Even on a sunny day it would be. There's no television and I can't find a sound system or speakers anywhere, and there are no magazines or newspapers. Not that I can imagine reading in here or relaxing with a friend.

The room is vast and unlived in, and as I stand silently and look around I detect a vague spectrum of other odors. Musty upholstery. Mothballs. Dust is on every surface and suspended in the overhead light, and I entertain stronger doubts about Chanel Gilbert's housekeeper.

THE LIVING ROOM hasn't been used or cleaned in quite a while, I tell Marino as I wander toward a menagerie of antique silver animals arranged on a pedestal table.

A horse, a grouse, a bison, a fish with glassy eyes, intricately handcrafted but tarnished and cold, and I see nothing whimsical. The decor is splendid but static and impersonal except for what I think of as talismans, symbols and tools of divination, and the clocks. Several are as old as the house including a lantern clock and a Swiss Gothic one.

"I can't imagine the housekeeper has been keeping this place up properly," I add, and I'm keenly mindful of the tactical team and what it's doing.

"The master bedroom's way in the back if you keep following the hallway." Marino walks to a window and pushes aside a panel of the deep red French jacquard curtains. "It's a long haul to the front door if you're in bed and someone rings the bell." He looks out at the dark rainy afternoon, and I hear the downpour and the wind but nothing else.

"I don't know what they pay Elsa Mulligan or how many hours she works but they aren't getting their money's worth." I continue making the point because Marino isn't interested in my domestic acumen, and he should be.

I try to envision Elsa Mulligan based on how she's been described, imagining her large framed glasses, her spiky black hair. Hyde commented that his first reaction was he assumed she was a family friend from Los Angeles, and she seems an odd choice for a housekeeping job. Clearly she isn't thorough or industrious, at least not about cleaning. If she shows up at eight o'clock every morning then what does she do while she's here? What she told Hyde strikes me as yet one more story we're supposed to believe that isn't adding up.

"Assuming Chanel was in the back of the house and wearing nothing but a robe you have to wonder how her body ended up near the front door," Marino is saying while my mind runs along multiple tracks, and I listen for creaking floors, for closing doors, for voices. "There's no way maybe the housekeeper moved the body in there?"

"Chanel wasn't killed in one place and then dragged or carried into the foyer if that's what you're asking."

"But the wiped-up blood we could see when you sprayed the marble," Marino considers. "Maybe there's other bloody areas that have been washed up."

"I suspect the goal of cleaning up blood in the foyer was to give us an initial impression of an accident. If you fall off a ladder you aren't going to leave impact blood spatter all over the place." I look around and listen for the tactical team. "If you want to lure people down the wrong path at the onset then you'd better clean up any blood or other evidence that doesn't fit with whatever it is you're staging," I add as we wait for any sign that there are four big men inside the house with us.

I listen to the rain and the clocks. Gusting wind rattles the windows. I hear nothing else.

"And this person knew you'd find wiped-up blood and figure it out eventually." Marino gets closer to saying what by now I'm sure is the inevitable and unfortunate truth. "There's no question Chanel was murdered where she was found. It's obvious, right?"

"Based on the blood pattern, yes," I reply. "She received her fatal injuries while she was down on the marble floor. That doesn't mean that's where the encounter started."

"Like someone got her on the floor without much of a struggle and started slamming her head."

"Based on my initial examination, the CT scan and what Luke told me that's the way it looks."

"We've seen this before, Doc." Marino doesn't mean in general.

He's alluding to blunt force trauma deaths that occurred in the past year when a Realtor named Patty Marsico was beaten to death in Nantucket, and young Gracie Smithers died similarly on a rocky shore in Marblehead.

"Carrie Grethen has a habit of bashing people's brains out like that." He's on her trail, locked in with no turning back.

"In several homicides we're aware of at any rate."

"The one in Nantucket last Thanksgiving." He heads there as a crow flies. "Then the one in Marblehead in June. She mixes up her MOs. Beatings, a stabbing, shootings with a PGF, a spear gun. Indoors, outdoors, on land, on a boat, underwater. Whatever the hell she feels like."

He leans close to the handcrafted silver fish on the pedestal table, nudging the articulated tail with his purple nitrile-sheathed knuckle.

"This is kind of strange. It's actually a box." Anger hardens his tone as he carefully picks it up and the tail moves, the eyes staring at me. "A heavy one, must be solid silver. Except I can't open it because it's glued shut. I can smell the glue so it wasn't applied all that long ago. Maybe while we were gone. Maybe while the clocks were being wound. I don't hear anything loose inside." As he shakes it a little. "So here's what I have to say, Doc. What happened to Chanel Gilbert is personal. It's sexual. This isn't about a burglary or some other crime that got out of control and ended in murder. It's obvious what we've got is sick and demented, and we're being jerked around and we know by who. Of course that's just me talking. I'm not that kind of expert. I'm not Benton."

I've paused by the fireplace to look at the clocks, at the bookcases filled with leather-bound books on either side of the wide stone hearth. "It's all about power," I tell him as he squats by the scene case and begins pulling out trays. "Everything with her is about power. That's what she loves. It's what sexually excites and drives her. You don't have to be a profiler to figure that out."

Marino finds a small plastic bottle labeled ACETONE and returns to the small table next to the cherry sofa with black leather cushions. He picks up the silver fish box in his gloved hands.

"Let's hope it's not a bomb." He's almost joking. "If it is then I'll just kiss my ass good-bye." He finds camera equipment.

"And mine by the way."

"Someone glued the lid on and I don't think it was all that long ago. I want to know why." He starts taking photographs of the box. "The other alternative is to bring in the bomb squad. Maybe Amanda Gilbert would like to watch. Let's see what else we can do to put her on the friggin' warpath."

He digs in the scene cases for fingerprint powder and brushes. I peruse old books as he checks the silver box for latent prints, finding not so much as a smudge. He swabs for DNA and he's getting angrier and more aggressive. He's feeling manipulated and mocked. I know when the pressure is building inside Marino, and he's about to blow.

"I mean you think it's her." He angrily rips open a packet of swabs. "By now you don't have any second thoughts." It's not a question. He's telling me as if there can be no doubt. And there isn't. We know.

"Yes," I reply.

"And you've been thinking it all day."

"It's been on my mind since I started getting the videos." I slide books off shelves, opening them, looking for any indication they meant something to someone. "I think it's a foregone conclusion who we're dealing with."

"But usually you'd be on the phone to Benton." Marino dips a swab in acetone. "And except when we were leaving Lucy's house you haven't been in touch with him at all. Not even before you knew he was up in the helicopter. You've been shutting him out of everything."

I offer no answer or explanation. I'm not going to discuss Benton with him, and I continue to scan musty-smelling books that without exception are arcane. Fly-fishing. Hunting dogs. Gardening. Stone masonry in nineteenth-century England. I've come across similar miscellaneous collections in homes accessorized by interior decorators who buy antique books by the yard.

"Most of what you're seeing is impersonal," I inform Marino but he's distracted. "Except for the hourglasses, the spinning wheels, the candles, the iron crosses, and the clocks," I add and he isn't paying attention. "They're not part of the decor. They seem collected for some reason, possibly a symbolic one." I say nothing more.

Marino has the silver box open and is walking toward me. His face is an angry dark red. He holds both halves of the silver box in one gloved hand, pointing the fish's head away from us. He touches his finger to his lips at the same instant I hear movement in the central hallway.

"Looks like she read strange stuff." Marino makes bland small talk, alerting me that there's a problem.

We've been talking inside this house and shouldn't have been. We've been discussing this case and Carrie, and someone has been listening. I can very well imagine who.

"I don't think anybody's been reading these books," I add to our mundane discussion as the small black device inside the fish box continues to record us.

The eyes are actually pinholes for the mini-recorder lens and microphone, and I'm reminded of the electric pencil sharpener in Lucy's Quantico dorm room. I remember the dragon in her rock garden and the garnet Mona Lisa eyes that seemed to follow me. I feel the hair prickle on my arms and the back of my neck even as I act as if nothing is wrong.

"I doubt these were collected because someone wanted to read them," I'm saying to Marino as he carries the silver box and its concealed recording device to the other side of the room. "I suspect what you're seeing is an example of the L.A. influence. It's as if much of her home was designed like a movie set with eclectic antiques, rugs and old paintings of people and places that likely had no connection to anyone that matters."

"And that means what to you besides Chanel Gilbert comes from Hollywood money?" He opens a paper evidence bag as we continue to talk as if nothing is abnormal.

"It tells me she parked herself here. But she lived somewhere else. Possibly metaphorically." I feel a presence and turn around.

The four officers in black ballistic gear are in the doorway.

CHAPTER 35

MARINO FOLDS THE TOP OF THE BROWN PAPER BAG, sealing it with red tape.

"Battery operated, wireless, and probably installed not all that long ago." He says this to Ajax, who suggests they call in the cyber investigation unit to sweep the house for surveillance devices.

"We should get that going ASAP," he adds.

"Not until we're done and the hell out of here. I don't need any more cops stomping through." Marino finds a Sharpie in the scene case.

"Thanks a lot."

"I wasn't talking about you. I meant the geek squad, and while they're at it they also should look for anything capable of jamming radio signals and rerouting cell phone traffic." Marino uses his teeth to pull the cap off a Sharpie.

"Someone might be listening. Where there's one device there are probably others," Ajax warns him. "These days I assume there's cameras everywhere."

"Let them listen. Screw whoever it is including the Feds. Hello, Feds," Marino says loudly, rudely. "So nice of you to join us."

"Nothing caught my attention when we were looking around but that doesn't mean you've got privacy. Like I said, I never assume I've got privacy except hopefully in my own home." Ajax is talking to both of us. "And even there we got cameras. But I know where they are in that case."

"Maybe Chanel Gilbert didn't have privacy either. Maybe she was being spied on." Marino just keeps on talking. "Or maybe she was blocking any attempt at someone spying on her. No matter which it is we should be asking the same question. Who the hell was she and what was she involved in?"

"You're clear in here," Ajax lets us know but his eyes are riveted to me now.

I know what his opinion is. He doesn't have to say it and out of respect for me he won't. But he wears his doubt like a sandwich sign and there can be no question what he would advise if asked. He'd point out that if the situation merits a special response team searching the property then I shouldn't be here.

To tactical operators, to troops involved in the active warfare of military and sting operations, I'm nonessential personnel. If the order on any given day is kill or be killed? Then justice and the way something might play out in court are low on the list. They may not be on the list at all. The Ajaxes of the world aren't the excavators, the scientists who have to interpret and decipher what they discover. Special ops shoot the cobras. It's up to me to figure out if it was merited. That's my job. I walked off it earlier today. I won't again.

"No sign of anyone upstairs or down," Ajax continues to brief us. "In fact if you ask me it doesn't look like most of the house has been lived in for a while. Other than the master bedroom at the back of this floor. Someone's definitely using that. Or was."

He waits near the doorway, the three other cops behind him in the hallway, their forearms resting on the matte black stocks of the rifles across their chests, barrels pointed down, their night vision goggles flipped up on their helmets. When they shift their weight or move they are subtle and silent. They're agile and nonreactive. They're disciplined, stoical, what I consider the perfect hero blend of selflessness and narcissism. You have to love yourself if you're going to fight gloriously and bravely, if you're going to survive at any price while protecting a person or a people with your life. It's a contradiction. It seems illogical. It's not a stereotype or a cliché when I say that special ops aren't like the rest of us.

"So unless there's anything else?" Ajax asks Marino.

"Nothing right now except for whatever's happened to Hyde." He finishes labeling the bag and puts the cap back on the Sharpie, tosses it into the top tray of the open Pelican case. "I heard from Lapin but still nothing from Hyde. We know he made a phone call from here before he left this morning and it's just more of the same crazy crap. We ping his phone and it comes back to a cell tower right here that doesn't exist. It sounds to me like someone is scrambling, jamming radio signals, turning this location into a dead zone for communications."

"Unless he uses his phone again we won't get anything else." Ajax joins his team in the hallway. "If you don't hit SEND? There's no signal and we can't find you. It's unusual that he's not used his phone for the past three hours. Unless you're sick, disabled or someplace that makes you turn it off, you're going to use your phone for something."

"No shit," Marino says.

"Are you sure his phone's not here somewhere?" one of the other cops asks. "Any possibility he might have dropped it, set it down and doesn't have it with him? I mean we didn't see it anywhere. But that doesn't mean it's not here. What happens when you call his number?"

"It goes straight to voice mail like the phone's turned off or the battery's dead." Marino tries Hyde's number again. "Straight to voice mail just like it's been doing."

"It's on the air that we're looking for him and his car," Ajax says. "Everybody's looking from here to Timbuktu. I'll get a couple backups on the perimeter so you two don't get lonely."

"We won't be here much longer." Marino slides his phone back into a pocket. "The Doc wants a walk-through of the important areas, and then we're out. I need the backup units to stay in place until we find Hyde, until we figure out what happened to the victim's Range Rover. No one unauthorized steps foot on this property or inside the house unless I say."

"Roger that," Ajax says. "You know where to find me."

Marino and I watch them leave, disappearing down the hallway, past the staircase, into the foyer. I listen for the front door to shut. I can barely make out the sound of their SUV starting up. I'm keenly aware that we're alone again, and I feel the emptiness and the silence as Marino returns to the foyer. He leaves the taped-up paper bag and other evidence near the door.

"You heard what he said," I say as he walks back to me. "If there's one covert device there could be others."

"I would count on it. Ready?" He snaps shut the scene case and picks it up.

Back into the hallway and the next right is the dining room, small with a low ceiling, the table built of an old barn door and surrounded by eight rustic brown leather chairs. Overhead is a Tiffany pendant chandelier, and I scan the dark oil pastoral scenes beneath gallery lights. The paintings depict cows and rolling hills, and meadows and mountains, seventeenth- and eighteenth-century English and Dutch. The dishes in the Georgian break-front cabinet are very old Chinese porcelain, and I detect the hand of a decorator again.

Pale gold damask draperies are drawn over the glass sliders, and I part the heavy satiny fabric. I look out at a narrow side yard hemmed in by a wrought-iron fence. Rain splashes deep puddles that are like small ponds, and rose petals litter the lawn like pastel confetti. The fence terminates at a tall dense boxwood hedge at the back of the property. I notice loose bricks and large stones, a hint of ruins possibly from an outbuilding in an earlier more gracious era, and I'm reminded of the people of New England. They'll work around and build on the past. But they'll never get rid of it.

Then I hear it again. A muffled thud. As if someone just slammed a door a floor below us in the cellar.

"What the hell was that?" Marino's hand drops to his gun. "Stay here," he orders me, as if I'd ever consider such a thing.

"I'm not staying anywhere alone in this house." I follow him past the staircase, and he opens the door I saw him use this morning, flipping on lights.

"I'm checking," he says.

"I'm right behind you."

The wooden stairs leading down are very old and scuffed, and the walls are stone. I feel as if I'm descending into the bowels of an old English castle as I take one steep step at a time, slowly, pausing every other second and careful with my leg. The air is cool. I smell dust. I detect fluctuations in light and shadow as if clouds are passing over the sun. But there are no clouds down here. There's no sun. The cellar is subbasement and there are no windows.

"What's moving?" I ask Marino. "There's a light barely moving on the wall."

"I don't know." He's in front of me with his gun drawn.

Ten steps and then a landing, and four more steps and we're inside an empty windowless space of stone and plaster walls, and I scan stone-pillared archways and a rough stone floor covered with rush mats. Suspended by braided fabric cords from the high cave-like ceiling are ceramic funnel lamps, and the one closest to the bulkhead doors is swinging slightly.

We silently stare up at it, then at the double doors, the wood gray on this side, repainted many times, and I notice dried water spots. The doors were opened at some point when it was raining. They're built into the wall about four feet off the ground and accessed by a stone ramp that is bone dry and very clean. I notice that the latch lock is modern and the key is in it. There's no sign that the doors are alarmed, and Marino pushes them with a Tyvek-covered shoe. They don't budge. He looks up at the lamp swaying imperceptibly now as if touched by a spirit or a draft.

"What we just heard wasn't these doors shutting," he decides. "If someone had just gone out this way they wouldn't be locked. Not with the key still inside. And rain would have gotten in. There'd be water and dirt that washed in from the flower bed."

Not if the person cleaned up afterward.

Marino holds his Glock in his right hand, the barrel pointed down as he walks to another door, this one in the far wall, a normal pedestrian door painted white. He climbs the four stone steps leading up to it.

"Locked and dead bolted." His Tyvek-covered feet make a slippery sound on stone as he returns to me. "I don't know why the hell this light was moving unless something ran into it, maybe flew into it. This joint probably has bats."

"We definitely heard what sounded like a door shutting, and we've heard it more than once today. Are you suggesting bats are responsible for that too?" I say as my phone rings, and I'm surprised I have a signal down here.

I look at the display. It's Jen Garate. She's parking on the driveway and I tell her to meet me at the top of the steps near the supercans at the east side of the house.

"Why is there a roll of crime scene tape in the flower bed by those big wooden doors?" she asks. "I assume you noticed it?"

"Stay away from the front of the house," I tell her. "Meet me exactly where I just told you and don't touch anything."

I USE TYVEK as an umbrella, holding a disposable lab coat over my head as I step outside on the landing. The rain is steady but not as hard, the sky lighter to the south.

I block the open door. I hope if we stay out here we won't be overheard by any interior surveillance devices that might be hidden somewhere. Beyond that there's nothing I can do, and it's not the first time I've worried about drop cams, nanny cams and other home security devices that are increasingly common and easy to use. When I work a crime scene these days it always enters my mind that what we do and say may not be private.

Jen Garate climbs out of the CFC SUV she's parked in front of my truck. Dressed in rain gear she trots toward me, her rubber boots splashing through water as if she's having great fun. She's loud on the wooden steps. She's excited as we exchange keys, her wet fingers fumbling and pushy.

"Don't go into the back of the truck except to remove the packaged evidence," I instruct her, and I'm not friendly or about to let her into the house.

That's what she wants. It's obvious she's desperate to come inside.

"They're in the first locker." I'm all business as I explain. "Receipt the packages to Ernie after you've left the truck in the evidence bay. He'll take it from there."

"I need more details about what happened to it." Her long dark hair is tied back, her eyes intensely blue beneath her baseball cap as she stares past me into the kitchen.

"I've given you the information you need for now."

"I'm happy to come in and help," she says. "It must be complicated or you wouldn't have been here earlier and come back. Marino's with you?"

"He is?" It's my way of reminding her that she's not to interrogate me.

"Hey don't mess with me cuz I know he's with you." She's teasing seductively, talking fast as if she's on speed. "I've heard his radio chatter. That officer he's looking for? What's his name? Hyde as in Doctor Jekyll? Just so you know, it's on Twitter that Cambridge P.D. is looking for him, that there's an APB because it appears he's vanished off the radar and they can't find his police cruiser. Do you know what happened?"

"I'm not the one listening to radio chatter. You tell me." I don't answer her questions, and I don't like the way she continues looking past me and inching closer to the open door.

"I can finish up in here with Marino so you can get back." She doesn't offer but says it like a directive, and I feel my dislike of her intensify.

Jen Garate is pretty in a bad girl way, midthirties with olive skin and a full-bodied figure that she loves to flaunt. When she applied for the job I didn't give much thought to her tattoos and Gothic jewelry or her snug skimpy clothing, and none of that is my real problem with her. What I have come to object to and resent are her invasiveness and histrionics. Everything she does is motivated by her own brand of exhibitionism. She can be digging up skeletal remains or recovering a dead body from a river and she somehow makes it a sexy spectator sport.

"Please get the truck back as discussed," I tell her, "and I'll see you and everyone shortly I hope."

She lingers on the top step as rain smacks her rain suit, dark blue with FORENSICS in yellow on the back. A sly smile, a smirk creep over her face.

"Sorry to hear about Lucy," she says and I don't react.

I play dumb as Marino's heavy footsteps enter the kitchen.

"What do you mean you're sorry about her?" I ask Jen calmly, as if there is nothing on earth that might bother me right now.

"Well from the way I hear it the helicopter buzzing her house this morning wasn't hers."

"And where might you have heard such a thing?" I ask and Marino is behind me in the kitchen.

I step inside next to him, both of us out of the rain and leaving her in it.

"Is Lucy in trouble?" Jen stares at him. "I sort of have a right to know. I mean even you have a right to know, Pete. Doesn't matter that you aren't at the CFC anymore. You and Lucy are really close. So if she's in trouble with the Feds don't you think you should be aware? That everyone around her should be?"

"What makes you think she's in trouble?" he asks.

"BAPERN."

The Boston Area Police Emergency Radio Network includes more than a hundred different local agencies, and the state police and the FBI. I can't imagine why anything about Lucy or her property would have been broadcast over BAPERN.

"I know the FBI had a chopper up and it was pretty obvious where it was," Jen explains. "Lucy's big spread in Concord."

"Oh yeah? And why would the Feds be talking about one of their tactical helicopters over BAPERN?" Marino glowers at her. "The answer is they wouldn't. They'd be on the Air Traffic Control freq."

"It wasn't the Feds talking. It was the Concord cops. Plus your big truck was complained about." She directs this to me. "You blocked in an FBI car or something? Apparently a Concord cruiser checked out why the chopper was flying over Lucy's house and there was talk about our truck blocking an FBI car."

"No shit," Marino says snidely. "And guess what? It's not our job to answer your questions. You need to leave."

"I'm not asking questions. I'm telling you stuff you clearly don't know."

"We don't need your help."

"Maybe you're not smart enough to ask for it." She stares defiantly at him and I can't believe it.

He slams the door shut in her face. The last thing I see is Jen Garate's mouth dropping open as she protests. I move to the window over the sink. I stand there looking out as she goes down the steps. She follows the walkway and drives off in the big white truck, and I feel satisfaction when the tires slide off the bricks and bump through mud. She overcorrects, fishtailing slightly. I drive the damn thing better than she does.

CHAPTER 36

THE OLD SAYING THAT YOU ARE WHAT YOU EAT has morbid implications if you're me. I can tell a lot about people from what's in their cupboards and trash.

Marino and I are searching the kitchen now as I caution him about Jen. It's not the first time and likely won't be the last. The empty trash can is exactly as we left it, no bag inside, the plastic liner pulled up far enough to keep the lid open.

"I just wish you wouldn't," I'm saying.

"You know me. I'm always honest." He shuts a drawer of pot holders and dish towels.

"Please don't give her any reason to sue the CFC, calling it a hostile workplace, for example, because people like you slam doors in her face. I don't care if it's honest."

"I don't like her and it's not because she has my old job."

Inside the refrigerator I scan shelves of bottled water and

juices, and white wine, sticks of butter and condiments. I think about Chanel's gastric contents. It would seem she ate a seafood dish, possibly a creole gumbo, stew or soup shortly before she was murdered. But I don't see fresh vegetables such as peppers and onions or anything that suggests she cooked such a thing, and there's no take-out box. I begin to wonder about the trash that's disappeared. I mention it in a guarded way to Marino, knowing our every word may be monitored.

I let him know I'm not seeing anything that might indicate someone has eaten or prepared food in recent memory. The only exception is the cold-pressed fresh juices. There are five glass bottles of them, deep red concoctions. I open one and smell ginger, cayenne pepper, kale and beets. I seriously doubt the perishable drinks are available in any grocery store I've been to in the Cambridge area, and I'm again reminded that this house isn't even two miles from mine. It's barely ten minutes from my office. It's possible Chanel Gilbert and I shopped, gassed up our cars, ran errands in some of the same places.

"A lot of these fresh juice companies deliver," I'm saying to Marino. "And this particular brand isn't one I've ever seen in a store."

He picks up a bottle of the dark red juice, turns it in his hand, inspecting the label. The name of the company is 1-Octen. It occurs to me the bottles look like the ones I saw in a bag in the back of the red Range Rover.

"No company address anywhere, no expiration date. Sort of looks like a computer-generated label, sort of homemade?" He returns the bottle to the shelf, takes off his gloves and dips into a pocket for his phone. "And now I'm Googling it and nothing. There's no such company. A freaky name. Maybe as in *octane*? Like a high-octane super fuel or food?"

"Or in *one-octen-three-one*," I suggest. "The molecular composition for the odorant that depending on other things causes blood to smell metallic."

"Blood?"

"This particular blend of juice obviously is heavy in beets, explaining the deep red color. Like blood, like the essence, the fluid of life. Beets are high in iron, and iron is what we smell when blood touches our skin. One-Octen is an odd if not distasteful name for a food."

"Maybe Chanel Gilbert bottled it herself. Like I said it sort of looks homemade."

"Then we need to find a juicer, a food processor, a Ninja. And I don't see anything like that here in the kitchen."

"Well maybe she was into vampires in addition to all the occult shit everywhere," he says sarcastically.

"It appears that she or someone was vegan and on a gluten-free diet." I'm looking in the pantry now. "Nothing with wheat. No cheese, fish or meat in her refrigerator or freezer. Lots of herbal teas and nutritional supplements. Again there's nothing perishable except the juice."

I refrain from telling him about Chanel Gilbert's gastric contents. Vegans would abstain from shrimp or any seafood and yet that seems to be the last thing she ate before she was murdered. Was she out at a restaurant last night? Was the food delivered or brought to her by someone she knew? Are remnants of her last meal in the trash that's missing? Was she really vegan? I don't give voice to such questions. I don't want anyone spying on us gifted with autopsy details.

I retrieve an evidence bag from the scene case, deciding to take a bottle of the red juice with me because it's inconsistent with the context. The juices are fresh. Nothing else is. It's as if nobody has been living here for a while and yet someone has been. I'm seeing things that contradict each other. I'm picking up mixed signals. Suddenly and in unison the clocks begin to chime. It's three P.M. Next there's a burst of radio chatter.

Marino turns up the volume, adjusts the squelch, and there's a report of a fight in progress in a parking lot on North Point Boulevard.

"Two white males, possibly juveniles in a late-model red SUV. One has on a baseball cap, the other a sweatshirt with a hood, apparently intoxicated and arguing outside the vehicle . . . ," the dispatcher is saying, and a marked unit responds that it's in the area, then another one does.

Marino tucks the radio back in a pocket. "Come on, Doc," he says to me with a sigh. "Let's get this over with."

WE HEAD DOWN a hallway of wide board pine flooring that I suspect is original to the house.

The walls are stucco and hung with more old dark English art. A doorway leads into an oak-paneled library that's a gallery of underwater photographs illuminated by vintage mirrored sconces that have been electrified. Built-in bookcases are crowded with more antique leather volumes most likely purchased as decor, and for a moment I stand in the doorway conducting my usual high recon as Lucy calls it.

I take in the exposed dark timber beams in the white plaster ceiling, the wood-burning stove built into a deep stone fireplace. The wide board floor is covered with rush mats just like the ones in the cellar, and between the two curtained windows is an inlaid mahogany and satinwood writing desk. The computer that was on it has been taken to the labs, Marino informs me.

I begin to walk around the library table. It's at least ten feet long with a parquetry top and an elaborately hand-carved base. In the center is an empty crystal decanter, several small glasses, and another clock tick-tocking, this one tortoiseshell, gilt and colorful enamel, possibly late eighteenth century and musical. I check my watch. It's now exactly four minutes past three P.M. The clock has been synced with the others.

"Was there any other indication that Chanel Gilbert worked in here? What else was on the desk?" I begin looking at the framed photographs of sea turtles, eagle rays and barracuda.

There are rainbow parrot fish, Spanish lobster, a queen conch and a goliath grouper near the shadowy carcasses of sunken ships. The water is vivid shades of green and blue, and sunlight filters through it from the surface.

"In here we collected the computer, one of these Mac Pro desktops." Marino watches me look around at dive scenes vibrantly reflected in the mirrored sconces. "Plus we got her phone. She also has a router but there was no point in taking that, the TV and other electronics. Not at that time."

"What about a laptop, an iPad, any other devices?"

He shakes his head and I wonder who doesn't have a laptop or an iPad these days. But we don't discuss it. I take my time perusing the sea creatures and sunken vessels as another bad feeling billows up from the darkest depths of my psyche. It slowly comes to me that what I'm seeing is familiar.

I look more closely and begin to recognize the scattered remains of the Greek steamer *The Pelinaion* that sank during World War II. I know *The Hermes, The Constellation* and many other shipwrecks in the Bermuda Triangle. Where I've been diving many times. Where I was shot on June 15. Exactly two months ago to the day.

"You didn't say anything about these." I indicate the photographs, and I don't mean to sound accusatory but I can't help myself.

Where I was shot.

"Paintings of cows, photos of fish." Marino shrugs as he looks around. "What's the big deal?"

Where I was shot!

"The diver here. Here. Here . . ." I walk around pointing, my right thigh throbbing. "It's the same person. Isn't this her? Isn't this Chanel Gilbert?"

The woman looks young and fit in a three-millimeter-thick black wet suit with double white stripes around the right thigh. Her fins and mask are black, and her hair is brown, and then I notice the zipper. It stops me in my tracks, startling me. I search my memory for what I saw in the video my dive mask recorded. I remember the double white stripes on the leg of the wet suit Benton was wearing as he tried to place the regulator into my mouth, and then I catch myself.

How can I be sure it was Benton? He's always said he helped me to the surface after I was shot. I've never had a reason to doubt him until today, until this very minute, and I envision what Lucy played for me inside the boathouse. In truth I couldn't identify the diver in the video. I couldn't swear it was Benton, and I didn't notice the person's wet suit zipper either. But in these photographs I'm looking at now the wet suit looks the same as what I saw earlier today—and the zipper is in front. Most are in back with a very long pull tab so you can reach around and zip yourself up.

Chest zippers are relatively new. Some people find them preferable because the neoprene isn't as restrictive when a zipper doesn't run the length of the wet suit in back. I tend to associate chest zippers with tactical divers, with the police and military, and no wet suit Benton or I own zips in front. It wasn't him in the video. It wasn't my FBI husband. I don't know who it was or why the person was there or if the diver I'm looking at right now in these photographs inside Chanel Gilbert's library saved my life and now is dead.

I walk around and study every photograph, estimating that the woman in them is medium height and weighs approximately 130 pounds. She's looking directly into the camera, and I continue superimposing that image on what I saw earlier today. I'm almost certain they're the same person but when I examined the dead body this morning, the hair was so bloody it was difficult to tell the color.

The nose was broken, the eyes almost swollen shut. The photo on Chanel's driver's license wasn't recent and her face was fuller, her hair lighter and longer. But I believe she and the diver are one and the same. This can't be a coincidence. In fact it's part of the plan. Not my plan. Not Marino's plan. Carrie's plan.

The Bermuda Triangle. Where I was shot.

I say this to Marino and he instantly dismisses it. "You were shot off the coast of South Florida. It didn't happen in the Bermuda Triangle." He glances around, looking for surveillance devices we're not going to see.

"You draw a line from Miami to San Juan, Puerto Rico, to Bermuda and that's the Bermuda Triangle," I reply and geography isn't my bigger point.

Did Lucy know her?

She was in Bermuda last week. When she landed at Logan her private jet was searched by Customs agents. That's what I want to ask Marino about but I'm not going to say it. He stares at me, then at the photographs on the wall, and I overhear traffic on the handheld radio he has jammed into the back pocket of his borrowed black tactical pants. The reported altercation on North Point Boulevard was unfounded. The police have cleared the parking lot.

"Obviously Chanel was familiar with wreck diving in Bermuda." I point to a photograph of the female diver swimming close to a nurse shark. "The more I look? The more I'm sure that's her unless she's got an identical twin."

"I don't know anything about her being a scuba diver," Marino says. "Only that she must have liked underwater photography or her mother or the decorator did."

"It's easy enough to find out."

There should be certification cards for the Professional Association of Diving Instructors (PADI) or for the National Association of Underwater Instructors (NAUI). She would have taken courses. She would have certifications and her name should be on membership lists. She should have dive gear in the house unless she kept it someplace else, and I bring that up again.

"Does she have other homes?" I ask and my stubborn calm is shaken.

"Good question."

What I really want to know is if she and Lucy were recently together in Bermuda. Lucy said she went there to dive but she wouldn't do that alone. Lucy would never dive without a dive buddy, and maybe her buddy was Chanel Gilbert—the person Lucy described as a friend of Janet's. We have to find that out. The electronic devices collected from here have been receipted to Lucy's lab or will be before the day is out.

I can't have her going through Chanel's computers, her phone, her thumb drives and any surveillance equipment if the two of them had a personal relationship. Even as I entertain such thoughts a part of me knows better. Lucy may not return to my office. Not ever. I don't know what's going on with her right now. I have no idea what might happen next and how far the FBI might go to ruin the rest of her life.

But I say none of this to Marino because if I do I'll be saying it to anybody else who might be listening. I'd be saying it to Carrie. I might be saying it to the FBI, and it occurs to me next that Lucy may not know Chanel is dead. That's assuming she knew her at all. We've not released her identity yet and I decide I'd better make sure there's nothing on the Internet. I call Bryce again. The connection is bad. I ask him where he is.

CHAPTER 37

THE RECEPTION'S NEVER GOOD IN HERE," HE SAYS. "You know because of the magnetic field? Imagine a flock of starlings lifting out of the trees all at once? This big black cloud of demonic birds and that's what it's like when all these little electrons fly around and mess up your phone? I could call you on a landline if you prefer."

"That won't work," I reply.

"You're breaking up a little so I'll make this quick."

"I'm the one calling you, Bryce."

"Hello? Doctor Scarpetta, hello? Can you hear me okay? It's Fort Knox in here."

"I have only a minute."

"Sorry. There I've moved. Can you hear me better? Whoa I almost feel a little woozy. Well probably from oxygen deprivation. I do think it's worse after he's vacuumed down the chamber, sucking all the air out and maybe that changes the level in the lab. How could it not? I'm sitting down and just realized I've not eaten a single thing today. Well kale chips that had been in my drawer too long."

My chatty chief of staff is with Ernie inside the trace evidence lab with its thick steel-reinforced concrete walls, ceiling and floor. That's why the cell phone reception is never good in there. It's not because of the Scanning Electron Microscope (SEM) or Fourier Transform Infrared spectroscopy (FTIR) or any other high-tech instrument we use in the identification of unknown materials. They can't possibly make Bryce woozy. But he doesn't need the assistance of any special circumstances, locations or equipment to spin himself into a dizzying state.

"You go first with updates." I'm mindful that any covert recording devices inside the Gilbert house can monitor only my side of the conversation.

What Bryce is saying won't be overheard. Unless my cell phone has been tapped. Unless Carrie has hacked into it or the FBI has. I will myself to be cool and calm, to concentrate on what I'm doing and why I'm here. But it's getting more difficult, close to impossible. Chanel Gilbert dove the Bermuda Triangle. Lucy was just in Bermuda. Now Chanel has been murdered and Lucy's property has been raided by the FBI. A police officer is missing, and Marino and I are alone again inside this house where clocks are mysteriously wound, the table set, and doors open and shut on their own it seems. It's as if we can't escape gravity here. It's pulling us in like a black hole.

"Well, the headline is the way-cool thing Anne found," Bryce launches in about why he's in the trace evidence lab.

"I hope you don't mean it literally as in something that's in the news."

"No! But it's so exciting it should be in the news and I'm sure it will be huge when it eventually hits."

"Not now. Not until I say."

"You're talking like someone has a gun pointed at your head or you've been turned into bad animation in a bad Lego movie. I take that to mean Big Brother's watching you not that there's such a thing as privacy at all anymore. So I'll do the talking. Anne found a weird piece of glass sticking to blood and I'm thinking good God what could have happened? How did this thing get on Chanel Gilbert's body? I mean it's true she lived in a house that goes back to when they were still hanging witches on the Common. But unless you saw other stuff like this inside her . . . ?"

"Other stuff?"

"The mineral fingerprint that showed up on SEM."

"Can you be more specific? I assume Ernie's with you . . . ?"

"Okay hold on."

In the background I hear Ernie's voice, then Bryce is back with the answer. "Specifically sand quartz, soda ash and limestone. In other words glass. With trace amounts of silver and gold." He parrots what Ernie is saying to him. "Almost undetectable traces. But that could be from dirt obviously."

"What dirt?"

"Well the bit of broken bead's been somewhere the sun don't shine all these hundreds of years. Gold and silver could be in the dirt and therefore not really part of the glass but then again they certainly could be. You can't see it with the naked eye, what he calls *a whisper of precious metals*. Which is such a poetic way to put it. There's also lead."

"Has he identified something that might tell us where this particular item had been before it somehow ended up where it did?" I'm mindful of my every word and tempted not to be.

She wants to control you.

"A teeny tiny piece of a cockroach wing which is why I mentioned dirt as in nasty spaces and hidey-holes where critters congregate," Bryce says. "Oh my God maybe the source is the actual house? Holy shit. Are you noticing insects? Is it slovenly? I hope it doesn't get out about Amanda Gilbert that her daughter lived like one of these hoarders on TV with their filth and dead pets and bugs everywhere . . . ?"

"Tell Ernie I'm going to call him directly."

"Wait a minute. He's saying something. What . . . ?"

I hear Ernie's voice in the background again. I make out the word *millefiore,* Italian for *a thousand flowers.* He's referring to a type of bead made centuries ago in Venice and used as currency.

I HANG UP on Bryce and enter the number for Ernie's lab. Suddenly my favorite microscopist is in my earpiece, and the sound of his familiar voice is a comfort and a relief.

"It goes without saying this isn't something I usually come across, Kay, but it's familiar," he explains. "I'm not an archaeologist and don't pretend to be but over the years I've become sort of an armchair one, a Sherlock at rooting through society's detritus. When you've worked enough cases there isn't much you don't see, including remnants from the past. Like minié and musket balls that mistakenly end up in the labs or buttons and bones that turn out to be from the American Revolution."

"Which is what you think this is from. The past."

"I've seen similar artifacts. You know how much I've always loved digging things up microscopic and otherwise, and you may remember a couple years ago I took my family to Jamestown, to the excavation there. We got a personal tour of the site, got to go through the lab and see all the artifacts. That's one reason the piece of glass from your scene at Brattle Street is familiar. It's reminiscent of trade beads our early colonists used to snooker the Indians. Especially beads that were blue like the sky. I guess they were passed off as good luck or magical."

"You're talking about a time period of the late fifteen hundreds, early sixteen hundreds," I reply.

"Your broken bead might be that old."

"Any details you can give me, Ernie."

"What we've got is a decent-size fragment that's multifaceted, made from three layers of glass, probably by molding it over the heat of an oil lamp as opposed to drawn or blown glass that requires a proper work space and equipment like a kiln. Once upon a time making beads was a cottage industry sort of like minting your own money, and typically the finishing touch was adding dots of colored glass or thin threads of gold, copper, silver, a pièce de résistance for the perfect gaudy bauble."

"How big?" I continue to talk in a vague way but pressure is building inside me and heating me up.

"Five by three millimeters from a bead that I'm guessing was about the size of a small pearl. Probably about nine or ten millimeters, which is consistent with what they called trade or slave beads. Supposedly Christopher Columbus swapped them for supplies and permission to sail through unfriendly waters. Don't be impressed. I just found it on the Internet. Beads like yours were also the major currency for the slave trade in West Africa. You know hand over some fancy trinkets and sail off with a ship full of gold, ivory and stolen human beings."

"You referenced colors." There can be no question that what he's describing isn't remotely similar to the quartz-like metamaterial I found on Lucy's property.

"Shades of blue with a little bit of green," Ernie says and I think of the cockroach wing.

I've seen no insects dead or alive inside this house except for the flies, and I'm reminded of the dust bunny inside my clean truck. I think of the debris adhering to the pelt-like fletching of the arrow left as a gory surprise. Evidence that's transferred from another location, and maybe that's true of the glass fragment too. Nothing I've seen so far would give me reason to think the broken bead came from inside this house, at least not from the rooms we've searched.

"Call me as soon as you have anything else," I tell Ernie. "Jen should get to you soon . . ."

"She already did the minute she left the truck in the bay, and I need to get to that after a while too. Do you have any special instructions beyond what Bryce has passed along?"

"Work as fast as you possibly can."

"I'm slitting open one of your packages as we speak."

"I'm curious about a possible shared origin." I'm so cryptic I'm almost unintelligible, and I'm getting angry. "Does that make sense?" I'm like an engine about to overspeed.

"Loud and clear. You want to know if some or all of it could have come from the same location."

"And what type of one. As detailed and as quickly as possible."

"If I can tell you where and give you an exact address I will." He's teasing and he's not.

Ernie will get on this immediately because he knows me. We've worked together for years. He's patient and he listens, and it's just a shame I can't say the same about Bryce. I get him back on the phone.

I tell him in a no-nonsense way, "I have ten seconds. When I was here this morning I didn't see anything similar to what you and Ernie are describing."

"You probably wouldn't have."

"Where was it?" I resist saying the words *glass* or *bead*. "Where exactly on the body?" I'm on the verge of venting my temper.

Don't give her the satisfaction.

"Like I said in blood. Matted inside her bloody hair," Bryce says.

"Okay. Harold thought he saw something like that and then he couldn't find it."

"Well Anne found it on CT. It lit up like Times Square but itty-bitty like a split pea. It's so awesome to see it magnified five hundred times on SEM. You can make out the tool marks on it from where it was gripped while the glass was melted," he says cheerfully, as if we're having a happy conversation.

"Bryce, I need to be sure that Chanel Gilbert's name and any other information about her and the case haven't been released publicly."

"Certainly not by us. You know of course it's on Twitter."

"I didn't know that."

Lucy must know she's dead.

"Oh yes. As of just a little while ago. But I'm not surprised. Nothing's secret anymore," Bryce reminds me.

"What's being said?"

"Just that the daughter of the famous producer Amanda Gilbert was found dead in Cambridge this morning. I don't know who tweeted it. I guess a lot of people have."

I get off the phone and find myself staring at a photograph of a hammerhead shark. A big one with dead eyes and bared teeth. The diver is almost on top of it. She's not afraid. She might be smiling.

Don't give her your fear. Don't give her what she wants.

In another photo the same diver is removing a tangle of fishing line and a hook from a tiger shark's mouth. Chanel Gilbert. Brave and adventuresome. Kind to animals it would seem. Fearless. Sure of herself. Maybe overly confident. Maybe nothing phased her until she was beaten to death on her marble floor, and I envision a blitz attack. She didn't see it coming.

She was in the foyer barely dressed and didn't feel physically threatened. I found no defensive injuries that might indicate she attempted to protect herself. Then suddenly she was on the floor being knocked senseless. She was trusting for some reason. She was unguarded and thought she had nothing to fear or she wouldn't have been in her foyer almost naked. It's unlikely she would have been in such a state of undress and vulnerability were the person she was with a stranger.

She knew her killer.

The blood pattern shows she was murdered where she was found. But that doesn't mean her body didn't lie there for a while. That would explain the time of death not making sense, and another image comes to me. Carrie returning to the foyer and enjoying the afterglow. She may have lived with the dead body in situ for hours or days.

Their relationship was sexual. At least to her.

"See these?" I point at the photographs.

"Yeah I think you're right." Marino is looking over my shoulder. "It's Chanel Gilbert. Obviously she was a big diver."

"She doesn't seem to be afraid of much."

"Or else she was stupid. Anybody who tries to get the hook out of a shark's mouth is stupid if you ask me."

"I doubt she was stupid and we need to seriously question who she really was." I look at my watch and it's close to four.

"Her dental records . . . ," he starts to say.

"Yes they seem to confirm she's Chanel Gilbert but I think it's like everything else we're seeing, Marino. Nothing is what it appears to be. Including her."

I walk out of the library before he can answer. I don't wait for him to pack up his scene case.

"Hey! Wait up!" he yells but I'm not waiting for him or anyone.

He hurries after me, clutching the scene case, his Tyvek-covered feet thudding and sliding along the wooden hallway. It dead-ends at the master wing, an addition with oak floors and paneling that are different from what I've seen in other rooms. The stylistic elements are Gothic Revival, possibly mid-nineteenth century, the doorway an elaborate pointed arch. Inside are cluster columns and decorative molding. The drapes are drawn.

I flip on the lights and I'm a specter, a quiet vengeful presence working my fingers into a pair of black nitrile gloves. I don't move from the doorway as I look inside at the messy antique bed ornately carved with animals that watch over the room like gargoyles.

CHAPTER 38

THE COVERS ARE PULLED BACK AS IF CHANEL GILbert just got up and will return any second. That's assuming she was the one sleeping in here. That's assuming she was sleeping alone.

She—or someone—didn't bother to make the bed or even straighten it. She didn't get dressed. What happened? Did someone unexpected appear at the door? Was her killer already inside the house? The questions are landing fast, one after another, and I wonder if it was Chanel's habit to sleep nude. Did she get up and put on the black silk robe she was wearing when her body was found? Was she naked for some other reason?

I smell the stench of decomposing flesh but it's an olfactory phenomenon like a phantom pain. It's remembered. It's imagined. The odor has dissipated and I can't really smell it in this remote part of the house. But the thought of it is a reminder of an unavoidable fact that has gnawed at me all day. The advanced rate of decomposition argues that Chanel Gilbert didn't die late last night and definitely not this morning. Postmortem artifacts don't lie even during a heat wave when the air-conditioning has been turned off.

But the meaning of such morbid phenomena can be misinterpreted if we're given bad information, and I believe we have been, and that thought leads me to her gastric contents. The shrimp, rice, onions and peppers had barely begun to digest. A seafood creole or stew would be an unusual choice for breakfast but that doesn't mean much. People eat all sorts of things at whatever time suits them. What I can say with certainty is she ate lunch or dinner or a snack, she possibly had a beer or a glass of wine, and very soon afterward something happened. She died. Or she was so traumatized and distressed that she went into fight-or-flight mode and the blood rushed to her extremities. Either way her digestion completely stopped.

This could suggest she ate a meal with her assailant, possibly inside this house, possibly at the kitchen table that now has been set with a collector's plate taken off the wall. Possibly Chanel got up after her meal and moments later was beaten to death. Had she been out to dinner and was attacked at some point after she returned home it's likely her digestion would have been further along, and next I think of the missing kitchen trash bag. I play out a scenario of someone bringing take-out food to the house. It might have been Chanel. It might have been her killer—it might have been Carrie Grethen.

I imagine Chanel eating and possibly within minutes being attacked or dead, and I find it curious that evidence of her last meal isn't in the kitchen trash. It isn't in the supercans at the side of the house. There's no restaurant receipt anywhere either. But I don't really need evidence like that no matter how helpful it might be. Chanel's stomach contents tell me what she ingested before she died. I don't know if her killer correctly anticipated what we would find on autopsy. Perhaps even Carrie isn't well versed in the nuances of digestion.

Were it not for what the housekeeper claims I would place Chanel Gilbert's murder a good twenty-four hours earlier than we're supposed to believe. Not this morning or yesterday but possibly the midday or night before. In other words as early as Wednesday. The same day Bryce had our CFC vehicles washed and detailed. Possibly the same day the truck's taillight was tampered with.

The housekeeper is mistaken or lying.

"What really happened here?" I mutter to the empty room.

The wide board flooring is centered by an Oriental rug, the ceiling beamed. The ivory silk drapes are drawn, and behind them are blackout shades pulled down.

"Uh-oh." Marino is right behind me. "When you start talking to dead people it's time to call it a day."

I walk inside and smell flowers and spices. I follow my intuition and my nose. The scent leads me to a chest of drawers.

"I'd like to open these," I say to Marino.

"Be my guest."

"Did you look when we were here the first time?"

"I didn't have a reason to go through all her personal stuff, not that there was time. She was just an accident. Then we had to rush to Lucy's place."

"Well we're back."

"Yeah no shit."

I FEEL HIM STARING AT ME. I sense his heavy mood, his edginess as I find what I'm looking for in the first drawer I try.

It's empty except for a ceramic ball-shaped pomander. I pick it up and recognize the perfumes of lavender, chamomile, lemon verbena and something else I don't expect and can't pinpoint. It's subtly pungent and that's odd for a household fragrance.

"They could have had something together." Marino doesn't take his eyes off me. "And I think you know what I'm talking about, Doc. I don't want to get into it more than that."

I do know what he's talking about and he doesn't need to get into it. I intuit his meaning not from what he says but from the way he says it. Marino is suggesting that Chanel and Carrie might have been acquainted. They might have been more than that. He's coming around to this point of view on his own.

"The pomander is an antique but the potpourri definitely hasn't been it in very long. It's fresh." I verify to him that it appears someone in addition to Chanel has been using the house.

This suggests more of the same unpleasantness to put it mildly. If Carrie knew Chanel and Chanel knew Lucy then that links the three of them. Chanel has been murdered. Carrie's existence can't be proven. That leaves Lucy hung out to dry by the FBI. I worry that might be the reason for everything but I can't fathom why.

"A pom-what?" Marino sets down the scene case.

"A container used to hold potpourri, scent pellets, sachets." I open other drawers. "This pomander is old. It's not a reproduction and looks about the same era as when this addition was built, around the time of the Civil War, possibly earlier or a little later. I can't say for sure. But definitely not seventeenth century. And certainly not modern."

I walk my gloved fingers through neatly folded athletic clothes, maybe half a dozen tank tops and pairs of tights. Ladies size small. Some of them still with the tags. None of it inexpensive.

"Mid- to late eighteen hundreds is my guess." I continue to tell Marino what I see and think. "The important point is the dried herbs, flowers or oils used are fresh or they wouldn't smell this potent."

"Do you want it to go to the labs?" He flips up the clasps on the scene case.

"Yes . . ." My thought is stalled by the sudden sensation that I'm inside a pub.

I stop everything for a moment and concentrate. Then it occurs to me.

"I smell hops," I say to Marino and whoever else might be listening.

"As in beer?"

"As in the brewing of it." My voice is strong and audible, and I realize I sound aggressive.

Maybe two can play your game.

"Sounds like wishful thinking. I sure as hell could use a couple beers right now," Marino says.

"Hops has other uses, including medical," I explain blandly, as if I have no feelings about it.

He sniffs the air near where I'm standing. "I don't smell it but that's nothing new when I'm with you. I think you were a bloodhound in another life. It will be interesting to see if Chanel had something wrong with her. If she might have been sick."

"I don't believe so. At least there was nothing evident on gross examination. We'll see what shows up on histology but Luke would have mentioned it if he'd found any sign of her having a disease or some other serious problem."

"Well not that I'm an expert," Marino says, "but a lot of the stuff we're seeing in this house is what I associate with someone worried about bad luck or bad health or dying."

Carrie made a pact with God that she wouldn't suffer a similar fate.

I hear her talking in the video, telling the story of her life as if I might have compassion for anything she's ever been through. And I don't. I'm beyond feeling humane or understanding. I don't care, and I see her pale skin and short platinum hair as she reads from her script and holds up a bottle of her special protective potion that supposedly keeps her young.

"Possibly what we're seeing indicates a health concern or a disabling problem of some sort, possibly one that causes discomfort, pain or some type of embarrassment such as a tic, a tremor or a deformity," I continue to explain to Marino but it's directed at her. "We might infer that this person has an atypical belief system—in other words delusions—about the healing power of plants and other things that occur naturally such as metals."

Copper.

"The hops plant is actually a cousin of cannabis and has been used to shrink tumors, to help with sleep." I set the pomander on top of the dresser. "I suspect Chanel or someone staying here has suffered from insomnia, anxiety, depression or some other mood instability." I imagine Carrie's reaction if she's listening.

She's not a good sport about narcissistic injuries. She handles them poorly. Usually with murder.

"But medical marijuana doesn't fit with that. It's not a superstition. It's not quackery," I add. "Is that where it's been kept? Not exactly a foolproof place to hide it."

Marino has the small closet open and I notice very little hanging inside, just a few shirts and jackets and cedar planks to discourage moths. He's lifting a mahogany apothecary box by its tarnished silver handles. He sets it down on the rug and opens the faded red-velvet-lined lid. It's not locked. It doesn't appear there was a concern about someone possibly stealing Chanel's medication assuming this was hers.

Inside the box the wooden partitions and tiny drawers are filled with eyedropper bottles of cannabis tinctures and infused chews, and plastic containers of bud. Indica. Sativa. Various blends of cannabidiol (CBD). I pick up a bottle. The company name is Cannachoice. There's nothing on the label that might tell us where it was manufactured but I agree with Marino's earlier assessment.

"This isn't from around here." I return the bottle to its proper drawer. "I'm pretty sure there are no dispensaries in Massachusetts selling anything like this, and there's no way caregivers are getting access to tinctures of such high quality. I seriously doubt you could find anything like this on the entire East Coast. Maybe someday but not now."

"I'm guessing California." Marino is back to assuming the wealthy well-connected mother is the source.

"It could have come from there or Colorado. Possibly Washington State." I pick up another bottle, a blend of fifteen parts CBD to one part THC, and the plastic seal around the neck is broken.

I unscrew the cap and pull out the dropper. The tincture inside is thick and golden. It smells sweetly herbal and is nothing like some of the home-brewed extracts I've seen, black tarry pastes that are too bitter to hold under your tongue or mix with food or drink, and the memory of why I researched all this is jolting. It catches me by surprise swiftly, sadly, powerfully.

Not that long ago I learned more about medical marijuana than I ever thought I needed to know, talking to experts, scouring the Internet and ordering what legal products I could when I learned that Janet's sister was diagnosed with stage 4 pancreatic cancer. I talked to physicians who specialize in alternative medicine. I read every journal article I could find. Nothing I could procure legally was going to help Natalie, and I felt absolutely awful about it. I still do when I remember the late-night discussions, the unfairness, the distress, and Lucy's combative language when I said we'd done as much as we could. Legally we had.

Fuck 'em. Watch what's next, was her answer, and I remember when she said it she and Janet were sitting on the circular bench around the big magnolia tree in my backyard. The sun was going down and we were drinking a small batch bourbon, and they were talking about the chemotherapy. Natalie couldn't eat. She could scarcely hold down water. She was in pain, anxious and depressed, and what she needed was medical marijuana. It isn't legal in Virginia. It is here in Massachusetts, but to date there's no appropriate product available. Just bud, which is riskier to bootleg according to Lucy.

Weed is harder to hide from drug dogs and disapproving people, she pointed out.

We were having dinner at my house when she said this after the conversation had turned angry. Lucy made threats and I don't want to be asked about it under oath. I can imagine the likes of a Jill Donoghue ripping into me:

Doctor Scarpetta, does your niece ever make statements to you about having no respect for the law?

Only when they're stupid laws.

That's a yes?

Partly.

What has she said exactly?

Which time?

How about recently?

She said that she doesn't obey stupid laws made by stupid corrupt people. That wasn't very long ago.

And a red flag didn't go up?

Not literally.

Logistical and legal technicalities aren't going to stop Lucy if she's made a decision, and by her way of thinking the end justifies the means. Always. Without fail. It doesn't matter how she gets to that point, and I can imagine what she did these past few months when Natalie was dying. Lucy has never told me. I've never asked. She flew her private jet to Colorado. She flew it and her helicopter in and out of Virginia but she didn't tell and I didn't ask, and ordinarily I could call her and we could talk about it.

I would ask her about Cannachoice and if she knows where it came from. Because she might and it's important information since there are bottles of it here at a murder scene possibly masterminded by Carrie Grethen. Ordinarily I would be on the phone with Lucy asking a lot of questions. But things aren't exactly ordinary, and if a trap has been set then I intend to make sure it isn't my niece who's caught in it. I don't know if the FBI is still on her property. I don't know if Erin Loria is right there trying to question or Mirandize her or who knows what. I don't want to make matters worse.

Besides, I tell myself, pretty soon we'll have an embarrassment of riches when it comes time for chatting while she's staying at my house. Lucy, Janet, Desi and Jet Ranger will be with Benton and me, and we'll have Sock, our rescued greyhound, with us too. All of us will be together for quite a while, and I'm comforted by the thought with no substantiating evidence whatsoever that it will come to pass.

I'm not obtuse. I'm not naïve. But it's as if I'm hovering over my destiny, looking down at the awful dark shape of something I can't bear to get close to or identify, and I know I'm fooling myself. I'm in denial about what matters most, and that's Lucy and Benton. It's Marino. It's everyone I care about.

"Let's take all of this in to the lab," I decide about the contents of the antique apothecary chest. “We’ll have it analyzed and see exactly what’s in it.”

I move closer to the bed and smell the same spicy floral scent over here but something has been added.

Peppermint.

CHAPTER 39

BOTH PILLOWS LOOK SLEPT ON. UNDER THE LEFT one closest to the bathroom is a drawstring black satin pouch.

It appears to be a homemade sachet, and it seems more of the same. I'm reminded of the cold-pressed juices, the candles in the living room and the clocks being wound. Someone is industrious, working with fresh fruits, vegetables, herbs and homeopathic remedies but there's no evidence any such concocting has gone on inside this house. Not any area we've searched so far.

It's a skin regeneration preparation . . . Just use something so you don't completely destroy your sweet tender skin, Carrie filmed herself saying.

She's obsessed with her health, her youth and most of all her power, and she's skilled at ranging about freely without leaving a trace. Unless it's a trace we're supposed to find. Like the recording device inside the silver box. Like latent blood that reacts to a reagent, and she knows I'd look. She knows how I think and work, and I'm suspicious about what all of this means and how dangerous it could be to remain inside this house.

She wants you here.

There can be no doubt about it.

You should leave now.

I pull the bedcovers back farther and look closely at the linens, a high-thread-count polished off-white cotton with a pale gray duvet. I pull the covers down the rest of the way and find a black silk pajama top inside out. Chanel was nude because she took her pajamas off. Or someone did, and where are the bottoms? They weren't in the drawers or with the body. I ask Marino to remind me what the housekeeper Elsa Mulligan said. She claimed Chanel left here yesterday at around three or three-thirty P.M. I recall Marino telling me this and he confirms it. He says that's what Hyde told him when we responded to the house the first time at around eight-thirty this morning.

"Like I already told you the housekeeper and Hyde talked for a few minutes," Marino says. "That was it."

"And then she was gone by the time we got here." It seems an increasingly important detail. "What happens if you try to call her? Do we know if you can really reach her?"

"I haven't tried yet. We've been a little busy. Allegedly she mentioned Chanel was staying in and working last night," he repeats the same story. "Allegedly there was no indication she might be expecting anyone, and allegedly she'd broken up with a boyfriend last spring. Allegedly she and Chanel met in New Jersey a couple years ago."

"That's a lot of *allegedlys*."

"Hell yeah there are. You got that right. At this point I don't trust a goddamn thing."

"Has anybody talked to her alleged former boyfriend? Do we know for a fact there's a former boyfriend?"

"Carrie Grethen was in New Jersey two months ago, right before she went to Florida," he repeats that point.

"And that was my next question. Did Hyde ask the housekeeper how she and Chanel met? Or was the information volunteered?"

We know Carrie was in New Jersey as recently as two months ago. We know that earlier than that she murdered a woman there, shot her to death while she was getting out of her car at the Edgewater Ferry. I can't help but wonder if it's another taunt that the alleged housekeeper happened to mention New Jersey. It's an emotional subject for me. I was in Morristown when I learned that Carrie Grethen is alive and killing people for her twisted reasons. When Lucy told me we were sitting in the very bar where Carrie had been.

"I don't know because I didn't witness them talking." Marino continues to explain that he didn't question the woman who claimed to be Elsa Mulligan. "I was with you in that damn truck of yours."

"And what might happen if you tried to call Elsa Mulligan right now?" I have a feeling I know the answer.

Nothing will happen. You won't get hold of her.

"I'm not going to until we finish up here," he says. "But I know what you're getting at. There's something off about the whole thing with her."

"That's right. There is." My eyes slowly move around the room, looking for any hint of covert surveillance devices.

I'm not going to find them unless Carrie wants me to, and I feel the change that has come over me. It's rare and always happens the same way. I don't recognize the transformation until it's already taken place, irreversibly, finally. Like an engine flaming out. Followed by an instant eerie silence. A floating sensation. A perfect calm. Then the warnings flash bright red and horns blare and sirens scream that I'm about to crash. But it's Marino's radio I'm hearing. He has it in his hand, adjusting knobs.

"Something at the River Basin," he announces in an annoyed, jaded way. "The same red SUV with the same damn drunk juveniles it sounds like. Only now one of them maybe has a gun."

"What kind of red SUV?" I hear myself ask before I think the thought.

"Late model, maybe high end. That's all I know based on radio traffic."

"The same juveniles and red SUV have been called in several times and there's no more detail than that? What kind of SUV?" I ask that again.

"No other info," Marino says. "Usually there would be a plate number, a make and model or something."

I'm thinking about the missing red Range Rover and I mention it. I'm the first to say it's unlikely kids stole it out of this driveway in a downpour after the police were at the house most of the morning. I'm quick to admit that it sounds like the calls to 911 about a late-model high-end red SUV and rowdy kids might be completely unrelated.

"But what if they aren't and what if they're false?" I ask. "What if it's a game?"

We know who might play a game like that and why, and the River Basin is near here. It's only minutes from the Gilbert house.

"I guess we have to think of every worst-case scenario," Marino says, and he gets on his radio. "Anything further on the red SUV and subjects in it?" he asks the dispatcher and he's not flirty this time. "We got a plate number, a make and model?"

"Negative. Nothing further." The dispatcher—Helen I presume—

sounds somber too as if there's been an announcement somewhere that all is wrong in the world.

"Do we have a phone number for the complainant?" Marino's jaw muscles are clenching.

She recites a number that has an exchange I don't recognize. But it's not local. Marino tries it and it rings and rings and rings.

"No voice mail set up," he tells me. "Probably some bogus disposable phone. Probably kids having a great time messing with the police."

"You hope so at any rate."

"Well it's better than the alternative that someone's out joyriding in a murdered lady's red Range Rover."

"Or that Chanel's killer is the one calling nine-one-one. Or that her so-called housekeeper is."

"You're thinking they're the same person?" His eyes are on me, and we know we're both considering the possibility.

It's shocking to contemplate. It would mean that Carrie murdered Chanel Gilbert and at some point when it suited her called 911. Then she answered the door when Officer Hyde showed up. She stayed just long enough to answer a few questions but was long gone by the time Marino and I got here. One look into Elsa Mulligan's eyes and I would have known it was Carrie. Marino might not have, but it was only two months ago when I watched her shoot me.

"I'm thinking we should finish up. Let's try ALS on the bed. Maybe she wasn't in it alone before she died," I suggest.

He opens what is actually a heavy-duty toolbox made of tough black plastic. He finds a kit that contains an Alternate Light Source, a set of what looks like small black flashlights of different bandwidths.

"What do you want to start with?" He sets a box of gloves on the floor and grabs a new pair.

"UV."

Body fluids can fluoresce in the long wavelengths of black light illumination, and Marino selects that light for me. He hands me amber-tinted goggles and I put them on. The lenses glow violet and I begin painting invisible light over the bed, starting at the head of it. The pillow on the left side that had the sachet under it turns dark like a void.

"Whoa," Marino says. "I've never seen that before. Why does it look black? The other pillow and sheets don't. What could turn black in UV like that?"

"Usually blood would be the first thing that comes to mind," I reply. "But obviously the pillowcase isn't covered with blood."

"Hell no. When the light's off it looks perfectly clean. Just a little rumpled like someone's slept on it."

"Let's start taking photographs, and then all of these linens will need to go to the labs." As I'm saying this I hear the same thud, as if a heavy door just slammed in a remote area of the house, possibly the cellar.

"Jeez that's starting to freak me out," Marino exclaims.

Then we hear it again. The same sound. In fact it's exactly the same.

"Makes me wonder if it's the wind blowing something like a loose shutter." Marino's eyes are darting around the bedroom, the top of his head sweaty.

"It doesn't sound like a shutter."

"I'm not going to look right now. I'm not leaving you alone."

"I'm glad to hear it." I direct the UV light over other areas of the bed as he collects his camera.

He finds the thick plastic filters tinted amber, yellow and red that must be held over the lens if we're going to capture the fluorescence in photographs.

"The good news," he says, "is Ajax and his guys wouldn't have left if there was even a chance someone's in here. If they saw the slightest thing they'd be taking apart this house."

I try a higher wavelength. "What about Hyde? Any news at all about him?"

"Nope."

"And his car?"

"Nothing so far."

"And his wife has no idea? Nobody close to him has heard from him?"

"Not a peep," Marino says as small stains light up milky white.

"Dried sweat, saliva, semen, vaginal fluid maybe . . . ," I start to say when I'm jolted by the alert tone on my phone.

The C-sharp cord that I've heard three times so far today.

"Wait a minute." Marino lowers a yellow filter from the camera lens. "How's that possible?"

"It's not." I take off a glove and dig out my phone.

We're supposed to think it's Lucy's In Case of Emergency line but it can't be. She doesn't have her phone. The FBI does. Even if she's already gotten another phone it won't have the same number.

"And it's being spoofed anyway just as it has been," I tell Marino emphatically. "This is the same thing that's happened three other times today, the first time when I was inside this house early this morning. This is exactly what it looked like." I show him what's on the display of my phone.

The message has no text, only an Internet link, and I step away to give myself some privacy. I turn my back to him as I click on the link, and I'm instantly struck by the absence of a *Depraved Heart* title sequence this time. Then I realize why. The video hasn't been produced. It hasn't been scripted or edited. It isn't a recording. It's live and Carrie's not in it.

Janet is. I watch her in the small display. She's in the middle of something, clipping her phone to the waistband of the faded scrubs she had on earlier, walking over to Lucy. They're inside the basement, what we refer to as the bomb shelter only we don't mean it in an ominous way but rather as an affectionate nostalgic reference to a past that I shouldn't think about right now. As I'm watching. In real time. As if I'm there.

Control your thoughts.

When I first met Benton he worked in the Behavioral Science Unit, his elite squadron of psychological profilers located inside Hoover's former bomb shelter. I used to descend into the bowels of the FBI Academy to meet about cases and I wasn't above trumping up excuses. When I wanted to see Special Agent Benton Wesley there was no extreme I wouldn't go to, and on numerous occasions Lucy was with me. She knew what was going on. She'd known for years that Benton and I were more than colleagues. She understood what it meant.

He was married with children. Professionally it was a conflict for the chief medical examiner and the head of the FBI's profiling unit to be sleeping together. Everything we were doing was wrong. It would have been considered shameful and unethical but nothing was going to stop us, and the unexpected reminder of that is powerful. I'm overwhelmed by a reaction I couldn't have anticipated and I realize how hurt I am. Everything I've been through and the day is far from over, and where is he? Benton is with his tribe. The FBI is his tribe. Not his family. Not me. I was almost murdered two months ago and he's with them. How could he be loyal to them after what's happened? How could he be okay with what they're doing to Lucy?

Focus!

In those early days when I carried my official business to Quantico and descended into that dank dismal cave it was the most glorious place on earth. When I ached for him. When I could think of nothing but him, the same way Lucy feels about Janet, the way both of them feel. They love each other. They always have even when they were apart all those years. They think nothing about breaking rules any more than Benton and I did, and we broke them all the time. That's what happens when people have affairs, and as I watch what's live-streaming on my phone I know I'm being shown this for a reason.

I steel myself for what it might be as I remember that the security cameras Lucy installed have backup batteries and built-in hard drives. They can continue to run and record without the server, without external power. The FBI didn't shut down Lucy's network even if they assume they did. They aren't in control of it even if they think they are. They couldn't possibly outsmart her but someone has.

Her security system and communications network have been hijacked. They're being used to broadcast what she's doing in the privacy of her home. Lucy doesn't realize it's happening. She can't possibly have a clue. She'd never allow such a thing I keep telling myself. She's being spied on the same way she was in 1997 and has no idea now any more than she did then. And yet it seems incredible that my shrewd, stubborn, brilliant niece could be duped by anyone.

Especially more than once.

Doubts are growing by leaps and bounds as I watch Lucy and Janet crouch by an area of gray flooring, examining large stone tiles as if there's something wrong with them. I recognize the huge space they're in, what Lucy calls her *naughty Santa's workshop* that is professionally outfitted with built-ins and any piece of equipment or tool one might need for gunsmithing, automotive work, hand-loading ammunition.

I hear Marino breathing and feel his heat. He's crept close and is looking over my shoulder. I step away and tell him absolutely not. Under no circumstances can he watch. It's bad enough that I've been compromised. He doesn't need to be compromised too.

"Jesus Christ. Inside their own house?" He can't tear his eyes away. "Who else is seeing this?"

"I don't know but not you." I cover the phone with my hand. "There's nothing for you to see. Stay over there and don't look."

CHAPTER 40

THERE ARE NO WINDOWS, AND THE OVERHEAD LAMPS inside the machine shop are an intense candlepower on a par with an OR. I can see Lucy and Janet in vivid detail. I can make out the expressions on their faces and their every gesture as they hover by the same area of flooring, the bright lights harsh on them, unkind and glaring, and that's the way life feels right now.

Exposed, unsafe and rife with deceptions and brazen lies as I witness my niece and her partner in the privacy of their home. They're deliberating, talking somewhat tersely, cryptically in the midst of workbenches, with vises and tall red roll-around tool-boxes, a CNC mill and lathe and a table saw, a surface grinder, a shaper, drill press and welding machines.

I don't know for a fact what they're pondering but I can make an educated guess. They've hidden something down here, probably Lucy has. Drugs, firearms, maybe both, and as I watch my niece and listen to her I realize her FBI sweats from her academy days still seem ironic to me but not in the same way.

They're not the chest-thumping taunt they were hours ago when I first saw her trotting toward me on her driveway. They look wilted and faded, sweat splotched and tired in their soft cotton grayness, drooping and defeated like a faded old battle flag on a windless day. Lucy looks rather pitiful really, and her demeanor has completely changed. She's fast talking and aggressive, about to fly apart and I know what that means. It's the way she gets when she's desperate. Which is almost never.

"Didn't I tell you nobody would ever know? And they were walking in and out of here all day without a clue. I told you there was nothing to worry about." Lucy is full of bravado and I don't buy it.

She's scared.

"There's everything to worry about." Janet is quiet and controlled but I sense something else. "They've predicted you'll do this."

"So you've said fifty times."

"And I'll make it fifty-one times, Lucy. They can anticipate with pretty good certainty what your post offense behavior is going to be."

"I've not committed an *offense*. They fucking have."

"Do you want me to talk like a lawyer right now?"

"No I don't."

"I'm going to anyway. Erin Loria knows how you're wired. She's well aware there's no way you'd ever allow us to be left in the position they've just put us in—of not being able to defend ourselves. She knows you're not going to sit on your hands and let us be hurt or killed."

"Why is it my behavior and not both of us? Since when do you sit on your hands either?"

"They took my guns too," Janet says as if that answers the question.

But it doesn't. It simply raises another legal problem. What right did the FBI have to confiscate anything belonging to Janet? There wasn't a warrant for her, not that I know about. Of course if they took her firearms then they'll simply say they needed to test them. What if Lucy had used them in the commission of a crime? What if Janet had for that matter? Agents walking out the door with Janet's belongings is no different from them walking out with my computer and anything else they seized from the guest bedroom. They'll assert that when people live together or stay under the same roof then anything on the property is fair game. The FBI can't know what's mine, Janet's or Lucy's if all of it is in the same location.

I'm not all that surprised the FBI might have decided to send Janet's guns to the lab. But her mention of it to Lucy strikes me as a strategic sidestep, a non sequitur, a lawyer-speak that is far more deliberate than it might seem. Janet is choosing her words with precision and care, and maybe that simply comes naturally to her when times are stressful. But it strikes me that she's creating a record, as if someone is listening, and someone is. I am. But who else?

Then she uses the word *criminal*. She says that what's happened is criminal but she doesn't make her meaning clear. Is she referring to what Lucy has done or what the Bureau has? And Lucy's response is that a person's rights are honored only in the breach.

"Justice won't do us any good if we're dead," she says, "and they'll make sure the truth never comes out. If we're murdered it will have been sanctioned by our own government. Hell yes it's criminal. They basically have put a hit on us."

"Technically, legally I'm sure they haven't," Janet replies. "I guarantee you they didn't hire Carrie, they didn't contract with her to hurt Kay last June or kill us. What they've done is far more clever and diabolical. It's an open invitation to commit a violent act, and yes it's willful negligence. It's a complete disregard for human life, the absolute definition of a depraved heart crime," she adds to my disbelief. "It should be criminal. But it's the FBI, Lucy. And there's no accountability unless there is a perceived political obstruction such as an embarrassment to POTUS."

An embarrassment to the president of the United States would have to be a public event. If it's not public then he can't be embarrassed. I imagine what sort of political obstruction Janet might be thinking about and come up with one right away. Gun control is an acutely polarizing issue in this country with the majority of Americans literally up in arms over the prospect of losing their Second Amendment right.

If it ever came out that our government disarmed citizens who then ended up murdered? The fallout would be significant. Such a horrendous story would bring new energy to the battle over gun control. It would galvanize conservative voters. It would become a raging agenda in the upcoming presidential election.

"It's so fucked up. No matter the truth about Pakistan, about missing guns, about anything, nothing justifies this," Lucy rants on. "There are better ways to handle it. What they're doing is personally vindictive and destructive. There's a child and a dog in this house. What did they ever do to deserve . . . ? Well it's evil and it isn't even necessary."

"That depends on who you ask," Janet says. "I'm sure to someone it's necessary."

"To Erin."

"Directly, yes it's necessary to Erin Loria. But this is higher up than her. It's higher up than Benton. When you're talking about a cover-up of this magnitude it's at the cabinet level. It's agency directors who get involved in ugly lies and conspiracies, the Watergates, the Benghazi disaster not to mention making deals with terrorists, exchanging the release of prisoners at GTMO for a deserter. The U.S. doesn't need any more humiliations, scandals, botched missions, constitutional violations or casualties, and if the collateral damage is you or me or Desi? If it's all of us? To DoJ, to DoD, to the White House that's a nothing price to pay as long as the public doesn't know. As long as it never gets out."

What she and Lucy are intimating is egregious beyond comprehension and yet I don't doubt it could happen. Lucy seems to think that Carrie Grethen has been given an assignment. Or maybe an invitation is a more accurate way to put it if she's been recruited to kill Lucy, maybe to kill everyone around her. And to make it easy? Let's leave them on fifty isolated acres with no weapons. Let's leave them on a remote estate the FBI has vacated and left wide open for an attack that will be interpreted as random, as the lightning strike of a violent psychopath.

But not a lightning strike by Carrie Grethen. I have a strong suspicion the FBI isn't about to acknowledge that she's alive and well. They give every impression to the contrary. She's not officially considered a fugitive. She's not on the Ten Most Wanted list. Her case isn't active with Interpol. On their website Carrie has been a black notice for the past thirteen years. In the international law enforcement community it would appear she's considered just as dead today as she was when it was assumed that she went down in a helicopter.

"They'll chalk it up to a home invasion," Lucy is saying to Janet, and my chest is tight. "One of those unfortunate things that's related to my having money. Then the attention of the public will move on. Nobody will remember what happened to us or care."

My heart is pounding as I stand inside a dead woman's bedroom fifteen miles away from Concord, which may as well be a million miles from Lucy's house. I couldn't possibly get there fast enough if Carrie has somehow breached the perimeter, if she's gotten inside and is watching them even as I'm watching all of it. She's stalking her quarry, about to pounce while I'm her audience it occurs to me horribly, and this is what she's been leading up to, the grand finale.

She wants me to see what she does to them.

"Marino?" I don't turn around or give a hint of what's going on inside me. "I need you to get on your phone."

My voice catches as if I'm a little hoarse. But I'm perfectly steady. I don't sound frantic.

"What is it?" He steps closer.

"Try Janet. If you can't get her try Benton, the FBI, the state police . . ."

"What the hell is it? Are you talking about Carrie?"

"Yes that's exactly who I mean. I'm concerned she might be inside Lucy and Janet's house or is about to be inside it."

"Shit! Why would you . . . ?"

"Do it now, Marino."

"Even better I'll get some cars from Concord P.D. ASAP. They can be there in two minutes. And I'll try Janet . . ."

"If there's no response they should break down the gate, the front door. Whatever it takes. Janet and Lucy are okay but I'm not sure they will be for long."

"I'm on it. Where are they?"

"Downstairs."

"The bomb shelter?"

"Yes. But not Desi. I don't see him."

"They must not be worried if he's not with them," Marino says and he's right.

Why is Desi alone?

He's not with them and yet I've never seen Lucy more worried than she is right now. It doesn't make sense. She and Janet are devoted to him. If anything they're overly protective. So why isn't he with them? They don't want him to witness what they're doing. That's the obvious answer but it's not a good enough one, and I hear Marino on his phone as I watch Lucy crazed by panic and rage like a snake at the first metallic touch of the shovel blade. That's what comes to mind as I spy. Another second goes by. Then two. Then ten, and she steps on various stone tiles as if they might be loose. She lightly jumps up and down on them.

"Completely undetectable. You can walk across these tiles all day long like those assholes did and you can't tell." Lucy jumps again for good measure.

She's obsessed with the FBI. She's fixated on outsmarting the Feds and that's not wise. Lucy knows better. Certainly Janet does.

"And even if they'd ever found this, which I knew they wouldn't, they'd still have to go under a certain undetectable area of the metal flooring and dig down about three feet for the gun case," Lucy says. "I hate to tell you I told you so."

"I agree they shouldn't have put us in this position," Janet says strangely.

It's as if she's disassociating herself from whatever she and Lucy may have done earlier that has caused them to be in this part of the house right now. Janet continues to make comments in a stiff stilted way as if she knows someone is listening.

"But you don't have to do this," she's saying and I continue to be bothered by the way she sounds and acts. "Let's go upstairs, pack up and get to Kay's."

It's subtle but I see it. Janet is performing. It's as if she's onstage and doesn't want to be. Like a deer in the headlights, it occurs to me, and I wonder if Erin Loria talked to her alone. I wonder what the FBI might have said to Janet while they were searching the property. They might have made a deal with her. If so it won't be one that has a good payoff for Lucy. I know about such bargains. You can have immunity as long as you throw your own mother under the bus, and my vigilance kicks up another notch.

"Let's go upstairs," Janet encourages Lucy but she isn't pushy about it. "I don't want you getting into any more trouble."

Lucy stares at her incredulously. "What's going on with you? I'm not leaving us with no damn way to protect ourselves. We agreed this morning we wouldn't let them do that to us. What's wrong with you? You of all people know what she's like."

"I never really knew her," Janet says and I'm stunned.

Of course she knew Carrie. Janet knew about their relationship at the time. There have been endless conversations about it since.

"What's wrong with you?" Lucy has her hands on her hips. "You sure as hell met her back then. Remember the time we were having lunch in the Boardroom and she sat at our table and didn't say one word to you or even look at you?" She's angry and accusatory. "And the time you and I were talking in my dorm room and she walked in without knocking like she was hoping to catch us. What do you mean you never really knew her? What are you talking about?" Lucy is getting more upset.

"In the ERF, the Boardroom, out running, in passing in other words." Janet's voice is flat and disconnected. "I'm not sure I'd recognize her."

"You've seen the photos. I've used computer age progression and showed you what she'd look like today. And besides you remember her. You'd recognize her. Hell yes you would."

"I recognize her behavior. But literally I've not seen her to quote *recognize* her."

"Are you being funny?"

"I'm being a lawyer. I'm telling you how I would feel compelled to answer the question of whether I've seen her."

"Because this isn't a game," Lucy says, and I think I smell it. "They lie and say there's no evidence she exists and you're going to help them out by saying you haven't seen her?"

"I haven't seen her since the late nineties. Not probably. Absolutely and it's the truth," Janet says, and I'm sure I smell it.

I remember the loamy musky scent. More olfactory fool's gold, and of course I'm not smelling it now but it wasn't just Lucy. It was Janet too. When I hugged both of them it entered my mind that they'd been doing yard work. Until I remembered they don't do yard work. They smelled as if they'd been digging in the soil.

Both of them did.

Not just Lucy. But also Janet, who was in her scrubs, and I was surprised by her messy hair, her dirty nails and that she was wearing what essentially are her pajamas. She didn't bother to get dressed this morning. She got out of bed and got busy. She got sweaty and dirty. She didn't clean up before Erin Loria appeared at the front door and that was deliberate. Janet wanted to look surprised. She wanted to look raided without a moment's advance warning. She intended to look caught, ambushed and demoralized. But she wasn't really. Neither was Lucy.

They knew the FBI was coming.

"I'm not getting Janet," Marino says behind my back. "It goes straight to voice mail."

JANET'S PHONE DOESN'T RING. I'm watching it on her waistband and the display isn't lighting up the way it should if someone is calling her. I also don't hear it.

Marino is trying her number and her phone is silent. She's not checking it and I wonder if it was working earlier. The video opened with Janet clipping her phone back on the waistband of her scrubs. What was she doing with it before I started watching and why doesn't it seem to be working now?

"Okay. I'm trying again. And I think Janet might have her phone off. Or the FBI might have taken it from her." Marino has no idea what I'm seeing.

He isn't watching the live feed and can't know that I'm looking at Janet and her phone even as he's trying to call her.

"She may have the ringer off or the battery could be dead but the FBI doesn't have her phone," I say to Marino because I'm looking at it. "Are the police en route?"

"They sure as hell should be. Let me check."

"Don't push me away," Janet is saying to Lucy. "Don't act like I'm the enemy. That's what they want. That's especially what Erin wants. Come on. Let's go back upstairs." She pulls Lucy by the hand but she won't budge. "We'll get a few things and go to Kay's house. Come on. We'll get there and have a drink and a nice dinner and everything will be better," says Lucy's partner, her lover, her soul mate, colleague and best friend.

They've been each other's best everything on and off since the beginning of their FBI careers when they first met at Quantico. For a number of years they lived together, and I've always thought Janet is wonderful for Lucy, ideal, maybe perfect. They have much in common and are similarly motivated and trained. But Janet is more flexible and easygoing. She's as patient and deliberate as the Sphinx, she likes to say, and she's bright and grounded. She's not an impulsive or angry person and doesn't seem to have a lot to prove.

I was distraught when they broke up. But time heals as it passes and about a decade did. Then Janet came back. I don't know how it happened exactly, only what I've been told and that it seemed a miracle. I suppose it still does, and I think back to when Lucy ordered her to move out not all that long ago. The spring, I think, and how cruel that must have been.

It was about the same time Janet learned her sister was dying, and in the blink of an eye it must have seemed that everything was lost. It would be a hard thing to forgive. I understand Lucy's fear that Carrie would target Janet and Desi. But I also believe what Lucy decided to do about it was hurtful and unfair. Janet has let it go, just as she's let so many things go. Sometimes I halfway wonder if she's a saint.

"I told you not to follow me down here." Lucy walks to a workbench. "Everything isn't going to be better but it's also not going to get as bad as it could. Go upstairs." She opens a drawer. "I bet Desi would like some popcorn and a movie. Why don't you put *Frozen* on again? I'll be right up with a few friends and we'll go," she adds and *friends* is a euphemism for *guns*.

Lucy has hidden weapons from the FBI.

She's fighting for her life, for what in her mind is everybody's life while Janet in cool contrast is reluctant and somewhat removed. I sense something else beneath her flat calm, beneath her unconditional love and loyalty. For a flicker I feel a wavering of trust. Just as quickly the feeling is gone. Janet is uncomfortable. Understandably so I tell myself. If she's acting detached and a little flat and uncooperative it's to counterbalance Lucy, who at the moment is her polar opposite emotionally. Her fists are loosely clenched. Her entire body is tense as she threatens and curses the federal government.

I watch her open more drawers in a workbench that fills an entire wall. I can see a hydraulic lift in the background and there's a car on it, her Ferrari FF, Tour de France blue. The all-wheel-drive supercar is what she was driving two months ago when I was shot. She was talking about it with Jill Donoghue earlier today when they were going over possible alibis for where Lucy was when I almost died.

"You can't let them dictate how you behave. It doesn't matter what they've done." Janet is firm but calm, and she's something else. "Let's go upstairs before it's too late. You don't need to do this."

"I'd rather be judged by twelve than carried by six." Lucy means she'd rather be on trial than dead. "If we don't have any way to protect ourselves? You know exactly what's going to happen. This is wrong, Janet. It's outrageously disgusting. The FBI wants us murdered."

"I realize Erin has set it up that way. Don't give her what she wants."

"How convenient. If we're dead then Erin is rid of her biggest problem in life."

"That's what she thinks at any rate. So you know what we do? Let's leave and go to your aunt's house. Let's talk to Benton about it," Janet says, and then it lands hard on me.

I realize what I've been picking up. Janet won't look in the direction of any surveillance camera. Lucy in contrast is looking wherever she wants. At cameras and away from them. It's obvious to me that she doesn't assume the FBI is spying on them. Lucy clearly doesn't think she's being picked up by her own security system but Janet is wary and cautious. She avoids looking in the direction of the cameras and yet she's talking openly and that's confusing to me. Why would she mention Erin Loria by name? Why would she mention POTUS, Benghazi and cover-ups?

"We can't be emotional." Janet doesn't take her eyes off Lucy.

"I'll be whatever I want," Lucy says. "Wait and see what I do. They can go to hell if they think we're going to be left here with nothing. Not a handgun. Not even a damn steak knife. She leaves us here like this so we can't protect ourselves or Desi or even Jet Ranger against the worst dirtbag imaginable. And they know her. They sure as hell do because they created her."

The Feds created Carrie Grethen like Frankenstein. Marino said that earlier and he was quoting Lucy.

She walks over to the area of flooring she was jumping on a few minutes ago. Metal rings against stone as she sets down a pry bar and a small shovel. She pulls her gray T-shirt over her head, balls it up and drops it on top of the workbench. She's sinewy and strong in her sports bra and running shorts, and I feel her raw vulnerability as I wonder where the cops are.

"Have you heard from the Concord police?" I ask Marino. "Are they there yet?"

CHAPTER 41

THE MUSCLES OF HER SHOULDERS AND UPPER ARMS flex as she finds a folded tarp and opens it near the area of flooring she was jumping on a few minutes ago.

I'm reminded of how supremely fit and disciplined Lucy is. She rarely drinks alcohol. She's vegan. She runs and works out daily with weights and TRX bands. I catch a glimpse of the small dragonfly on her flat lower abdomen and think about what the whimsical tattoo hides. Carrie scarred her. Carrie marked her for life. Carrie might be inside the house. She could be no more than a room or two away. Lucy and Janet have no idea and I can't reach them.

"I've not heard shit." Marino answers my question about the Concord police. "Let me try my guy there again."

I'm not intimate with every nook and cranny inside the house Lucy built after we relocated to Massachusetts some five years ago. But I'm familiar with where she and Janet are right now and know that the entire area is monitored by surveillance devices. Lucy is technically sophisticated and meticulous. So is Janet. It was only months ago they began talking about adopting Desi and upgrading the security system.

"Really?" Lucy puts on a pair of thick leather work gloves. "They come in here and do this and we're not supposed to have any recourse?" She picks up the pry bar. "Talk about an unfair fight."

"There are no words for how unfair this is," Janet says.

"The *kurz* is going to be planted somewhere around here. You know that right?"

"Did Erin say something that made you think she was planting evidence?"

"She wanted me to think it and start packing my bags for going down the river."

"Where would she have hidden it?"

"Maybe out there in the woods where somebody's been but the cameras aren't picking up anything," Lucy says. "Maybe it's buried out there like Blackbeard's treasure so the FBI can magically dig it up and send me to prison. Maybe Carrie was out there in the woods watching Erin hide the damn thing. That would almost be funny."

"When for a fact did you ever see Erin with the MP5K?"

"I didn't see it and wouldn't have known about it. But Carrie had to brag. She just couldn't resist rubbing it in."

"So it's what Carrie said as opposed to what you saw." Janet is a lawyer but I wouldn't expect her to sound like one during a supposed private moment with her partner.

"She'll make it look like I had it all along when in fact she did." Lucy is talking about Carrie stealing the machine gun I saw slung around her neck in the first video. "She restored it to its original condition, turned it into a deadly little Valentine on February fourteenth, 1998, for her vapid former beauty queen. And then nine years later and we know what happened."

"Erin didn't come right out and say that to you." Janet seems to be building a case.

"She said enough for me to get the drift."

"And of course she didn't record the conversation."

"They never do."

"Did you ever see Erin with the machine gun in question? Think hard, Lucy."

"No. After I told Carrie to stay away from me she bragged. She claimed she got the MP5K back into working order and that she taught Erin how to shoot it, clean it, that sort of thing. That was her Valentine's Day present, a day on the range with a dangerous weapon, and Erin was such a damn ditz. She couldn't even reload a damn pistol magazine. She couldn't push the cartridges down unless she used a speed loader or had someone load it for her. I can't imagine her shooting a machine gun."

"But she did. Carrie taught her how to shoot a gun that Erin now claims came from you. In other words Erin is lying. And she's planting evidence." Janet is open and bold about Erin Loria, and it's deliberate but I don't think Lucy has caught on.

"That's what Carrie said at the time," Lucy replies and I have no doubt that Janet has seen the *Depraved Heart* videos. "Erin was talking about the former prime minister of Pakistan being assassinated. I knew exactly who she meant. Who else could it be? And that can mean only one thing. Carrie's talking to the damn FBI. She's talking to Erin. She may have turned over the MP5K to her for that matter, possibly recently."

"And then suddenly frag from a bullet magically matches,"

Janet makes her next comment a matter of record, a damning record depending on who she's targeting. "Why was the comparison even made? Especially now?"

"It's the very sort of thing Carrie would orchestrate. If nothing else all she has to do is tamper with various databases such as the NSA, the FBI, Interpol, whatever strikes her fancy. She could falsify a forensic report, fake a hit," Lucy says as I think of what Jill Donoghue asked me this morning.

She wondered if I'd ever heard of *data fiction*. And that seems to be what Lucy is describing.

"She could do that easily and she also knows people in the intelligence community. Now it's making sense why DoD showed up at your house pretending to be the tax collector," Janet says and I envision the dark man in the cheap suit who claimed to be a revenue officer for the IRS.

"Carrie reenters the U.S. finally and makes sure she's going to drop a bombshell," Lucy says. "She hacks into databases and creates political pandemonium."

We don't get badges, guns, nothing fun like that, said the man who introduced himself as Doug Wade.

He lied to Jill Donoghue and me. Everyone is lying.

"Carrie finds a way to ensure that frag recovered from the assassination is a match with a machine gun that was once in the custody of the FBI," Lucy says. "You realize how long she's been sitting on this?"

"And that's classic," Janet says.

"It's what she does. She gathers things as they happen and holds on to them for as long as it takes. Then she launches her next attack."

"The timing's not an accident." Janet stares at Lucy and avoids looking anywhere else.

"Of course it's not an accident."

"Suddenly there's a match between the MP5K and bullet frag. Suddenly Erin Loria transfers to Boston and is chasing you to the gates of hell."

"Which is what Carrie always threatened. She said when I reach the gates of hell don't let them slam me in the ass on my way in," Lucy says and I hope I'm misunderstanding what she and Janet are implying.

They seem to be suggesting that the missing MP5K may have found its way to Pakistan by late December of 2007. The gun could link the United States to the assassination of former Prime Minister Benazir Bhutto.

ULTIMATELY SCOTLAND YARD got involved in the case. I remember it was determined that Bhutto died from blunt force trauma caused by a terrorist attack on her vehicle.

Bullet fragments would have been analyzed. They would have been compared with any weapons recovered, and maybe one of them was an unusual machine gun once in the FBI's possession. Benton had it. Then Erin Loria did, even if only briefly. It would be like Carrie Grethen to make sure the gun creates havoc, especially if the biggest loser is the American government, specifically the Department of Justice.

What a terrible thing to do to an FBI agent who's not particularly bright or formidable, and as much as I dislike Erin Loria I wouldn't wish that on her. I can only imagine the international outrage. Even the Bureau might suffer damage if it came out that former beauty queen Special Agent Loria now married to a federal judge was at one time in possession of a machine gun used in the murder of a former world leader. Maybe she's trying to save her own ass at my niece's expense. If someone has to go it won't be Erin Loria. Or that's what she thinks.

"Carrie has to be talking to someone in government," Lucy is saying. "How else would they know about the *kurz*?"

"You're basing this on a few vague questions Erin asked," Janet replies. "That's my impression since I wasn't present."

She says it as if she's creating documentation, and I wonder who Janet is really talking to right now. Lucy? Or the FBI? Or is Janet talking to me?

"Why else would Erin want to know where I was on December twenty-seventh, 2007? She asked me about the machine gun I had quote *stolen and hidden* in my dorm room. So where'd that come from if not from Carrie?" Lucy works the curved edge of the pry bar between the edges of two tiles.

"I can imagine her saying something like that."

"Erin asked me what happened to what she called an MP5K *prototype,* which it wasn't. It was just a very early model, so early it has a single-digit serial number."

"It would be just like Carrie to let Erin play around with something long enough to taint her," Janet says. "Carrie has created a liability. But not just for Erin."

"Also Benton." Lucy doesn't hesitate to say his name.

But so far Janet hasn't so much as alluded to him. I continue to sense she's being careful. She's talking as if she knows the conversation isn't private.

"Imagine if a gun you'd once had illegally even if only for a day was implicated in the assassination of Benazir Bhutto?" Janet adds.

"Even if Carrie's lying and planted false reports it's still a bad story if it gets out."

"Forgetting the PR nightmare," Janet says, "there's not going to be any statute of limitations loophole in a case like that, and that's exactly why that DoD idiot was here. The FBI is a stalking horse for the DoD, and we've seen our share of cases like that. You think you're doing one thing when you're really doing something else."

"Now it's the Pentagon after me," Lucy says, and she sounds more annoyed than anything else.

"Something is." Janet has yet to look at a camera or in the direction of one.

I can't stop replaying in my mind the first thing I saw when I clicked on this video link. Janet clipped her phone back to the waistband of her scrubs. She'd been doing something with it. Then it didn't seem to work anymore. I called it and it didn't ring.

She activated the surveillance system. Then she turned off her phone, making sure no one could reach her.

"This is funny though. Was I right?" Lucy pries up another tile. "Their ground-penetrating radar in their overkill chopper wasn't going to find anything down here."

I hear stone rubbing against stone as she slides tiles out of the way, and then she lifts out three more. Under them are a sheet of steel and a control box of some type. Lucy enters a code and presses a button. An electric motor hums to life. The metal subflooring begins to move, to open like a hatch.

She drops in the pry bar, the shovel, and they disappear in the void and clatter loudly at the bottom. There's a ladder, and Lucy climbs down into a subterranean hideaway that I've never known about before now. It's like her sound-masking boathouse and her Cone of Silence rock garden. It's like so much I'm finding out. I hear the shovel scraping. Who else is seeing this or will? It's an incredible thought that Janet might be the one spoofing Lucy's ICE phone number and making sure I'm watching.

If only I could talk to Lucy right now.

"Everything all right?" Janet calls down to her. "You okay?"

"Roger that." Lucy's voice is muffled, and she's out of range inside this secret place where she stashes possessions that are on the warrant but were missed.

Lucy knows exactly how federal agents conduct searches. When she puts her mind to it she can outsmart their every procedure, protocol and technology. I watch her lifting ammunition boxes up through the opening, setting them on the floor and pushing them to one side. She lifts out a sleek assault rifle with a silvery metallic finish, a Nemo Omen Win Mag .300 that she gently sets on the tarp.

This is followed by another one with a different finish on the receiver, and I recognize firearms that Lucy calls deadly works of art. I've shot them before, and I watch her continue to obstruct justice. It doesn't matter that I don't blame her. It's of no consequence that what the FBI is doing to her is an outrage. Her behavior is criminal and they'd arrest her instantly if they knew, and I watch as she climbs up out of the pit. The motor starts again as she closes the hatch. A buzzer sounds loudly. Someone is at Lucy's front gate.

Please God let it be the police.

"Who's here?" Janet walks over to a security monitor.

Lucy picks up the two assault rifles, lightweight and as precise as a laser beam. They shimmer in shades of silver, copper and green.

"I think it's a cop," Janet says. "What are the cops doing here?"

"Shit," Lucy says. "Now what?"

I can't make out what's on split screen. It's too far away. Janet touches the display and asks how she can help the person. Next I hear a man's voice. He sounds familiar. When he starts coughing like a chain smoker I realize it's the same state trooper who showed up here at the Gilbert house early this morning. I thought he'd gone home sick. I guess he didn't but it sounds as if he should have. Trooper Vogel. I still don't know his first name.

"Who am I speaking to, ma'am?" He coughs again as Janet answers him. "We got a report and want to make sure everything's okay in there."

"We're fine," Janet says. "What report?"

"Ma'am, I need you to open the gate. We'd like to come in just to be sure everyone's okay."

"Open it," Lucy tells Janet.

"I'm opening the gate," Janet says to the security monitor.

"We'll see you at the front door," Trooper Vogel says as Lucy uses her foot to shove ammo boxes across the floor to a workbench.

Then I see it again. Janet removes her phone from her waistband and types with her thumbs, probably unlocking the keypad. Instantly my display goes dark. The live-streaming stops. When I click on the link again it's dead. I look up and am shocked to see Benton standing in the bedroom doorway, checking something on his phone, his earpiece winking bright blue. I stare at him, startled and alarmed. I have no idea how long he's been there or why or how he got in.

"They're safe, Kay." Benton is dressed the same way he was when I left the house this morning. "Concord P.D., the state police, our agents are on Lucy's property as we speak or are about to be with additional backup on the way."

"The police are already inside the house?" I don't believe that's possible.

"They're on the way." He walks in.

"That's not the same as being with them—physically being

with them right this second. You know who we're dealing with, Benton."

"Lucy, Janet, Desi, Jet Ranger, everyone's accounted for and safe." His amber eyes are locked on me and he knows damn well who I mean. "Nothing is going to happen to them."

"How can we be sure of that yet?"

"Because I'm telling you, Kay. They aren't alone and won't be." He looks alert and unflappable but I have no doubt he's been through it.

This can't have been a good day for him and I see the hints of stress and fatigue in the messiness of his thick silver hair and the tightness around his eyes and mouth. The suit is one of my favorites, pearl gray with a very narrow cream stripe, and it's badly wrinkled. His white shirt is wrinkled. Probably from the five-point harness he was wearing inside the helicopter it occurs to me.

"We have to make sure they're fine," I persist. "She'll want you to think they are, and when everyone is feeling safe you know what happens."

"I do know what happens. I know how she thinks," he says, and I realize it's not the FBI that has Chanel Gilbert's house under surveillance.

If the Bureau were spying on this place then Benton would know about it. He wouldn't talk freely. He would talk in an off-tilt scripted way—the same way Janet has been talking. Or he'd say nothing at all. If anyone is spying it's Carrie, and I'm fast reaching the point of not caring. She seems to know everything about us anyway.

CHAPTER 42

HE SHUTS THE DOOR, AND WE'RE ALONE INSIDE Chanel Gilbert's bedroom.

Or someone's bedroom.

I can't be sure whose.

"I know you're upset," Benton says. "I can understand how you might feel abandoned and misinformed by me right now."

"I'm upset? Words I might use are *unhappy, confused, concerned, manipulated.*" I don't want to sound like this. "Who was she, Benton? I saw the dive pictures in the library. Who the hell was she?"

He doesn't say a word.

"I saw the tactical wet suit she had on. Black with a chest zipper, and that's what I saw in the video my dive mask took. You and I don't wear chest zippers. Our wet suits don't have two white stripes on the leg but it appears hers did based on what I noticed in the framed photos of her wreck diving in the Bermuda Triangle. Do I need to refresh your memory further?" I continue to talk despite a presumed lack of privacy.

I have to know if the person who saved my life in Fort Lauderdale this past June is dead. Murdered. Probably beaten to death by Carrie.

"Her dental records have confirmed her identification," I say to Benton. "But that doesn't mean anything. Who was she?"

"I understand how things might look," Benton finally answers.

"Maybe you'd like to tell me who Doug Wade is while we're at it."

"I'm not sure who you mean."

"I mean the man I met on Lucy's property who isn't really with the IRS. He's with the Department of Defense, and DoD wouldn't be involved unless this is more about national security than some trumped-up criminal case against Lucy . . ."

"We can talk about this later . . ."

"But I can't imagine why you might think I'm upset. Why should it upset me that I can't trust a damn thing anybody does or says right now?" I'm emotional and that's the last thing I want to be. "How did you get in here? Did you take her Range Rover and not tell the police? Or maybe a fake IRS agent took it."

"Her Range Rover?" Benton frowns.

"A red one that was here earlier and now is gone." I feel tears touch my eyes and I fight them back. "But I don't believe the recording device in the silver box is yours." I realize how angry I am, and I need to back off before I lose control. "It was too sloppily done even for the FBI. That was a scare tactic. It's psychological terrorism for us to be working a case like this and worry every second that we're being spied on. You wouldn't wind the clocks."

"I wouldn't do what?"

"Or leave candles. You wouldn't play a game like that with me. Your colleagues might. But you wouldn't and you also wouldn't permit it."

"What game, Kay?"

"There's more than one, Benton."

"I don't know anything about a silver box."

"I'm relieved to hear it." I don't care who else does.

"What candles?" Benton asks.

"You'd have to walk into the living room to notice the scent. I assume they're still there unless they've vanished right under our noses the way the kitchen trash did. New white votive candles that I suspect were recently put there, possibly while we were on Lucy's property, and the clocks were wound. Candles scented with my favorite fragrance, Benton. The one you always get for me on my birthday."

"We didn't do it. We haven't been on this property until now."

"And you would know that for a fact. You know everything your colleagues are doing. Well I could tell you a lot of things they might not know that go back a very long time. Dangerous things."

He says nothing. He doesn't ask me what dangerous things I might be referring to, and he watches me quietly and glances at his phone.

"I think I know what's happened," I say to him, and his silence is my answer.

He knows about the recordings. He's seen them.

"Of course the FBI didn't sneak in here and set up this place with me in mind, with me in mind personally, intimately." I feel myself getting angrier as I get more rattled.

Benton, what have you done?

"Why would they go to all the trouble to find special Italian candles?" A current of fear runs through me. "They didn't . . ."

"Kay?"

"But you're not going to share that with me. I'm sure I'll have to find out everything on my own. I have to find out for myself what you know or don't. You're not going to admit it to me if you're to blame for Lucy being raided, for Marino and me being followed by one of your damn helicopters."

"Are you finished, Kay?"

"I've barely started, Benton."

"I meant in here. Are you done working in here because I'm not leaving unless you're with me. You're not staying here without me."

When he's extremely serious and intense, I'm reminded of how tall he is. He seems to tower over me when he leans into a conversation, his strong chin lifted, his keen features predatory like an eagle, a hawk.

"We don't have much time," he says next.

"Who else is with you?"

"I told them to drop me off. I was coming in alone. We should go."

"You told your FBI colleagues that. The ones you were flying with right before the weather turned awful. The ones who are trying to trump up a reason to ruin Lucy's life or possibly even end it." I won't let him forget that unforgivable fact. "Your colleagues who are doing the bidding of the Pentagon, and that's exactly what must be happening. Otherwise DoD wouldn't show up on Lucy's property pretending to be the IRS." I say it boldly because I'm convinced he already knows.

"We can't get into this now." His face is somber, his eyes intense. "We have maybe fifteen minutes before they're back with others."

THE FBI will be all over this house. They've taken charge of the investigation as Marino and I suspected. I know what happens next.

It doesn't matter that I have federal jurisdiction. You can't legislate collaboration and the FBI isn't exactly known for working and playing well with others. They'll take over this scene and then they'll take over the evidence. They can do whatever they want.

"The house hasn't been swept yet," I say to him. "We're possibly being monitored. But then why am I the one telling you?"

"I'm glad you did." He says it with dry ice irony.

"We should probably assume it at every scene these days." I begin stripping the bed, and he doesn't reply. "But then you would know that too." I glance up at him. "It's hard not to know something if you're the one who did it."

"Did what, Kay?"

But I'm the one who's silent this time as I carefully fold the pillowcase that turned black in UV light. Paper rattles loudly as I package evidence and Benton watches. I feel his eyes on me. I sense he's busy with his phone. Another scheme, another manipulation, I can't help but think as I uncap a Sharpie and smell the bright odor of ink. I take off my gloves. I close the scene case and pick it up.

Non fare i patti con il diavolo, my father used to say.

"One thing I was taught when I was growing up"—I meet Benton's eyes—"is don't make a contract with the devil. The very act of acquiescing will land you in a pit you can't climb out of. Or is it too late?"

Benton continues to stand in front of the closed door. Judging by the blank look on his face he has no idea what I'm talking about. But it isn't true. I feel strongly that it isn't. He may not know everything going on but he knows most of it. He's responsible for some of it at the very least, and I find it remarkable to contemplate the position I find myself in. I can't tell what is Carrie's bad behavior and what is the federal government's or my husband's.

"Is what too late, Kay?" Benton asks.

"Whatever you've done," I reply. "And that includes the videos I've been watching today, watching against my will I might add. Since I didn't exactly ask for them. Nor has anyone confessed to sending them. And if you know what I'm talking about and I suspect you do?" I add and the more I allude to the *Depraved Heart* videos the quieter he gets.

He knows.

"Well I just hope you're sure, Benton. Because you're playing with fire. You shouldn't dance Carrie Grethen's dance or get into her dialogue." I hold his stare for a beat and hear distant footsteps in the hallway.

What's done is done, and Benton isn't going to listen. I can look at him and tell it's too late to stop whatever he's put into motion.

"I have evidence rounds to make and cases to check on." I move past him as footsteps in the hallway get closer, and I hear Marino's voice. "You can ride with me to the office. Unless you'd rather wait for your colleagues," I say to Benton as I open the door.

"You need to hold on." Marino is firm but low-key for him. "Ma'am? Let me . . . ? It's real important they know what you just told me."

"You're damn right it's important!" Amanda Gilbert rolls toward us like a gale and I almost don't recognize the famous producer.

She looks considerably older than her sixty-some years. Her dyed red hair is disarrayed around her shoulders, her face haggard, her eyes dark pools of grief and something else I try to pin a label on before it's too late.

"Get out." Her voice trembles as she jabs a finger at me. "I want everybody out of my house."

I feel her hatred and fury, and they're not what I expect in a scenario like this. She just walked through a foyer spattered with her daughter's blood, and there are no tears, only anger and indignation.

"The housekeeper," Marino says to Benton and me. "There isn't one."

"What do you mean *there isn't one*? Not at all?" I ask. "Then who did Hyde talk to when he first got here this morning?"

"I got no idea," Marino says.

"Whoever the person is she knew Chanel." Benton states it as a fact.

"There's no housekeeper? Did your daughter clean the house herself?" I ask Amanda Gilbert this but it's Marino who answers.

"Apparently Chanel hadn't been here since the spring," he says. "And she prefers to pick up after herself."

"Where was she?" Benton asks her mother but I'm convinced he already knows, and it's terrible to think about how badly I've been fooled and for how long.

"Who the hell are you?" she demands and he tells her.

Then he asks, "Did she have a red Range Rover?"

"Not that I'm aware of."

"There's one registered in her name. I guess you're not aware of that either."

"What are you implying? Identity theft?"

"Who notified you about your daughter's death?" Benton asks and he's definitely not implying identity theft.

What he's hinting at is spying. The murdered woman might have been Chanel Gilbert. But she was also someone else. Her mother probably has no idea who and what her daughter really was.

"I found out because she e-mailed me." Amanda Gilbert jabs her finger at me, and it's not true. "The coroner e-mailed me. A politician in other words. And I'm supposed to trust a fucking elected official?"

I certainly didn't send the e-mail, and Bryce swears our office didn't either.

"I'm actually not a coroner. And I wasn't elected. I wonder if you could let us see the e-mail," I say to her quietly, carefully.

She finds it on her phone and shows it to Marino, and when he looks at me I know the truth. The CFC e-mail has been hacked. Possibly Carrie has hijacked my e-mail account and is in my office database, and if so that will be ruinous in ways I can't begin to calculate. There can be no other explanation unless Lucy signed onto my e-mail account and sent a message to Amanda Gilbert. I seriously doubt that.

There's no reason for Lucy to have known about Chanel's death until news of it appeared on Twitter not so long ago. I try to imagine what Carrie's endgame might be as Benton asks Amanda Gilbert how long she's owned this house. As if he doesn't already know the answer to that, and I feel certain he does.

"Where has she been? I'm supposed to answer that again?" Amanda Gilbert is openly hostile toward each of us but seems to distrust me the most.

"Again?" Benton watches her carefully, and I suspect the questions he's asking are for our benefit and not his.

"It's none of your damn business! I have nothing else to say to the fucking FBI!"

Nothing else? I think. She's talked to one of Benton's colleagues. She's talked to someone, and Benton does us the favor of asking her who.

"I don't remember the name."

"You don't remember which agent contacted you?" he asks. "A man? A woman?"

"Some woman as dumb as a box of hair."

Erin Loria.

"She sounded stupid and southern," Amanda Gilbert says.

"It would be helpful if you'd tell me what you discussed," Benton says before Marino has the chance.

"Well by all means let me be *helpful*." Her voice shakes, her eyes swimming with tears. "Chanel is a professional diver and a photojournalist who constantly travels and gets involved in assignments she doesn't talk about."

She's more than that if she was in Fort Lauderdale when I was shot. If Chanel is the diver in the video my mask recorded then she was present at the shipwreck when Carrie almost killed me. The implication is obvious, and I suspect it's the truth. Chanel Gilbert was some sort of operative, possibly working for military intelligence or Homeland Security. Lucy and Janet knew her and I suspect Benton did too, and what that means is Chanel witnessed the attack.

And now she's been murdered.

She could have sworn to Carrie's existence and Lucy's innocence. But Chanel Gilbert or whoever she was isn't around to tell.

Maybe that's why she's dead.

"This is my damn house," Amanda Gilbert is saying shakily, furiously. "I grew up in this damn house. It was my family home. My father sold it after I left for college and when it went on the market several years ago I decided to buy it for Chanel and her eventual family. I thought maybe she might settle down and have some peace and quiet, that maybe she'd stop running around and disappearing."

"What about Bermuda?" Marino asks her. "I'm wondering if you have a place there."

"I have a lot of places at my disposal. And Chanel has managed to use all of them as whistle-stops. She was hardly ever here. She's not been anyplace for long ever since she was discharged from the Navy with PTSD."

"A disorder she possibly treated with medical marijuana?" I suggest, and when she doesn't answer I add, "Although based on what I've seen she didn't get her medication locally."

"Ma'am," Marino says to her, "I know how difficult this is. But you need to help us out by answering our questions. We're supposed to believe your daughter never had a housekeeper, that she tends to straighten up after her own self. Well let me ask you this. Who was Elsa Mulligan?"

"Who?"

"The lady who said she's your housekeeper," Marino replies. "The one who found your daughter's body?"

"I've never heard of any such person." She nails her attention on me, her eyes wild. "Who really found her? It wasn't some fictitious housekeeper that's for damn sure! So who was it? Who was inside this house . . . ?" She's raised her voice until she's yelling.

Carrie has been staying here.

"There is no damn housekeeper! There is no such damn person!"

"The candles, the spinning wheels, the iron crosses and crystals." I draw her attention to that. "Was your daughter superstitious or into the occult."

"Hell no!"

"Your decorator, for example, didn't place these items in here?"

"I don't know what items you're even talking about!"

"You'll see them when you walk into the living room," I reply and I can't stop thinking about Carrie.

The neighbors could have been seeing her for weeks, months

and would have been none the wiser. They wouldn't know the young woman driving the red Range Rover wasn't the owner of the house. Carrie has been helping herself to whatever she wants. That's why there are potpourris and special charms in rooms she inhabited, and I have a hunch about why the pillowcase turned black in ultraviolet light.

I've heard of bed linens treated with copper oxide, especially pillowcases. Impregnating a fabric with nanoparticles of copper is supposed to help combat wrinkles and other signs of aging, and there can be no doubt how Carrie feels about her youthful appearance.

She's been sleeping in Chanel's bed.

"Someone's been in and out according to the neighbors," Marino is saying. "We've got reports of the red Range Rover being spotted on the driveway. Who the hell was in it?"

"How dare you! How dare all of you! How could they let you in?" She steps closer to me and I smell alcohol and garlic on her breath. "Your niece seduced my daughter! She murdered my beautiful daughter in cold blood and they let you inside the house? They let you tamper with evidence!"

She clutches my arm, her grip like iron. Tears flood her bloodshot eyes and spill down her blotchy puffy face.

"Do you have any idea what my attorneys will do to you, to Lucy Farinelli, to the entire fucking lot of you?" she shrieks as she begins to cry uncontrollably.

CHAPTER 43

I'M AWARE OF MY LEG AS I SIT ALONE INSIDE THE SUV Jen Garate left for me. The ache is as deep as bone. Pain throbs in rhythm with the rain slowly thumping the roof and sliding down the windows.

The Ford Explorer is white with the CFC crest, the scales of justice and caduceus in dark blue symbolizing what I'm supposed to represent and fight for, what I'm sworn to uphold and never violate. Justice and do no harm. Yet nothing is just. I want to harm someone. If I were given a polygraph I would fail if I said I didn't want Carrie Grethen dead. I do. I want her eliminated for good by any means possible. My eyes don't stop moving. My nerves, my pulse have been humming all day like high-voltage power lines. I'm constantly checking the mirrors, my Rohrbaugh pistol in my lap. As I wait. As I wonder.

Maybe it's part of the master plan for me to be driving this next.

Maybe it was anticipated like the truck I selected this morning, and I consider that the SUV may have been tampered with too. Maybe it will go haywire on the highway or blow to the moon. Maybe that will be next and the way my time on this planet ends. I'm no longer sure of anything, not the natural course or progression of events or who's to blame. Is this what's supposed to happen? Is it preordained? Or does it just feel that way? Is it Carrie or someone else?

Don't doubt your own mind.

Then I think about Lucy as stress spikes and arcs like electrical glitches and overloads. What can any of us believe? What's true? Who's to say? I don't know what's been manipulated and schemed with more ugly surprises on the way, and I watch and wait for Marino and Benton. They're inside the house with a mother made berserk by grief and rage. She has enough power and money to give me as much trouble as she wants. Based on her demeanor she will try, and her accusations replay in my thoughts like a discordant chorus that won't stop.

Who planted the idea that Lucy had seduced and murdered her daughter? Why would Amanda Gilbert bring up my niece for any reason? Why would the Hollywood producer have heard of her? Unless Lucy and Chanel really did know each other but that seems strange too. If Chanel was a spy then why would Lucy know her? What business might they have had in Bermuda, and I remember Lucy saying the person she met there was Janet's friend. Chanel Gilbert may have known Janet first.

I'm not sure what that might mean. But I have no doubt someone gave the mother a reason to worry that I might tamper with evidence. I don't have to look very hard to know who. Erin Loria is after Lucy. I can imagine the aggressive self-important FBI agent with her southern roots and twang calling Amanda Gilbert and feeding her all sorts of propaganda, miscommunications and outright lies. But why exactly? To ensure we're sued? To frame Lucy and get me fired? To turn all of us on each other and watch us self-destruct? What is Erin Loria's real agenda?

I seriously doubt it has anything to do with law enforcement, with her damn job, and all these things float up from my deepest darkest trench of distrust. I can't be certain who's telling me the truth, including my own husband, my entire family really, and I adjust the defogger, clearing the glass. I'm grateful that the rain is on its way to stopping and the wind is calmer. Thunder beats a distant retreat. I can scarcely hear it anymore and to the south clouds are breaking up, flattening the way they do when their violent drama is spent.

I keep up my scan as I glance at my e-mails, my messages. When my phone rings I realize how easily I startle right now. I'm hypervigilant and jumpy. I recognize the number calling me but I'm puzzled.

"Scarpetta," I answer.

"I hate to start out by saying *you're not going to believe this*," Ernie launches in without a hello.

"Why are you calling from the firearms lab?" I reply.

"I'm about to get to that but first on the list?" he says. "The metamaterial you sent in may be from Lucy's camera system, which I'm guessing is *Star Trek* high-tech."

"I asked her that and she said it wasn't," I'm quick to answer.

"Not that I've ever seen anything quite like this associated with a security system," he says.

"Lucy told me she'd never seen the metamaterial before but she suspected it might be quartz or calcite."

"It is," he verifies. "Specifically a laser-quality calcite that is typically used in high-grade optics like camera lenses, microscopes, telescopes. But again, the hexagonal shape of this is very odd."

"So we can't know what the metamaterial might be from unless we locate a possible source for comparison."

"Exactly right," he replies. "Which brings me to your buffalo fiber. I'd sure like to know the source of it because you can bet it's old and interesting."

"Did you say buffalo?"

"As in 'Home on the Range' and nickels from my grandfather's day."

"Buffalo have fibers?"

"The same way sheep do. For the sake of simplicity I'll call what I found a hair. But technically it's a fiber and a first-time match in my animal reference library," he says proudly, almost lovingly. "Which is why I've been building it all these years. You're always waiting for that one oddball something to show up . . ."

"Buffalo aren't exactly indigenous to this area." I stare straight ahead at a black SUV backing toward me on the flooded driveway.

Not SWAT, I think. It looks like a limo.

"I think if we consider the context, Kay, this hair goes back a long time," Ernie says. "Possibly from a buffalo skin, a rug, a robe that's inside someplace or possibly was in an earlier era. The Cambridge house where your truck was parked when you found the dust bunny, the arrow? It's really old."

"Yes. More than three hundred years." My attention is riveted to the SUV, a Cadillac Escalade with dark tinted windows and a livery license tag.

It's slowly backing toward me, starting and stopping, taillights flaring red as Ernie tells me he's been doing some *poking around*. He's been excavating as he puts it, and he reminds me for the hundredth time at least that he should have been an archaeologist.

"What have you dug up?" My eyes are on the black SUV getting closer.

"That the Gilbert house was built by some rich Englishman who owned a shipping company," he says. "According to what I've come across the place started out as a sizable estate in Cambridge's rural days when there was nothing much there but a small college called Harvard. The original property included a smokehouse, a guesthouse and servants' quarters, a kitchen, and one article said cows were kept in the basement out of the harsh winter weather. They'd take them outside to graze then return them to built-in stalls."

"I can only imagine the trace evidence in such a place." I see where he's going with this.

"Trace evidence like the broken piece of Venetian glass that could be from a trade bead," he says, "which could be related to the shipping company. As could furs."

But where might such fragile ephemerae have been preserved this long and out of view? I've yet to see anything on the property that could be a time capsule. The house has been renovated and enlarged over the centuries, and the outbuildings are gone with not much left but the broken bricks and stones scattered beneath a backyard hedge I noticed through a window. Then the FBI helicopter thunders through my mind and I remember what Lucy said about ground-penetrating radar. The FBI was searching Lucy's property for anything buried. Maybe the place to be searching is here.

I resist the impulse to get out of my SUV, to begin looking around. Benton and Marino will show up any minute. It wouldn't be wise to wander the grounds alone, and I stay put with my doors locked as Ernie tells me what he's found out about the early American fur trade. He says unusual fibers beneath a buffalo's undercoat can be spun into a fabric similar to cashmere, and this is one reason the skins were a popular export until the end of the nineteenth century.

"Bottom line?" he adds as I watch the Escalade inch closer, faltering, lurching, as if something is wrong with the driver. "Everything we're finding seems to be from the same context."

Water sloshes around the oversize tires, beading on the glossy black paint. The wipers have been turned off, the back windshield fogged up and I don't know how the driver can see. I'm about to bolt out of my SUV when the Escalade halts inches from my front bumper. It has me blocked in when it couldn't be more obvious that I'm not merely parked here. I'm on official business with the engine running, the lights on. Not to mention I'm sitting inside.

I keep my eyes on the Escalade. I wait for someone to get out of it.

NO ONE DOES. The driver's door doesn't open and I decide the limo is Amanda Gilbert's. Perhaps it dropped her off then drove away for some reason. Now it's back.

"Where exactly did you find this buffalo fiber?" I ask Ernie.

"The arrow fletching," he replies. "The dyed blond hair."

"Human?"

"As you suspected, I'm sorry to say, because the implication is a pretty bad one. The hair is saturated with glue, so you can imagine what's stuck to it," he replies. "I can't say whose hair. Hopefully DNA will tell us soon. Of course we might be talking the DNA of one of our early ancestors. The tissue and hair could be really old I suppose."

"They aren't. The excised scalp is dried but not mummified and has a slight odor of decomposition. My guess is it's been in someplace moderately cool and dry but is relatively fresh."

"How fresh?"

"Days old. Possibly weeks," I reply. "Again it depends on where it's been since it was removed from someone's head."

"Postmortem? Because I sure as hell hope so. But knowing her? That wouldn't be as much fun."

Ernie has examined tool marks and other evidence we believe were left by Carrie Grethen during the commission of her various violent acts that in the past year include at least six homicides. He knows what she's capable of. He doesn't doubt her existence. He doesn't find it convenient or politically advantageous to blame Lucy for her crimes. He has no compulsion to engage Carrie in a battle that is ours to lose, and I worry that's exactly what has happened. What she's set in motion may be too far gone to remedy.

Non fare i patti con il diavolo. Non stuzzicare il can che dorme.

"At this moment I can't promise it occurred postmortem," I tell Ernie.

Don't make a contract with the devil. Don't tease a sleeping dog, my father used to say.

"The victim could still be alive," I explain. "A partial scalping isn't necessarily a fatal injury."

"So she's gotten rid of someone else or is going to," Ernie replies.

"This isn't about a need to eliminate people as a matter of convenience or expediency." I feel hatred stir in my deep dark place. "It never is with her even if she shoots the person from a mile away. It's about power and control. It's about what feeds her insatiable compulsions that inevitably cause profound pain and annihilation to anyone in her path."

"I sure as hell hope she's not torturing someone she's holding captive somewhere," Ernie then says.

Given the opportunity Carrie is fond of removing flesh. If she's in the mood she doesn't wait for her victim to die before she goes to work with a sharp blade or in one case I know of a well-honed chisel. It all depends on who and what strikes her fancy, and she can be impulsive. Benton says she can be whimsical, a word far kinder than I would apply to the likes of her. But he's right about her ability to turn on a dime, as I've heard it defined.

If Carrie has a fatal flaw it's her emotionality. She can't stop until she's over the cliff. Based on her history, that can take years before she vanishes again or we mistakenly assume she's dead.

"When I can look at the tissue microscopically," I tell Ernie, "I should be able to say whether there was a vital response. I should be able to say with certainty whether the injury is postmortem or not."

"Any idea who she might have targeted?"

"Whoever it is she's taunting us with it," I reply and on and off I've been thinking about the boy.

What has happened to Troy Rosado? What did Carrie do with him after she murdered his politician father, shooting him to death from aboard his own yacht while he was waiting on the water's surface to begin his dive? I tell Ernie to make sure the DNA lab is aware of my grim suspicion. It would be like Carrie to partner with a disturbed teenage boy, to seduce him into doing her bidding. Then to thank him the way she does. Which is hideously.

"What do you know about the glue on the arrow?" My anger rolls to a boil. "Do you have a chemical analysis of that yet? Anything special?"

"Cyanoacrylate, good ole Super Glue."

"What else?"

"So far it's quite the trace evidence bouillabaisse." Ernie sounds cheerful as he talks about the trash in life that he considers treasure. "Bovine hair, and remember I mentioned people used to keep cows in the basement. Also deer hair, which isn't unusual. And I've found wool, cotton lint and other natural fibers, pollen, and pieces and parts of cockroaches and crickets. Plus potassium nitrate. In other words saltpeter in addition to sulfur, carbon and traces of iron, copper and lead that have sort of permeated everything," he says and I understand why he's in the firearms lab.

Saltpeter, sulfur and carbon are the basic components of gunpowder. Specifically black powder.

"What's really strange are tiny globules of metal that was molten at some point," Ernie says. "It's what I commonly see on skin, especially around burns in electrocutions."

"Possibly part of gunshot residue?" I think of the granule I saw that looked like a black sugar crystal.

"The molten metal is copper and unrelated to GSR in my opinion. Like I said I associate it with electrical burns we see in fatal electrocutions. I'm putting you on speakerphone now," Ernie says. "We'll let a real gun nut weigh in."

"You're sure it's not gunshot residue, both burned and unburned powder that we typically see in shootings?" I rephrase my question. "In other words could the residue be from something contemporary? Is there some crazy reason GSR could have been inside my truck? And maybe that's why it's showing up in the lab?"

"I'd say no. I'd say it categorically." It's not Ernie talking now. "No one has cleaner forensic vehicles than we do and if the black powder in question is burned it would be very fragile. Chances are we wouldn't be finding it."

The deep midwestern voice belongs to Jim, the chief of the firearms lab.

"Burned black powder is extremely corrosive," he explains. "Especially when it's exposed to moisture, for example condensation that forms when a gun barrel is cooling. There's a chemical reaction that forms sulfuric acid, and if you don't know that and don't clean your black powder pistol right away? The barrel is fouled like you wouldn't believe. I'm talking within hours. What we've got here isn't burned powder. It's definitely not GSR."

In contrast unburned black powder can remain viable indefinitely if it's protected in an abandoned armory or is sealed by rust inside an old weapon, and that's what Jim and Ernie believe we're talking about. Unburned powder that could be hundreds of years old, and I think of the stories I've heard about antique firearms loaded with ammunition that people assume is inert until the gun accidentally goes off.

"How many cannonballs have you seen used as doorstops or hanging from gates especially during your Virginia days?" Jim says.

"If I had a dollar for every one," I reply.

"Most people have no idea a cannonball from the American Revolution or the Civil War could still explode, that they're basically decorating their house with a bomb."

"Could the black powder possibly be modern?" I ask the question again because it's critically important. "Even remotely possible? How can we be sure someone isn't using it to build an explosive device?"

"BP"—as Jim refers to black powder—"isn't child's play. Using it to build a bomb would be impractical and dangerous."

"As is true of everything it all depends on who you're talking about."

"Listen I'm the first to say we should never underestimate any potential disaster. Better safe than sorry. And sure. The person could make BP. When I was a kid I used to make my own, was a regular Betty Crocker in the garage. It's a damn wonder I lived long enough to vote and buy booze."

"The person I'm most concerned about may do her own gunsmithing, may reload her own ammo," I say to him and Ernie. "If so there would be traces of gunpowder, lead, iron and copper in her work area and possibly elsewhere. That's why I'm asking if we're absolutely certain the black powder is of antiquity and not from a location where someone might be building a weapon of mass destruction."

"I personally think it's an old remnant from the same era the other trace evidence is from." It's Ernie who says this, and I search my memory.

CHAPTER 44

I CAN'T RECALL SEEING BLACK POWDER IN ANY MA-chine shop Lucy has ever owned or worked in. I don't remember seeing its modern substitute Pyrodex either.

My niece has always been into extreme technology and has been tinkering and tampering with electronics and machines since she could walk. She isn't the sort to care about firing a flintlock gun or a muzzle-loader. She's never been particularly interested in things that are old. She'd rather read a book about physics than history. She doesn't collect antiques. She's not particularly sentimental about the past.

Lucy does her own handloading of ammunition and has for almost as long as she's been shooting her very fine guns. I've always preached safety first and would be very unhappy if Lucy worked with black powder. It's easily ignited. It's highly unpredictable and I've worked my share of explosive catastrophes when someone decides to make a dirty bomb and arrives at the morgue in heavy-duty plastic bags. I remember my surprise in the early days of my career when I realized that the first question in such cases is who are the bombers versus their victims.

It wasn't always obvious at first that the eviscerated, handless, headless body I examined turned out to be what was left of a cruel intention that literally blew up in the perpetrator's face. Now and then evildoers do it to themselves. I won't say it's poetic justice. But I think it.

"How many granules did you find?" I ask Ernie as I wonder if Carrie knows what we've discovered.

Or is the evidence in question something she left deliberately? Because it could be. It very well may be. If so what is it she's hoping we'll conclude and act on? I don't want to engage with her. I don't want to dance but I'm doing it even as I tell myself to resist. I shouldn't have started but I did, and the synchronizing isn't mine. I didn't choreograph it. I wasn't invited. I was recruited and tricked. But it doesn't matter at this point.

I fatti contano più delle parole. Another thing my father used to say.

"Five," Ernie answers my question. "Two in the dust bunny. Three in the fletching, the dyed human hair glued to the arrow. By the way? Jim had to head out to a deposition. He said to call if you need anything else."

Actions count more than words. I'm demonstrating it even as I'm sitting here. If I didn't want to play along I should have returned to my office hours ago. But that's not who I am and Carrie knows it.

"And I've just e-mailed you a couple photos," Ernie says.

"Hold on." I log on to the laptop built into the console.

I open the images Ernie has sent and at a magnification of 100X the BP granules look like broken pieces of coal, black and irregular. At 500X they look like meteorites big enough to land a spacecraft on, rugged and jagged, no two shapes alike. They're mingled with other debris, what looks like thick cables and cords and crystals in vivid colors. Dirt is only dirt when we don't see it up close. Under magnification it becomes a ruined world of broken edifices and habitats and the disintegrating remains of past lives that include bacteria and beetles and human beings.

"Well it's definitely not like smokeless powder, not like any manufactured propellant I've seen." I save the photographs in a folder. "Those granules come in a variety of shapes and sizes that are uniform and don't occur in nature. They don't look anything like what you just showed me. But I have to ask you again, Ernie. Old or new? What if someone makes BP? Will it look the same as it did centuries ago?"

"She could be making the stuff," he says as I watch the Gilbert's front door open. "Cooking it herself, sure she could. Jim says most people into BP these days are do-it-yourselfers, and it's risky as hell but not all that hard. Just saltpeter, sulfur and carbon with a dash or two of water and voilà, you've made a cake. And I always add the caveat of not trying this at home."

Amanda Gilbert emerges first on the front porch, and I feel a deep sense of doom rumble through me like an earthquake.

"When it's dry you break it up and force it through screens or whatever's handy in the kitchen like a spaghetti strainer." Ernie continues his deadly cooking lesson while my thoughts keep bumping into Carrie Grethen.

How cruel and cunning it would be to resort to a low-tech black powder bomb loaded with vicious frag like ball bearings and nails. I'd much rather be shot. So would most people. Carrie no doubt would be amused by the thought of such a mutilating way to die. Or maybe her goal is to maim and torment, to terrorize, to rip us apart one inch, one limb, one portion of scalp at a time.

I watch Amanda Gilbert, Benton and Marino talking on the front porch out of the rain as Ernie tells me about other microscopic fragments that he considers significant. It's possible the black powder was once stored in oak kegs, he's decided. It could go back to the American Revolution or the Civil War. Unless it's homemade? The BP Ernie has found can't be modern. He's quite certain it isn't but I'm withholding judgment. If I'm mindful of nothing else this day it's to be very careful of assumptions.

"I'm thinking about an outbuilding, a cellar?" He again wants to know if we've searched everywhere. "It's significant that I've yet to find anything consistent with contemporary times. Nothing synthetic for example such as polyester or nylon fibers."

"We checked the basement." I look out my side window at Amanda Gilbert arguing with Marino on the front porch. "And it's empty and clean. It isn't closed or sealed off. It's accessible by bulkhead doors that open into the yard."

"It could be a place that in an earlier life was an armory and later was turned into something else," Ernie suggests. "Just keep that in mind when you're looking around."

Amanda Gilbert, Benton and Marino are making their way down the front steps in the gentle steady rain. I tell Ernie I have to go as a chauffeur climbs out of the Escalade, and he's a Mister Magoo squinting, his big ears sticking out from his uniform cap.

I watch him open the back door for Amanda Gilbert and I'm not surprised by his erratic driving, his starting and stopping earlier. Marino and Benton climb inside my SUV and in typical fashion Marino picks the front seat. He doesn't ask. I pull out after the Escalade, keeping my distance.

"WHAT JUST HAPPENED?" I drive slowly over flooded bricks.

"She's pissed as hell." Marino pats his pockets the way he does when he needs a cigarette. "That's what's happened. She'll probably sue all of us."

"Here's what I can and will tell you," Benton says behind my head as we pass other old mansions where Chanel Gilbert's wealthy well-connected neighbors live.

But before he can continue, I interrupt. "Did Amanda give you any reason why she thinks Lucy has something to do with Chanel's murder?"

"Maybe that's why the FBI raided Lucy's property." Marino is turned in his seat so he can look at me as we talk, and as usual I have to tell him to buckle up. "Erin Loria's the snake in the woodpile in other words. But what I can't figure out is how she could have known anything about it so early. You assholes had your chopper up before we even knew it was a murder." He directs this at Benton.

"You're right. We didn't know about the murder but were aware of the relationship," Benton answers.

"Whose relationship?" I ease the SUV to a stop at Brattle Street.

"We have airport surveillance from Lucy's trip to Bermuda. We know when she landed at the FBO there and when she returned to Boston. We know that in fact Chanel Gilbert was on the private jet with her."

"Wait one damn minute." I look at him in the rearview mirror, and his eyes meet mine. "Lucy flew Chanel back from Bermuda?"

"Yes."

"You're absolutely sure?"

"Chanel Gilbert was on the manifest, Kay," he says. "And when agents boarded the plane at Logan they checked passports as you'd expect. There's no question who was on Lucy's jet."

"Quite to the contrary. I think there are plenty of questions about who was on it." I concentrate on my driving, careful to avoid deep puddles and big branches that are down.

I try not to give in to what I'm feeling. It's bad enough that Lucy might have met Chanel in Bermuda. But if Lucy flew her to Boston then that likely makes Lucy a suspect in Chanel's homicide. It could explain some of what's happened today. But I don't believe it explains all of it.

"Are we absolutely certain it was Chanel on the jet?" I ask him again. "As opposed to someone pretending to be her? Or maybe I should wonder if someone was impersonating Chanel Gilbert. Who the hell got murdered if it wasn't her?"

"We're sure of her identity," Benton says, answering nothing.

He may be sure of her identity. But that doesn't mean he's telling us the truth about it.

"Did she work for you?" I ask him point-blank. "Was she undercover FBI?"

"Not for us. But with us."

"I'm getting the feeling that after she left the Navy she didn't merely do photography," I reply wryly and with an edge. "But she may very well have suffered from PTSD. I would imagine working for some intelligence service like the CIA is very stressful. When were she and Lucy on the jet?"

"They landed in Logan day before yesterday, Wednesday," Benton says.

"I assume you checked the catering in addition to the manifest," I reply.

"Why do you ask?"

"Do you know what catering Lucy requested for her guest?"

"Shrimp stir-fry and brown rice." His eyes are on mine in the mirror. "In addition to the usual things you'd expect Lucy to have on board. Nuts, raw vegetables, humus, tofu. Her standing order."

"Someone ate Chinese food cold? Not that I haven't done it a million times right out of the carton," Marino says and I slow down as water blasts the undercarriage of the SUV. "But not on a private plane. Lucy's doesn't have a big galley and she refuses to have a flight attendant. Stir-fry seems a weird thing for catering."

"Chanel's gastric contents are consistent with her eating shrimp, rice and vegetables but the timing is off," I reply. "Her meal had barely begun to digest. She certainly didn't eat it during the short flight from Bermuda to Boston. But what I'm wondering is if she might have taken it home for later. If she'd been out of the house for months as her mother claims then there wouldn't have been anything in the refrigerator, nothing much to eat."

"Which is what we saw when we went through the kitchen," Marino agrees.

"Except for the fresh juices, and we can't assume those were hers. In fact I'm suspicious they aren't," I reply. "What time did Lucy's plane land at Logan?"

"Shortly after one P.M." Benton says. "And you're right. Chanel didn't eat on the plane. The pilots remember her carrying some of the catering off of it. They had to dig around and find a bag for her."

"You've talked to the pilots." I pick up on what he just said and he pauses as if he has to sort through information he might not want to share.

Then he says, "Yes."

"I'm curious about why you were inspired to do that, Benton. What were you hoping to discover? Were you asking the pilots about Chanel Gilbert? Or were your questions about Lucy and whatever the Customs agents might have been looking for when her jet was searched after it landed at Logan?"

"It wasn't Customs. It was the DEA."

"I see. Well the story gets only more unfortunate and offensive. Let me guess. The DEA showed up because there was a suspicion Lucy had found a way to get medical marijuana to Janet's dying sister?"

"It seems Lucy may have gotten it from Chanel Gilbert."

"Then how did it end up inside an old wooden box in the closet?" Marino asks. "Who the hell put it there if Chanel's not been here since last spring?"

"Last spring was about the time Lucy and Janet realized they needed something to help Natalie. What you've found may have been in the wooden box since then," Benton says. "Beyond that I don't know."

"And that's the explanation for how Janet, Lucy and Chanel knew each other?" I ask. "Because of Natalie and MMJ?"

"It's not," Benton says. "It's incidental to it. Medical marijuana has nothing to do with how the three of them were acquainted but it did turn into something they had in common. Again because of Natalie."

I begin to wonder if Janet may have introduced Lucy to a spy. I ask myself why Janet would know someone like that.

"Her mother must get the stuff for her in California or wherever," Marino says.

"I think Chanel was perfectly capable of getting anything she wanted," Benton says. "But to answer you, Kay?" He meets my eyes in the mirror. "Lucy was transporting *product* shall we say into Virginia. It is believed she was supplying it to Natalie the months before she died."

"Maybe if the Feds spent their time and resources on real crimes?" I reply. "What a different world it would be."

"Fortunately they didn't find weapons or contraband when they searched Lucy's plane," Benton says.

"What the hell?" Marino exclaims. "Your FBI assholes are just trying to trap her in anything you can possibly come up with? Because that's what it's sounding like."

Benton has no answer for that. At least not one he's going to offer. Instead he brings up what we've suspected all along. I'm not surprised but it's brutal to hear him confirm it so bluntly. The FBI believes Carrie Grethen is a fabrication, a diabolically ingenious one that Lucy conjured up *when she went rogue*. Pressure points. Triggers. Turbulence in a domestic life that's already shaky, and Lucy is unstable. She's always been unstable. *And let's face it she's a sociopath, Kay.*

CHAPTER 45

"THIS ISN'T ME TALKING," BENTON ADDS AS IF IT will make me feel better. "It's everyone else."

By everyone else he means the same people he always does. His people. The Feds. I'm aware of Marino next to me in the passenger's seat, his portable radio upright on his thigh. He's gotten interested in something and is turning up the volume.

"This is wrong beyond words and you know it, Benton." I continue glancing at him in the rearview mirror.

"I don't disagree."

Then I remind him of the H&K machine gun, an early model with a wooden forestock. I remember it was at my house in Richmond once.

"You had it in a briefcase that I assumed you locked inside the gun safe. You must have let Lucy borrow it at some point," I explain what I vaguely recall.

"Why would I let a child borrow anything I might keep in a gun safe?"

"Lucy wasn't a child," I reply but it's nagging at me that the chronology is off.

"If you're talking about the MP5K? Then Lucy would have been about ten. At the most twelve when it was presented to my unit," Benton says and I think back to when he showed up with the ominous briefcase, which he said was straight out of James Bond. "I happened to have it with me one night when I came to your house. I showed it to you because it was a novelty."

"Did you ever report it missing from my house after you locked it in the gun safe?"

"I never locked it in your gun safe, and it was never mine, Kay."

"But it was in your possession at one time."

"Me personally?" His face is unreadable in the rearview mirror.

"Yes."

"Only once. Very briefly in 1990, which was when I brought it to your house." He has that look he gets when he knows that what I'm about to say is incorrect.

"Because ultimately it was connected to the assassination of Benazir Bhutto," I tell him, and I'm distracted by Marino's radio.

A female officer is at the River Basin. She sounds keyed up as she requests backup and a detective.

"And you believe that?" Benton's reflection looks amused. As if I said something funny.

"Carrie had it. Then Erin Loria did. Ultimately it ended up in Pakistan," I say to him as Marino goes through his recent calls, looking for a number. "Erin Loria could be in a lot of hot water and I think that might be one reason she's framing Lucy."

"I don't know who you've been getting your information from," Benton says. "But the machine gun you're talking about was a prop my unit was given as a thank-you when the movie folks were filming *Silence of the Lambs* at Quantico in 1990. A couple of us got fun Hollywood toys like tommy guns, handcuffs, wanted posters. When Lucy showed up for her internship many years later she saw the MP5K prop in my office and asked if she could borrow it. Which was fine since the gun was completely useless not to mention legal," he adds and I feel foolish. "It was a real MP5K but the barrel had been plugged, the firing group removed and even the receiver was cut."

"Is it possible Carrie got hold of it and rebuilt it, got it back into working order?" I ask as Marino talks on his phone.

"Yeah I heard," he's saying to another officer. "What's going on?"

"It would have been hard but yes she certainly could have." Benton's eyes are on me as I continue to glance at the mirror.

"That would be a pretty shrewd setup wouldn't it? Someone gives a machine gun to the FBI profiling unit. And the head of it lets my nineteen-year-old niece borrow it. Then Carrie steals it and years later it's used to commit an international crime that would cause our government unthinkable embarrassment and bad relations if the truth got out. Not to mention wrecking a few careers. In particular Erin Loria's. Am I right, Benton? Is it true about Bhutto?"

"Erin certainly might think it's true. In my mind it's uncertain at this time if it's a bluff or an example of record tampering. Either way you're right. There's a massive perception problem if word gets out."

Data fiction.

"We should talk about this later," he says.

"The way things are going there may not be a later." I don't want to sound incensed but I do. "If that damn MP5K is ever connected even indirectly to Lucy? It makes no difference that the gun was a movie prop at one time. Maybe it was refurbished. Carrie could have done that blindfolded I'm guessing," I say and Benton is quiet. "And what a lot of trouble she could cause whether the records have been tampered with or not. Who's going to prove they've been tampered with or even admit it because that alone is a massive public perception problem. You know what they say about revenge. It's much better served cold. So why not wait years, almost a decade or even longer to decimate everyone you hate."

"I knew what Carrie did at the time," Benton says. "Lucy had to explain why the MP5K wasn't returned to the display case in my unit. She said Carrie had it and wouldn't give it back, and then they broke up and that was that. There's paperwork about the gun or *prop* disappearing. Of course it could be returned to working order and Lucy knew that too. Even as a teenager she was too smart to be hoodwinked."

"Erin Loria probably wasn't. She probably isn't."

"I won't argue with you."

"If a movie prop became a working firearm again and it now appears it was used to assassinate someone"—I give him a scenario—"Erin might truly believe she's in serious trouble."

"Especially if Carrie's done things to make her paranoid," Benton agrees, and he knows far more than he's saying.

"Which might explain her leading a raid on Lucy's property. It might explain one of the most bogus search warrants I've seen in a while. Whose idea was it to transfer Erin Loria to Boston?"

"After you were shot in Florida she requested it."

"I'm sure she did. Probably about the same time she fell into the trap of believing a former movie prop she'd once been in illegal possession of was suddenly matched to frag recovered from an assassination in 2007," I reply. "But even if going after Lucy was Erin's idea the Bureau has to be cooperating or nothing would be happening. So in essence the FBI deliberately moved Erin Loria here to sic her on Lucy."

"I don't deny that's true," Benton says as Marino orders me to floor it.

"Cambridge Street over to Charlestown Ave." His voice is loud and urgent. "The old gravel quarry."

THERE'S NO GOOD REASON for him to have driven his cruiser to the River Basin, especially in this weather. He wasn't responding to a call. He wasn't meeting anyone. Not officially.

Officer Park Hyde, unit 237, never contacted dispatch. He didn't telephone, radio or inform anyone by any means we know of that he was headed to the navigation locks of the Charles River Dam where boats pass through to enter the Boston Harbor. The abandoned quarry is a foreboding isolated place under the best of conditions, and I can only imagine the reaction of the officer who discovered Hyde's marked car concealed between mountains of sand. Unlocked. The battery dead. Hyde not inside the car. But the trunk is malfunctioning. It seems no one can open it.

"I don't understand why she can't get inside it," Benton says to Marino.

"She?" I inquire.

"Officer Dern," Marino says. "She's on the juvenile crime squad, which is probably one of the reasons she responded. She probably figured she'd be familiar with the little assholes joyriding in the red SUV we're still trying to locate."

"Yes a late-model high-end red SUV which very well may be the one missing from the Gilbert house," I reply. "The Range Rover that is supposedly registered to Chanel Gilbert," I add. "I assume that Carrie stole her identity?"

"She would assume any identity she wants if it serves a certain purpose," Benton says. "What's happening at the River Basin?"

"The call where one of the subjects supposedly had a gun?" Marino says. "Well then there was another call reporting shots fired in the old gravel quarry."

"*Supposedly* shots were fired," Benton reminds us. "We can't say for a fact who's been making these calls to nine-one-one."

"The officer went there and got out of her car to look for any sign that the red SUV and dirtbags had been there. She was walking around when she found Hyde's police car. You probably can't see it unless you're on foot. I'm familiar with the area and you're not going to drive close to huge mountains of sand and gravel that have been there forever. We always joke that you'll disappear into a sinkhole. I'm pretty sure the car was deliberately dumped there by someone who didn't want us to find it for a while. There's no way in hell Hyde drove it there."

"I don't understand why Officer Dern can't open the trunk," Benton says. "Unless it's been sealed shut somehow."

"She says it's been glued," Marino replies and I think about the silver fish-shaped box he opened with acetone. "So maybe there's another camera inside, right Doc?" His jaw muscles are clenching. "Or some other prize in the Cracker Jacks like a murdered cop?"

"I think we can figure out what we're supposed to assume is inside the trunk," Benton says as if we shouldn't be so sure.

"If Hyde's in there he's likely dead," I tell them. "But let's not assume it, and we also have to be concerned that gunpowder, specifically black powder has turned up. While it might be very old and not a danger to anything or anyone we can't be certain."

"Happy Fourth of July." Marino picks up his phone to make a call. "Carrie wants to turn this day into a damn fireworks display. Fuck that."

I listen to him get Officer Dern on the line and order her not to touch the trunk. He barks at her to move back from the car. I can tell she's putting up an argument. Every cop worth his salt has only one concern and that's Officer Hyde's safety. If he's inside the trunk they need to get him out now. What if he's still alive?

"You hear any movement?" Marino asks Officer Dern as he cracks his window open and lights a cigarette. "Is there any sign someone might be inside? Okay. We'll be there in three minutes." Then he's off the call and saying to Benton and me, "How could he be in the trunk and not be kicking or banging around to get out? She told me she doesn't hear anything. You'd probably better get Harold and Rusty there ASAP in case what we suspect turns out to be true."

"How about you call them," I reply. "And while you're at it tell them to bring a power drill and grab a borescope camera probe from the firearms lab. I assume the bomb squad has what it needs but just to be sure."

"You can't take out the damn trunk with a damn water cannon unless you want to kill whoever might be inside." Marino is frustrated as hell.

"That's why you drill a hole and take a look," I say to him as I drive fast toward the river. "And I don't mean *you* literally, Marino. If there's loose black powder anywhere I wouldn't want to introduce a power drill unless it's a bomb squad doing it."

"How much time do we got?" he retorts. "The answer is nothing to waste if there's even the slightest chance Hyde is alive."

"What we know for a fact is the trunk has been glued shut for a reason," Benton says. "Not a good one. If it's not a dead body inside then we should be worried about some other ugly surprise like a bomb."

"Why glue the trunk shut then?" Marino says. "Why not let some poor cop pop the lid and boom? End of story."

"If you can't open the trunk easily then more people get involved. The more people the more collateral damage," Benton replies. "Maybe twelve people get taken out instead of one."

"Or that's what we're supposed to conclude," I decide.

CHAPTER 46

MARINO COULDN'T BE MORE DISTRACTED. IT'S worse as we approach the old warehouses, the storage bins, the defunct belt conveyors and bucket elevators up ahead.

A high fence and foothills of gravel and sand rise above rusty railroad tracks and soaring stretches of I-93 and U.S. 1. Beyond are the cable-stayed Zakim Bridge and the Boston skyline, the tops of the towers and buildings dissolving in the fog. The rain isn't hard but it's constant. The basin will be muddy and low-lying areas will be underwater.

I glance in the rearview mirror at Benton. He meets my eyes and his are lusterless and grim. If he's in contact with his FBI colleagues I can't tell.

"What's going on with your division?" I ask him as Marino looks out his side window, on a call with the head of his department's bomb squad.

"Fifteen, twenty minutes?" Marino says. "Yeah usually we don't need to touch nothing and can stand there until we turn into skeletons. But not when a cop might be dying inside the damn trunk. Yeah get here ASAP but I'm going to start without you. Yeah you heard me loud and clear." He ends the call and drops his phone into his lap.

"Should I expect to see some of your compatriots here?" I ask Benton. "Because I hope not."

"I haven't told them anything," he says, and Marino whips around long enough to glare at him.

"Bullshit." Marino stares out his window again and says, "One of my guys is missing or dead and your Boston Field Office doesn't know?"

"It's not up to me to notify them unless you ask," Benton says to the back of Marino's head. "If you're inviting me to help and thereby inviting my office to assist, that's a different matter."

"When do I ever invite and when the hell do you ever wait for an invitation? The answer is you guys do whatever the hell you want."

"This isn't about *you guys*. It's about me trying to help," Benton says. "And what I'll tell you in no uncertain terms is this is a game. That doesn't mean it's not a deadly one."

"You've already been so much damn help today I don't know how I'll ever thank you," Marino says sarcastically, rudely. "I mean flying around watching Lucy's place get raided and her belongings hauled off. And all the planning that went into that because you guys had to know where she was and when and what would be the best time to spring a little ambush like that. Assuming the DEA didn't get her first."

I turn onto an unpaved access road, and emergency lights are a rolling wave of red and blue.

"You've probably been hatching plots for days and weeks, and I'm sure you never passed along any intelligence you happened to have access to." Marino keeps his tirade going. "After all it's only family we're talking about. Why should you tell us a goddamned thing?"

Benton is quiet. He knows when not to take verbal swings at Marino, who is keyed up and furious.

"Right now plain and simple we may have an officer down." He isn't going to stop. "And I sure as hell don't need the friggin' FBI's assistance. In fact maybe if you assholes had kept your nose out of what's going on Carrie Grethen wouldn't have just murdered someone else, this time a cop."

"Be careful . . ." Benton says but Marino cuts him off.

"Be careful? Be careful! It's a little fucking late for that," Marino yells at him, and I realize what this is about.

Marino is terrified. He's afraid we're going to die. He's trying not to panic, and anger is his remedy. It's safer than debilitating fear.

"Are you telling me you've been careful, Benton? Let's talk about Erin Loria. If she was a cop she'd be a fucking bad one. As an FBI agent I guess she's typical, a lying, manipulative bitch who has an axe to grind and an old score to settle. To put her on Lucy's case is like asking John Wayne Gacy to babysit your kids."

"I've made it clear I had nothing to do with Erin coming here," Benton says.

"Well what a strange coincidence that Lucy knew her from their Quantico days."

"I doubt it's a coincidence."

"Jesus Friggin' Christ! You have this way of saying shit like it's normal. You *doubt it's a coincidence*? And you just sit back and watch it happen like a fucking wooden Indian."

"I don't just sit back and watch anything unless I have a reason," Benton says as I park a generous distance from at least half a dozen police cars, marked and unmarked.

The three of us get out and I walk around to the back of the SUV, my boots crunching through gravel and swishing through puddles. The smacking of the rain is slower and softer, and cops in slickers and rain suits are huddled a good hundred feet from Hyde's cruiser. It's rain spattered and splashed with mud. It looks empty and dead. Whatever we do we run a terrible risk. I see no option that doesn't include a potential horrific consequence, and Marino has every good reason to react the way he is.

Usually when an explosive device is suspected the bomb squad will render the vehicle safe by hauling it away inside a containment vessel. They might use a portable X-ray machine to determine if there's an explosive device inside, and if so they take out the power source, probably with a water cannon. But what Marino said is true. In the process Hyde probably wouldn't survive assuming he's inside the trunk and not already dead.

Rusty and Harold are here and I trot to their van as it bumps through mud. They park and I open the tailgate as they climb out in rain suits. I reach for the borescope, the power drill in their black plastic carrying cases, and then Marino is grabbing them from me.

"I'll take care of it." He's ordering me around the same way he was Officer Dern.

"You realize if she has a remote control or some other means to detonate a bomb . . ." Benton directs this at him as he walks closer to us.

But Marino isn't going to listen.

"Someone's got to do this. If Hyde's unconscious and maybe bleeding to death then we don't have time to waste. Maybe he's suffocating in there and I'm sure as hell not waiting for the bomb squad," Marino says over my protests but I'm not going to stop him. "And you need to clear the area, Doc."

"Absolutely not," I reply. "I think right now might be a good time to have a doctor present."

"I'm not asking you. Get the hell out of here now!"

"I'm not going anywhere, and you need to wait for the bomb squad. If Officer Hyde is inside the trunk it's unlikely he went in willingly and is still alive. He may have been in there most of the day. Your life is a sure thing right this minute and his certainly isn't. Let someone in a bomb suit drill a hole in the trunk. If this is a trap, Marino, you're walking right into it."

"And if I don't who will?" His eyes are wide and glassy, and I can see what passes behind them, the dark shape of finality and fear.

Marino knows this might be it for him. He would risk everything for an officer he barely knows because that's what cops do. The brotherhood of the badge, I think, and I understand his motivation but I can't possibly agree with it.

"I'm in charge of this scene and I'm ordering you to leave," Marino says to me and I continue to ignore him. "Rusty, Harold, you need to back up, maybe pull the hell way back out of the way in case I start drilling and the police cruiser blows."

"You don't have to ask us twice," Rusty says and he and Harold hurry back into the van. "We'll be a couple blocks from here." It's Harold who shouts this. "Just call when you're ready."

"Unless you hear a big bang. In that case take to the hills." Marino starts walking alone toward the Cambridge police cruiser abandoned between huge mounds of sand and gravel.

He pauses. He turns around and stares right at me, and when it's apparent I'm not climbing back inside my SUV and driving away he gets on his radio. I can't hear what he says as he walks toward the cruiser with his back to me. But instantly a uniformed officer strides in my direction, a young cop I've seen before.

He politely, firmly tells Benton and me that we need to leave the scene now, and when that gets no response he warns us. If we don't drive away immediately we'll be interfering with a police investigation. As if he really might haul an FBI agent and a chief medical examiner in handcuffs, and I'm not paying any attention as I watch Marino stop walking again. He turns around and looks back at us as the rain smacks and splashes more slowly. But it seems louder. It seems more ominous.

"GO!" he bellows. "GET THE HELL OUT OF HERE!"

If it happens he doesn't want me to see it.

He walks on. Benton and I get back inside the SUV, only this time he's in front, and we watch in unbearable silence. Marino has reached the rear of the police cruiser now. He's up to his ankles in mud, and he sets the carrying cases on the highest driest ground he can find, and he opens them. I see him pick up the cordless drill and attach a battery pack. He walks around the trunk, squatting, standing, studying every detail as he determines where to make the hole.

The first bite of the steel drill bit into metal and the car is going to explode.

"It's not what we think," Benton says as Marino targets the top of the trunk lid, exactly in the middle. "This isn't what we think, Kay. It's what *she* thinks. This is her fantasy and we're obliging her by playing it out."

"Are you suggesting the car isn't going to blow up? That it's a bluff?"

"I don't know the answer. But I do know her. I think it's a bluff but I couldn't possibly suggest such a thing. We should leave."

"Carrie's fantasy? And you know what that is, Benton? Isn't it really dangerous to assume you can think and feel like her?"

I'm so worried about Marino I don't know whether to scream or cry.

"Do you see how treacherous it is if you believe you can divine her fantasies?" I hear the high-pitched whine of the drill turning on.

I WAIT FOR THE SHARP THUNDEROUS CRACK, the billowing black explosion. But there's nothing.

"I know the formula for defining who and what she is and does," Benton is saying. "And she thinks she can do the same with us."

"But she can't." I roll up my window and shove the gear into reverse. "She can't possibly, not accurately. She doesn't have a Rosetta stone that can help her decipher people like us no matter what she believes in her wildest delusions. Carrie is missing too many moral pieces. A conscience for example."

"Don't ever undersell her shrewdness, Kay," Benton says.

"And don't you undersell her malignancy, her sickness. She isn't us." I back up and nose out, driving away as I wait for the worst to happen. "And she can't possibly think and feel exactly like us."

"Meaning she's capable of miscalculating."

"As are we," I reply, and he doesn't argue but he doesn't agree with me either.

I can't hear the drill bit grinding through metal anymore as I drive away slowly through the flooded River Basin, looking in my rearview mirror. I watch Marino until he's a small figure I can scarcely recognize. Then he's gone as we round a bend and I wonder if I'll ever see him again.

"Sickness?" Benton returns to that. "You know better than to assume she's crazy."

"I'm referring to her physical health." I may never see Marino alive again.

For an instant I'm too upset to speak. I can barely breathe as I listen for the noise of the world coming to an end. Not the entire world. But mine. Will it be a big bang or a whimper? How does death announce itself when it's our turn at last? Of all people I should know. But I don't. Not today. Not like this.

"What about her health?" Benton asks me again, and I can't abide what I believe he's done.

"Ernie detected trace amounts of copper in the dust bunny, the fletching," I reply. "He says it permeates the samples I collected."

"I guess it could be from the copper arrow," Benton says but his mind is going through something else, making another dangerous calculation that will probably turn out wrong. "Staying there is what she expects us to do."

"As opposed to what we're actually doing, which is driving away and waiting for Marino to die?" Bile is coming up the back of my throat.

"We have to ask ourselves what she calculates we'd do." Benton's hands are loosely curled around the phone in his lap, and every other second he's looking at what's landing in the display. "To start with she'd predict you'd say what you just did," he adds, and he's in a different character, the one who takes over when he conjures up the devil, when he invites evil to be part of the discussion.

"If it's true she has a blood disorder and it's not being treated," I say to him, "then she could be in trouble."

Even as I ask this the same doubts nag at me. Why would Carrie want me to know that her health could be compromised?

Why would she use her self-produced video recordings to reveal that she has a potentially life-threatening gene mutation that killed her mother and her grandmother—if Carrie was telling the truth. Why would she want me to know she suffers from polycythemia vera. By telling me that, she's given me reason to suspect she's physically compromised beyond any injury I might have inflicted on her at the bottom of the sea in Fort Lauderdale last June.

I explain to Benton that if Carrie hasn't been having regular blood draws she may be suffering from headaches and exhaustion. She could have weakness, visual disturbances and serious complications that could kill or incapacitate her. Such as a stroke, and it seems impossible to consider that a monster like her might ultimately be defeated in such a mundane way.

"I've checked with area doctors, phlebotomists and clinics to see if someone even remotely fitting Carrie's description has been getting blood removed," Benton says to my disappointment and surprise. "And the answer seems to be no. But she's masterful at disguises and creative options."

"Then you've seen the videos." I confront him again about the *Depraved Heart* recordings and he doesn't say a word. "How long have you known about them and her blood disorder." I push harder.

"I know about her suffering from polycythemia vera," he says.

"Am I to assume you've had access to lab values that show an increased hematocrit and bone marrow packed with red cell precursors?"

He says nothing.

"The answer's no. So in other words, Benton, I don't see how you could have known. Unless you witnessed the same thing I did on recordings she covertly made."

He's seen them. But he's not going to say it.

"If she's been in this area for the better part of a year as we suspect then she has to have some means of removing a unit or pint of blood every month or two," I then say, because he's not going to discuss what he's orchestrated and misrepresented. "Unless she's found a different way to take care of her problem."

"She could have," he says and right now I know my husband and I don't.

I'm reminded I couldn't do what he does for a living. I've never been motivated to form alliances and détentes with miscreants, with monsters. I don't pretend to understand them. I don't want to be their friend and tend to resist the temptation of believing I can think like them. I probably can't. Maybe I wouldn't if I could or maybe I already can and refuse to face it. But the love of my life, the man I sleep with is a very different story.

"How the hell has this happened?" I talk very quietly, scarcely audibly as I listen for a boom or bang, what might be a bomb going off.

"It's happened exactly according to plan," Benton says, and he channels people like Carrie or at least he comes disturbingly close to it.

In his own baffling way he doesn't judge those he pursues and he doesn't hate them either. They're nothing more than sharks or snakes or other deadly creatures in the grand pecking order and food chain of things. He accepts that their behavior is predetermined as if they have no will of their own. He has no feelings about them. Not feelings the rest of us can begin to understand.

"She presents us with a choice and believes she knows exactly what we'll decide," he says as I head to the office. Finally at almost five-thirty.

At least at the CFC I'm only minutes from the River Basin should the worst happen and in typical fashion I begin to envision what that scene would look like. Then I stop myself. I can't bear to imagine Marino dead, much less blown apart. He's always joked about knowing far too much about death and how humiliating it can be. He wouldn't want people laughing at his autopsy pictures.

You'll make sure they don't pass them around and make fun of me, right Doc? Because I've sure as hell seen them do it with other people . . .

"Who's at the Gilbert house? Anybody yet?" I ask Benton as he scrolls through something on his phone.

"We've got agents on location."

"Ernie wonders if there's an area of the house we don't know about that might explain some of the evidence we're identifying. Your agents might want to look around the property for some area that isn't readily visible," I'm saying when his phone rings.

"Yes," he says and then he listens. "It has to be coming from somewhere," he finally replies curtly, not particularly nicely.

He gives the cross street address of where we are and ends the call.

He turns to me and says, "We've got four agents there and all of them heard the same thing. Some weird slamming noise they can't identify."

"Marino and I both heard something similar a number of times." I continue checking my mirrors for the filthy smoke plume of a black powder bomb going off.

I listen for an alert tone on the scanner that might indicate an emergency but I see and hear nothing that might hint at what's happening with Marino. I keep telling myself he must be all right or I'd know. He must have drilled a decent-size hole by now and has the borescope's long camera probe fed through so he can see what's inside.

"You mind swinging by there?" Benton asks and I don't understand.

"Excuse me?"

"The Gilbert house. Let's see what they're talking about. The noise has to be coming from somewhere."

CHAPTER 47

I TURN ON BINNEY STREET AS MORE MINUTES PASS. I've heard nothing about Marino and I can't stand it.

"What's going on with him?" I ask Benton as we drive back toward the Harvard campus. "It shouldn't take any time at all to know what's inside the trunk. To thread the camera head through he'd need about nine or ten millimeters, a hole about that size which isn't that big. He must know by now what's inside," I add and it hasn't escaped my notice that I'm not hearing sirens.

I've heard nothing on the scanner that might indicate Hyde has been found inside the trunk and a rescue squad is responding. I've heard not a peep from Rusty and Harold.

"Lucy and Janet are safely out of their house," Benton says, as if that's what we're talking about, and he's skimming through messages on his phone, using some encrypted FBI app that allows him to communicate safely, privately. "I suggested the best place to drop them off for now is your office. I didn't think they should be at our house yet or anywhere else until we have a better idea what's going on."

"What about Desi and Jet Ranger?"

"All of them are safe, Kay. I have a text from Janet. She says Desi and Jet Ranger will wait in your office. When you get there everybody will be waiting, and that's a big relief to hear."

"It's nice she texted you. She must know we're together right now. Somehow."

"Why do you say it like that?" he asks as he stares straight ahead.

"She didn't text me. She must figure you'd tell me. Janet would know how worried I am," I reply and Benton doesn't answer. "It's easy for me to forget that the two of you were friends before she knew Lucy. In fact you introduced them to each other."

"It was one of my better decisions."

"She signed up with the FBI because of you."

"And I'm very glad because she might not have met Lucy, and I'm not sure where we'd be right now if it wasn't for Janet."

"And she's texting you but not me." I make that point again. "She hasn't asked you to pass along to me that they're okay, and that's surprising because she knows what I'm feeling. I was on their property this morning. She's aware of my concern to put it mildly."

"We've always had a special closeness."

"Even during the years they were broken up and out of contact."

"Janet kept up with her through me," he says. "She's always been Lucy's biggest protector."

"Including now."

"Yes." He looks at me. "It would be good if you'd leave it at that."

"I can't possibly. I couldn't help but notice that Janet seems very aware of the cameras inside their house, 'specially in the machine shop, where Lucy was removing tiles from the floor, pulling out rifles the FBI missed. I had a funny feeling Janet knew they were being filmed."

Benton doesn't reply, and I hear Carrie's voice in my mind. I see her gleaming eyes as she talks into the camera.

And you know the evolutionary purpose of psychopathy now don't you?

"If I didn't know better I'd think Janet was trying to hurt Lucy. Not help her," I hear myself say to Benton as I remember the recordings I watched. "Because I'm not sure how it helps Lucy's case if she's caught on video obstructing justice, committing a felony."

"A video that could be very destructive if it ever became public," Benton says. "The Democrats in particular don't need to further inflame the NRA for example by showing two young women fearing for their lives and the life of their child because the FBI rolled in and took all of their guns for no good reason."

We've never had a substantive conversation. Not even a cordial one. And that's shocking when one considers what you could learn from me.

Carrie was talking to Benton. Long years ago she made the recordings with him in mind, and I say that to him as we drive through the Harvard campus, past the Yard with its old brick walls and wrought iron.

"As I think back to everything I watched in her *Depraved Heart* secret recordings it makes sense that she was never talking on camera with me in mind," I say to Benton. "She was talking to you."

"A supreme narcissist like that and she assumes I want to know the slightest detail about her." He confirms he's seen the recordings but there's more to it than that.

"YOU DID THIS. You and Janet." I'm accusing Benton and at the same time I'm strangely relieved.

I've been lied to for the best of reasons. Benton's first loyalty is his family.

"The two of you are trying to save our family and in doing so may get all of us destroyed." I hope this is the truth.

"I'm not going to get us destroyed, Kay," he says. "Neither is Janet. And you need to leave it at that."

"And what about Lucy's involvement? How much is she in on all of this, Benton?"

"You need to leave it, Kay," he says but I can't.

"You've created a record that you hope will clear Lucy's name while showing that Erin Loria is a compromised agent who is trying to entrap her." I glance over at him and my misgivings grow. "The recordings from 1997 are real and they aren't."

"They're edited."

"You turned them into fiction to manipulate."

"I turned them into what they needed to be. We're in the next election cycle. The Bhutto story would be very unfortunate timing," he says. "And it's all the more believable because Janet is on film saying things that are unhelpful and damaging for Lucy. That's what makes it authentic. Janet is saying things that could incriminate Lucy. But it won't matter by the time the Bureau has to deal with the rest of it. The timing is terrible, and Carrie knew it would be when she tampered with records relating to the Bhutto case."

"For the FBI, for the current administration, yes, the timing is bad," I reply. "But not for Carrie. She wouldn't give a damn about what you just said beyond her ecstasy that she's managed to orchestrate a disaster. So who put Janet up to filming what happened in their basement?"

I think back to when I was inside Chanel Gilbert's bedroom and realized Benton was standing in the doorway. I now have no doubt he was watching the same live-streaming video I was. He and Janet are partners. Lucy may be their partner too. The three of them are in on this and I'm the odd person out. Benton admits nothing but it's making sense.

"What about the other videos," I then say, "the ones Carrie is supposedly responsible for? I just need you to say that you're the reason for them—that you're the one who made sure they were sent to me."

"We have spousal privilege." Benton looks at me. "We don't ever mention this conversation. But yes. And Janet has been helping."

"And the timing of my getting these little cyber bombs that I was supposed to worry were from Lucy's In Case of Emergency line? You must have planned this for quite a while and I'm trying to figure out the connection between your sending these to me and Chanel Gilbert's ending up dead."

"Her murder is Carrie's timing. Not ours," Benton says. "But is there a connection? Yes. It would appear that she's known for a while who and what Chanel Gilbert was. When you consider Carrie's previous ties to Russia and what we know she was doing over there for at least the past decade? It's no surprise that she would have encountered some of our people from the intelligence community."

"Were Carrie and Chanel personally involved?"

"It wouldn't surprise me."

"I assume you pulled the trigger on making sure the *Depraved Heart* videos were sent to me because you knew Lucy was getting raided this morning," I then say and Benton doesn't answer me. "I just need to know you had nothing to do with Chanel being killed . . ."

"Jesus, Kay. Of course not." He holds my stare and again says, "You need to leave it. Suffice it to say that the information in those recordings you've watched will derail what Erin Loria is trying to do to Lucy. And now is a good time to trust me. We shouldn't talk about this anymore."

"Stupid me not to figure it out." I turn the wipers off because the rain has almost stopped. "The red flag should have been that Carrie confessed she has a blood disorder, that she might have a physical impairment. I don't have to be a profiler to intuit that she wouldn't want to come across as weak. Not to me. But she couldn't resist making such a confession to you."

"Transference. It's not so different from what happens between a patient and a psychiatrist."

I look at him. "How long have you had these recordings. Benton?"

"Pretty much since they were made."

"Lucy figured it out?"

"Not at first. If you listen to them unedited Carrie refers to me by name. Not you."

"Then Lucy has seen them too. You, Janet and Lucy are all in this together. I thought so. Okay. At least I know."

A soupy grayness blurs lights and obliterates the tops of tall trees and buildings. Harvard Square is almost deserted and shrouded in fog.

"I think it's safe to say that all of us need to be in this together," Benton replies.

"The MP5K was a movie prop and the firearms reports linking it to an assassination were probably faked," I then say. "And the videos as it turns out are propaganda . . ."

"They're not," Benton interrupts. "The footage is genuine and Carrie did hide cameras in Lucy's dorm room."

"You've had the recordings for seventeen years and suddenly decided to edit them into clips that were sent to me." I follow the trail to where I'm sure it leads. "You're using Carrie's own covert recordings against her, and that presupposes she's seen the *Depraved Heart* clips too."

"It's safe to suppose that."

"Then that can mean only one thing. Carrie Grethen is into everything," I say to Benton, and the Gilbert driveway is up ahead. "She's seeing everything we do."

"Now you're hitting the mother lode," he says.

"Data fiction."

"That's what this is about," he says. "That's Carrie's big coup. Yes she's seeing and manipulating pretty much everything and has been for a while."

We bump and splash over the same old pavers, through the same deep standing water and puddles. I park behind three Bureau SUVs in the driveway, near the front of the house.

"Do you have contact with your people?" I cut the engine. "Because in light of everything else let's not venture inside until we know your agents are alive and well and accounted for."

I don't need to repeat what happened in South Florida two months ago. I don't need to find out the hard way that Carrie has killed our backups.

"I'm giving you a heads-up that a couple of the same agents who were on Lucy's property are here because of the presumed connection between Lucy and Chanel," Benton says, and he goes on to explain that the four agents inside have spread out.

Other than the peculiar thudding noise that sounds like a heavy door slamming they've found nothing unexpected. That's what Benton says Erin Loria has reported to him, and we're on the porch now. He tries the front door. It's unlocked. The alarm system is disarmed. I hear a chirp as we open the door but it's not the alarm system. It's Benton's phone.

He looks at the display. He places his hand on my arm and shows me an image sent to him, a photograph the borescope took of the inside of the trunk. There's nothing there but the usual police gear neatly stowed. I can make out a first aid kit, a roll of toilet paper, a stack of paper towels, spray bottles of all-purpose cleaner, Windex, jumper cables. Benton opens the door and we step inside the foyer, and the odor of decomposition is fainter now, and we hear the thud again.

It's muffled but loud. It's what we've heard before, and then it happens another two times in rapid succession.

BOOM! BOOM!

A heavy slamming that sounds faintly metallic, and it seems louder than I remember it, as if the volume has been turned up. Benton and I look around. We don't hear or see a sign of anyone. He reaches under his suit jacket and slides out his gun, and we walk through the foyer. We stop every few steps and listen, and as we get closer to the door that leads down into the basement I hear voices. Benton opens the door, and Erin Loria sounds distressed.

CHAPTER 48

THE FIRST SIGN OF TROUBLE IS THAT THE LIGHT over the stairs no longer works. I have a flashlight in my shoulder bag, and I dig for it and my nine mil as I hear Erin Loria yelling somewhere below us inside the pitch-dark cellar.

"FBI! Come out now with your hands up in the air!"

I paint the light on the stairs, on the cave-like walls, and at the bottom I try more light switches but they aren't working either. If there are other agents inside the house there is no indication of it. I feel we are alone. I feel we have made what may prove to be the worst mistake of our lives.

"FBI! Come out now with your hands up in the air!" Erin Loria's voice is a recording, and then the sound again, the booming thud and it seems to be coming from the rear of the basement, past the bulkhead doors toward the back of the house. "FBI! Come out now with your hands up in the air!"

Carrie is mocking us with a recording of Erin Loria reciting what sounds like a line from a campy cop movie. The FBI agents aren't down here or if they are there's no sign of it, and I realize as I shine the light around the empty cellar that we are where we're supposed to be. We're here as planned but not our plan. It's her plan.

"Stay right behind me," Benton says under his breath.

There is no other place for me to be. I can't run and I can't stand still in the dark while he walks around with his gun. Then the light touches an area of stone that is out of alignment with the wall around it, and this is deliberate too. I draw Benton's attention to what appears to be a secret opening, and we walk toward it as the thudding sounds again, a heavy slamming as we get closer. Benton pushes the wall with his foot, and it moves, and the thudding sounds again as we find ourselves staring into the dark mouth of a tunnel that is very old, possibly as old as the house.

I smell the stale cool air of a closed-up space, and I shine the light through the arched opening to the left of us. The boom sounds again and the tunnel lights up as if a bomb has gone off. Troy Rosado's shrieks are drowned out by the sound, and it's not possible he could be heard anywhere else in the house. He's underground, chained by his wrists to iron rings in the wall. Another boom and a flash of glaring light, and I see his crazed eyes, his short dyed blond hair. He's naked except for a towel tied with rope around his narrow hips like a Tarzan loincloth.

Dangling barely within reach is a malignant mobile comprised of a small green teddy bear . . .

Mister Pickle.

And a Swiss Army knife . . .

The one from Lucy's dorm room.

There's also a silver key, a bottle of water and a candy bar.

They're connected by bare copper wires that have been rigged in such a way as to shock Troy if he grabs for a drink or food or a way to free himself. More bare wires dangle from the ceiling and touch his head, shoulders and back like jellyfish tentacles, and I can smell his foulness as we get closer. In the background a stainless steel industrial freezer has glass panels on the double doors, and I can make out the units of blood inside hanging from racks, scores of pint bags, dark red and frozen.

She's been drawing her own blood.

I notice a work area set up. Tools. A food processor. Empty glass bottles. Draped over an old wooden worktable is a pair of black silk pajama bottoms. A naked dress form mannequin on a metal stand looks like a faceless torso, and I see the silvery glint of mirrors everywhere.

Troy makes a grunting noise as he suddenly lunges at the mobile. His spastic fingers graze the Swiss Army knife and it swings perilously as the thudding sounds and he screams and the light pops like a camera flash.

"Troy?" I call out to him, and his eyes widen and he looks around in deranged fear.

I know why we've been lured here. Carrie expects us to save him. But she will exact a price that I'm already deciding I won't pay. He may be the only witness who can claim that Carrie is alive and responsible for what's happening, and I feel certain that's the choice I'm supposed to make. I need Troy for Lucy, and I can see Benton going into his mode like a fighter plane revving up for an air strike.

"Troy? Over here. Turn around and look behind you." It's Benton talking to him now, and I touch his arm.

"Benton, don't." The pressure in my grip communicates that he shouldn't get any closer.

I see the bare wires and the water on the stone floor, and I tell Benton that we can't reach Troy without running the risk of being electrocuted. But Benton is in the same mode Marino was in moments ago. You do your job. You risk your life. You sacrifice if that's what it takes because that's what people like us are sworn to do.

Troy reaches a shackled hand up toward the silver key. He swats at it feebly, spastically as if he's half awake during a terrible dream. Then he tries to grab the knife, and each time the mobile stirs it completes an electrical circuit. There's a boom and a blinding flash and Troy screams. As he jerks his head I notice the gaping linear wound running down the back of it, a dark gory crust where part of his scalp has been cut from the crown of his head to the nape of his neck.

His narrow white chest rapidly moves in and out as he almost hyperventilates from panic. His gaunt face is patchy with stubble and a fuzzy mustache, and he cowers at the sound of approaching footsteps. But we don't see anyone. No one seems to be in here except the three of us, and I realize what we must be hearing is another recording that is being infernally piped in wherever Carrie decides. The footsteps sound again and seem to be closer, and Troy's reaction is Pavlovian. His reflex is to react with terror.

"No! Please no!" He begins to make whimpering sounds like an infant, tiny cries interspersed with gasps as metal clanks and scrapes against stone. "No," he begs as his legs go out from under him.

He slips on the wet stone floor and struggles to regain his balance. He seems too exhausted to stand as the weight of his body threatens to pull his arms out of their sockets. He's collapsed like a rag doll, and then he's standing again, swaying and looking around blindly. He flaps at the key again and hits the bottle of water, and it knocks into Mister Pickle and the thudding slams and booms and the light flashes each time Troy is shocked.

"Not again! Please!" he spits through the space where his front teeth used to be. "Please don't hurt me anymore. Please . . ." He cries convulsively and can barely speak. "Please . . . !"

He cowers, turning his naked back to us, and the long linear burns covering it and his shoulders are puffy and different shades of red. He grabs at the key hanging almost in reach of his shackled hands, and then another boom. He shrieks and collapses, balling up on the wet floor like a threatened centipede.

"NO! NO!" he screams. "Please. I'll be good. Please let me go. I'll do anything. NOOOO!" His screams rip the air as the thudding sounds again and again, and I remember what Lucy said to Janet a little while ago about the gates of hell.

Don't let them slam me in the ass on my way in, Lucy repeated what she claims Carrie used to say to her, and that's the sound that comes to mind each time. The gates of hell slamming. A prison door banging shut. Troy sobs convulsively and I understand what Carrie has set up. I'm aware of the choice I'm supposed to make and that it's a damnation, a punishment tailored just for me, and I notice the dust balls on the floor.

I notice the water everywhere, shining and glinting when my light skims over dirty stone. There's a bucket filled with a liquid near Troy's bare feet. I suspect he keeps kicking it over, possibly while trying to move it close, and I can see how dried and cracked his lips are. He's dehydrated and hungry, and Benton wants to save him.

"Benton, do not get any closer," I say as Troy is shocked again, and I realize that every time we've heard the slamming sound it's him being tortured.

By now he's so brainwashed and conditioned he no longer seems able to discern between real and remembered pain. When the recording booms he shrieks and cowers no matter what, and I smell ammonia. I smell the fresh stench of his bowels opening up as he soils himself and the floor beneath his filthy bare feet with their long curled nails, as if this once beautiful boy is being turned into a beast like a goat.

"We have to get him out of here somehow before he's electrocuted," Benton says to me as he looks around, and I know what he has in mind.

He wants to find a junction box. He's looking for a circuit breaker. He's inches from the wet area of the floor, and I have no question what he intends to do. Benton is going to try to rescue this kid who assisted in murdering his own father, a kid who sets fires, bullies and sexually assaults whomever he pleases. Troy Rosado is garbage and I'm not allowed to have an opinion like that. He's done nothing in this life but hurt people and I'm not supposed to feel that either.

"Keep still." Benton is going to save him.

"DO NOT get any closer," I warn.

Troy has been made psychotic by fear and pain, and he weakly flaps a hand around. Groping the air for the small silver key dangling from a long copper wire. Groping for the knife, and Mister Pickle dances slowly in the air. He looks exactly as I remember him, the same way he did in the first video I watched this morning. The memory of it is awful, and I'm frantic for a way to stop what's happening.

"You need to stay still," Benton says to Troy. "You need to be still so we can get you out of here, son."

But Troy has been deconstructed and the person who may have existed before is gone. He can't comprehend what we're saying or doing, and he continues to flap his hands at the key, at the bottle of water, at the candy bar, at a silly toy bear I rescued from a junk shop in Richmond decades ago.

The demonic mobile is alive around his head as he continues to shock himself and shriek, and my attention fixes on the bucket, and I bend over and pick it up. It's full of water, and I step in front of Benton, my feet barely an inch from the wet area of stone flooring.

"What are you doing?" he exclaims.

I'll be damned if either of us is going to die. I'm sorry if Troy might, and I dash the water on him, on the wires dangling over him, and they spark and pop as they short out. Silence and darkness, and the recorded slamming sounds have stopped. I smell singed hair and flesh as I grab the silver key dangling over Troy's head. I unlock his shackles. I lower his limp body to the floor and begin CPR.

ONE WEEK LATER

SIGHTS AND SOUNDS ARE TRIGGERS.

Water splashing into the sink. The clicking of an induction burner turning on. The screen door banging. Glasses and silverware clinking. Bottles clanking. Backfires on the street. Mundane events are evocative of what's been uncommon and abnormal.

"What are you having?" I ask Benton as I obsess over tomorrow's front page of the *Boston Globe.*

I don't want to get into a disagreement. I don't want to care and I'm trying not to spend my energy on anger. Benton has told me all about that story and other ones, and he should know since it was his Boston division that planted them. Waving the flag. Taking the credit.

FBI TRAPS MASS MURDERER IN SECRET TUNNEL

Those are the sorts of headlines and sound bites we're hearing with more on the way, and it's all a lie. It's all utter bullshit. The FBI didn't trap Carrie Grethen. Troy Rosado isn't a mass killer. He didn't murder FBI agents or police. He's also not responsible for what happened in the cellar, not for any of it. He was nothing more than a victim. But the FBI can't resist spin doctoring. They might just have invented data fiction and are about to be done in by it.

"I don't know." Benton moves bottles around, checking labels. "I'm torn. Maybe I shouldn't drink anything. Tomorrow's going to be a hell of a day after that damn story breaks."

It includes photographs of the tunnel, which dates back to the late 1600s when hundreds of acres were settled by a wealthy Englishman named Alexander Irons. Married with eight children and many servants, he had much to protect. Extant original property records indicate he kept secret cellars full of food, gunpowder and weapons, and a fortune in silver, gold and furs. There were rumors in his day that he might have been involved in privateering, a polite word for piracy.

We know for a fact he had subbasement cow stalls, which look like an ice cube tray of windowless cells with stone sides and dirt floors. They're below the house about halfway between Carrie Grethen's torture chamber and the hedge in back where I noticed loose bricks and stones.

"What I'd love is a martini but I'm afraid that will do me in for the night." Steam clouds up as I empty a pot of boiling water and pasta into a strainer in the sink.

"Booze booze everywhere and not a drop to drink." Bottles clink as Benton looks through a cabinet of single malt whiskeys and small batch bourbons. "I don't know. What goes with prosciutto di Parma and mortadella?"

"Everything. But there's a sparkling Malvasia if you'd like." I shake the strainer over the sink, draining all of the water out. "That's good with the antipasto. Or there should be a Freisa d'Asti." I pour the steaming tagliatelle into two big bowls. "Something light and fresh would be nice."

"Not for me." More bottles clink. "I think I need something strong."

"Nothing heavy, ponderous and peaty." I tear up basil leaves and their fresh bright scent makes me happy until I remember why I shouldn't be. "I'm in the mood for something easy."

We've been chatting about cocktails for the past hour, going back and forth and around and around as I cook a comfort food dinner of *Ragù alla Contadina* and also a vegan version of it. It's as if we can't make decisions about the smallest things but we talk about recent horrors easily. We decisively discuss running away and starting all over and we explore incarceration, disability and death in detail. But we can't decide between wine and whiskey. We don't know what we want.

"It's weird when you can't think of anything that might make you feel soothed." Benton has said this repeatedly over recent days and it's more an observation than a complaint. "Not that we don't feel stressed on a regular basis but usually it doesn't last this long. It's not relentless. I have more empathy for people who feel like this all of the time. It's no wonder they medicate with cigarettes and booze."

"Medicating sounds good right about now." I dribble unfiltered cold-pressed olive oil over pasta, tossing it with wooden spoons. "I'm not sure I remember feeling soothed it's been so long." I blend in fresh grated Parmesan Reggiano, crushed red pepper and the basil.

"I know how to soothe you."

"Promises promises." A second bowl of pasta is for Lucy and Janet, and I leave out the cheese. "As I said it's been so long."

"Well we can't have that. Don't get too sleepy tonight." Benton finds glasses in another cupboard. "A red, maybe a Valpolicella would be civilized I suppose." He goes to the wine cooler, opens the door and shuts it without selecting anything.

He returns to the liquor cabinet and illustrates exactly what my father meant about actions telling the truth, about people speaking with their feet. Benton sets two crystal tumblers next to a bottle of Scotch, Glenmorangie aged eighteen years. He pulls out the cork with a quiet pop.

"No worries about my being sleepy." I stir crushed plum tomatoes into the sauce, and the kitchen is filled with the savory aroma of onions, garlic and fresh herbs from earthenware pots on the sunporch. "If anyone wants wine I recommend the Rincione. You can go ahead and open a bottle. It should breathe before Jill gets here."

"She'll drink the hard stuff I'm pretty sure," he says and I hate the reminder.

"Let's put a Freisa d'Asti on ice. Maybe we can pretend this will be a festive dinner full of pleasant conversations as opposed to an interrogation we'll pay for by the hour."

"Try not to be negative about her."

"Oh I'm not negative. Just realistically unhappy about spending an evening with her."

"She's trying to help. She would do anything for us, Kay. I consider her a friend."

"I understand that it's not her fault I dread seeing her. She can't help it that I don't want to hear her voice right now. I'm sure it's not her choice that she represents everything wrong in our lives. It's through no damn fault of her own that I associate her with everything I care about being taken and destroyed."

"Nothing's been taken and destroyed, Kay." Benton's voice is gentle, his eyes soft and I can feel his love for me. "We won't allow anything that matters to be taken from us."

"I don't want Desi to be frightened by what she says."

"We'll protect him. I promise. But he's been hearing it, Kay. He's actually taking things in stride."

"Maybe better than I am." I stir wine into the sauce. "But I don't want him worrying that his Aunt Lucy could go to jail. Or worse that she's bad, that she used her Swiss Army knife to break into the back of my truck, and that her childhood teddy bear was involved in torture."

Tool marks on the flathead screwdriver matched what was used to remove screws in the taillight. The red Swiss Army knife and Mister Pickle are evidence that could be used against Lucy. I have no doubt this was part of Carrie's plan, and I don't expect to have a pleasant evening.

"Let's just get through this." Benton kisses me and pours our drinks.

Jill Donoghue is on her way here and the visit isn't social. For the most part it will be miserable as we fill her in on what has occurred and what we should expect, which is nothing less than anarchy. There are possible criminal charges to explore, and of course I'm waiting for Troy Rosado to sue now that he's no longer in critical condition.

The rest of them are dead, and I can't stop seeing their bodies piled in an old cow stall. I see them vividly when I least expect it. The images are there in my mind like a huge graphic painting, a gruesome mural that wraps around the walls. I see death and destruction and a future that offers little hope as we face the ugly fact that everything we've built in our careers has been compromised. Possibly it's been perverted and completely destroyed. Worst of all is the thought that every case we've worked will be overturned and evil people will be free to pick up where they left off.

"A little more ice please." I set down my whiskey tumbler. "And make mine a double."

"She just pulled up." Benton is peeking out the window by the breakfast table.

"She's early." I turn off the stove.

I take off my apron and absently run my fingers through my hair. There's no mirror in the kitchen and it's just as well. I know I look like hell. The first part of this past week I didn't leave the office. I didn't sleep. It wasn't just the caseload and associated complications, which are massive. I didn't dare vacate the premises or close my eyes while Amanda Gilbert was on the prowl and the Feds were everywhere.

The FBI has been frantic in its investigative and PR efforts to determine how it was possible that four of their agents including Erin Loria were murdered without a struggle. They must have been lured downstairs the same way Benton and I were, and somehow Carrie electrocuted them, possibly by tricking them to step on the same wet flooring Benton was about to walk across when I short-circuited the electrical booby trap that I'm now certain would have killed him.

I will always wonder what I was hearing. For the rest of my days I know I'm going to wonder and anguish. The boom, the thuds happening in quick succession, and as I remember them I'm haunted by the fear that what I was hearing was those four agents dying. I'll never know but will always worry that Carrie was killing them even as Benton and I were inside the Gilbert house.

She dragged the bodies deep into the tunnel, piling them into the same stall where we eventually would find Hyde. At least he died more humanely than the others, stabbed in the back of the neck with the copper arrow that was then planted inside my truck. It's unlikely he knew what hit him. He didn't suffer. His spinal cord was transected. He was blessed with instant death.

"Maybe we could have a little music?" I take the tumbler of Scotch from Benton after he's dropped a few more ice cubes in it. "It might not soothe us but it will help." The liquor heats up my nose and the back of my throat. "Maybe *The Magic Flute*."

"So in good operatic fashion we can be reminded of the ordeals that lead to enlightenment." Benton heads to the sound system in the hallway closet. "Before we're cast into the eternal night."

Momentarily the *Overture* begins. I chop celery to the crashing of big brass answered by argumentative piccolos and scurrying strings.

"THE FBI AND CFC DATABASES have been hacked." Benton carries a platter of cured meats and bread to the teak table in the backyard where all of us sit. "There's no telling what else."

"You're thinking we're going to discover that she's into other databases." Jill Donoghue picks up her drink, and I can smell the Scotch's sherry finish as I walk past her and hand out small plates and napkins.

"Yes." Benton sits back down next to Janet who is watching Lucy horse around with Desi, Jet Ranger and our rescued greyhound Sock.

Lucy grabs a green rubber ball off the lawn and tosses it, and when she darts and dodges playfully I catch a glimpse of the .40 caliber pistol in her ankle holster. Jet Ranger runs several steps and that's enough exertion for him. He sits as Sock wanders off to his favorite rest stop of rosebushes and Desi races to the ball laughing hilariously. He hurls it back to Lucy as the screen door bangs shut and Marino emerges drinking a bottle of Red Stripe beer. He wears a pistol on the waistband of his jeans. Janet and Benton also are armed, and I'm reminded that no one close to me is very far from a gun at any given time. We don't know where Carrie is. We have no clue.

"We can't trust that cases haven't been tampered with and turned into data fiction." Donoghue is presenting the case as she sees it.

"That's the point," Janet says. "Every single record or report she might have accessed will be questioned. Defense attorneys will have a field day."

"I know I would."

"Not *would* but *will,*" Benton says to her.

"People will get out of prison."

"Right and left" is his answer.

"Dirtbags who will want to send Benton and Kay a thank-you note." Janet is sipping the sparkling wine, her eyes on Lucy and Desi.

"I would think that's a very real threat," Donoghue says. "You can't know who might come around, and these days it's easy to figure out where somebody lives."

"Classic Carrie payback," Janet says.

"And that's what this is about?"

"It's about her need to overpower. It's about her need to be a god," Benton says, and one place we might go is California.

We could move there and be safer than we are here. That's a given. But the prospect of uprooting is overwhelming, and I don't believe it will do any good. We can't escape Carrie. If she doesn't want us to find her we won't, even if she's breathing down our necks. It seems impossible we could be inside the same house with her and not have any idea. But that's what happened. For the better part of the past six months she was belowground in a tunnel that had been sealed off since the Civil War. Lucy suspects Carrie found out about it the same way other people have. It's in old documents. You just have to look.

"And the ultimate in taking power," Benton describes to Donoghue, "is to stalk, to steal someone's identity and then finally take the person's life."

"Which is what she did to Chanel Gilbert." Donoghue stares off thoughtfully, watching Lucy play tug-of-war with Sock.

"Leave it. Leave it!" Lucy says, and he drops the green ball and looks bored.

I smell the perfume of the roses along the back wall behind our Cambridge house, and the breeze is cool for August. The sun burns bright orange over rooftops and trees, and soon I need to go back inside and finish preparing dinner but it's not just that. I don't want to sit here. It's hard for me to listen to the stories. I've heard them multiple times and they don't get better in the retelling.

Chanel Gilbert was a Navy underwater photographer who left the military to work for the U.S. Central Intelligence Agency. One of her aliases was Elsa Mulligan, the name Carrie called herself when she "found" the body and claimed to be the housekeeper. It's a bad story, the worst of stories, and it's all connected to cyberterrorism, to data fiction. The man murdered in a Boston hotel this summer, Joel Fagano, was also CIA. He and Chanel Gilbert were colleagues, both of them spies. Janet knew Chanel before Lucy did, and no one has told me what that means.

"We don't exactly know when Carrie alerted to Chanel." Benton continues to talk about what really can't be explained, not entirely.

"Probably it was when she began working as an adviser to the Ukrainian security service," Janet offers. "Beyond that who knows why anybody ends up on Carrie's radar."

"It's as subjective and personal as picking out who to date." Marino takes a big swallow of beer. "It's sort of like being attracted to someone. That's what I've always figured."

"People are more the same than they're different." Benton remembers his drink, and ice rattles quietly. "They fall in love with someone who looks like them. Chanel was fit and into extreme sports. She was compellingly attractive in an androgynous way. She would have appealed to Carrie's narcissism."

"So she takes on at least one of Chanel's identities and even takes over her property here in Cambridge? Plus she manages to get a Range Rover—an SUV the police, the FBI still can't find? You have to admit she's unbelievably brazen, doesn't seem to have a fearful bone in her body." Donoghue sounds annoyingly impressed.

It enters my mind that she'd probably like nothing better than to represent a notorious monster like Carrie.

"The best place to hide is in plain view," Benton says. "Neighbors saw a red Range Rover in and out. They caught glimpses of a young woman. Why would they think anything was amiss? Carrie's probably pulled stunts like this countless times all over the world."

"So she hijacked Chanel's life or lives," Donoghue says. "Then what made Carrie decide to kill her right after she returned here from Bermuda?"

"It might simply have been a matter of practicality," Benton says. "Chanel hadn't been here for a long time. So Carrie appropriated her property and then murdered her when she showed up."

"Something made her decide it though." Lucy walks back to us and sits. "And my theory is when Carrie hung around after she shot you"—she directs this at me, reaching for the bottle of Freisa d'Asti in the ice bucket—"she watched Chanel help you to the surface, basically save your life and that marked Chanel for death."

The same way Carrie marked you, and I push that from my mind. I don't want to imagine Lucy's tattooed dragonfly. I don't want to envision Carrie slashing her with the same Swiss Army knife that she fashioned into a cruel mobile some seventeen years later.

"I'm not saying she wasn't going to annihilate Chanel eventually," Lucy adds.

"She would have," Benton says. "But when she watched Chanel save Kay's life it pushed her over the edge. As much as we can simplify what is anything but simple when you're dealing with an offender like this."

Two months and one week ago when I almost died I didn't know that other dive boats in the area belonged to special ops. In retrospect I'm not at all surprised because Benton knows how dangerous Carrie is. He wouldn't allow us to dive a hundred feet down into dark murky water without making sure we were safe. As it turned out we weren't. Certainly the two police divers weren't. The tactical divers were a day late and a dollar short, to quote Marino. But they helped save my life after I was shot—specifically Chanel Gilbert did.

"Why might that have prompted Carrie to kill her?" Donoghue is asking. "I'm trying to understand the reason."

"You're probably not going to," I reply.

"Jealousy. Resentment." Benton sips his drink. "Chanel was the hero. She stole Carrie's thunder. That's as close as we're probably going to get to what goaded Carrie into it. There's no fortune cookie formula."

"That's the hard part," Lucy says. "We don't know the details and might never. For example I'm not sure of the relationship between Carrie and Chanel."

"Did they have one?" Donoghue asks.

"That's what I'm getting at," Lucy says. "They could have."

"One of the problems with people in the intelligence community is they never seem to know whose side they're on," Janet says as I get up to see about dinner, and I just can't listen anymore. "It's a squirrely way to live," she adds, and I carry my drink toward the back door.

Janet and Lucy ask if they can help but I say no. I tell everybody I'll get dinner on the table and they're to relax and enjoy their cocktails and antipasto. I open the screen door and feel something cold poke against the back of my injured leg, and I stop to turn around and pet Sock's long velvety snout.

"I see. So you're not going to stay with our company," I say to him as I let him inside the house. "Well there's not much you can help me with but I'm happy for the company."

I continue to talk to my shy brindle greyhound as I open a drawer inside one of the refrigerators and select various greens, both tart and sweet lettuces and two of my cherished homegrown tomatoes. A rinse and a whirl in the salad spinner, I explain cheerfully to Sock, and a dash or two of coarse ground pepper and sea salt.

"And we save the vinegar for last so it doesn't wilt everything." I continue talking to a dog who doesn't answer or bark, and then I hear the back door bang again.

I'm startled and just as quickly I remember I'm home and I'm not alone. I hear quick quiet footsteps in the hall. I'm cubing tomatoes as Desi walks into the kitchen, and he wants to know why I'm crying. I blame it on the Vidalia onion I'm just now peeling but Desi is a perceptive little boy. He stands in the middle of my kitchen with his hands on his hips, his mussed-up brown hair in his big blue eyes.

"Aunt Janet says I'm helping you set the table." He opens a drawer and begins gathering silverware. "Do you want to eat on the sunporch or are you afraid?"

The sunporch is enclosed in glass.

"What might I be afraid of?" I scan a selection of vinegars and decide on a Bordeaux.

We're not sitting on the sunporch.

"The bad lady who hurt you," Desi says. "She might see us through the windows if we eat on the sunporch. Is that why you're crying?"

"She could see us sitting in the yard," I remind him.

"I know. You can't stay here anymore can you?" He slides out a chair from the breakfast table and sits down. "But you'll take me with you."

"Where are we going?"

"We have to stay together, Aunt Kay," he says and technically I'd be his Great-Aunt Kay if I were a blood relative.

"You know where the dining room is. Out this door and to the left." I hand him plates and folded napkins. "We'll be fancy and eat in there."

"That's not why."

"We'll turn on the chandelier and pretend we're royalty."

"I don't want to pretend. You don't want us sitting near windows. That's why we're not eating on the sunporch, isn't it? I don't want that bad lady to hurt us."

"No one is going to hurt us." I collect glasses from a cupboard and follow Desi out of the kitchen, and I think about the way we lie to children.

I can't tell Desi the truth. I won't have him live in fear. We're not safe. But for him to know that solves nothing. It makes things only worse.

"Now I'm going to show you a trick." I turn on the overhead alabaster chandelier inside the dining room. "That's assuming you might want to learn a trick." I close the draperies in big windows overlooking the side yard.

"Yes! Please show me!"

I get place mats out of the breakfront and help him set the table. I teach him how to fold linen napkins into a tree. A flower. A horse. A bow tie. By the time we make an elf hat he's giggling. He's laughing hysterically. Then I fold a napkin into a heart. I put it on a plate.

"This is your place," I say to him. "And you know what that means don't you?" I wrap my arms around him.

"It means I sit here!"

"It means I've given you my heart."

"Because you love me!"

"Yes." I kiss the top of his head. "I think I might. Maybe just a little bit."